10/08

Please Return to:
Belmont Senior
Center Library

THE SACRED BOOK OF THE WEREWOLF

also by Victor Pelevin

THE HELMET OF HORROR: THE MYTH OF THESEUS AND THE MINOTAUR

HOMO ZAPIENS

4 BY PELEVIN

BUDDHA'S LITTLE FINGER

A WEREWOLF PROBLEM IN CENTRAL LONDON

THE LIFE OF INSECTS

THE BLUE LANTERN

OMON RA

THE YELLOW ARROW

VICTOR PELEVIN

The Sacred Book
of the
Werewolf

*translated from the Russian
by Andrew Bromfield*

VIKING

FIC
PEL

VIKING
Published by the Penguin Group
Penguin Group (USA) Inc., 375 Hudson Street,
New York, New York 10014, U.S.A.
Penguin Group (Canada), 90 Eglinton Avenue East, Suite 700,
Toronto, Ontario, Canada M4P 2Y3
(a division of Pearson Penguin Canada Inc.)
Penguin Books Ltd, 80 Strand, London WC2R 0RL, England
Penguin Ireland, 25 St. Stephen's Green, Dublin 2, Ireland
(a division of Penguin Books Ltd)
Penguin Books Australia Ltd, 250 Camberwell Road, Camberwell,
Victoria 3124, Australia
(a division of Pearson Australia Group Pty Ltd)
Penguin Books India Pvt Ltd, 11 Community Centre, Panchsheel Park,
New Delhi – 110 017, India
Penguin Group (NZ), 67 Apollo Drive, Rosedale, North Shore 0632,
New Zealand (a division of Pearson New Zealand Ltd)
Penguin Books (South Africa) (Pty) Ltd, 24 Sturdee Avenue,
Rosebank, Johannesburg 2196, South Africa

Penguin Books Ltd, Registered Offices:
80 Strand, London WC2R 0RL, England

First American edition
Published in 2008 by Viking Penguin,
a member of Penguin Group (USA) Inc.

1   3   5   7   9   10   8   6   4   2

Copyright © Victor Pelevin, 2005
Translation copyright © Andrew Bromfield, 2008
All rights reserved

Originally published in Russian by Eksmo, Moscow.
English translation first published in Great Britain by Faber and Faber Limited.

Publisher's Note
This is a work of fiction. Names, characters, places, and incidents either are the product of the author's imagination or are used fictitiously, and any resemblance to actual persons, living or dead, business establishments, events, or locales is entirely coincidental.

LIBRARY OF CONGRESS CATALOGING IN PUBLICATION DATA

Pelevin, Viktor.
[Sviashchennaia kniga oborotnia. English]
The sacred book of the werewolf / Victor Pelevin ; translated by Andrew Bromfield.
p.   cm.
Summary: A novel about a fifteen-year-old prostitute who is actually a 2,000-year-old werefox who seduces men with her tail and drains them of their sexual power. She falls in love with an FSB officer who is actually a werewolf.
ISBN 978-0-670-01988-5
I. Bromfield, Andrew.   II. Title.
PG3485.E38S8713 2008
891.73'44—dc22
2008015563

Printed in the United States of America

The Sacred Book
of the
Werewolf

Commentary by Experts

The present text, which is also known under the title of 'A Hu-Li' is in fact a clumsy literary forgery, produced by an unknown author during the first quarter of the twenty-first century. Most specialists are agreed that this manuscript is of no interest in its own right, but only for the manner in which it was launched into the world. The text file entitled 'A Hu-Li' was supposedly found on the hard disk of a laptop computer discovered in 'dramatic circumstances' in one of Moscow's parks. From the militia report describing the discovery it is quite clear that the whole incident was deliberately staged. Indeed, to our mind the report provides useful insight into the virtuoso techniques employed in modern PR.

The report is authentic, incorporating all the requisite stamps and signatures, although the precise time at which it was composed is no longer known – the upper section of the title page was cut off when the report was bound into a file before being despatched to the archives at the end of the calendar year, as required by standing instructions. It appears from the report that the interest of members of the militia was attracted by strange natural phenomena in the Bitsevsky Park in the Southern Administrative District of Moscow. Members of the public observed a bluish glow above the treetops, ball lightning and a large number of five-coloured rainbows. Several of the rainbows were also spherical in form (according to the testimony of eye-witnesses, the colours in them seemed to shine through each other).

The epicentre of this strange anomaly was an extensive waste lot at the edge of the park, where the ramp for bicycle jumping is located. The half-melted frame of a 'Cannondale Jekyll 100' bicycle was discovered close to the ramp, together with the remains of its tyres. The grass around the ramp was burned to a distance of ten metres, with the burnt area taking the form of a regular five-pointed star, beyond which the grass remained unaffected. Certain articles of female clothing were discovered beside the bicycle frame: jeans, a pair of trainers, a pair of panties with the word 'Sunday' on them (evidently from a weekly set) and a T-shirt with the letters 'ckuf' on the chest.

Judging from the photographs in the report, the third letter of this word appears to resemble the Cyrillic letter 'И' rather than the Latin 'U'. We may therefore assume that what we are presented with here is not an anagram of the English word 'fuck', as M. Leibman asserts in his monograph, but a representation of the Russian word 'скиф', i.e. Scythian. This surmise is confirmed by the phrase 'yes, we are asiatics' on the back of the T-shirt – a clear allusion to Alexander Blok's poem 'Scythians', which, to all appearances M. Leibman seems not to have read.

Also found with the articles of clothing was a rucksack containing a laptop computer, as already mentioned in the report. None of these items had been damaged, and no signs of exposure to fire were discovered on any of them, which indicates that they were planted on the site of the incident *after* the five-pointed star was burned into the grass. No criminal investigation was initiated as a result of this event.

The subsequent fate of the text that was (supposedly) discovered on the hard disk of the laptop is well known. It initially circulated among occult fringe groups, and was later published as a book. The original title of the text, sounding exactly like the Russian phrase for 'so fucking what?', was considered obscene even by our modern-day literary hucksters, and so it was published under the changed title of *The Sacred Book of the Werewolf*.

This text is not, of course, deserving of any serious literary or critical analysis. Nonetheless, we would like to note that it presents such a dense interweaving of borrowings, imitations, rehashings and allusions (not to mention the poor style and the author's quite exceptional puerility), that its authenticity or genuineness do not pose any question for serious literary specialists: it is interesting purely as a symptom of the profound spiritual decline through which our society is currently passing. And for serious people who have made their way in the world the pseudo-oriental pop-metaphysics that the author is unable to resist flaunting before other dismal failures like himself cannot possibly evoke anything more than an intense feeling of compassion.

We should like to assure Muscovites and visitors to the capital that cleanliness and public order in Bitsevsky Park are always maintained well up to the mark and the militia of Moscow stand guard over the peace and security of citizens walking there by day and night.

Finally, and above all, my dear friends, may there always be room in your lives for a song of joy!

Tengiz Kokoev,
Major, head of the 'Bitsa Centre' Department of the FSB

Maya Marmeladoff, Igor Shitman,
PhD in philological science

Peldis Sharm,
Presenter of the TV programme 'Karaoke Homeland'

Who is your hero, Dolores Haze,
Still one of those blue-caped starmen?
                                    Humbert Humbert

The client I had been directed to by the barman Serge had been waiting in the Alexander Bar of the hotel National since seven-thirty in the evening. It was already seven-forty and the taxi was still crawling along, shifting from one traffic jam to another. I had a dreary, depressed feeling so deep in my soul that I was almost ready to believe I had one.

'I want to be forever young,' Alphaville sang yet again on the radio.

I wish I had your problems, I thought. And immediately remembered my own.

I don't really think about them that often. All I know is that they reside somewhere out there in the black void and I can come back to them again at any moment. Just to convince myself one more time that they have no solution. And thinking about that for a moment leads to interesting conclusions.

Let's just suppose I solve them. What then? They'll simply disappear – that is, they'll drift away for ever into the same non-existence where they reside for most of the time anyway. And the only practical consequence will be that my mind will stop dragging them back out of that black void. Doesn't that mean my insoluble problems only exist because I think about them, and I recreate them anew at the very moment when I remember them?

I

The funniest of my problems is my name. It's a problem I only have in Russia. But since I live here at the moment, I have to admit that it's a very real problem.

My name is A Hu-Li. When this is spelt in Russian letters – 'А Хули' – it becomes a Russian obscenity.

In the old days, with the pre-Revolutionary Russian alphabet, I was able to avoid this, at least in the written form of my name, by writing it as 'А Хулï'. On a seal given to me in nineteen-thirteen by a certain wealthy patron of the arts from St. Petersburg who knew the secret, it is condensed into two symbols:

$$\text{ДX̣}$$

It's an interesting story. The first seal that he ordered for me was carved on a ruby, and all five letters were incorporated into a single symbol.

$$\text{X̣}$$

He gave me that ruby when we were sailing on his yacht in the Gulf of Finland and I threw it straight into the water the moment I looked at it. He turned pale and asked me why I hated him. He didn't, of course, really think that I hated him. But it was just a time when theatrical, soulful gestures were the fashion. Indeed, as it happens, they were responsible for the First World War and the Russian Revolution.

I explained that it was possible to lay all the letters on top of each other and fit them on a small gemstone, which wouldn't be too expensive, but then you couldn't tell which letter came first. A day later the second version was ready, carved on an oblong opal – 'with a teasing mysterious "AH"', as the patron noted elegantly in the poem appended to the gift.

That was the kind of people there used to be in Russia.

Although, in fact, I suspect that he didn't write the poem himself, but commissioned it from his friend – the gay poet Mikhail Kuzmin – since after the Revolution I was visited by a gang of cocaine-intoxicated queers from the Cheka, looking for some diamonds or other. Then they moved a load of plumbers and laundrywomen into my flat on Italianskaya Street and took away the final prop of my self-respect, the old Russian letter 'i' that rendered my name printable. So I never did like the communists from the very beginning, even at a time when many brilliant minds believed in them.

My name is actually very beautiful and has nothing to do with its apparent Russian meaning. In Chinese 'A Hu-Li' means 'the fox named A'. By analogy with Russian names, you could say that 'A' is my first name and 'Hu-Li' is my surname. What can I say to justify it? I was given the name at a time when the obscene phrase didn't exist in the Russian language, because the Russian language itself didn't even exist yet.

Who could ever have imagined in those times that some day my noble surname would become an obscene word? Ludwig Wittgenstein once said that names are the only things that exist in the world. Maybe that's true, but the problem is that as time passes by, names do not remain the same – even if they don't change.

We foxes are fortunate creatures, because we have short memories. We only remember the last ten or twenty years clearly, and everything from before that slumbers in the dark void that I've already mentioned. But it doesn't completely disappear. For us the past is like a dark room from which we can extract any memory we wish by making a special and rather painful effort of will. This makes us interesting to talk to. We have a lot to say about almost any subject; and apart from that, we know all the major languages of the world – we've had enough time to learn them. But we don't go picking at the scab of memory without any need, and our everyday stream of thought is virtually the same as people have. The same applies to our operational personality, which renders a fox virtually indistinguishable from a tailless monkey (our ancient term for humans).

Many people cannot understand how this is possible. Let me try to explain. In every culture it is usual to link particular aspects of a person's appearance with specific character traits. A beautiful princess is kind and compassionate; a wicked witch is ugly, and she has a huge wart on her nose. And there are more subtle connections that are not so easy to formulate – the art of portrait painting is constructed around them. These connections change over time, which is why the great beauties of one age are a puzzle for another. Anyway, to put it simply, a fox's personality is the human type with which the present age associates her appearance.

Every fifty years or thereabouts, we select a new simulacrum of the soul to match our unchanging features, and that is what we present to people. Therefore, from the human point of view, at any given moment our inner reality corresponds completely to our external appearance. It's a different question altogether that it's not identical with the genuine reality, but who's going to understand that? Most people don't have any genuine reality at all, all they have are these external and internal realities, two sides of the same coin that the tailless monkey sincerely believes has actually been credited to his account.

I know it sounds strange, but that's exactly how it is: in order to make ourselves acceptable to our contemporaries, we adopt a new personality to match our face, exactly like altering a dress to suit a different fashion. The previous personalities are consigned to the lumber room, and soon it becomes a strain for us to remember what we used to be like before. And our lives consist of jolly trivia, amusing fleeting moments. I think this is a kind of evolutionary mechanism designed to make mimicry and camouflage easier for us. After all, the best kind of mimicry is when not only your face becomes like others' faces, but your stream of thought becomes like theirs too.

To look at I could be anything from fourteen to seventeen years old – closer to fourteen. My physical appearance arouses feelings in people, especially men, that are boring to describe, and there's no need – nowadays everybody's read *Lolita*, even the Lolitas. Those feelings are what provide my living. I suppose you could say I earn my living as a swindler: in actual fact I am anything but a juvenile. For the sake of convenience I define my age as two thousand years – the period that I can recall more or less coherently. This could possibly be regarded as coyness – I am actually significantly older than that. The origins of my life go very, very far back into the depths of time, and recalling them is as difficult as lighting up the night sky with a small torch. We foxes were not born in the same way as people. We are descended from a heavenly stone and are distantly related to the king of apes, Sun Wukong himself, the hero of *Journey to the West* (although I can't really claim this is all actually true – I have no memories left of that legendary time). In those days we were different. I mean internally, not externally. We don't change externally as we grow older – apart, that is, from the appearance of a new silver hair in our tails every 108 years.

I have not made such a significant mark in history as others of my kind. But even so, I am mentioned in one of the greatest works of world literature, and you can even read about me if you like. To do that, you have to go to the bookshop and buy the book *Anecdotes of Spirits and Immortals*, written by Gan Bao, and find the story of how the governor of Sih during the late Han period searched for the commander of his guards, who had fled. The governor was told that his officer had been led away by an evil spirit, and a detachment of soldiers was sent to look for him.

To this day, reading what comes after that never fails to excite me (I carry the page with me as a talisman):

... the governor and several dozen soldiers on foot and on horse-back, having taken the hunting dogs with them, began prowling about outside the walls of the city, tracking down the fugitive. And indeed, Tsao was discovered in an empty burial crypt. But the were-creature had heard the voices of the people and dogs and hidden. The men sent by Sian brought Tsao back. In appearance he had become entirely like the foxes, almost nothing human remained in him. He could only mutter: 'A-Tsy!' ('A-Tsy' is a name for a fox.) About ten days later he gradually began to recover his reason and then he told his story:

'When the fox came the first time, a woman who was most beauti-ful appeared in the far corner of the house, among the hen-roosts. Having named herself as A-Tsy, she began enticing me to herself. And so it happened several times, while I, without intending to, followed her summons. There and then she became my wife and that very evening we found ourselves in her home ... I do not recall meeting the dogs, but I have never felt so glad.'

'This is an evil spirit from the mountains,' the Taoist sooth-sayer said.

'In "Notes on the Glorious Mountains" it says: "In deep antiquity the fox was a dissolute woman and her name was A-Tsy. Later she was transformed into a fox."

'This is why were-creatures of this kind most often give their name as A-Tsy.'

I remember that man. His head was like a yellow egg, and his eyes looked like two pieces of paper glued on to the egg. His ver-sion of the story of our affair is not entirely accurate, and the narrator is mistaken when he says I was called A-Tsy. The head of the guards called me by my first name, 'A', and 'Tsy' came from the sound that he began making involuntarily when his vital energy fell into decline: while we talked he sucked in air very noisily, as if he were trying to pull his dangling lower jaw back into place. And what's more, it's not true that I was once a dissolute woman and was then transformed into a fox – things like that simply don't happen, as far as I'm aware. But even so, I get the same thrill from re-reading this passage of ancient Chinese prose as an old actress does from looking at the very earliest photograph that she has kept.

Why am I called 'A'? A certain Confucian scribe with a predilection for boys, who knew what I was, but nonetheless had recourse to my services until the day he died, thought up an interesting explanation. He said it was the very shortest sound that a man could make when the muscles of his throat ceased to obey him. And it is true that some of the people over whom I cast my web of hallucination have just enough time to make a sound something like a muffled 'A-a . . .' This Confucian scribe even wrote a special sheet of calligraphy as a gift for me – it began with the words 'A Hu-Li, willow in the night above the river . . .'

It might seem that living in Russia with a name like mine is a rather sad fate. Something like living in America and being called Whatze Phuck. Yes, the name does lend my life a certain tone of gloom, and there is always a certain inner voice ready and willing to ask – 'So what the fuck were you expecting from life anyway, A Hu-Li?' But as I have already said, this is the very least of my concerns, not really even a concern, since I work under a pseudonym. It's more like a humorous comment – although the humour, of course, is black.

Working as a prostitute doesn't really bother me either. My shift partner at the Baltschug hotel, Dunya (she's known as Adulteria in the hotel) once defined the difference between a prostitute and a respectable woman as follows: 'A prostitute wants to get a hundred bucks out of a man for giving him a good time, but a respectable woman wants all his dough for sucking all the blood out of him.' I don't entirely agree with this radical opinion, but it does contain a certain grain of truth: morals in modern Moscow are such that the correct translation of the phrase 'for love' from the slick humour of the glamour magazines into legal terminology would be 'for a hundred thousand dollars plus a pain in the arse'. Why bother paying any attention to the opinion of a society dominated by a morality like that?

I have more serious problems. Conscience, for instance. But I'll think about that in some other traffic jam, we're almost there now.

* * *

A top hat is a badge of caste indicating membership of the elite, no matter how we might feel about that. And when you are met at the entrance to a hotel by a man in a top hat who bows low and opens the door for you, you are elevated thereby to social heights that impose serious financial obligations towards those who have been less fortunate in life.

Which fact is immediately reflected in the menu. Taking a seat at a table by the bar, I immersed myself in the drinks list, trying to locate my niche among the forty-dollar whiskies and fifty-dollar cognacs (and that's for just forty grams!). The names of the long drinks arranged themselves into the storyline of a high-tension thriller: Tequila Sunrise, Blue Lagoon, Sex on the Beach, Screwdriver, Bloody Mary, Malibu Sunset, Zombie. A ready-made proposal for a movie. So why am I not in the movie business?

I ordered the cocktail called Rusty Nail – not in honour of the impending meeting, as anybody of a psychoanalytical cast of mind might be inclined to think, but because in addition to scotch, its contents included the incomprehensible Drambuie. One should experience something new every day of one's life.

There were two of my co-workers sitting in the bar – Karina, an ex-model, and the transsexual Nelly, who moved here from the hotel Moscow after it was closed. Nelly had just recently hit the big five-oh, but business was still going pretty well for her. Just then she was swarming all over some gallant Scandinavian type, while Karina was sitting on her own, finishing off a cigarette that wasn't her first by a long way – that was obvious from the lipstick-smeared butts in the ashtray. I still haven't finally figured out why that happens, but it kept happening all the time: Nelly, an ugly freak who spent her previous life in the Komsomol, earned more bucks than the young girls who looked like supermodels.

There could be various reasons for this:

1) Western man, who has imbibed the ideals of equal rights for women with his mother's milk, is not capable of rejecting a woman because of her age or her external imperfections, since he sees her above all as a person.
2) For the thinking Western man, to satisfy his sexual needs with the help of a photographic model means to follow the dictates of the ideologues of consumerist society, and that is vulgar.
3) Western man regards social instinct as so far superior to biological instinct, even in such an intimate matter as sex, that his primary concern is for the individuals least capable of competing in the conditions of the market.
4) Western man assumes that an ugly freak will cost less, and after an hour of shame, he will have more money left for the payments on his 'Jaguar'.

I did as the barman Serge said and didn't even look in his direction. In the National everybody reports on everybody else, so you have to be careful. And anyway, right then I wasn't much interested in Serge, I was more concerned about the client.

There were two possible candidates for the position in the bar; a Sikh wearing a dark-blue turban who looked like a chocolate Easter rabbit and a middle-aged man in a three-piece suit with glasses. They were both sitting alone – the man in glasses was drinking coffee and surveying the rectangular courtyard through its glass roof, and the Sikh was reading the *Financial Times*, swaying the toe of his lacquered shoe in time to the pianist, who was masterfully transforming the cultural legacy of the nineteenth century into acoustic wallpaper. The piece concerned was Chopin's 'Raindrops', the same composition that the villain in the film *Moonraker* is playing when Bond appears. I used to adore that music. Leo Tolstoy's wife, Sofia Andreevna, was right to entitle the rebuttal of her husband's 'Kreutzer Sonata' that she worked on in her final years as 'Chopin's Preludes' . . .

I'd prefer the one in glasses, I thought. He was obviously not saving up for a 'Jaguar', he already had one. For his kind the whole thrill is in spending money, they get more excited over that transaction than all the rest, which doesn't even have to happen at all, provided you can get them drunk enough. But that Sikh would be really heavy work.

I smiled at the man in glasses and he smiled back. That's great then, I thought, but just after that the Sikh folded his financial newspaper, got up and came to my table.

'Lisa?' he asked.

That was my pseudonym for the day.

'That's right,' I said happily.

What else could I do?

He sat facing me and immediately started abusing the local cuisine. His English was good, not the kind people from India usually have – genuine Oxford pronunciation, with that dry tone to it reminiscent of a Russian accent. Instead of 'fucking' he said 'freaking', like a Boy Scout, and it sounded funny, because he stuck the word into every second sentence. Maybe swearing was against his religion, there was some little point like that in Sikhism, I thought. He turned out to be a professional portfolio investor, and I only just stopped myself from asking where his portfolio was. Portfolio investors don't like jokes like that. I know that, because every third client of mine at the National is a portfolio investor. Not that there are all that many portfolio investors at the National, it's just that I look very young, and every second portfolio investor is a paedophile. I don't like them, to be quite honest. It's strictly professional.

He began with extremely old-fashioned compliments, saying how he couldn't believe his luck; I was like the girl from the romantic dreams of his childhood – that was what he said. And then more in the same vein. Then he wanted to see my passport, to make sure I wasn't under age. I'm used to requests like that. I had a passport for foreign travel – false, naturally – in the name of 'Alisa Li' – it's a common Korean surname and it suits my Asiatic face. The Sikh looked through it very carefully – he was obviously concerned about his good name. According to my passport I was nineteen.

'Do you want a drink?' he asked.

'I've already ordered,' I replied. 'They'll bring it in a moment. Tell me, do you say that to all the girls, about the romantic dream of your childhood?'

'No, only to you. I've never said anything like that to any girl before.'

'I see. Then I'll say something to you that I've never said to any other man before. You look like Captain Nemo.'

'From 20,000 Leagues under the Sea?'

Oho, I thought, what a well-read portfolio investor!

'No, from the American film The League of Extraordinary Gentlemen. There was one extraordinary gentleman who looked just like you. An underwater karate specialist with a beard and a blue turban.'

'Why, was the film based on Jules Verne?'

They brought my cocktail. It turned out to be small – only sixty grams.

'No, they gathered together all the supermen of the nineteenth century – Captain Nemo, the Invisible Man, Dorian Gray and so on.'

'Really? That's original.'

'Nothing original about it. An economy based on brokerage gives rise to a culture that prefers to resell images and concepts created by others instead of creating new ones.'

That was a phrase I'd heard from a certain left-wing film critic who stung me for 350 euros. Not that I entirely agreed with it, it was just that every time I repeated those words in conversation with a client I felt the film critic was paying me back a few bucks. But it was too much for the Sikh.

'I beg your pardon?' he asked with a frown.

'The point is, the Nemo character looked remarkably like you. A moustache and beard . . . he even prayed to the goddess Kali in his submarine.'

'Then it's not likely that we have much in common,' he said with a smile. 'I don't worship the goddess Kali. I'm a Sikh.'

'I have a lot of respect for Sikhism,' I said. 'I think it's one of the most advanced religions in the world.'

'Do you know what it is?'

'Yes, of course.'

'You've probably heard that Sikhs are men with beards who wear turbans?' he laughed.

'It's not the external attributes of Sikhism that I find attractive. I really admire its spiritual side, especially the fearless transition from reliance on living teachers to reliance on a book.'

'But that's the case in many other religions,' he said. 'It's just that instead of the Koran or the Bible, we have Guru Granth Sahib.'

'But nowhere else do they address the book as their living mentor. And apart from that, nowhere else is there such a revolutionary concept of God. I'm impressed most of all by two features that distinguish Sikhism radically from all other religions.'

'Which ones?'

'Firstly, the acceptance of the fact that God didn't create this world for some exalted purpose, but exclusively for his own amusement. No one before the Sikhs ever dared go that far. And secondly, its God-finding. As distinct from other religions, in which there is only God-seeking.'

'And what are God-finding and God-seeking?'

'Do you remember the aporia with the execution on the square that is often referred to in the commentaries on the Sikh sacred texts? I think it goes back to Guru Nanak, but I'm not absolutely certain.'

The Sikh stared at me, opening his brown eyes wide, which instantly made him look like a crayfish.

'Imagine a market square,' I continued. 'Standing at the centre of it is a scaffold surrounded by a crowd, and they're beheading a prisoner on it. A fairly ordinary scene for medieval India. And for Russia too. Well then, God-seeking is when the best people are horrified by the sight of blood on the axe and start seeking for God and the result is that a hundred years and sixty million corpses later they get a slightly improved credit rating.'

'Oh yes,' said the Sikh. 'That's a tremendous achievement for your country. I mean the improved credit rating. So what's God-finding then?'

'That's when they find God right there in the market square, as the teachers of the Sikhs did.'

'And where is he?'

'In this aporia God is both the executioner and his victim, but not only. He is the crowd round the scaffold, the scaffold itself, the axe, the drops of blood on the axe, the market square, the sky above the market square and the dust under people's feet. And, of course, he is this aporia and – most importantly of all – the person who is listening to it . . .'

I'm not sure that this example can really be called an aporia, since it doesn't contain an irresolvable contradiction – although that might be in the very fact that God is discovered in the midst of blood and horror. But the Sikh didn't object to the term. He opened his eyes even wider, so that he looked even more like a crayfish, but a crayfish who has finally realized why he's surrounded by all these immense beer mugs. While he pondered what I'd said, I calmly finished off my cocktail – I still hadn't found out what Drambuie was. I must say the Sikh looked a real picture – he seemed to be teetering on the brink of enlightenment, as if a slight nudge would be enough for the unstable equilibrium of his mind to shift suddenly.

And that was what happened. The moment my glass touched the table, he recovered his wits. He took a Diners Club Platinum Card with a hologram of Che Guevara out of his wallet and tapped on the table with it to call the waiter, then he put his hand over mine and whispered:

'Isn't it time to go to the room?'

* * *

The name National suggests a hotel representative of national taste. In Russia this taste is eclectic, which is reflected in the decor: the carpet on the stairs is covered with classical fleurs-de-lys, the stained glass in the windows is art nouveau, and it is hard to discover any principle at all in the selection of paintings on the walls – churches, bouquets of flowers, forest thickets, old peasant women, views of Versailles, with Napoleon suddenly turning up in the middle of them all, looking like a blue parrot with a gold tail . . .

But actually it's only at first glance that the pictures have nothing in common. In fact they all share the most important artistic attribute of all – they're for sale. As soon as you remember that, the remarkable stylistic unity of the interior becomes clear. And in addition, you realize there is no such thing as abstract art at all, it's all very concrete. A profound thought, I even wanted to make a note of it, but that would have been awkward with a client there.

We stopped at the glass door of room number 319 and the Sikh gave me a sultry smile as he slipped his key card into the lock. He had a VIP suite – they cost 600 dollars a day there. Behind the double door there was a small businessman's sitting room: a striped sofa with a high back, two armchairs, a fax and a printer, a palm tree in a tub and a small cupboard with antique tableware. The window offered a panoramic view of a street from which the Kremlin could be seen. That's category 'B'. There's a category 'C' there too – that's when the window looks out on to a street from which you can see the other street, from which the Kremlin is visible.

'Where's the bathroom?' I asked.

The Sikh began unfastening his tie.

'Are we in a hurry?' he asked playfully. 'Over there.'

I opened the door he had indicated. Behind it was the bedroom. Almost the entire space was taken up by an immense double bed, and the small door into the bathroom was in the corner of the room: I didn't even notice it at first. That was the way it should be, the dimensions of things proportionate to the place they occupy in life. The suite approached the ideal, since it was structured precisely like the VIP life. Work represented by the businessman's sitting room – receive a fax, send a fax, sit on the stripy sofa for a while, look at the palm tree in the tub and when you get fed up with the palm tree, turn your head and look at the tableware in the cupboard; personal life represented by the bedroom with the bed stretching from wall to wall: take a sleeping pill and sleep. Or else what was happening now.

I went into the bathroom, turned on the shower and started getting ready for work. It wasn't difficult – I simply lowered my trousers a bit and freed my tail. I only turned on the water as camouflage.

I feel I have now reached the point where certain explanations are required, otherwise my narrative will seem rather outlandish. So let me pause for a while to say a few words about myself.

Foxes don't have any sex in the strict sense of the word, and if we are referred to as 'she', it's because of our external resemblance to women. In actual fact we're like angels – that is, we don't have any reproductive system. We don't reproduce because we don't grow old and we can carry on living until something kills us.

As for our appearance, we have slender, shapely bodies without a trace of fat and magnificently defined musculature – the kind that some teenagers who do sport have. We have fine, silky, gleaming hair that's a bright fiery-red colour. We are tall, and in ancient times that often used to give us away, but nowadays people have become taller and so this feature doesn't make us stand out at all.

Although we don't have any sex in the sense of the ability to reproduce, all of its external signs are present – you could never take a fox for a man. Straight women usually take us for lesbians. Lesbians usually go nuts. And it's not surprising. Beside us even the most beautiful women look crude and unfinished – like a carelessly dressed block of stone beside a completed sculpture.

Our breasts are small and perfectly formed, with small, dark-brown nipples. At the spot where women have their most important dream factory we have something similar in appearance – an imitative organ with a function I'll tell you about later. It doesn't serve for childbirth. And at the back we have a tail, a fluffy, flexible, fiery-red antenna. The tail can become larger or smaller: in the sleeping state it's like a ponytail about ten or fifteen centimetres long, but in the working state it can reach almost a metre in length.

When a fox's tail increases in length, the ginger hairs on it grow thicker and longer. It's like a fountain when the pressure is increased several times over (I wouldn't draw any parallels with the male human erection). The tail plays a special part in our lives, and not only because of its remarkable beauty. I didn't call it an antenna by chance. The tail is the organ that we use to spin our web of illusion.

How do we do that?

By using our tails. And there's nothing more to be said about it. I have no wish to conceal the truth, but it really is difficult to add anything else. Can a person who isn't a scientist explain how he sees? Or hears? Or thinks? He sees with his eyes, hears with his ears and thinks with his head, and that's all. Likewise we create illusion with our tails. It feels just as simple and clear to us as the other examples. But I won't attempt to explain the mechanics of what happens in scientific terms.

As for the illusions, they can be of various kinds. Everything here is determined by the personal qualities of the fox, her imagination, mental strength and other distinctive features. A great deal also depends on how many people have to see the illusion simultaneously.

There was a time when we could do a great deal. We could create illusions of magical islands and make crowds of thousands see dragons dancing in the sky. We could create the appearance of a huge army approaching the walls of a city and all the city dwellers would see this army in exactly the same way, right down to the details of its equipment and the hieroglyphs on its banners. But those were the great, incomparable foxes of antiquity, who paid for their wonderworking with their lives. In general, since those days, our kind has declined rather seriously – probably because we are always so close to people.

Of course, my powers are nothing like those of the great foxes. Put it this way – I can make one person see anything at all. Two? Almost always. Three? That depends on the circumstances. There aren't any precise rules here, everything is decided by the feel of things: I sense what I am capable of more or less like a rock-climber standing in front of a crevice in the mountains. He knows where he can jump from one side to the other, and where he can't. If you don't make the jump, you fall off and tumble into the abyss – the analogy with our enchantment is very precise.

It's best not to exceed your own limits, because a hallucination that is not strong enough to subdue another person's mind gives the whole game away. The mechanism involved is complicated, but the external result is always the same – when a person suddenly escapes from hypnotic control (slips off the tail, as we say), he suffers a seizure, with unpredictable consequences. More often than not he tries to kill the fox, who is entirely defenceless just at that moment.

The point is that our sport involves a certain provocative detail. In the non-working state, our tails are really small, and so we hide them between our legs. For the antenna to work at full power, it has to be unfurled. To do this, you have to lower your trousers (or raise your skirt) and spread your tail into a fiery-red plume. This increases the power of suggestion by several orders of magnitude, and that's the way all serious questions are decided.

The need to expose yourself could give rise to awkward and ambiguous situations, but – fortunately for foxes – there is one helpful feature to the process. If you can expose yourself quickly enough, the subject will forget everything that he has seen. There's a kind of twilight zone, ten or twenty seconds that disappear from the memory, and we have to manage the manoeuvre within that time frame. They say the same thing happens when someone faints – when they come round, people don't remember what happened immediately before their fainting fit.

And now for the final thing I ought to tell you. We eat ordinary food (fairly close to the Atkins Diet). But in addition to that, we are capable of directly assimilating the human sexual energy that is released during the act of love – whether real or imaginary. And while ordinary food simply maintains the chemical equilibrium of our bodies, sexual energy is like our most important vitamin, the one that makes us enchanting and eternally youthful. Is this vampirism? I'm not sure it is. We simply pick up what the irrational human being carelessly discards. And if he is so profligate that he actually kills himself, does that mean that we're to blame?

In some books it says that foxes don't wash – supposedly, that's how they can be recognized. It's not because we're dirty creatures. It's just that the excess sexual energy transfuses us with the immortal nature of the primordial Yang principle and our bodies clean themselves through the corresponding influx of Yin. The faint odour that our skin gives off is actually extremely pleasant and reminiscent of Essenza di Zegna eau de cologne, except that it is lighter and more lucid – without that hot, sensuous breath of the mistral in the distant background.

I hope that now the reasons for my actions will be clearer. And so, I turned on the water, so that my client would hear the noise, then unfastened my trousers and lowered them slightly to free my tail. And then, trying not to hurry, I counted to three hundred (a notional five minutes) and opened the door.

* * *

19

Popular expositions of the theory of relativity often ask the reader to compare the pictures that would be taken by two cameras – one in an independent system of coordinates and the other on the head of an astronaut. In our case it would be more correct to say 'in the head' rather than on it. What would the camera in the Sikh's head have shown? The door of the bathroom opened and the girl of his romantic childhood dreams stepped into the room. With a blindingly white towel wrapped round her body.

After she came out of the bathroom, the girl went over to the bed, threw back the blanket and dived under it, blushing ever so slightly: everything pointed to the fact that she hadn't been in the business long and still hadn't acquired the professional shamelessness of the trade. That was what the Sikh saw.

I don't know if the rooms in the National have cameras set in an independent system of coordinates. The staff there claim that they don't. But if they did have, then they would have shown the following:

1) the girl wasn't wearing any towel. She hadn't even thought of getting undressed, but merely slightly lowered her trousers, releasing the red plume of her tail.
2) the girl didn't walk into the room, she crawled into it on all fours and her tail swayed in the air before freezing above her back in a ginger question mark.
3) she looked less like a bride than a beast prepared to pounce – there was a fierce, intense look in her green eyes and there wasn't even a trace of a smile on her face.
4) since in modern Russian the word 'bride' signifies something very close to 'a beast prepared to pounce', there is no contradiction here anyway.

The Sikh looked at me, raised his eyebrows and swayed on his feet. When a person is overwhelmed by the hypnotic shock, a shadow of something like faint revulsion passes across his face, like when a bullet just clips someone's skull: if anyone has seen the documentary footage of Vietnamese executions, then he'll know what I mean. Only after my bullet the client doesn't fall down.

With a smile on his face, the Sikh staggered towards the empty bed, pulling off his jacket on the way. I waited until he had made himself comfortable in it, then sat on the chair beside it and opened my handbag.

I'm trying to improve myself morally, and so I avoid looking at the client once the paid time has begun. I feel ashamed even to describe what happens to a man during his encounter with a fox. Ashamed above all for the man, since he looks quite terrible. And a little awkward for myself too, since all this doesn't just happen of its own accord.

I'm not writing for the yellow press, so I won't go into the scabrous details, but simply say that a man's behaviour is especially unattractive when he starts to realize his sexual fantasies. The fact that he is performing alone increases the obscenity of it to the second power. And if the man concerned is wearing a blue turban and is so hairy that his beard seems to cover his entire body, then it is quite fair to say it is raised to the third.

Maintaining an illusion is considerably easier than breaking into someone else's mind in order to establish it. Everything is decided in the first moment, after that it's all pretty routine. But even so, while the client is in the world of his illusions, it's best not to go too far away from him, because you have to perform the functions of a nurse. As I've already explained, looking at the patient is rather unpleasant, so I usually take a book with me, and that was what I did this time. I settled down beside the bed and opened Stephen Hawking's *A Brief History of Time*, which includes a lot of interesting things about various systems of coordinates. I've already read the book from cover to cover several times, but I still haven't got fed up with it, and every time I laugh as if I were reading it for the first time. I even have a suspicion that it's a postmodern joke, a kind of scam. The very name Stephen Hawking is suspiciously reminiscent of another horror writer by the name of Stephen King. But the horrors here are of a different kind.

The Sikh turned out to be relatively quiet. He muttered something in his native language and squirmed about in the very centre of the bed. There was no need to be concerned that he might fall out on to the floor. But even so, like a good nurse, I glanced at the patient occasionally. When he got fed with embracing the upper half of an empty space, he started pressing himself against it from the side. Then he moved back to the top again.

It's hard to get used to this sight. People have muscular spasms, and at such moments the client looks as if he really is lying on an invisible body. His entire weight is supported on his awkwardly twisted wrists, or sometimes on his fingers. Normally a man could never deliberately hold himself in that position for even a few seconds, but in a trance he can stay in it for hours. Similar phenomena are repeatedly described in the literature on hypnosis, so nobody will give me a Nobel Prize for the discovery. And I don't need human fame anyway. I don't need anything from human beings except love and money.

I have always felt that the means for maintaining eternal youth that has been laid open to me on the Great Way of Things is rather shameful, although I reject all accusations of vampirism. I take no satisfaction in stealing another being's life force and I never have done. Moral satisfaction, I mean. There is no way to vanquish the physiological aspect, but that is not subject to moral judgement: even someone with immense compassion for animals can tuck into a bloody steak for dinner with his stomach gurgling, and there's no contradiction involved. And apart from that, unlike people, who kill animals, I haven't taken anybody's life for centuries now, at least not deliberately. Accidents happen, but a night spent with me is less dangerous than a flight in a Russian helicopter in conditions of average visibility. People fly in helicopters in conditions of average visibility, don't they? Of course they do. I'm the same kind of helicopter – only, as Bruce Springsteen put it, I can take you higher.

And apart from that, I don't believe that it's personal when I draw energy from someone. A man who eats an apple doesn't enter into a personal relationship with the apple, he just follows the established order of things. I regard my role in the food chain in a similar fashion.

The energy that serves for the conception of life does not belong to people. Entering into the act of love, a human being becomes a channel for this energy and is transformed from a sealed vessel to a pipe that is connected for a few seconds to the bottomless source of the life force. I simply require access to that source, that's all.

'And now lie on your tummy, sweetheart,' the Sikh said. 'It's time to try something a bit more serious.'

Anal sex is the favourite sport of portfolio investors. There's a simple psychoanalytical explanation for this – just try comparing the prison slang term 'shoving shit' with the expression 'investing money' and everything should be clear enough. Personally, I'm all in favour of anal sex. It generates an especially large discharge of the life force from the male organism, and that's the best time for gathering energy.

Setting aside my book, I closed my eyes and performed the usual visualization – the yin-yang symbol, surrounded by eight blazing trigrams. Then I pictured myself as the dark half of the symbol and the Sikh as the white half. A white dot began to glow in the centre of the dark half, and a similar black dot appeared in the centre of the white half.

The white began growing darker and black growing lighter, until they swapped places. Dilettantes believe that this is the most advantageous moment to disconnect, but I always work with the method known as 'the bride returns the earring' – the poetic name given to it in the Middle Kingdom six hundred years ago.

If you steal someone else's life energy, it's important not to provoke the wrath of heaven and the spirits with your greed. Therefore, I allowed the situation to proceed into the phase of reverse development. The flow of energy halted and then turned back on itself. My visualization began changing rapidly. A black dot appeared in the centre of the light half of the yin-yang symbol and a similar white dot appeared in the centre of the dark half. And it was only when the dots had become clearly visible that I broke the energy link and dissolved the visualization in the void.

After a big win in a casino, the right thing to do is not to leave – it's better to lose a little, in order not to provoke resentment and anger. And it's the same in our line of work. In ancient times many foxes were killed purely because of their greed. But then we realized we had to share! Heaven does not frown so darkly when we show compassion and return part of the life force. It might seem like splitting hairs, but the difference here is exactly the same as that between an armed robbery and a privatization auction. Formally speaking, in the latter case there is no crime for the spirits to punish. But there's still no way you can trick your own conscience, so it's best just to leave it out of things.

The Sikh got up off the bed and wandered into the bathroom. When he came back out, he lay down, lit up a cigarette and began speaking in a relaxed voice, telling the pillow beside him some story out of his life. After coitus, men become garrulous and benevolent for about half an hour, owing to the release of dopamine into the brain as a reward for fulfilling their duty. I didn't pay much attention to what he was saying. I wanted to finish reading about how a black hole behaves when gravitational collapse reduces its diameter to a distance shorter than the event horizon.

I thought I could detect an erotic subtext to these astrophysical models, and my conviction was growing that Stephen Hawking wasn't writing about physics at all, but about sex – only not about squalid human intercourse, but the grandiose cosmic coitus that gave birth to matter. Surely it's no accident that this great explosion is referred to as the 'Big Bang'. All the most sacred mysteries of the universe are concealed in the darkness of black holes, but it's impossible to look into a singularity because it doesn't emit any light, like a bedroom when the lamp's switched off . . . Basically, I thought, astrophysicists are nothing but voyeurs. Except that voyeurs sometimes manage to glimpse someone else's act of love through the gap between the curtains, but physicists have been cheated by fate, and they have to imagine absolutely everything as they stare into ink-black darkness.

When he'd finished smoking and talking, the Sikh set to work again – he settled on his side and went at it for a long time. The regular creaking of springs was like a soothing lullaby. And I committed the most stupid blunder a fox can possibly commit during working hours. I fell asleep.

I actually only dozed off for a moment and then immediately woke up again. But that was enough. I sensed I'd lost contact with the Sikh and when I looked up, my eyes met his, staring wildly. He could see me just as I was, sitting on a chair with my trousers lowered and my tail sticking up behind my back. And that is a sight no one should ever see, apart from the mirror and the spirits.

* * *

The first thought I had was that I was facing a Taoist exorcist. This was a totally absurd idea because:

25

1) The last Taoist capable of hunting foxes lived in the eighteenth century.

2) Even if one of them had managed to hold out until modern times, he would hardly have been able to disguise himself as a bearded Sikh with an Oxford accent – that would have been 'too freaking much'.

3) Since I work according to the method 'the bride returns the earring', Taoists have no formal right to come hunting me.

4) Taoists never come three times in a row.

But the powerful fear of exorcists of evil spirits is built into our genes, and in moments of danger we always think of them. Some time I must tell you a couple of stories about those guys, then you'll understand the way I feel.

A moment later I realized this was no Taoist, but simply my client, who had slipped off the tail. It was an appalling sight. The Sikh was opening and closing his mouth like a fish just landed on a riverbank. Then, in an attempt to gain control of the body that wouldn't obey him, he lifted his hands up in front of his face and began clenching and unclenching his fingers. Then he groaned hoarsely several times and suddenly bounded to his feet.

At this point I finally unfroze and made a dash for the bathroom. The Sikh came rushing after me, but I slammed the door in his face and locked it. In moments of danger my mind works quickly; I realized immediately what I had to do.

Every bathroom in the National has a red and white cord hanging out of a little hole in the wall. I don't know what it's connected to, but if you tug on it, ten seconds later the phone in the room will ring, and a minute after that someone will knock on the door. I pulled the cord and dashed back to the door of the bathroom.

The next few minutes were rather nerve-racking, while I waited for security to arrive, and shuddered at the furious blows on the door, counting to myself and trying not to hurry. The Sikh was pounding as hard as he could, but I managed to hold him back without too much trouble – he wasn't a large man.

The phone rang after exactly twenty seconds. Naturally, the Sikh didn't answer it. When the blows stopped after a minute or two, I knew there were other people in the room. They were just in time – the door was already coming off its hinges. I heard the sound of furniture being overturned, the tinkle of broken glass and a garbled shout that sounded liked 'kali ma!' It was the Sikh shouting. Then there was silence, broken only by the distant honking of car horns.

'That's fucked it,' said a man's voice. 'He's a goner.'

'Lucky he didn't take us with him,' said another voice.

'True enough,' the first voice replied.

It was better to let them know I was there myself than wait for them to find me. I called out in a plaintive voice:

'Help!'

The door opened.

There were two hulks standing in the doorway of the bathroom – dark glasses, suits, flesh-coloured wires dangling from their ears . . . A regular cult of Agent Smith, I thought. And, incidentally, that would make a great religion for security men – after all, the Roman legionaries worshipped Mithras, didn't they?

One of the security men began muttering to himself – the only words I could make out were 'three nineteen' and 'call'. He wasn't talking to me.

As far as I'm aware, their microphones are hidden behind the lapels of their jackets, and that's why it often seems like they're talking to themselves. Sometimes it looks very funny. I once saw one of these goons searching a woman's toilet – opening the doors of the cabins and chanting: 'There's no one here . . . There's no one here at all . . . The window's blocked off by a party wall . . .' If I hadn't known what he was doing, I might have thought he was pining over some failed lovers' assignation and pouring out his grief in iambic pentameters.

'Did you pull the cord?' the second security man asked.

'Yes,' I said, 'but where's . . .'

The security man nodded towards an open window. The glass was broken.

'Over there.'

'You mean . . .' I said, making big round eyes, 'he's . . .'

'Yeah,' said the guard. 'Came at us like a lunatic the moment he saw us. Was he doing drugs?'

'What drugs? I've been working here for a year now. Everybody knows me, I've never had any problems.'

'Well, now you do. What did he want from you?'

'I didn't really understand,' I said. 'He wanted me to give him something called a fisting. I said I didn't know how, and then he started . . . Well, anyway, I hid in the bathroom and pulled the alarm. And you saw everything else.'

'We sure did. Got any ID on you?'

I shook my head. Give your passport to these guys and you'll never see it again.

'Maybe I could go? Before the fuzz gets here?'

'What do you mean, go? Are you crazy? You're the main witness,' the security man said. 'You'll have to testify about what you were doing here.'

That definitely wasn't part of my plans. I evaluated the situation. While there were only two of them there, I still had a chance of avoiding any hassle. But it was getting slimmer every second – I knew the room would soon be packed with people.

'Can I go to the toilet?'

The security man nodded, and I went back into the bathroom. I had to act quickly, so I didn't hesitate for a second. I dropped my pants and freed my tail, bent over and opened the door. I did it very abruptly, and the guards immediately turned to look at me.

I believe a man reveals what he's really like in that second when he's already seen a fox's tail but not yet fallen under its hypnotic influence. A client usually has enough time to express his response to what he's seen. And that's enough to tell you who you're dealing with.

All the crude, narrow-minded losers screw their faces up into grimaces of sullen disbelief. But the faces of people who have the potential for inner growth express something like delighted surprise.

One of the security men wrinkled up his forehead and frowned. The other gaped in amazement (I could see his eyes even through his dark glasses) and opened his mouth like a little child who's just seen the birdie the photographer promised him. It looked really sweet.

Of course, I couldn't completely remove my imprint from their memories – to do that to someone, you have to shoot them in the head with a pistol. All I could do was change the context of the memory – I planted the suggestion in their minds that they'd met me in the corridor on their way to the suite. Then I made them go into the bathroom. As soon as the door closed behind them, I picked Stephen Hawking's book up off the floor, dropped it in my handbag, pulled up my trousers and skipped out into the corridor.

There was another security man standing on the stairs. When he saw me, he gestured for me to go over to him, and when I reached him, he ran his hand over my buttocks, forcing me to squeeze my tail in between them as tightly as I could. In any other situation the least he would have got for that was a bruise pinch. But right then it still wasn't clear how everything was going to work out, so I just slapped him on the hand. He wagged his finger at me, and then this gesture flowed smoothly into a different one, as his index finger and thumb connected and started rubbing against each other.

I understood. Girls like me usually hand over a hundred dollars on the way out, but under the present circumstances of *force majeure*, it was being suggested that payment should be made on the spot. I took a portrait of Benjamin Franklin out of my purse and the guard grabbed it with the same finger and thumb that had just been rubbing against each other. There was a certain kind of beauty in the economy of movement – from threat to reminder to acceptance. As the Japanese swordsman Minamoto Musashi said: 'You can tell a master from his stance.'

I walked down the stairs decorated with fleurs-de-lys and made it out into the street without any further adventures. A crowd, including several militiamen, had already gathered to the left of the exit – that was clearly where the unfortunate Sikh was lying. I walked in the opposite direction and a few steps later I was already round the corner. Now all I had to do was stop a taxi. One pulled over almost immediately.

'Bitsevsky Park,' I said. 'The equestrian complex.'

'Three hundred and fifty,' the driver answered.

Today was his lucky day. I jumped into the back, sat down and slammed the door, and the taxi carried me away from the disaster that had seemed inevitable only five minutes earlier.

I had nothing to reproach myself for, but my mood had been spoilt. Apart from the fact that an entirely innocent man had died, I'd lost my job at the National – it wouldn't be wise to show my face in there for the foreseeable future. That meant I'd have to look for other ways to earn a living. And starting from the very next day – my funds were running low, and the hundred dollars I'd given the security guard had thrown my budget into deficit.

An acquaintance of mine used to say that the evil in our lives can only be overcome by money. It's an interesting observation, although not entirely flawless from a metaphysical point of view: what we should really talk about is not victory over evil, but the opportunity to buy it off temporarily. But without money evil is triumphant in just a couple of days, that's proven fact.

I could have got rich, if I earned my living dishonestly. But a virtuous fox must support herself only by prostitution and never, under any circumstances, exploit her hypnotic gift for other purposes – such is the law of heaven, which it is not permitted to transgress. Of course, sometimes you have to. I myself had only just fuddled the brains of two security guards. But you can only do that kind of thing when your life and freedom are in danger. A fox should not even think about gullible money couriers. And if the temptation becomes too great, you have to inspire yourself with examples from history. Jean-Jacques Rousseau could have been swimming in money, but how did he earn a living? By copying out music.

Getting a spot in another hotel wasn't easy, and for the foreseeable future I could only see two alternatives: streetwalking and the Internet. The Internet seemed more attractive, after all, it was at the cutting edge of modern progress, and selling myself on its fibre-optic sidewalks would be stylishly futuristic. How interesting, I thought, everybody's always going on about progress. And what does it all mean? Just that the oldest professions acquire an electronic interface, that's all. Progress doesn't alter the nature of the fundamental processes.

The driver spotted my gloomy mood.

'What's up,' he asked, 'someone upset you, love?'

'Aha,' I said.

He'd been the last person to upset me, when he named a price of three hundred and fifty roubles for the journey.

'Don't you pay 'em any heed,' said the driver. 'You know how many times a day people upset me? If I thought about it every time, my head would be like a great big balloon full of shit. Pay 'em no heed, I tell you. By tomorrow you'll have forgotten all about it. And life's a long business, you know.'

'I know,' I said. 'But how do you do that – pay no heed?'

'Just don't, that's all. Think about something you enjoy instead.'

'And where do I get that from?'

The taxi-driver squinted at me in the mirror.

'Isn't there anything you enjoy in your life?'

'No,' I said.

'You don't mean that.'

'Yes I do.'

'All nothing but suffering, is it?'

'Yes, and so's yours.'

'Well, now,' the taxi-driver laughed, 'you can't know about that.'

'Yes, I can,' I said. 'You wouldn't be sitting here otherwise.'

'Why?'

'I could explain. Only I don't know if you'd understand.'

'Well, get you!' the driver snorted. 'Do you think I'm more stupid than you are? I reckon I ought to be able to understand, if you can.'

'All right. Do you understand that suffering is the material out of which the world was created?'

'Why?'

'That can only be explained with an example.'

'Well, give me an example then.'

'Do you know the story of Baron Münchhausen, who pulled himself out of a bog by his own hair?'

'I do,' said the driver, 'I've even seen the film.'

'The foundations underlying the reality of this world are

32

very similar. Only you have to imagine Münchhausen suspended in a total void, squeezing his own balls as hard as he can and screaming in unbearable pain. Look at it one way and you feel kind of sorry for him. But look at it a different way, and he only has to let go of his own balls and he'll immediately disappear, because by his very nature he is simply a vessel of pain with a grey ponytail, and if the pain disappears, then he'll disappear as well.'

'Did you learn that at school?' the driver asked. 'Or at home?'

'Neither,' I said. 'It was on the way home from school. It's a long journey, I get to see and hear all sorts of things. Did you understand the example?'

'Sure I did,' he replied. 'I'm not stupid. So why's your Münchhausen afraid to let go of his balls?'

'I told you, then he'll disappear.'

'Maybe it would be better if he did? Who the hell needs a life like that?'

'A good point. And that's precisely why the social contract exists.'

'Social contract? What social contract?'

'Every individual Münchhausen can decide to let go of his own balls, but . . .'

I remembered the Sikh's crayfish eyes and stopped. One of my sisters used to say that when a client slips off the tail during an unsuccessful session, for a few seconds he sees the truth. And for a man this truth is so unbearable that the first thing he wants to do is kill the fox responsible for revealing it to him, and then he wants to kill himself . . . But other foxes say that in that brief second the man realizes that physical life is a stupid and shameful mistake. And the first thing he tries to do is to thank the fox who has opened his eyes. And after that he corrects the error of his own existence. It's all nonsense, of course. But it's clear enough how these rumours get started.

'But what?' the driver asked.

I remembered where I was.

'But when there are six billion Münchhausens holding each others' balls arm over arm, the world is in no danger.'

'Why?'

'That's very simple. Münchhausen can let go of himself, as you so correctly observed. But the more someone else hurts him, the more he hurts the two that he's holding on to. And so on for six billion times. Do you understand?'

'Shee-it,' he said and spat, 'only a woman could come up something like that.'

'I have to disagree with you again,' I said. 'It's an extremely male picture of the universe. I'd even call it chauvinistic. There's no place in it for a woman at all.'

'Why?'

'Because women don't have any balls.'

We drove on in silence.

No point in denying it, sometimes it happens that you lay something heavy on someone, and your own heart feels lighter for it. Why is that? It's a mystery. Never mind, let him think a bit, it's never done anyone any harm.

* * *

The next morning the business with the Sikh was in the news. It wasn't what I went onto the net for, but some lousy worm had set my home page to 'rumours.ru' and I'd never got around to changing it. I forced myself to read the article right through to the end:

BUSINESSMAN FROM INDIA KILLS HIMSELF
IN FRONT OF SECURITY GUARDS

The public will soon start thinking of the National hotel as a high-risk zone. With the terrorist attack that took place right outside its door still fresh in the memories of Muscovites, another alarming incident has just taken place: yesterday a forty-year-old businessman from the Indian state of Punjab killed himself by jumping from a fifth floor window. At least that's the story of the two security guards employed by the hotel who were with him at the time the tragedy occurred. They claim that the guest from India summoned them by pulling the special alarm cord, and then when they entered the room, for no apparent reason he took a run and jumped out of the window. He was killed instantly when he hit the surface of the road. It has been established that shortly before his death the businessman had received a visit from a female denizen of the demimonde.

Why the fifth floor, I wondered, when his suite was number 319? Ah yes, they had that swanky European way of numbering the rooms – the first two floors didn't count, so number three nineteen was on the fifth floor . . .

Then my thoughts moved on to that mysterious French word 'demi-monde' – the 'half-world'. Why, I wondered, wasn't it the quarter-world? If you followed that method of word formation, consistently you could define the precise depths to which a woman had fallen. After two thousand years my denominator would probably have been pretty impressive . . .

And then suddenly, at long last, I started to feel ashamed of my own insensitivity. A man with whom I had, in a certain sense, been intimate, had died, and here I was counting floors and doing fractions. The intimacy may have been arbitrary, hallucinatory and temporary, but it was still appropriate to feel some compassion, even if it was as insubstantial as our intimacy had been. Yet I didn't feel any at all – my heart flatly refused to generate it. Instead I started thinking again about the reasons for the previous day's outrageous events:

1) The reason could lie in the astral background of the hotel National, where the dancer Isadora Duncan and the KGB's founder Felix Dzerzhinsky hung side by side in the photo-gallery of 'honoured guests'.
2) What had happened could have been a karmic echo of one of those bloody business rituals they're so fond of in Asia.
3) It was an indirect consequence of India's recoil from the teaching of the Buddha in the Middle Ages.
4) The Sikh had been a worshipper of the goddess Kali after all – why else would he have shouted 'kali ma' as he threw himself out of the window?

I have to explain that sometimes I have as many as five inner voices, with each of them conducting its own inner dialogue: and as well as that, they can start to argue with each other over anything at all. I don't get involved in the argument, I just listen and wait for a hint at the right answer. These voices don't have any names, though. In that sense I'm a simple soul – some foxes have as many as forty of these voices with very long and beautiful names.

The old foxes say these voices belong to the souls that we consumed during the primordial chaos: according to legend, these souls made their home in our inner space by entering into a kind of symbiosis with our own essential nature. But that's probably all just fairy tales, because every one of the voices is mine, although they're all different. And if you follow the old foxes' logic, you could say I myself am a soul that someone else consumed some time in the depths of ancient antiquity. All this is no more than pointless juggling with the various summands, it makes no difference to the sum total that is A Hu-Li.

These voices mean that foxes don't think in the same way as people: the difference is that several thought processes develop in our minds instead of just one. The mind follows several different paths at the same time, keeping an eye open to see which will lead to the light of truth first. In order to convey this peculiarity of my inner life, I designate the various levels of my inner dialogue as 1), 2), 3) and so on.

These thought processes don't intersect with each other in any way – they're absolutely autonomous – but my consciousness is involved in each one of them. Some circus performers juggle a large number of objects at the same time. What they do with their bodies, I do with my mind, that's all. This peculiarity means I have a tendency to draw up lists and break everything down into points and sub-points, even when, from the human point of view, there's no real need for it. Please accept my apologies if you come across such lists broken down into points in these pages – it's exactly the way everything happens inside my head.

Picturing the dead Sikh to myself as accurately as I could, I recited the requiem mantra three times and went to reuters.com to find out what was going on in the world. Everything in the world was just the same as it had been for the last ten thousand years. I rejoiced briefly in the headline 'America Ponders Mad Cow Strategy' and then went to my mail server.

Together with an invitation to increase the length of my sexual organ and a zip file that I didn't open, despite the alluring subject of the message ('Britney Blowing a Horse'), there was a quite unexpected pleasant surprise waiting for me – a letter from my sister E Hu-Li, who I hadn't heard from for ages.

I had known sister E since the times of the Warring Kingdoms. She was a terrible rogue. Many centuries ago she was famous throughout the whole of China as an imperial concubine by the name of Flying Swallow. As a result of watching her fly, the emperor lived for twenty years less than he could have done. After that E Hu-Li was punished by the guardian spirits, and she began keeping a low profile, specializing in rich aristocrats, whom she milked dry in the peace and quiet of their country estates, away from the eyes of the world. For the last few hundred years she'd been living in England.

It was a very short letter:

Hi there, Ginger,

How are you? I hope everything's going well. Sorry to bother you for such a trivial reason, but I need to consult you urgently about something. According to my information, in Moscow there's a Shrine of Christ the Saver that was first demolished completely, leaving not a single stone in place, and then restored to look just the way it used to be. Is this true? What do you know about it? Please answer quickly!

Heads and tails,

E.

Strange, I thought, what's all this about? But she had asked me to reply urgently. I clicked on the 'reply' button.

Hello, Carrot-Top,

Up here in the north everything's still the same as ever. I'll write in more detail some time, but meanwhile here's the answer to your question. Yes there is a Cathedral of Christ the Saviour (that's the correct form) in Moscow. It was blown up after the revolution and restored at the end of the last century. There really wasn't a single stone left standing – for a long time there used to be a swimming pool where it had been. But now the swimming pool has been filled in and the cathedral has been built again. The cultural significance of this event is highly ambiguous – at one of the demonstrations I saw the slogan:

'We demand the restoration of the Moscow swimming pool,
barbarously destroyed by the cleptocracy!' Since I personally
have never visited either the first or the second facility, I have
no opinion of my own on this subject.
Heads and tails,
A.

I sent the letter and went to the site whores.ru.

It looked very picturesque – even most of the pop-up ads were subject-related:

SEE PARIS AND LIVE!
DUREX ANAL EXTRA STRONG.

SUVs had appeared even among the condoms. The market was seeking out new approaches and niches: I came across 'Occam's Razor' condoms with a portrait of the medieval scholast and the slogan: 'Pluralitas non est ponenda sine necessitate' – 'One should not multiply entities without necessity'. I used to know William of Occam personally. I remember him chasing me round his house in Munich, and two centuries after that the Reformation began – for some reason the two entirely unrelated events have fused together in my memory. But I had no time now for reminiscences – I had to compose an ad for myself quickly, and to do it I had to familiarize myself with already existing examples.

Fortunately, there was a huge number of them. I found one feature of the genre rather amusing: many of the girls brightened up their notices with a few inserts in verse that had nothing to do with the list of services on offer – it was a kind of verbal piercing, and I decided to have a go at it as well.

An hour later my text was ready. A demanding critic might perhaps have described it as an eclectic compilation, but I wasn't trying to make a name for myself in literary circles. My announcement began like this:

I'm a bright and nimble maid,
Mistress of the intimate trade!

Just the way you like it, a bright smile and slender waist,
Service classical and anal, passion geared to every taste.

The second couplet, separated from the first by an empty line, was not linked to it by rhyme or rhythm – they were like two different earrings in the lobe of one ear. It looked and sounded really authentic, just like what the other girls did. The lines of verse were set in bold script and the information followed:

A FAIRY-TALE CUM TRUE!
Small breasts for big money. A little ginger kitten is waiting for a call from a well-to-do gentleman. Classic sex, deep and royal head, anal, petting, bondage, whipping (including the Russian Knout), foot fetish, strap-on, sakura branch, lesbo, oral and anal stimulation, cunnilingus (including compulsory), role-swapping, two-way gold and silver rain, fisting, piercing, catheter, copro, enema, gentle and heavy domination, Mistress and Slave Girl services. Face control. Visits by arrangement. Many things are possible. Almost everything. Shag me and forget! If you can . . .

A fine little kitten, I thought when I reread what I'd written. I must admit I didn't really understand what the bandage was doing in there and why anyone would want a sakura branch up his ass. I didn't have a very clear idea of what fisting was, either, but judging from what the other announcements said, it was either oral or vaginal, which made it the same kind of filth as all the rest. I supposed it must mean shoving in the fist? Did that mean it could be *per oris* too? In one of the announcements I even saw the following list: 'fellatio, PR, cunnilingus'. What did that mean? Or 'strap-on'? It sounded like something cosmic, from the romantic sixties of the last century. But, fortunately, I didn't have to know what strap-on was – the only thing needed was to introduce myself to the client.

I don't think anyone but a fox can understand how I could provide a 'strap-on' service without even knowing what it is. It's not easy to explain that kind of thing, all you can do is offer analogies. I sense a client's consciousness as a warm, spongy sphere, and in order to send the poor soul into the world of his dreams, first I have to make a little dent in the very hottest spot of that sphere with my tail, and then make the little dent smooth itself out and ripple across the surface of the sphere. That will just be a strap-on. But if I gently force the dent to fold back over on to itself so that it becomes a tender little nipple, that will be the kind of strap-on the client will remember and drool over until his mind finally drowns in the cold ocean of Alzheimer's disease.

The same thing applies to fisting, light domination and all the rest. If, say, you want to take an elderly transvestite with higher musical education and a gold tooth in his mouth, and beat him to death with a baseball bat, even then I can assist you with your dubious project. But it's better for me not to know everything that's going on in someone else's mind – it's easier to keep my own soul pure that way.

That's why I had no doubts about my ability to cope with the list of services advertised, no matter what they might be. But there was still something missing in the text. I thought for a moment and then, after 'A little ginger kitten is waiting for a call from well-to-do gentleman' I wrote in:

Transsexual, versatile, penis 26x4. Always following the rules means denying yourself all the pleasures! We need to know how to commit the follies that our nature demands of us.

Ah, if only they knew what our true nature is, I sighed, and took out 'Transsexual'. As the chef of the Grand Duke Mikhail

Alexandrovich used to say, before the revolution: 'You can't spoil gruel with butter, but you can spoil butter with gruel.' Something else was required . . . After thinking about it for a while, I decided to replace 'Mistress and Slave Girl services' with 'Mistress, Slave Girl and Ray of Light services'. That didn't impose any additional physical exertions on me, not even imaginary ones, but it opened up wide scope for fantasy.

Fantasy . . . A courtesan I used to know in China during the Late Han period often used to say that a man's weak spot is the fantasies that fill his mind. When she got old, she was given to a nomad leader as severance pay, and he boiled the poor woman in mare's milk, hoping to bring back her youth. A weakness can sometimes become a terrible strength.

I could have gone on improving the text ad infinitum – everyone knows that for a real poet the process continues until the moment the publisher calls round to collect the manuscript. In this case I had to collect the manuscript from myself. And so I decided to put a full stop after the final touchingly artless couplet at the end:

> Turbulent stream, pining without affection,
> I promise you a passionate connection!

I'd never worked with the site whores.ru before. The procedure for posting information turned out to be the same as on other similar facilities, but there was one unpleasant difference. Posting plain text cost 150 dollars, photographs were twenty apiece. I had three of the WMZ cards that they accepted for payment on the site – a hundred, a fifty and a twenty. Obviously the whole thing was set up to suit these values. I could only post one photo – or else I would have to go to the nearest Metro station for a new supply of Internet money. I decided to make do with one picture, but to send it immediately, so that in the morning it would already be hanging out there on the wires. But I still didn't manage to send the photograph off quickly – I spent almost an hour choosing it.

The choice proved difficult because every alternative tinted the services in my list in a different hue, illuminating the *strap-on* and the *fisting* with new nuances of meaning . . . Eventually I settled on an old black and white photograph – me in front of a set of bookshelves, with a volume of Alexander Blok in my hands. The book was *The Snow Mask*, and the photo itself, taken in the 1930s, had a magical, mysterious air to it, as if it had captured the final glimmering of the Silver Age of Russian literature – which was very appropriate for the final service offered in my list. It was a good thing I'd had my most precious negatives and daguerrotypes digitized.

All that left me to do was choose my artistic pseudonym. I found a suitable list through Google and chose a name from the very beginning – Adele, which reminded me of the Russian word for hell – 'ad'.

It was a good quality photo and it took up half a megabyte. I clicked on the 'send' button. My little face obediently smiled, shot through the wires into the wall, was swept into the telephone cable and skipped along the electrical backbone of the street, to be intertwined with the other names and faces hurtling along from God knew where to God knew where else, as it dashed towards the distant network gateway.

* * *

The call in response to the announcement came the next morning, shortly after eleven. The client's name was Pavel Ivanovich. His interest had been caught by the line about the Russian knout. It turned out that he had his own Russian knout, in fact not just one of them, but five – four on a special carved wooden stand and one in his tennis bag.

Let me say straight away that I would quite happily have thrown all mention of Pavel Ivanovich out of my memoirs, but without him the narrative would be incomplete. He played an important part in my life, in the same way as a filthy, slimy pedestrian underpass might if the heroine happens to walk through it on her way to the other bank of the river of fate. And so I shall have to tell you about him, and I beg your forgiveness in advance for the unappetizing details. Some computer games have a 'Tx2' button, and after you press it time moves twice as fast as before. So now I'll press my little 'Tx2' button and try to boil him down into the least possible volume.

I think it was Diogenes Laertius who told the story about a philosopher who studied for three years to rid himself of all passion, paying money to every man who insulted him. When his period of study was completed, he stopped giving out money, but the habitual skills remained with him: one day he was insulted by some ignoramus, and instead of setting about him with his fists, he began to laugh. 'Well, did you ever,' he said, 'today I received for nothing what I'd been paying for three whole years!'

When I first read about this, I felt envious that I didn't have any similar practice in my life. But after I met Pavel Ivanovich I realized that now I did.

Pavel Ivanovich was an elderly scholar of the humanities who looked like a melted-down, hairy pink candle. Formerly he had been a *right-wing liberal* (I didn't understand what this outrageous word-combination meant), but following the common trend he had repented to such an extent that he had assumed personal responsibility for all the woes of the motherland. In order to soothe his soul, he had to take a flogging once or twice a week from *Young Russia*, which he had condemned to poverty by forcing it to earn a living by flogging old perverts instead of studying in university. And so he was caught in a closed circle,

44

which I might possibly have pondered on more deeply, if only he hadn't masturbated during the session. That destroyed all the mystery.

If he'd had a real sex worker from somewhere in Ukraine as his own *Young Russia*, she would never have agreed to be paid only 50 dollars for a one-hour session. Flogging someone is hard work, even when the procedure is merely a hypnotic suggestion. However, I began going to Pavel Ivanovich's place not just for the sake of the money, but also because he irritated me quite incredibly, provoking uncontrollable spasms of wild fury in me. I had to summon up all my willpower to keep myself in hand. For sheer practical reasons I ought to have gone for richer sponsors, but character has to be trained during the difficult periods of life, when the meaning of doing it is not obvious. That's when it does the most good.

So that I could understand my part in what was going on, Pavel Ivanovich gave me a detailed account of all the reasons for his repentance. I was going to take another 50 dollars an hour for this understanding, and I was just waiting for the moment to come when I could bring up the matter of the extra charge. But it never came – Pavel Ivanovich spoke at exceptional length:

'Between 1940 and 1946, my dear, the volume of industrial output in Russia fell by twenty-five per cent. And that was with all the horrors of war. But between 1990 and 1999 it slumped by over half . . . worse than Genghis Khan and Hitler taken together. And that's not just commie propaganda and lies. It's what Joseph Stieglitz writes – the chief economist of the World Bank and a Nobel Prize winner. Have you read *Globalisation and its Discontents*? What a terrifying book! And America doesn't even need the atom bomb, because it has the World Trade Organization and the International Monetary Fund . . .'

I actually began to forget what I was doing there in his apartment, and only the leather knout lying on the table between us reminded me of it. It soon emerged that Pavel Ivanovich's repentance was total, embracing not only the economic aspect of the Russian reforms, but also the cultural history of the last few decades.

'Did you know,' he said, staring keenly into my eyes, 'that the CIA actually financed the beatnik movement and the psychological revolution? The goal was to create an attractive image of the West for our youth. They wanted to pretend that America has fun. So they did – and for a while they even believed it themselves. But the funniest thing of all is that all these children of LSD generals who tried KGB and strove so hard to copy the beatniks really were doing just what the CIA wanted, that is, they were committing the very sin the Party accused them of! And they were the future intelligentsia, the nerve system of the nation . . .'

In speaking of the intelligentsia's debt of guilt to the nation, he kept using two terms that I thought were synonyms – 'intelligentsia' and 'intellectuals'. After a while I just had to ask:

'But what difference is there between a member of the intelligentsia and an intellectual?'

'There's a very big difference,' he replied. 'I can only try to explain it allegorically. Do you understand what that means?'

I nodded.

'When you were still very little, there were a hundred thousand people living in this city who were paid for kissing the ass of a loathsome red dragon – which you probably don't even remember . . .'

I shook my head. Once in my young days I really had seen a red dragon, but I'd already forgotten what it looked like – the only thing I could remember was my own fear. It was unlikely that Pavel Ivanovich had that incident in mind.

'Of course, those hundred thousand people hated the dragon, and they dreamed of being ruled by the green toad who fought against the dragon. So, anyway, they came to an arrangement with the toad, poisoned the dragon with lipstick that they got from the CIA and started living a new life.'

'But what have the intell –'

'Wait,' he said, raising his hand. 'At first they thought that under the toad they would be doing exactly the same as before, only they'd get ten times as much money for it. But it turned out that instead of a hundred thousand ass-kissers there was only a demand for three professionals working in three eight-hour shifts to give the toad a never-ending royal blowjob. And which of the hundred thousand those three would be, would be decided by an open competition, in which candidates would not only have to demonstrate their advanced professional skills, but also the ability to smile optimistically with the corners of their mouths while they were at work . . .'

'I'm afraid I've lost the thread.'

'Well, this is the thread. Those hundred thousand people were called the intelligentsia. And those three are called intellectuals.'

I have one quirk that is rather hard to explain. I can't stand it when anyone uses the word blowjob in my presence – outside the context of work, at least. I don't know why, but it just drives me wild. And in addition, Pavel Ivanovich's explanation seemed like such a crude, boorish hint at my own profession that I even forgot about the additional fee I'd been planning to ask for.

'Are you talking about a blowjob so that I can understand? On the basis of my experience of life?'

'Of course not, my dear,' he said patronizingly. 'I explain things in those terms because then I start to understand the point myself. And the point here is not your experience of life, but mine . . .'

The next time he started reading a magazine during his flogging. That was insulting enough. But when he started prodding the article with his finger and muttering, 'Why don't you just keep your mouth shut, you bastard,' I began to get annoyed and interrupted the procedure, that is, I planted the suggestion of a pause in his mind.

'What's wrong?' he asked in surprise.

'Tell me, are we doing a flagellation here, or is this a library day?'

'I'm sorry, darling,' he said, 'this interview's outrageous. It's absolutely incredible!'

He slapped his fingers down on the magazine.

'I've got nothing against detective novels, but I can't stand it when the people who write them start explaining how we ought to arrange things in Russia.'

'Why?'

'It's just like some underage prostitute who's been given a lift by a long-distance truck driver so she can give him a blowjob suddenly stops work, looks up and starts giving him instructions about how to flush the carburettor in a frost.'

Pavel Ivanovich clearly didn't understand just how insulting that sounds in a conversation with a sex worker. But I became aware of my upsurge of rage before it overwhelmed me, so that my soul was immediately flooded with a calm joy.

'What's wrong with that?' I asked in a perfectly natural voice. 'Maybe she's serviced so many truckers that she's picked up all the subtle points and now she really can teach him how to flush his carburettor.'

'Darling, I pity the kind of truck drivers who need to take advice from an underage blowjob provider. They won't get very far.'

'An underage blowjob provider' – that was what he said. Why, what a . . . I caught another outburst of fury in the very instant it began, and stopped the anger before it could manifest itself.

This was great. It was like jumping on to a surfboard during a storm and coasting along over the waves of destructive emotions that can't even touch you. If only it had always been like this, I

48

thought, so many people would have lived longer lives . . . I didn't argue with Pavel Ivanovich about the substance of what he said. It's best if we foxes who follow the Supreme Tao don't have any opinions of our own on such matters. But one thing was clear: Pavel Ivanovich was an invaluable exercise machine for training the spirit.

Unfortunately, I realized too late that the load was too heavy for me. The first time I lost control it didn't lead to any injuries. I was driven wild by a phrase about Nabokov (not to mention the fact that he had a photocopy of an article entitled 'The appearance of the hairdresser to the waiters: the phenomenon of Nabokov in American culture' lying on his desk).

I had loved Nabokov since the 1930s, ever since I used to get hold of his Paris texts from highly placed clients in the NKVD. What a breath of fresh air those typed pages were in Stalin's gloomy capital! I remember I was particularly struck by one place in the 'Paris Poem', which I didn't come across until after the war:

> *Life is irreversible –*
> *It will be staged in a new theatre,*
> *In a different way, with different actors.*
> *But the ultimate happiness*
> *Is to fold its magic carpet*
> *And make the ornament of the present*
> *Match the pattern of the past . . .*

Vladimir Vladimirovich wrote that about us foxes. That's exactly what we do, constantly folding the carpet. We watch the endless performance played out by bustling human actors who behave as if they were the first people ever to perform on the stage. They all die off with incredible speed, and their place is taken by the new intake, who begin playing out the same old parts with the same old pomposity.

49

Of course, the scenery keeps changing, sometimes far too much. But the play itself hasn't changed for a long, long time. And since we can remember more exalted times, we are constantly tormented by a yearning for lost beauty and meaning, so those words touched many strings at once . . . And by the way, that carpet from 'Paris Poem' was later inherited by Humbert Humbert:

Where are you riding, Dolores Haze?
What make is the magic carpet?

I know what make it is. It was woven in Paris on a summer day sometime around 1938, under gigantic white clouds frozen in the azure heavens, and it travelled to America in a roll . . . It took all the abomination of the Second World War, all the monstrosity of the choices that it dictated, for that carpet to be hung up in Humbert's reception room . . . and then this scholar of the humanities blurts out:

'Happiness, my darling, is such a contradictory thing. Dostoevsky questioned whether it was permissible if it was paid for by a child's tear. But Nabokov, on the other hand, doubted whether happiness could ever be possible without it.'

I couldn't tolerate a vile insult like that to a dead writer and threw the whip down on the floor. I mean I didn't just stop making Pavel Ivanovich think he was being flogged, I made him see the whip hit the floor so hard that it left a dent in the parquet. I had to scrape it out afterwards by hand, when he went to the shower. I always avoid arguing with people, but this time I just exploded and started talking seriously, as if I was with another fox:

'I feel insulted when someone confuses Nabokov with his characters. Or calls him the godfather of American paedophilia. That's such a profoundly mistaken view of the writer. Remember this – Nabokov isn't speaking for himself when he describes the

50

forbidden charms of a nymphet at such length. He speaks for himself when he describes in meagre terms, in the very merest hint, the impressive financial resources that allow Humbert to freewheel round America with Lolita. A writer's true heart speaks out very furtively . . .'

I remembered where I was and stopped. I took Lolita's story very personally and very seriously. For me Dolores Haze was a symbol of the soul, eternally young and pure, and Humbert Humbert was the metaphorical chairman of this world's board of directors. Apart from that, in the line of verse describing Lolita's age ('Age: five thousand three hundred days') it was enough to replace the word 'days' with 'years' and it would more or less fit me. Naturally, I didn't share that observation with Pavel Ivanovich.

'Go on, go on,' he said in amazement.

'Of course, what the writer was dreaming about wasn't a green young schoolgirl, but the modest financial security that would allow him to catch butterflies in peace somewhere in Switzerland. I see nothing shameful in such a dream for a Russian nobleman who has realized the vanity of the heroic feat of a human life. And the choice of subject for the book intended to provide that security offers less insight into the secret aspirations of his heart than what he thought about his new fellow-countrymen and just how indifferent he was to what they thought about him. And the fact that the book turned out to be a masterpiece isn't hard to explain either – talent is hard to conceal . . .'

As I concluded this tirade, in my own mind I cursed myself, and with good reason.

I'm a professional impersonator of an adolescent girl with big innocent eyes. Creatures like that don't utter long sentences about the work of writers from the last century. They talk simply in monosyllables, mostly about material, visible things. And now . . .

'Well, didn't you get carried away,' Pavel Ivanovich muttered in astonishment. 'Eyes blazing, eh? Where did you pick up all that stuff?'

'Here and there,' I said in a morose voice.

I swore a solemn oath to myself never to get into an argument about culture with him again, but only to exploit him for his proper purpose, as a gymnastic apparatus for developing my spiritual strength. But it was too late.

* * *

In modern society it is fatal to give way to social instincts acquired in other times, and in a culture that was very dissimilar. They're like gyroscopes trained on a planet which was blown to bits: it's best not to think where the course they indicate might lead to.

The people who lived in ancient China were highly spiritual. If I'd demonstrated that kind of knowledge of the classical canon to any scholar then, he'd have gone into debt in order to reward me with double pay and he would have sent a letter in verse to my home, bound to a branch of plum blossom. Perhaps my old memories had led me to expect something similar when I started talking to Pavel Ivanovich about Nabokov. But the result was quite different.

The next time we met, Pavel Ivanovich asked me to conduct the session on credit because he'd just bought a refrigerator. He expressed this request in the spirit of a secret accomplice, an old comrade tried and tested in journeys to the heights of the spirit. A poet borrowing a bottle of ink from a colleague might have spoken like that. I couldn't refuse.

The new refrigerator took up almost half his kitchen, it looked like the tip of an iceberg that had broken through the side of a ship and smashed into the hold. But nonetheless the captain of the ship was drunk and jolly. I'd noticed a long time before that nothing delights a member of the Russian intelligentsia (Pavel Ivanovich could hardly make the grade as an intellectual) as the purchase of a new electrical household appliance.

I don't like drunks, so I was acting a bit sullen. No doubt he put that down to the fact that the session was being conducted on credit, and he wasn't particularly demanding. We got down to work in silence, like a pair of Estonian yachtsmen who have sailed together for ages: he handed me the tattered knout that he kept in the tennis bag with Boris Becker's signature on it, got undressed, lay down on the sofa and opened a fresh copy of *Expert* magazine.

I guessed that what was going on had nothing to do with his disdainful attitude to my art, or even his love for the printed word. Clearly his contrition before Young Russia coexisted in his heart with other vibes about which I knew nothing, and he hadn't revealed all of his secrets to me. But I felt no urge to penetrate his inner world beyond the depth that had been paid for, and so I didn't ask any questions. Everything was going as usual – I was lashing his backside with an imaginary knout, thinking my own thoughts, and he was muttering quietly. Sometimes he would start to groan, sometimes to laugh. It was boring, and I felt like some odalisque in an oriental harem, waving away the flies from her master's fat carcass with regular sweeps of a fan. Then suddenly he said:

'Would you believe it, what a name for a lawyer – Anton Drill. How did he manage to survive with that . . . I bet the kids gave him hell in school . . . People with names like that grow up psychological deviants, it's a fact. They all need help from a psychotherapist. Any expert can tell you that.'

Of course, I shouldn't have got involved in the conversation – there was absolutely no point in taking the situation beyond the limitations of our professional relationship. The reason I didn't hold back is that names are a sore point with me.

'That's simply not true,' I said. 'It doesn't matter what name anybody has. I have a girlfriend, for instance, and she has a name that sounds very, very crude. So crude you'd laugh out loud if I told you it. It's almost a swearword, you could say, that kind of name. But she's a beautiful girl, clever and kind. A name's not a prison sentence.'

'Perhaps, my dear, you don't know your friend very well. If her name has an obscene meaning, then it will come out in her life. Just you wait, it will manifest itself yet. Everything depends on the name. There's a scientific hypothesis that every person's name is a primary suggestive command that contains the entire script of their life in highly concentrated form. Do you understand what a suggestive command is? Do you at least have some idea about hypnotic suggestion?'

'In general terms,' I replied, and mentally lashed him a bit harder.

'Ooh . . . According to this point of view, there is only a limited number of names, because society only needs a limited number of human types. Just a few models of worker and warrior ants, if I could put it like that. And everybody's psyche is programmed at a basic level by the associative semantic fields that their first name and surname activate.'

'Nonsense,' I said irritably. 'No two people in the world with identical names are the same.'

'Just as no two ants are the same. But nonetheless ants are divided into functional classes . . . No, a name is a serious thing. Some names are like time bombs.'

'What do you mean by that?'

'Here's a real-life story for you. There was a Shakespeare scholar called Shitman who worked in the Institute of World Culture. He was getting along just fine, until one day he decided to learn English so that he could read his author and benefactor

54

in the original . . . And he wanted to go to England – "to see London and die" as he put it. He started studying. And after a few lessons he learned what "shit" means in English. Can you imagine it? If he'd been a chemistry teacher, for instance, it wouldn't have been so awful. But for specialists in the humanities words mean a lot, Derrida pointed that out. It's hard to serve the cause of the beautiful wearing a decoration like that in your buttonhole. He began to feel as if the people in the British Council were giving him queer looks . . . In fact, just then the British Council couldn't care less about the local Shakespeare specialists, because they were being screwed by the tax police, but Shitman decided it was their personal attitude to him. As you can understand, my dear, when someone looks for confirmation of his paranoid ideas, he always finds it. Anyway, omitting all the sad details, he went insane in a month.'

By this point I was positively seething with rage. I felt he was trying to insult me, although there were no rational grounds for such an assumption – he couldn't possibly know my true name. But I remembered that the most important thing was to stay in control. Which I managed to do perfectly well.

'Really?' I asked politely.

'Yes. In the madhouse he wouldn't talk to anyone, just yelled so the entire hospital could hear him. Sometimes he yelled "same shit, different day", sometimes "same shite, different night". He obviously hadn't wasted his time studying English. In the end they took Shitman away in a car with military number plates – the special services needed him, let's put it that way. And nobody knows what's become of him now, or if they do know, they're not telling. So much for a midsummer night's dream, my little darling. And they say nothing depends on a name. But it does, and how. If your friend has an obscenity in her name, sooner or later her path leads to only one place. It's the madhouse for her. And by the way, Shitman was lucky, the special forces found a use for him. You must have heard about our madhouses. You can get a blowjob for a cigarette in there . . .'

Spiritual training using a human irritant is like a game of chance in which everything is staked on the kitty. The winnings are very big. But if you can't take the heat and you lose control, you lose absolutely everything else too. I could have put up with doing the session on credit, even with his theory of obscene names, if only he hadn't thrown in that blowjob for a cigarette. I wasn't prepared for that.

'Sweetheart!' Pavel Ivanovich screamed. 'Sweetheart, what's wrong? What are you doing, you snake? Militia! Anybody! Help!'

When he started calling for the militia, I came to my senses. But it was too late – Pavel Ivanovich had received three lashes that even Mel Gibson wouldn't have been ashamed of. And even though those three lashes were only hypnotic, the blood that had started running down his back was real. Of course, I regretted what I'd done, but that always happens a second later than it ought to. And anyway, in my heart I played another cunning trick – knowing I would be overwhelmed by repentance at any moment, and adopting the inner stance of a repentant sinner, I said in a final vengeful, voluptuous whisper:

'That's for you from Young Russia, you stupid old fart . . .'

As I review my life now, I find many dark spots in it. But the sense of shame I feel for this is exceptionally keen.

* * *

Many shrines in Asia surprise the traveller by the contrast between the bare poverty of their empty rooms and the multi-level splendour of their roofs – with their upturned corners, precious carved dragons and scarlet tiles. The symbolic meaning here is clear: treasure should not be stored up on earth, but in heaven. The walls symbolize this world, the roof symbolizes the next. Look at the building itself and it's a hovel. But look at the roof and it's a palace.

I found the contrast between Pavel Ivanovich and his 'roof' – the modern Russian term for protection – equally fascinating, even though there was absolutely no spiritual symbolism involved. Pavel Ivanovich was merely a petty philological demon. But the roof over his head . . . But then, all in good time.

The call came two days after the lashing, at eight-thirty in the morning, too early even for a client with special oddities. The number that lit up didn't mean a thing to me. I'd been up since four o'clock and already managed to get a lot of things done, but just in case I drawled in a sleepy voice:

'Hello-o . . .'

'Adele?' a cheerful voiced asked. 'I'm ringing about your advert.'

I'd already taken the announcement off the site, but someone could easily have saved it for future reference, clients often do that.

'Let a girl get some sleep, eh?'

'Triple rates for short notice. If you're there in an hour.'

When I heard the words 'triple rates', I stopped being difficult and wrote down the address. One of my Latin American sisters told me that the Panamanian general Noriega liked to drink whisky non-stop all night long, and early in the morning he would send for one of the six women who he always had around him to have sex – my sister knew this, because she was one of them. But that's Panama – cocaine and hot blood. For our latitudes such early morning passion was a little bit strange. But I didn't sense any danger.

For the sake of speed I took the Metro and in fifty minutes I was already there. The client lived in the quiet centre of town. When I walked into the courtyard of the building I wanted (a tall concrete candle with pretensions to architectural originality), I thought at first that I'd made a mistake and this was the back entrance to some bank.

There were two guards standing by the metal gates in the wall. They looked at me in glum incomprehension and I showed them the piece of paper with the address on it. Then one them of nodded towards an unobtrusive porch with an intercom on it. I walked up to the intercom.

'Adele?' the voice in the speaker asked.

'In person.'

'Come up to the first floor, the last door,' said the intercom. 'You'll see when you get here.'

The door opened.

It didn't look much like a block of flats. There wasn't any lift, or any real stairway either. That is, there was one, but it ended on the first floor, running straight up to a black door with no spy-hole or bell, but with the tiny lens of a TV camera glinting in the wall beside it. As if someone had bought up all the flats from the first floor up and made a single entrance. But that's a vulgar comparison, owing to the absence of any legitimate culture of large-scale property ownership in Russia. I didn't have to ring – as soon as I reached the door, it opened.

Standing in the doorway was a solidly built man of about fifty, dressed like a bandit from the nineties. He was wearing an Adidas tracksuit, trainers and gold – a bracelet and a chain.

'Come in,' he said, then turned round and walked back down the corridor.

It was a strange place that looked like some kind of business premises. One of the doors in the corridor was half open. Through the gap I could see a nickel-plated metal pole that disappeared down through a circular hole in the floor. But the client closed the door and I didn't get a good look at anything.

'Come on in,' he said, letting me past him.

The bedroom at the end of the corridor looked perfectly civilized, only I didn't like the smell – it smelled of dog, quite unmistakably, like in some dogs' love hotel. As well as a bed, the room contained a low coffee table with a drawer and two armchairs. There was a bottle of champagne on the table, with two glasses, and standing beside them was a telephone with a large number of keys and a blue plastic document folder.

'Where's the shower?' I asked.

The man sat in a chair and indicated the one beside it.

'Wait, there's no hurry. Let's get to know each other first.'

He smiled paternally, and I decided I must have got stuck with one of those *soulful* clients. Those men who don't just want your body for their two hundred bucks, but your soul as well. They're the ones who really wear you out. To stop a soulful client getting carried away, you have to be morose and unsociable. Let the nice man think the girl's got adolescent problems. During the period when their personalities are taking shape, teenagers are unsociable and uncommunicative, as every paedophile knows very well. Therefore, that kind of behaviour rapidly inflames a pervert's lust, which results in a saving of time and is helpful in obtaining better payment for your work. But the important thing here is to shut yourself in the bathroom in good time.

Some foxes who live in America and Europe take a scientific approach to the use of this effect. That is, they think they take a scientific approach, because they prepare by reading the literature that 'reveals the soul of the modern teenager'. They are particularly fond of reading alleged fifteen-year-old authors who specialize in removing the panties from the inner world of their generation with a shy blush on their cheeks. It's ridiculous, of course. Teenagers don't have any common internal dimension – just as people of any other age don't. Each of them lives in his or her own universe, and these insights into the soul of the young generation are simply the market's simulacra of freshness for the consumer who's surfeited with anal sex on video, something like the chemical scent of lily-of-the-valley for toilets. A fox who wants to imitate the behaviour of a modern teenager accurately shouldn't read those books: instead of making you look like a teenager, they'll turn you into an old theatrical queer acting out a travesty.

The correct technique is quite different. And like everything that really works, it's extremely simple:

1) In a conversation you should look off to one side, best of all at a spot on the floor about two metres away.
2) Never answer what people say with more than three words, not counting prepositions and conjunctions.
3) Every tenth utterance, or thereabouts, should break rule number two and be slightly provocative, so that the client doesn't get the feeling he's dealing with an imbecile.

'What's your name?' he asked.
'Adele,' I said, squinting at the floor.
'How old are you?'
'Seventeen.'
'You sure you're not lying?'
I shook my head.
'Where are you from, Adele?'
'Khabarovsk, in the Far East.'
'And how are things back in Khabarovsk?'
I shrugged.
'Okay.'
'So why did you come here?'
I shrugged again.
'Just felt like it.'
'You're not very talkative.'
'Can I go to the shower?'

'Hang on. We have to get to know each other first. What are we, animals?'

'It's two hundred dollars an hour.'

'I'll bear that in mind,' he said. 'Doesn't it disgust you doing this kind of work, Adele?'

'I have to eat.'

He picked the folder up off the table, opened it and spent a while looking at it, as if he were checking some kind of instructions. Then he closed it and put it back on the table.

'And where do you live? Are you renting a place?' he asked.

'Uhu.'

'And how many of you are there in the flat, apart from the madam? Five? Ten?'

'That depends.'

At this stage the ordinary pervert would already have reached boiling point. And it looked like my employer wasn't too far away from it either.

'Are you really seventeen, little girl?' he asked.

'Yes, daddy, I am,' I said, raising my eyes to look at him. 'Seventeen moments of spring.'

That was a provocative outburst. He snorted in laughter. What I should have done then was to go back to the short, vague phrases. But it turned out he knew how to be provocative as well.

'All right,' he said. 'If that's the way our chat's going, it's time for me to introduce myself.'

An official ID card appeared on the table in front of me, open. I read what was written in it very carefully, then compared the photograph with his face. In the photograph he was wearing a uniform jacket with epaulettes. His name and patronymic were Vladimir Mikhailovich. He was a colonel in the FSB.

'Call me Mikhalich,' he said with a smirk. 'That's what people who know me well call me. And I hope we're going to get to know each other very well.'

'To what do I owe the pleasure, Mikhalich?' I asked.

'One of our consultants complained about you. Apparently you upset him. So now you'll have to recompensate for it. Or recompense for it. Do you know which is right?'

* * *

He had a stereotypical appearance: a strong chin, steely eyes, a shock of flaxen hair. But a certain trapezoidal quality in the plebeian proportions of his features made his face look like the West's cliche of its Cold War opponent. Movie characters of that kind usually drank a glass of vodka and then ate the glass as a snack, muttering through the crunching that it was 'an old Russian custom'.

'Fuck it,' I muttered. 'A freebee?'

'Hey,' he said, offended, 'don't you confuse the FSB with the pigs. You'll get your money all right.'

'How many of you are there?' I asked in a tired voice.

'Just one . . . Well, two at the most.'

'And who's the other one?'

'You'll see in a moment. And don't worry, I won't cheat you.'

He pulled out the drawer of the table and took out a box with all sorts of medical bits and pieces – little jars, cotton wool and a pack of disposable syringes. One syringe was loaded – the bright-red cap on the needle made it look like a cigarette someone has dragged on so furiously that the flame has extended all the way along it.

'I not shooting up with you,' I said. 'Not even for quintuple fees.'

'You fool,' he said merrily, 'who's going to give you any?'

'And I want the money up front. Who knows what you'll be like in half an hour?'

'Here, take it,' he said and threw me an envelope.

Members of the Russian middle class often give me dollars in an envelope – the same way they get them when they receive their 'unofficial' salaries. It's exciting. As if you've been raised aloft on the wheel of social insight and offered a glimpse of the intimate linkages in your Homeland's economic mechanism . . . I opened the envelope and counted the money. The promised triple fee was there, plus another fifty dollars. Effectively the same level of pay as at the National. A client like that ought to be cherished – or at least I ought to pretend to cherish him. I smiled enchantingly.

'Okay, if I have to recompense, I'll recompensate. Where's the bathroom.'

'Just wait, will you,' he said. 'You've got plenty of time. Sit tight.'

'I . . .'

'Sit tight,' he repeated and started rolling up his sleeve.

'You said there'd be another one. So where is he?'

'Just as soon as I shoot up, he'll be here.'

He put a rubber strap round his biceps, then clasped and unclasped his fist several times.

'What are we shooting?' I enquired morosely.

I had to know what to prepare myself for.

'We're taking a ride down the Kashirksy Highway.'

I realized the syringe was full of ketamine, an extremely powerful psychedelic that only a psychopath or someone trying to commit suicide would ever inject into a vein.

'What, intravenously?' I asked, unable to believe it.

He nodded. I suddenly felt afraid. I couldn't even stand the ketamine junkies who injected it into the muscle. That stuff had a gloomy kind of effect on them. They became like trolls from beyond the grave, crushed by the weight of some eternal curse – like soldiers in the ghost army in the final episode of *The Lord of the Rings*. And this guy was about to take it intravenously. I didn't even know anyone did that. That is, I knew for certain that sane people didn't do it. A second stiff in less than a month was definitely the very last thing I needed. It was time to clear out.

'Listen, why don't I give you the money back,' I said, 'and we'll call it a day.'

'What's the problem?'

'It's okay for you, you'll be dead. But they'll drag me round the courts. I'd better go.'

'I said sit tight!' Mikhalich growled.

He got up, went over to the door, locked it and put the key in his pocket.

'Get up and you'll regret it. Understand?'

I nodded. He came back to the table, sat down and took a strange device that looked a bit like a Soviet-designed paper-punch out of his medicine box. The device consisted of two semi-circular plates connected by a simple mechanism. There was a large rubber sucker attached to the lower plate, and the upper one was stamped with a star and an inventory number, like a pistol. Mikhalich brought the two plates together, licked the rubber sucker obsessively and stuck the device on his fore-arm. Then he set the syringe in the gap, carefully introduced the needle into a vein and checked – the liquid in the syringe had turned dark-red. Then he touched a little lever on the strange device, and it started ticking very loudly. Mikhalich frowned as if he was about to take a leap into water, set his feet wide apart, bracing them more firmly against the floor, and pressed the plunger all the way into the syringe.

Almost immediately his body went limp in the armchair. For some reason it suddenly occurred to me that that was the way the high priests of the Third Reich had left the world. I listened to the mechanical ticking in alarm – as if it were a bomb that was just about to explode. After a few seconds there was a click, and the paper-punch and syringe sprang off his arm and fell on the floor beside the chair. A small drop of blood appeared in the crook of Mikhalich's elbow. A clever little invention, I thought. And then it suddenly hit me.

I have to explain one thing. I can't read people's thoughts. And no one can, because people don't have anything resembling a printed text inside their heads. Not many people are capable of noticing that ripple of thought that runs incessantly across the mind – even in themselves. So reading somebody else's thoughts is like trying to make out something written on muddy water by a pitchfork in the hands of a madman. I don't mean the technical difficulty involved, but the practical value of the procedure.

But thanks to our tail, we foxes often find ourselves in a kind of sympathetic resonance with somebody else's consciousness – especially when that other consciousness is performing an unexpected somersault. It's rather like the reaction of peripheral vision to a sudden movement in the dark. We see a brief hallucination, a bit like an abstract computer-animated cartoon. This kind of contact is no use for anything at all, and most of the time our minds simply filter out the effect – otherwise it would be impossible to ride in the Metro. Usually it's weak, but when people take drugs it's amplified – that's why we can't stand drug addicts.

When FSB colonels inject ketamine intravenously, strange things happen to them. The 'ride down the Kshirsky Highway' was no metaphor, but a rather realistic description: although Mikhalich's limp body looked like a corpse, his consciousness was hurtling along some kind of orange tunnel filled with spectral forms that he skilfully avoided. The tunnel kept branching sideways and Mikhalich chose which way to turn. It was like a bobsleigh – Mikhalich was controlling his imaginary flight with minute turns of his feet and hands that were invisible to the eye, not even turns really, simply microscopic adjustments of the tension in the corresponding muscles.

I realized that these orange tunnels were more than just structures in space, they were simultaneously information and will. The entire world had been transformed into an immense self-operating program, like a computer program, except that the hardware and the software couldn't be told apart. Mikhalich himself was an element of the program, but he possessed freedom of movement in relation to its other components. And his attention was moving through the program towards its beginning, towards a hatch behind which there was something terrible lurking. Mikhalich went flying into the final orange tunnel, reached the hatch and resolutely flung it open. And the terrible thing that was behind it burst out and went hurtling upwards – towards the light of day, up into the room.

I looked at Mikhalich. He was coming back to life, but in a strange, menacing kind of way. The corners of his mouth were trembling – little spots of either saliva or foam had appeared on them – and I could hear a sound like growling from somewhere in his throat. The growling kept getting louder, and then Mikhalich's body twitched and arched, and I sensed that in another second the mysterious, terrible power from the bottom of his soul would burst out and be free. I had no time to hesitate – I grabbed the bottle of champagne, swung it hard and hit him on the head.

To look at, nothing out of the ordinary happened. Mikhalich slumped down in the chair again, and the bottle didn't even break. But in his internal dimension, with which I was still in contact, something remarkable took place. The bundle of evil power that was rushing up and out from his inner depths lost control and crashed into a complex combination of thought-forms filling the orange tunnel. There was a flash, with pulsating stars and stripes of flame receding all the way to the horizon like the markings on an infinitely long runway. It was blindingly beautiful and reminiscent of a news report I saw in the 1960s of a trimaran speed-boat that crashed: the speedboat lifted up off the water, performed a slow, thoughtful loop-the-loop and shattered into small fragments against the surface of the lake. Almost the same thing happened this time, only instead of the speedboat it was the lake that was smashed into tiny pieces: the transparent structures filling the orange tunnel fell to pieces and went flying off in all directions with a melodic tinkling sound, fading, shrinking and disappearing. And then the whole universe of orange tunnels went dark and disappeared, as if the electricity lighting it up had been cut off. All that was left was a man lying limply in a chair and a melodic sound that was repeated over and over again until I realized it was the phone.

I answered it.

'Mikhalich?' a man's voice asked.

'Mikhalich can't come to the phone right now,' I said. 'He's very busy.'

'Who's that?'

I couldn't think of any short and simple answer. After a few seconds of silence the person on the other end of the line hung up.

* * *

What a crazy idea that was – to change the name of the KGB. One of the greatest brand names ever was simply destroyed! The KGB was known all over the world. But not every foreigner will understand what the FSB is. One American lesbian who hired me for the weekend kept confusing 'FSB' and 'FSD' all the time. 'FSD' is 'female sexual dysfunction', an illness invented by the pharmaceutical companies in order to launch the production of the female version of Viagra. Sexual dysfunction in women is a bluff, of course: in female sexuality it's not the physical aspects that are important, so much as the context – candles, champagne, words. And to be completely honest about it, the most important condition for the modern female orgasm is a high level of material prosperity. You can't solve that with a pill – as Bill Clinton said: It's the economy, stupid. But I'm digressing again.

Although the name of the KGB was changed, the personnel remained the same as before, disciplined and tough. Any normal man would have been out cold for a long time after a blow like that from a bottle. But Mikhalich started to come round quite soon. Perhaps that was because he received the blow in an altered state of consciousness – when the physical properties of the body are transformed, as any alcoholic can testify.

I realized he was conscious when I tried to take the key to the door out of his pants. When I leaned down over him, I saw he was looking at me with his eyelids half open. I jumped back immediately. I was frightened by what had happened to him after the injection – I'd never seen anything like that before, and I didn't want to take any risks.

'Phone,' Mikhalich whispered.

'What about the phone?'

'Who . . . who . . .'

'Who called?' I guessed. 'I don't know. Some man or other.'

He groaned. Amazing. After a blow like that an ordinary man would have been more concerned about the eternal questions. But this one was thinking about telephone calls. As the Soviet poet Tikhonov wrote, 'If we could make nails out of these men, everyone in Russia would have a happier life' (he later changed this to 'there would be no stronger nails in all the world', but the rough draft was exactly that, I've seen it).

'Give me the key,' I said, 'it's time I was going.'

'Wait a bit,' Mikhalich sighed, 'talk.'

'I don't talk to junkies.'

'Don't get clever . . .'

He spoke with an effort, leaving long pauses – as if every sentence were a high mountain he had to climb.

'Oh, sure,' I said in an offended tone. 'Don't get clever. That's what they said to Liuska too. And then when her client died on the sakura branch, she was arrested. Her lawyer said it was peritonitis, an unfortunate accident. But the investigator stuck the rupture of the colon on her, unpremeditated murder. Bung them three grand, then it'll be unpremeditated, otherwise you take the full rap. Give me the key, or you'll get it again. And I don't give a damn if you are from the FSB. Nothing will happen to me, it's self-defence.'

And at that I picked up the bottle again.

He made a sinister sort of sound – like a water sprite laughing somewhere in the depths of his millpond. Then he tried to say something, but all that came out was:

'Sit . . . si . . .'

'Listen, I'm asking you nicely one last time,' I said, 'give me the key!'

'Bitch,' he said surprisingly clearly.

These officers are such boors, you know. They simply can't talk to a girl in a civilized manner. I raised the bottle to hit him again, and at that point the door behind my back opened.

Standing there in the doorway was a tall young man wearing a dark raincoat with the collar turned up. He was unshaven, sullen and very good-looking – I noted that without any kind of personal involvement, with the cold eye of an artist.

The only thing that spoiled him a little were the arrogant, angry creases beside his lips. They didn't actually make me dislike him, though, they just seemed to establish some distance. But even with those arrogant creases he looked very, very attractive indeed. I'd say he was just a little bit like the young Tsar Alexander Pavlovich – as I recall he also had a fierce, wolfish look during the years immediately after he ascended the throne.

I was struck by the expression of his face. I don't know how to explain it. As if someone had been living with toothache for many years and become accustomed to taking no notice of it, even though the pain tormented him every single day. He had the kind of glance that's hard to forget as well: those greyish-yellow eyes imprinted themselves on your retinas and looked straight down into your soul for a few seconds. But the most significant thing about this face, I thought, was that it was a face from the past. There used to be a lot of faces like that around in the old days, when people believed in love and God, and then that type almost disappeared.

We looked into each other's eyes for a while.

'I was going to give him some champagne,' I said, putting the bottle on the table.

The visitor shifted his gaze to Mikhalich.

'Brought your daughter, have you?' he asked.

'Nah,' Mikhalich croaked from his armchair and even moved his arm (evidently the presence of the visitor had helped him to gather his wits). 'Nah . . . the whore . . .'

'Ah,' said the visitor and looked back at me. 'So this is the one . . . who offended our consultant?'

'That's her.'

'And what happened to you?'

'Boss,' Mikhalich mumbled in reply, 'the tooth, boss! Anaesthetic!'

The young man sniffed at the air and a grimace of disapproval appeared on his face.

'So they used ketamine for your anaesthetic, did they?'

'Boss, I . . .'

'Or did you call the vet in to have your ears docked?'

'Boss . . .'

'Again? I can understand it, out on the job. But why here? Didn't we have a talk on the subject?'

Mikhalich lowered his eyes. The young man glanced at me and it seemed to me his glance was curious.

'Boss, I'll explain,' said Mikhalich. 'Word of . . .'

I could physically feel what an effort the words were costing him.

'No, Mikhalich, I'll do the explaining,' said the visitor. He picked up the bottle of champagne off the table and hit Mikhalich over the head with it with all his strength.

This time the bottle broke and a geyser of white foam washed down over Mikhalich from his head to his toes. I was quite certain that after a blow like that he would never get up out of the armchair again – I know a thing or two about human anatomy. But to my amazement, Mikhalich just shook his head from side to side, like a lush who's had a bucket of water thrown over him. Then he raised his hand and wiped the spatters of champagne off his face. Instead of killing him, the blow had brought him round. I'd never seen anything like it before.

'All right, then,' said the young man, 'take a shower, then get in a taxi and go home. They can give you light broth. Or strong tea. But really Mikhalich, to do things right you ought to go on a barbiturate drip.'

I didn't understand what that phrase meant.

'Yes sir,' said Mikhalich. He struggled to his feet and staggered into the bathroom, leaving a trail of champagne drops behind him. When the door closed the young man turned to me and smiled.

'It's stuffy in here,' he said. 'Please allow me to show you out into the fresh air.'

I liked his polite manner.

We went out of the flat a different way. The steel pole I'd seen in one of the rooms turned out to lead to the ground floor. You see similar poles in fire stations and go-go bars. You can slide down a pole like that to a big beautiful fire engine and receive a medal 'for bravery at the scene of a fire'. Or you can rub your bottom and your breasts against it erotically and receive a few moist banknotes from the audience. So many different roads through life lie before us . . .

Fortunately, today I didn't have to do either of these things. Beside the pole there was a narrow spiral staircase – obviously for less urgent occasions. That was the way we went down, into a dark garage where there was a fantastic black car – an absolutely genuine Maibach. There couldn't be more than a few of those in the whole of Moscow.

The young man stopped beside the car and raised his head – so that his nose was pointed at me – then took a powerful breath in. It looked weird. But after that his face assumed a blissful expression – as if he'd been really moved by something, in fact.

'I'd like to apologize for what happened,' he said, 'and ask you to do me a favour.'

'What sort of favour?'

'I need to choose a present for a girl of about your age. I have no idea about ladies' jewellery and I would be very grateful for some advice.'

I hesitated for a second. Generally speaking, in situations like this, you should clear out at the first opportunity – but somehow I felt I wanted to continue the acquaintance. And I was wondering what the interior of the car looked like.

'All right,' I said.

But the moment I got into the car I forgot all about the interior – I was so struck by the pass on the windscreen.

I'd noticed a long time before then that the Russian authorities had a certain tendency towards kitsch: they were always attempting to issue themselves a charter of nobility and pass themselves off as the glorious descendants of empire with all its history and culture – despite the fact that they had about as much in common with the old Russia as some Lombards grazing their goats amid the ruins of the Forum had with the Flavian dynasty. The pass on the Maibach's windscreen was a fresh example of the genre. It had a gold double-headed eagle, a three-digit number and the inscription:

Lo and behold, this sombre carriage
Can travel everywhere in this town
A. S. Pushkin

What can I say? Okay, an eagle. Okay, Pushkin. (I think it was a quotation from *A Feast in the Time of Plague*.) But the feeling of pride in our great country that the FSB copywriters had been counting on failed to materialize. The problem was probably a wrong choice of period for the references. They should have gone for feudal chronicles, not imperial eagles.

'What are you thinking about?'

'Ah? Me?' I said, coming to my senses.

'Yes,' he said. 'When you think, you wrinkle up your little nose in a very touching sort of way.'

We were already driving along the street.

'By the way, we haven't introduced ourselves yet,' he said. 'Alexander. You can call me Sasha. I'm Sasha Sery.' That was interesting – 'sery' is the Russian word for 'grey'.

'And what's your name?'

'Adele.'

'Adele?' he asked, opening his eyes wide. 'You're not joking?'

I shook my head.

'Incredible. There's so much in my life that's linked with that name! You can't even imagine. Our meeting like this is fate. It's no accident that you've ended up in my car . . .'

'Do you have a fishing reel with you?' I asked.

'A fishing reel? What for?'

'You can wind me on to it after you finish stringing me along.'

He laughed.

'You don't believe me? About Adele?'

73

'No,' I said.

'I can explain what it's all about. If you're interested.'

'I am.'

And I really was interested.

'Do you know that game on PlayStation – Final Fantasy 8?'

I shook my head.

'I got almost all the way through it once – and that takes a long time. And then just before the end the enchantress Adele appeared. Very beautiful, a lot taller than a man. The animation's spectacular – she wakes up and opens her eyes, and she's covered in these rays of light, radiating out, a lot like the logo for Universal Studios, and she flies to Earth in her sarcophagus.'

'Where does she fly from?'

'The Moon.'

'Aha. And how does it all end?'

'I don't know,' he answered. 'That's the point. I couldn't defeat her. I did for all the rest, but not her, no way. So the game ended there . . .'

'Why is this memory so important to you?' I asked. 'There are plenty of games.'

'Before that I'd always succeeded at everything,' he said.

'Absolutely everything?'

He nodded.

'Oh, sure,' I said. 'Of course.'

'You don't believe me?'

'Why not? I believe you. I can tell from the car.'

A few seconds passed in silence. I glanced out of the window. We were approaching the beginning of Tverskoi Boulevard.

'A new restaurant,' I said. 'The Palazzo Ducale. Have you been there?'

He nodded.

'And what are the customers like?'

'Oh, the usual.'

'So what do people talk about there?'

He thought for a second. Then he answered in a ludicrous woman's voice:

'What do you think, is Zhechkov frightened to live in the dacha where Stalin's butcher Yezhov lived?'

Then he answered himself in an equally ludicrous bass:

'What do you mean? It's Stalin's butcher Yezhov who'll be shitting himself in his grave because Zhechkov's living in his dacha . . .'

'And who is this Zhechkov?' I asked.

He glanced at me suspiciously. Apparently Zhechkov was someone I ought to know. I'm losing the context, I thought, it happens every twenty years or so.

'I was just giving an example,' he said. 'The kind of thing they talk about there.'

I remembered Yezhov's dacha as it was in the 1930s. I used to like the plaster lions with balls under their paws who guarded the entrance – their faces had a slightly guilty expression, as if they could sense they wouldn't be able to protect their master. A thousand years earlier a lion looking almost exactly the same used to stand in front of the shrine of the Huáyán sect – only he was made of gold and on his side he had an inscription that I still remember by heart:

The cause of error by living beings is that they believe it is possible to cast aside the false and attain unto the truth. But when you attain unto yourself, the false becomes true, and there is no other truth to which one need attain after that.

What people there used to be around in those times! But nowadays is there anyone who can even understand the meaning of those words? All of them, every last one, have departed to the higher worlds. No one wishes to be born in this hellish labyrinth any more, not even out of compassion, and I'm wandering here

75

on my own in the dark . . .

We stopped at a crossroads.

'Tell me, Alexander, where are we going?' I asked.

'Do you know a good jeweller's anywhere round here? I mean really good?'

* * *

Every time I see a girl in a boutique with an admirer buying her a brooch that costs as much as a small aeroplane, I'm convinced that human females are every bit as good at creating mirages as we are. Perhaps even better. It's some going to pass off a reproductive mechanism as a delightful spring flower worthy of a precious setting – and to maintain that illusion, not just for minutes, as we do, but for years and decades, and all without the use of a tail. That takes real skill. Evidently women, like mobile phones, have some kind of inbuilt antenna.

This is what my internal voices say about that:

1) since a woman can pass off a reproductive mechanism as a wonderful spring flower, female nature cannot be reduced just to the bearing of children: it also includes at least the skill of brainwashing.

2) by its very nature a wonderful spring flower is exactly the same kind of mechanism for reproduction and brainwashing, only its meat is green and it brainwashes the bees.

3) apart from the woman, no one needs the precious setting, so it's pointless to discuss whether she is worthy of it or not.

4) mobile phones with inbuilt antennas have convenient shapes, but poor reception, especially in reinforced concrete buildings.

5) mobile phones with an external antenna are inconvenient, and their reception in reinforced concrete buildings is even worse.

Woman is a peaceful creature, she only hypnotizes her own male and inflicts no harm on birds and animals. Since she does this in the name of the supreme biological goal, that is, personal survival, the deception here is pardonable, and it's none of our foxy business to go sticking our noses in. But when a married man who lives every moment in a dream planted in his head by his wife, complete with elements of nightmare and gothic, suddenly declares over a glass of beer that woman is simply a device for bearing children, that is very, very funny. The man doesn't even realize how comical he is when he says that. In this particular case I'm not hinting at Count Tolstoy, whom I admire tremendously, I'm speaking generally.

But I'm wandering from the point. I just wanted to say that woman's hypnotic abilities are obvious, and anyone who has any doubts about that can easily lay them to rest by going into a shop that sells expensive trinkets.

I didn't realize until the final moment that Alexander was choosing a present for me. I simply had no reason to think anything of the kind. I assumed he needed to buy a souvenir for some glamorous little bimbo, and I gave him perfectly serious advice. So I felt quite exceptionally stupid when he finally held out the bag containing the two small cases that he had just paid for. I wasn't expecting it. And foxes have to foresee what a man will do – if not everything, then at least the things that affect us personally. Our survival depends on it.

The two identical small white boxes contained rings that cost 10,000 and 18,000 dollars – platinum and diamonds. The large stone was point eight of a carat, the small one point five four. Tiffany. Would you believe it – 28,000 dollars! How many times I'd have to strain my tail for that, I thought with a feeling that was almost class hatred. And the most important thing was that he didn't want anything from me. Apart from my phone number. He said he was flying to the north and he'd call when he got back.

It wasn't easy buying the rings. The sales assistant wasn't prepared to put through such a substantial transaction herself. Neither was the cashier.

'I can't do it without the manager,' she kept saying.

It was only when I got back home to Bitsevsky Park that I realized how tired I was – I didn't even have the strength to check my e-mails. I slept until the middle of the next day. I had suspiciously Borgesian dreams about the defence of a fortress – something like the storming of a city during the Yellow Turban rebellion. I was one of the defenders and I was throwing heavy javelins down from the walls.

No need to explain the symbolism to me, I can't stand that. Back in the 1920s I used to drive romantic Red Freudians crazy by telling them dreams that I invented: 'And then our tails fell off and they told us they were lying in a coconut hanging above a waterfall.' If I sometimes throw javelins in a dream, it doesn't mean I don't take in the symbolic significance of what's going on. And even less does it mean that I do take it in. I stopped collecting that sort of garbage a long time ago. Life's less cluttered that way.

After a rest, my head was working clearly and efficiently, and the first thing I thought about was the financial aspect of what was going on. My personal solvency index was now tinged a delicate green: the two rings had cost 28,000 in the shop, and that meant I could sell them for 18,000.

But it would be a shame to sell them – in the last hundred years I hadn't been given such pretty baubles very often. In Soviet Russia they were very strict about that kind of thing. Even in late Brezhnev times it was like that: if a man with a string bag walked off the street into a jewellery shop and bought a brooch for 30,000 roubles, the entire central press wrote about it indignantly for a week, asking what the competent organs were doing about it. In the era of stagnation, 30,000 really was a huge amount of money. But then why did they put the brooch in the shop window? As bait? There's really no other way to explain the indignation of the press – they laid down bait and, the fish ate it and just swam away.

At least, that was what the director of Moscow's Grocery Store Number One, who bought me the brooch, whispered in my ear with a passionate laugh. He was a careful man, but passion had made him a romantic. The poor fellow was executed by firing squad, and I felt sorry for him, although I still couldn't force myself to wear the brooch. It was a unique example of Soviet kitsch: diamond ears of wheat surrounding emerald cucumbers and a ruby beetroot. An eternal reminder of the only battle that Soviet Russia lost – the battle for the harvest . . .

After I finished admiring the rings, I decided to check my e-mails. There was only one letter in my inbox, but it was a very welcome one – from my sister U Hu-Li, whom I hadn't seen for an eternity.

Hi there, Red,

How are you getting on? Are you still into moral self-improvement? Searching for the exit from the labyrinths of the illusory world? I'd really like at least one of our big, ne'er-do-well family to find it.

But I've completely lost my way in those labyrinths. I'm still here in Thailand, although I've finally left Patthaya. In the last thirty years the sea has become really dirty. And apart from that, the competition from local women is so great that earning a living from the fox's trade is getting harder all the time. Everything here has been turned inside out – in most countries in the world people are delighted when they have a son, but here they're delighted when they have a daughter, and they say, quite literally: 'How good it is that we have a daughter, we won't go hungry in our old age!' If he heard that, Confucius would hang himself with his own sleeve.

The island of Phuket, where I live now, is still clean, but in a couple of years it will be the same as Patthaya. There are too many tourists. I've found a place to live on Patong beach and I work in Christine's Massage Parlour. We – the masseuses – sit on benches in a special room where the men can take a look at us, with our cheeks brightly rouged, looking like evil spirits. The pink, sunburned farangs (that's what we call the tourists from the West) come in off the street and choose a masseuse. After that, it's a separate room, and you know the rest. I'm regarded as a unique specialist in Thai massage, so my rates are higher than the other girls', but even so I still have to earn a bit on the side in the bars on Bangla Road, just five minutes away from my massage parlour. I get so tired during the day, and then I have to get dolled up in bright-coloured rags and go out on the stage. It's not even a stage really, just a counter that we walk around slowly from one pole to the other, girls with numbers on our breasts. And the farangs sit at the bar below us, drinking cold beer and take their time to choose. If I can put away fifty dollars a day working in two places, I'm doing well.

The very foundations of life have been perverted here. Thai girls are modest and as industrious as bees. Only in natural conditions bees fly from flower to flower, working hard collecting nectar. But if you tip a bucketful of sugar syrup out beside the hive, they go straight for the sugar, and none of them will fly to the flowers. That's exactly the way the West is destroying our tropical garden with its bodily secretions, drenching it with rivers of sweet dollar syrup from the hotels beside the sea. Your Russia is as great a sexual exploiter as anyone else here, and the fact that now she is no more than a raw-material appendage of the developed countries doesn't relieve her of her moral guilt. Although in a certain sense you could call Thailand a raw-material appendage too . . . Don't think that I'm waxing dogmatic, it's just that it was hot today, and I'm very tired.

By the way, about Russia. Just recently I was talking to our sister E, who came to visit us in Phuket with her new husband, Lord Cricket (the fool is perfectly happy). She told me something quite incredible. Do you remember the prophecy of the super-werewolf? She says that the place mentioned in the prophecy is Moscow. Her reasoning is certainly ingenious. The prophecy says that the super-werewolf will appear in a city where they will destroy a Temple and then restore it in its previous form. For many centuries, everybody thought that meant Jerusalem, and the coming of the super-werewolf was a prophecy that concerned the very end of time, something like the Apocalypse. But E Hu-Li is sure that we've simply been hypnotized by Judaeo-Christian symbolism – if there's a Temple, then it has to be the one in Jerusalem . . .

In fact, however, there are no references to Jerusalem in the prophecy. But not so long ago in Moscow they restored the Temple of Christ the Saver (if our sister E hasn't got the name confused), which was destroyed during the cultural revolution. And what's more, they restored it in the form in which it was originally built – she's relying on information she got from you there. I think you can expect her to visit you soon with her husband, who is totally obsessed with these mystical riddles.

This Lord Cricket is not only a mystic. He is well known in London as a patron and collector of art, and he deals with many art galleries. Apart from that, he was one of the leaders of an organization you have certainly heard of – the Countryside Alliance, which tried to prevent fox-hunting from being banned. I know how hard it is to let a character like that stay alive. But please remember that our little sister E hasn't yet decided who's going to be next. So gather your willpower up into a tight fist, just as I did. Take a detached view of what's going on – his lordship is obsessed with the search for were-

creatures absolutely everywhere, except in his own bedroom.
That's always the way with people. There's just one thing I
don't understand. How did he come to develop such an interest
in the supernatural? But then, the members of the exploiting
classes often resort to occultism in the attempt to find a justifi-
cation for their own parasitic existence.

I want to ask your advice. Should I move to Russia? I like
the Russian tourists – they're good-natured, they tip well and
fall asleep quickly because they drink a lot. I saw a beautiful
tattoo on the chest of one of them – Lenin and Marx with a
hammer and sickle – and he was still very young. He took a
real liking to me. He filmed me with his video-camera and then
advised me to come to Russia. 'With beauty like yours, you
could make a career,' he said. 'And not in some massage par-
lour, either. Hang about with our elite for a year or two and
you'll make enough money to last a lifetime.' He said every-
thing is different now in Russia. There are sweeping reforms
and the people have lots of money. Is that true? What is this
elite that I ought to hang about with? Apart from that, he said
your roubles have almost the same rate against the dollar as our
bahts, so I wouldn't suffer any great culture shock. Write and
tell me what it's like in Moscow and if there's a place there for
U Hu-Li.

Heads and tails,
U

My little sister U . . . I smiled as I remembered her – serious,
solemn and very sincere. She was probably the best of us, and so
she always ended up bearing the heaviest burden. She went
through the entire war of liberation with Chairman Mao, she had
medals from the Chinese National Liberation Army, and when
capitalism was restored in China she burned her party card on

Tiananmen Square and went away to Thailand. And now she wanted to come to Russia – she thought it was still the same old motherland of the October Revolution . . . The poor girl, I had to persuade her not to come. What if she really did, and ended up miserable and depressed among our northern snows? Or got involved with some kind of national bolsheviks? And when the national bolsheviks signed a contract with 'Diesel', she'd stay honest right to the end and then serve obscenely long sentences – it had happened to her so often already . . .

I spent a few seconds searching for an image that could reach her. Eventually I thought I'd found one. I put my hands on the keyboard.

* * *

Hello, Little Red,

You can't possibly imagine how pleased I was to hear from you up here in our snowbound back of beyond. You say you're fed up with Thailand? Try thinking about this: in the countries of the golden billion, people put money away for a whole year in order to come to your coconut paradise for just a couple of weeks. I understand that the life in the five-star hotels is very different from yours. But, after all, the sea and the sky are the same for all, and that's the real reason why they come to you from their neon catacombs.

You say life in Thailand is perverted because the visitors swamp the innocent natives with their poisonous dollar syrup and deprive them of the joy of simple labour. I respect your views, but try to look at things from a different angle: those same debauchers of innocence spend the whole year tearing each other's throats out in their offices in order to save up enough of that poisonous dollar slush. It's their lives that are really perverted, otherwise why would they come to your mas-

sage parlour, my sweet love? Low rates – yes, that is something that must be fought. But what point is there in these universal generalizations that end up with fifty million people getting killed every time?

You ask me what it's like here. To be brief, even the most hardened of optimists are now finding that any hope that the brown sea advancing on us from all sides consists of chocolate is melting away. And, as the advert puts it so wittily, it is melting not in their hands, but in their mouths.

In Moscow they are building skyscrapers, eating sushi by the ton and bringing billion-dollar court cases. But this boom doesn't have much to do with the economy. It's just that the money from all over Russia flows into Moscow and moistens life here a bit before it departs for off-shore hyperspace. I remember you once saying that the fundamental contradiction of the modern age is the contradiction between money and blood. In Moscow its sharpness is blunted somewhat because as yet the blood is spilled far away, and the money always belongs to someone else. But that's only a temporary state of affairs.

Life here is so distinctive, so unique, that it would take a clairvoyant like Oswald Spengler to grasp its true essence. From Spengler's point of view, every culture is based on a certain mysterious principle that manifests itself in a multitude of unrelated phenomena. For instance, there is a profound underlying kinship between the round form of a coin and the wall surrounding an ancient town, and so on. I think that if Spengler were to study modern-day Russia, what he would be most interested in would be the same thing that interests you – the local elite.

It is genuinely unique. You have been misinformed: no one has yet become any richer by 'hanging about' with those folks. You can only end up with less money than ever after putting yourself through that, otherwise the elite would not be the elite.

84

In ancient times in the Middle Kingdom every official strove to do good on the Great Way of Things. But here they all set up their own toll bars across the road and only raise them for money. And the essence of the social contract lies precisely in them raising their booms for each other.

The elite here is divided into two branches, which are called 'the oligarchy' (derived from the words 'oil' and 'gargle') and 'the apparat' (from the phrase 'upper rat'). 'The oligarchy' is the business community, which grovels to the authorities, who can close down any business at any moment, since business here is inseparable from theft. And 'the upper rat' consists of the authorities, who feed on the kickbacks from business. The way it works is that the former allow the latter to steal because the latter allow the former to thieve. Just think about the kind of people who have managed to create such a spellbinding formation in the middle of empty space. At the same time, there are no clear boundaries between these two branches of power – one merges smoothly into the other, forming a single immense, fat rat trying to swallow itself. Do you really want to hang about with this perpetually champing uroborus? That is what the alchemical symbol of the snake biting its own tail is called – but in our case the connotations are more urological in nature.

The reforms that you have heard about are by no means new. They have been going on here constantly for as long as I can remember. What they essentially come down to is the choice, from all the possible versions of the future, of the one that is the most disgusting. Every time the reforms begin with the declaration that a fish rots from the head, then the reformers eat up the healthy body, and the rotten head swims on. And so everything that was rotten under Ivan the Terrible is still alive today, and everything that was healthy five years ago has already been gobbled up. Instead of a bear, the 'apparat' or 'upper rat' here could have used a fish head on its banners.

Although a bear is a witty choice too: it is the international symbol of economic stagnation, and there is also the Russian expression 'greasing the paw'. The Eskimos have thirty words for describing different kinds of snow, and modern Russian has about the same number of expressions to describe giving a bribe to a state official.

But Russians still love their country anyway, and their writers and poets traditionally compare this order of things to a weight attached to the foot of a giant – otherwise, they say, he would start rushing along too fast . . . Oh, but I don't know about that. I haven't seen any signs of a giant for a long time, just an oil pipeline with a fat rat hanging over it, giving itself a royal autocephalic uroborus. It sometimes seems to me that the only goal of Russian life is to drag this rat across the snowy wastes, trying to make some geopolitical sense of all this and inspire the minor nations with it.

If you analyse another two interconnected aspects of the local culture – the strictly taboo vocabulary employed for daily communication between people here, and laws under which the generally accepted way of life is a crime (which means that the face of every citizen bears the indelible imprint of sin) – you have a brief description of the 'gestalt' that you are intending to visit. And this list could easily be extended indefinitely: it would include the metal doors with security locks on flats, metaphysical blockbusters in which good allows evil to feed, because evil allows good to feed, and so on. But enough of that.

Let me share with you my professional views on the prospects for a working girl here. There is a game played in the local prisons that the intelligentsia calls 'Robinson Crusoe' and the intellectuals call 'Ultima Thule'. What it consists of is the following: a man sits down in a tub of water so that only the head of his penis is visible on the surface. Then he takes out of a matchbox a fly whose wings have been pulled off in advance

*and releases it on to that little island. The essential content of
this northern amusement is watching the aimless wanderings of
the unfortunate insect across the foreskin (hence the name of
the game). It is a meditation on the hopelessness of existence,
loneliness and death. Catharsis is achieved here through the
stimulation of the head of the male member produced by the
rapid movements of the fly's feet. There is a version of this game
that the intelligentsia calls 'Atlantis', and the intellectuals call
'Kitezh of the spirit' (after the sacred underwater city in the
Russian folktale). But the details of that are so sombre that I'd
rather not spoil your sleep by mentioning them.*

*Believe me, my sister, if you come here, you will feel like a
wingless fly wandering over the islands of an archipelago, about
which everything important that there is to say has already
been said to mankind by Solzhenitsyn. Is it worth exchanging
your sea and sun for such a hard life? Yes, there is more money
here. But believe me, the local inhabitants all spend it on pretending to move a bit closer, if only in a state of
heroin-and-alcohol-induced stupor, to that torrent of happiness
and joy in which your life is spent.*

*And one last thing, since you have already mentioned the
super-werewolf. I'm absolutely certain that all the legends
about him should be understood metaphorically. The super-
werewolf is what any of us can become as a result of moral
self-improvement and the development of our abilities to the
greatest possible extent. You are him already, in potential terms.
Therefore, to seek him somewhere outside of yourself is to err. I
would not waste my time trying to convince E Hu-Li of this, or
her husband (it would be interesting to get a look at him while
it's still possible). But you, my little sister, with your clear mind
and truthful heart, should understand this.*

Heads and tails,

A.

There was a seventeenth-century Chinese comedy called *Two Foxes in One Town*. Moscow is a very big town, which meant there could be very big problems here. But it was not misgivings of that sort that stopped me, not at all – quite honestly, I was only thinking of my sister's happiness. If I laid it on a bit thick in my letter, then it was only out of concern for her – let her carry on warming herself in the sun a bit longer, happiness has nothing to do with money. And what I'd written about the super-werewolf was the most important thing of all, I was quite sure of that. Next time I would have to remind her always to work with the 'bride returns the earring' method.

An earring . . . I suddenly had a quite delightful idea that sent me dashing to the metal box where I kept my jewellery and all sorts of valuable bits and pieces. I found what I wanted immediately – the silver earrings were lying on the very top.

I opened my old Leatherman with the tiny pliers (one of the first models, they don't make them like that any more), carefully detached the hooks from the earrings, and soon I had something quite incredible lying on the palm of my hand. It was a pair of earrings in the form of diamond rings on silver hooks with a colour that almost merged into the platinum. The diamonds in the earrings were different, one a bit larger and one a bit smaller. I didn't think anyone had ever made earrings like that before. When people saw it, they'd steal the idea, I thought. But what could I do about that . . .

I put the earrings on and looked at myself in the mirror. It looked great. It was clear from the first glance that what I had hanging on my ears were not earrings, but finger rings. And apart from that, it was obvious that the rings were expensive – the diamonds glittered delightfully in the dusty beam of light that illuminated my humble abode. The most stylish part of it was the way an expensive item had been mounted to express emphatic contempt for its monetary value, a combination of the ideals of the financial bourgeoisie and the values of 1968 in a single unified aesthetic object which promised that its owner would put out for Che Guevara as well as Abramovich, and even vaguely hinted that she would only put out for Abramovich on a temporary basis, until Che Guevara moved in (of course, Che Guevara doesn't really have anything to do with the whole business, nobody's thinking of putting out for him – it's just that the girl thinks Abramovich is more likely to go for shiny bait like that). In a word, it was just what the doctor ordered.

But then I couldn't give a damn for the doctor. In two thousand years, I'd seen more than enough doctors like that – they make their prescription, and time after time the human heart believes in the same old deception, dashes straight at the cliffs of the world and is smashed to pieces against them. And then it dashes at them again, and again – just like the first time. When you live by the edge of that sea and hear the roar of its waves, you think what a blessing it is that each wave only knows about itself and has no knowledge of the past.

* * *

Of course, no one gives me rings and brooches like that because of the perfection of my soul, which it is beyond modern people's ability to perceive. The only thing they value is my physical attraction – poignant, ambivalent and overwhelming. I know its power very well – I have learned to understand it over many hundreds of years. But after the meeting with Alexander for some reason I had lost my usual self-confidence. I couldn't remember time ever moving so slowly – the two days while I waited for his call seemed like an eternity to me. The minutes crawled by from the future into the past like snails, I sat in front of the mirror, gazing at my reflection and thinking about beauty.

A man often thinks: there's a beautiful girl, a lovely flower, walking through the town in spring, smiling in all directions, and she's not even aware of how lovely she is. This thought naturally develops into the intention to acquire this flower who is unaware of her own beauty for considerably less than her market value.

Nothing could be more naïve. The man is aware of her beauty, but the girl, the lovely flower, is not? It's like a collective farmer from some remote village who has sold his cow and come to Moscow to buy an old Lada walking past the Porsche sales room, seeing a young salesman in the window and thinking: 'He's very green . . . maybe he'll believe that an orange Boxter is cheaper than a Lada, seeing as it's only got two doors? I must try having a word with him, while he's in the place on his own . . .'

A man like that is very funny, of course, and he has no chance at all of getting what he wants. But it's not all gloom and doom. There is good news and bad news for the collective farmer who has sold his cow:

1) the bad news is that he'll never buy anything for less than its market value. Everything's been worked out, checked and double checked. Abandon hope, all ye who enter here.
2) the good news is that this market value is considerably lower than he imagines it to be in his state of hormonal intoxication, multiplied by his inferiority complex and his lack of faith in success.

There'll be no new orange Boxter for him, of course – it will be bought by an amiable elderly gent from the Ministry of Social Development. But he might well be able to afford an old Audi. Only it's not an Audi that he needs, it's a tractor. The tragedy of this collective farmer, and that of all other men, is that they run after our beauty without understanding its nature. So many different things have been said about it – it's a terrible and appalling thing, which is also going to save the world, and so forth. But none of that throws even the slightest bit of light on the subject.

What a fox has in common with the most beautiful of women is that we live off the feelings we arouse. But a woman is guided by instinct, and a fox is guided by reason, and where a woman gropes her way along in the dark, a fox strides proudly forward in the bright light of day.

But then I must admit that some women cope rather well with their role. Only even if they want to, they can't reveal their professional secrets, since they themselves do not understand them at a rational level. But we foxes are quite consciously aware of these secrets – and now I'll tell you about one of them, the simplest and most important.

Anyone who wishes to understand the nature of beauty should first of all ask himself: where is it located? Can we say that it is somewhere inside the woman who is considered beautiful? Can we say, for instance, that there is beauty in the features of her face? Or in her figure?

Science tells us that the brain receives a flow of information from the sense organs, in this case from the eyes, and without the interpretations imposed by the visual cortex, this is simply a chaotic sequence of coloured dots, digitized into nerve impulses by the visual tract. Any fool can understand that there is no beauty in that, so it doesn't find its way into a man through his eyes. In technical terms, beauty is the interpretation that arises in the consciousness of the patient. As they say – in the eye of the beholder.

Beauty does not belong to a woman and it is not her specific quality – it is just that at a certain time of life her face reflects beauty, as a windowpane reflects the sun that is hidden behind the roofs of the houses. And so we cannot say that a woman's beauty fades with time – it is simply that the sun moves on and the windows of other houses begin to reflect it. But we know that the sun is not in the windowpanes that we look at. It is in us.

What is this sun? I'm sorry, but that's another mystery, and today I was only planning to reveal one. And in any case, from the point of view of practical magic, the nature of the sun is absolutely irrelevant. What matters are the manipulations that we perform with its light, and here lies an important difference between foxes and women. But, as in the previous case, I can only explain it by using an analogy.

There is a kind of lamp that people wear on their foreheads, on a special strap. They are popular with cyclists and potholers. It's very convenient – whichever way you turn your head, that's where the beam of light shines. I use one myself when I ride my bike at night in the Bitsevsky Park – it has three tiny, pointed bulbs that throw a spot of blue-white light on the asphalt surface of the path. Well then, beauty is the effect that arises in a person's consciousness when the light of the lamp on his head is reflected off something and back into his eyes.

In every woman there is a mirror, set from birth at a specific angle, and – no matter what the beauty industry might tell us – that angle cannot be changed. But we foxes can adjust the angle of our mirror across a very wide range. We can adapt to suit almost any cyclist. In this process hypnosis works hand-in-hand with flirting: the tail stays under our clothes and we only use it just a little bit to help ourselves. But every fox knows that 'little bit' is the key.

Especially for these notes I translated an excerpt from the memoirs of the Comte de Chermandois, a well-known eighteenth-century adventurer, in which he depicted my sister E Hu-Li for posterity. Chermandois met her in London, where he was taking refuge from the horrors of revolution. They started an affair, but it had an unfortunate ending – the comte died of a heart attack in strange circumstances. But here is how Chermandois describes the moment when a fox adjusts her mirror to direct the beam of reflected light straight into the eyes of her victim:

I cannot say that she was especially good-looking. On those occasions when I saw her after a long separation, I was amazed at how this skinny little creature with such fierce eyes could have become everything for me – love, life, death, the salvation of my soul. But she only had to meet my glance, and everything changed. First of all a startled doubt that she was loved would appear in those green eyes. At that moment it was obvious that there was nothing to love her for, and every time I experienced a wave of pity, merging into tenderness. But she soaked up those feelings like a sponge soaking up wine, and immediately blossomed into a tormenting beauty that could drive a man insane. A brief exchange of glances changed everything. A moment before it, I was not able to understand how this essentially unlovely woman could have enthralled me, and afterwards I could not grasp how I could have doubted even for a minute the magical power of her features. And the longer I gazed into her eyes, the stronger this feeling became, rousing me to ecstasy, to a state of physical pain – as if she had thrust a knife into a crack in the wall behind which I was trying to hide and, with a few swift movements of the blade, had loosened the brickwork so much that the wall had collapsed and I was left standing before her once again, as naked and defenceless as a child. I have studied this metamorphosis through and through, but I have still not learned to understand the nature of the fire that has seared my soul and reduced it to ashes.

Alas it is true: beauty is like fire, it burns and consumes, driving you insane with its heat, promising that in the place to which it drives its victim there will be calm, cool shade and new life –

but that is a deception. Or rather, it is all true – but not for the victim, only for the new life that will take the victim's place, and then also be consumed by this pitiless demon.

I should know what I'm talking about. The demon has served me for more than two thousand years, and although he and I have a long-established working relationship, I am a little afraid of him. The demon of beauty is the most powerful of all the demons of the mind. He is like death, but he serves life. And he does not dwell within me – I only release him from the lamp on the forehead of the beholder, like Aladdin releasing the genie, and when the genie returns to his prison, I pillage the field of battle. It is a hard lot, and the Buddha of the Western Paradise would hardly approve of what I do. But what's to be done about it? Such is the fate of foxes.

Not only is it our fate, it is also the fate of our little sister, woman. But only an insensitive and stupid male chauvinist could reproach her for that. After all, woman was not created from Adam's rib at all, that's simply a mistake the scribe made when the weather was too hot. Woman was created from the wound through which the rib was extracted from Adam. Every woman knows this, but I can only remember two who have ever admitted as much – the poet Marina Tsvetaeva ('from friends – for you, the lowdown on the mystery of Eve from the tree – here it is: I am no more than an animal wounded in the belly') and the Empress Tsy See, who was incredibly irritated by her own membership of the weaker sex (I won't cite her utterance, firstly because it is obscene and secondly because it is highly idiomatic and difficult to translate). But they gave Adam his rib back, and ever since then he keeps trying to stick it back into the wound – in the hope that everything will heal up and knit back together. No chance. That wound will never heal.

The Comte de Chermandois's remark about the knife blade and

the wall is a very telling image. We foxes actually do something of the kind – we feel for a man's secret heartstrings, and when we find them, we try to play the 'Ride of the Valkyries' on them, and that brings down the entire edifice of the personality. In fact, nowadays that's not so very terrible. The edifice of the modern personality is more like a dugout than anything else – there's nothing in it to collapse, and its conquest hardly requires any effort at all.

But then the spoils of conquest are insignificant too – the feelings of modern *eye-blinkers*, as Nietzsche called them, are shallow, and the barrel organs of their souls only play the 'Dog's Waltz'. Summon up in a man like that the most powerful hurricane that he is capable of containing, and the wind is only strong enough to blow a few hundred-dollar bills your way. And you still have to check to make sure they're not fake, torn or – God forbid! – issued before 1980. That's the way things are.

* * *

Alexander rang two days later, as he had promised. I was still asleep when I picked up the phone, but I had absolutely no doubt that it was him.

'Hello.'

'Ada,' he said, 'is that you?'

'Ada?'

I was quite sure I'd never called myself that.

'I'm going to call you Ada,' he said. 'We can take it as a diminutive from Adele, can't we?'

In Russian there could have been two polar opposite meanings concealed in the name Ada – 'ad A' (i.e. 'hell A') or 'A da' (i.e. 'Ah yes'). That was worrying. 'All right,' I said, 'call me that, if you like.'

'I want to see you,' he said.

'When?'

'Right now.'

'Er . . .'

'My car's waiting for you.'

'Where?'

'By the stands at the track.'

'By the stands? But how did you find out where I . . .'

'That's not difficult,' he laughed. 'Mikhalich will drive you.'

There was a loud knock at the door.

'There,' said Alexander's voice in the phone, 'that's him. I'm waiting for you, my little flower.'

He hung up. My little flower, I thought; well, well, he thinks I'm a plant. There was another knock at the door, more insistent this time. Consideration like that was almost insulting.

'Adele,' a familiar voice called from the other side of the door. 'Are you there? I can see from the reading I have that you are. Hey!'

He knocked again.

'You've got a sign here that says "No entry. Danger of death." So maybe you went in anyway and got killed? Are you alive? Answer! Or I'll break the door down!'

Idiot, I thought, then all the people will come running. But no, they won't, it's still too early . . . Even so, it was better not to risk it. I went to the door and said:

'Vladimir Mikhailovich, quiet! I'll open up in a moment, just let me get dressed.'

'I'm waiting.'

I got dressed quickly and glanced round my residence – I didn't think there was anything compromising in open view. But how had he managed to find me? Had he trailed me, or what?

'I'm opening up . . .'

Mikhalich came in and blinked for a few seconds as he got used to the darkness. Then he looked round.

'You mean to say this is where you live?'

'Well, yes.'

'What, in a gas-pipe junction?'

'It's not a gas-pipe junction. That sign at the door is just so that people won't start asking questions.'

'What's it supposed to be then?' he asked.

'How do you mean?'

'Well, every place has a function. What kind of premises is it?'

'I dislike premises,' I said. 'And I don't like it when people apply their own premises to me. It's an empty space under the stands. At first there was a storage space in here. Then they boarded everything off, built a transformer substation behind the wall and forgot about this part. Well, they didn't just happen to forget. Of course, I had to help them along a bit . . .'

I shuffled my fingers to make my point clear. Of course, what I should have done was wave my tail, but I wasn't about to initiate Mikhalich into all the details of my difficult fate.

'Do you have heating at least?' he asked. 'Aha, I see the radiators over there. But where's the toilet?'

'Why, do you want to go?'

'No, I'm just curious.'

'You have to go along the corridor. There's a shower there too.'

'You really live in this kennel?'

'Why is it a kennel?' I said. 'Its layout's more like a loft, the kind lawyers and political technologists have. Lofts are very fashionable. The ceiling's slanting, because the stand runs overhead. It's romantic.'

'But how do you manage without any light?'

'See that little pane of glass just below the ceiling? That's a window. When the sun rises, a very beautiful beam of light shines straight in here. And anyway, I can see pretty well in the dark.'

He cast another glance round my residence.

'Is that your junk in those sacks?'

'You could say that.'

'And the bike's yours too?'

'Yes,' I said. 'It's a good bike. Disc brakes, and the fork's made of carbon fibre.'

'Is the computer made of carbon fibre too?'

'Don't joke, you already guessed. It's a rare model, they only make them for Japan. One of the lightest laptops in the world.'

'I get it. So that's why it's standing on a cardboard box, is it? Instead of a table? Aren't you ashamed when you have visitors?'

His tone had begun to get under my skin.

'You know, Vladimir Mikhailovich,' I answered, 'to be quite honest, I couldn't really say what I care less about, the appearance of the things around me or the opinions of the people I meet. Both of them are over and done with far too quickly for me to be bothered.'

'A dump, that's what it is,' he summed up. 'Does the local militia know about this tramp's hideaway?'

'Are you going to tip them off?'

'I'll see how you behave. Right, let's go.'

We walked to the car in silence, apart from two occasions when Mikhalich swore – the first time when he had to squeeze through the narrow gap between two sheets of plywood, and the second time when he had to duck under a low partition.

'Please don't swear,' I said.

'I tore my sleeve. How do you drag your bicycle through here?'

'Easy. In summer I leave it outside. Who's going to bother climbing in here?'

'Yes,' he said, 'that's true enough.'

The car was standing outside the gates of the equestrian complex. That meant there was a chance that Mikhalich's visit would go unnoticed. But what difference did it make now? The local militia could carry on without noticing anything for another hundred years, but Mikhalich and his crowd knew everything. They'd never get off my back. I'll have to look for a new place to live, I thought, yet again . . .

After we'd driven away from the race track, Mikhalich suddenly handed me a scarlet rose with a long stem. I didn't even notice where he got it from, it was so unexpected. The rose had only just opened and there was still dew glistening on it.

'Thank you,' I said, taking the flower. 'I'm touched. But I ought to say straight away that the chances of anything between us aren't . . .'

'It's not from me,' he interrupted. 'The boss asked me to give it to you. He said you should think about what it means on the way.'

'All right,' I said, 'I'll think about it. What was that device you could see me on?'

He stuck one hand into his jacket pocket and took out a small object like a cigarette case with a little screen. There were a few buttons on the cigarette case, but overall it looked pretty unimpressive.

'It's a locator.'

'And what does it locate?'

'Signals,' said Mikhalich. 'Give me your handbag.'

I held out my bag. At the next traffic light he took hold of the strap, turned it over and showed me a little circle of dark foil smaller than a kopeck coin. It was very thin and held in place by a layer of glue. I would never have noticed it – or I'd have thought it was some kind of label.

'And when did you stick that on?'

'When we were on the way to the room to drink champagne,' he said with a chuckle.

'What for? Are you taking such a serious interest in me?'

'In general, yes,' he said. 'But it's not me any more. Never

99

mind, the boss will soon find out what you're up to. He's sorted out trickier specimens than you. By the way, I told him what kind of work you do.'

At this stage I didn't like what was going on at all, but it was too late to get worked up about it: we were already approaching the familiar building. The car drove into the courtyard and straight in through the metal gates of the garage, which immediately closed, cutting us off from the world.

'Get out, we're here.'

As soon as Mikhalich got out, I put the rose on his seat – its long thorny stem was almost the same colour, and there was a good chance that Mikhalich would just plonk his sturdy backside down on it.

'Take your shoes off,' he said when I got out after him.

'What's this, are you taking me to be shot?'

'That depends,' he chuckled. 'There are slippers over there by the lift.'

I looked around. A round hole in the ceiling, a steel pole, a spiral staircase – we were in a familiar place. But this time there was a light on in the garage and I spotted the door of a lift that I hadn't noticed the last time. Lying on the floor in front of it there were several pairs of various different slippers. I chose a pair of blue ones with round pompoms – they looked so touchingly defenceless that only a monster could possibly harm any girl who was wearing them.

The lift door opened and Mikhalich gestured for me to go in. There were two large triangular buttons on the panel, combined to form a rhombus. Mikhalich pressed the upper button, and the lift took off with a mighty jerk, carrying us upwards.

When the door opened a few seconds later, I was blinded by light coming from all directions. Alexander was standing there, engulfed in the bright swirling vortex. He was wearing a military uniform and his face was covered with a gauze mask.

'Hello, Ada,' he said. 'Please come in. No, Mikhalich, I'm sorry – I'm not inviting you. Today three would be a crowd . . .'

* * *

I'd noticed the penthouse on my first visit. Only I hadn't guessed that it was a penthouse – from below it looked like a dark knob on the end of the huge concrete pencil. It could have been taken for the housing of the lift motors, some kind of technical premises or a boiler room. But those turquoise walls turned out to be transparent from the inside.

Before I'd even taken it all in, they started turning dark before my very eyes, until they looked like bottle glass. I'd just been squinting at the bright sunlight, and all of a sudden in just a few seconds an entire house had condensed around me. It hadn't been visible before in the sunshine bouncing off all the mirror surfaces.

I learned later that it was an expensive technical gismo – the transparency of the walls was adjusted using special liquid-crystal membranes that were controlled by a computer system. At the time, though, what happened seemed like a miracle. Only since long, long ago the response that miracles provoke in me has been ironic, not to say contemptuous.

'Hi, Shurik,' I said. 'What's with the sideshow effects? No money for normal blinds?'

He was taken aback. But it only took him a second to recover and he laughed.

'Shurik,' he said. 'I like that. Well yes. Since you're Ada now, I suppose I'm Shurik.'

His light-grey double-breasted uniform jacket with a lieutenant general's shoulder straps and dark-blue trousers with wide red stripes looked a little theatrical. He came up to me, removed the gauze mask from his face, squeezed his eyes shut and drew in the air through his nose. I felt like asking why he was always doing that, but I thought better of it. He opened his eyes and his glance fell on my earrings.

'What an amusing idea,' he said.

'Great, isn't it? And especially beautiful because the stones are different. Do you like it?'

'It's all right. Did Mikhalich give you the flower?'

'Yes,' I answered. 'And he told me I should think about the meaning of the message. But I haven't come up with anything. Maybe you can tell me yourself?'

He scratched his head. He seemed disconcerted by my question.

'Do you know the folktale about the little scarlet flower?'

'Which one exactly?' I asked.

'I think there is only one.'

He nodded towards a desk with a computer and a silver figurine standing on it. There was a book lying beside the figurine, with bookmarks in several pages. The half-effaced red letters of the title on its cover read: *Russian Fairy Tales*.

'The story was written down by Sergei Aksakov,' he said. 'His housekeeper Pelagia told him it.'

'And what's it about?'

'About a beautiful girl and a beast.'

'And what's the little flower got to do with it?'

'It was the reason everything began. Do you really not know this fairy tale?'

'No.'

'It's long, but the gist is this: a beautiful girl asked her father to bring her a scarlet flower. The father found one in a magical garden a long way away and picked it. But the garden was guarded by a terrible monster. He caught the beautiful girl's father, and she had to become the monster's prisoner so that he would release her father. The monster was ugly, but kind. She fell in love with him, first for his kindness, and then simply in love.

And when they kissed, the spell was broken and the monster turned into a prince.'

'Aha,' I said. 'Do you have any idea what it's about?'

'Of course.'

'Yes? What is it about?'

'About love conquering all.'

I laughed. He really was quite amusing. He'd probably bumped off a few heavy hoods and ordered a hit on some banker, so now, with typical human presumption, he thought he was a monster. And he also thought that love would save him.

He took me by the arm and led me across to a futuristic divan standing between two groves of dwarf bonsais with miniature arbours, bridges and even waterfalls.

'Why are you laughing?' he asked.

'I can explain,' I said, sitting down on the divan and pulling my legs up under me.

'Okay, explain.'

He sat at the other end of the divan and crossed his legs. I noticed the edge of a holster peeping out from under his uniform jacket.

'It's one of those folktales that express the horror and pain of a woman's first sexual experience,' I said. 'There are lots of stories like that, and the one you just told me is a classic example. It's a metaphor of how a woman discovers the essentially bestial nature of man and becomes aware of her own power over that beast. And the little scarlet flower that her father picks is such a literal symbol of defloration, amplified by the theme of incest, that I find it hard to believe the story was told by a housekeeper. It was probably composed by some twentieth-century Viennese postgraduate to illustrate his thesis. He invented the story, and the housekeeper Pelagia, and the writer Aksakov.'

While I was talking, his expression turned noticeably gloomier.

'Where did you pick up all that stuff?'

'It's all truisms. Everybody knows it.'

'And you believe it?'

'What?'

'That this fairy tale is not about how love conquers everything on earth, but how defecation realizes its power over incest?'

'Defloration,' I corrected him.

'It doesn't matter. Is that what you really think?'

I thought about it.

'I . . . I don't think anything. That's simply the contemporary discourse of folktales.'

'So you're saying that because of this discourse, when someone gives you a scarlet flower you think it's a symbol of defecation and incest?'

'No, don't be like that,' I replied, a little embarrassed. 'When someone gives me a scarlet flower I . . . I'm simply pleased.'

'Thank God,' he said. 'And as for contemporary discourse, it's high time to take an aspen stake and stuff it back up the cocaine-and-amphetamine polluted backside that produced it.'

I hadn't expected such a sweeping generalization.

'Why?'

'So it won't defile our little scarlet flower.'

'All right,' I said, 'I understand about the cocaine. You mean Dr Freud. He did have that little peccadillo. But what have amphetamines got to do with it?'

'I can explain,' he said, and tucked his legs up underneath himself in a parody of my pose.

'Okay, explain.'

'All those French parrots who invented discourse were high on amphetamines all the time. In the evening they take barbiturates to get to sleep, and they start off the morning with amphetamines so they can generate as much discourse as possible before they start taking barbiturates to get back to sleep again. That's all there is to discourse. Didn't you know that?'

'Where did you get information like that?'

'There was a course at the FSB Academy about modern psy-chedelic culture. Counter-brainwashing. Oh yes, I forgot to say – they're all queers too. In case you were going to ask what the backside had to do with anything.'

The conversation was headed in the wrong direction, and it was time to change the subject. I prefer to do that abruptly.

'Alexander,' I said, 'explain to me, so I can understand, just what I'm doing here. Do you want to screw me or re-educate me?'

He shuddered, as if I'd said something terrible, leapt up off the divan and began striding backwards and forwards past the win-dow – or rather, not the window, but a rectangle in the wall that was still transparent.

'Are you trying to shock me?' he asked. 'You're wasting your time. I know there's a pure, vulnerable soul hiding behind your affected cynicism.'

'Affected cynicism? You mean me?'

'Not even cynicism,' he said, stopping. 'Flippancy. A failure to understand the serious things you're playing with, like a little child with a hand grenade. Let's talk frankly, to the point.'

'Okay, let's.'

'You say – the bestial essence of man, the horror of the first coitus . . . These are such terrible, dark things. If you want to know, even I am sometimes afraid to glance into those abysses . . .'

He really was funny after all – 'even I'. He went on:

'But you talk about it all like it was just peanuts. Don't you have any fear of the beast in a man? Of the man in the beast?'

'Not a bit,' I said. 'Mikhalich told you who I am, didn't he?'

He nodded.

'Well, then. If I had problems like that I wouldn't be able to do my job.'

'You're not afraid of the intimate contact with someone else's body – immense and ugly, living according to its own laws?'

'I simply adore it,' I said and smiled.

He looked at me and shook his head dubiously.

'I mean physical intimacy? In the very lowest sense?'

'For spiritual intimacy I charge an extra hundred and fifty per cent. How long can you go on chewing over the same thing? Do you always yatter on like this before you have a screw?'

He frowned.

'There's no need to talk to me as if I were a bandit. That's because of the FSB uniform, is it?'

'Maybe. Try taking it off. Including the trousers.'

'Why do you talk that way?'

'Don't you find me at all attractive?'

I lowered my head and gave him an offended look from under my eyebrows, screwing my eyes up slightly and pouting my lips. I worked on that look for over a thousand years, and there's no point in trying to describe it. It's my own patented brand of provocation – brazenness and innocence in the same armour-piercing package: it zaps straight through the client and then ricochets back to get him again. The only effective protection I know against that gaze is to look in the other direction. Alexander was looking at me.

'Yes, I do,' he said with a nervous twitch of his head. 'And how!'

I realized the critical moment had arrived. When the client jerks his head like that, the control centres of his brain are failing, and he can throw himself at you at any moment.

'I need to go to the bathroom,' I said. 'Where is your bathroom here?'

He pointed to a round wall of blue semi-transparent glass. There was no door – the way in was through a passage that curled like a snail's shell.

'I'll just be a moment.'

Once I was inside I took a deep breath.

It was beautiful on the other side of the wall. The gold stars on a blue background and the bath lined with mother-of-pearl reminded me of the baths at Pompeii – perhaps the designer had deliberately evoked that image. But the owner was unlikely to know about that.

It's risky to push a client up so far so fast, I thought, some day it will end badly. And maybe Alexander was injecting something, like Mikhalich? Or taking something by mouth? There must be some reason for the strange way he kept sniffing the air like that . . .

I took off my jeans and put them on the floor, then took a look at myself in the mirror. My pride and joy was like a Japanese fan painted to look like a red brush. It was beautiful. And against the starry blue background it looked simple fabulous. I was more sure of my powers than I had ever been – I was simply brimming over with energy, just a little bit more and the hairs of my tail would have started shooting out little balls of lightning. I remembered the funny Russian saying 'to hold your tail like a pistol', meaning to keep your spirits up. I don't know where it came from, but a fox must have been involved one way or another. Well then, I thought, all guns blazing . . .

When I reached the way out, I prepared for take-off by taking a few deep breaths, seized that one and only right moment when every cell in your body says 'Now!' and hurtled out of the bathroom like a tornado.

After that there was no time to think. I braked, turned my backside to the target, thrust my hands and feet hard against the floor and curved my tail above my head. I caught a glimpse of my reflection in one of the mirror surfaces – I looked like a menacing red scorpion prepared for battle . . . Alexander raised his eyes to look at me, but before he could even blink, my tail had delivered its precise, perfectly aligned, impeccably accurate blow to the very centre of his brain.

He put his hand over his eyes, as if to protect them against a blinding light. Then he lowered his hand and our eyes met. Something was happening that wasn't right. My tail simply wasn't able to sense him – and he was standing just a few steps away and looking at me as if he couldn't believe that anything so beautiful could possibly exist in all the world.

'Adele,' he whispered, 'my darling . . .'

And then the nightmare began.

He staggered, made a terrible howling sound and literally fell out of his own body – as if it were a bud that opened up into a sinister, shaggy flower in just a few seconds. It turned out that the man who was called Alexander was no more than a drawing on a door into the beyond. Now that door had opened, and the creature who had been watching me through the keyhole for a long time had come tumbling out.

Standing there in front of me was a monster, something halfway between a man and a wolf, with gaping jaws and piercing yellow eyes. At first I thought Alexander's clothes had disappeared. Then I realized that his tunic and trousers had been transformed together with him: his torso was covered with ash-grey fur, but his hind legs were darker, and I could see the irregular traces of the stripes on them. There was an elongated mark on the beast's chest, like the imprint of a tie that has slipped to one side. When my gaze moved lower I was horror-struck. I'd never seen how that place looked on a wolf that was aroused. And to my mind it looked more terrible than any gaping jaws.

At that point I realized I was still standing on all fours with my tail up in the air and my defenceless behind stuck out in his direction. Defenceless, because my antenna wasn't working and I had nothing to stop him with. I could guess how my pose might be interpreted, but I was paralysed – instead of jumping back, I kept looking at him over my shoulder. That happens in some dreams – you need to run away fast, but instead you go on standing there and there's just no way you can lift your leaden feet off the ground. I couldn't even wipe the idiot grin off my face – like a burglar caught on the job.

'Grr-rra-rra,' he said. 'Gr-rrrrra . . .'

'Hey, bro,' I babbled, 'wait. I'll explain everything . . .'

He growled and took a step towards me.

'Don't you even think about it, all right? I'm serious, you big grey wolf, slow down . . .'

He fell gently on to his front paws or hands and took another step towards me. Entirely different words were required. But where could I find them?

'Listen . . . Let's discuss everything calmly, eh?'

He grinned, opening his jaws wide and raising his huge grey tail, almost copying my working pose.

'Wait, grey beast,' I whispered, 'don't . . .'

He jumped, and for a second I thought the world had been covered by a terrible, low storm cloud. The next moment the cloud collapsed on top of me.

* * *

Lying on the divan, covered with something like the skin of an albino mammoth, I sobbed into the pillow, unable to understand how there could have been so many tears inside me – the pillow was already soaked on both sides.

'Ada,' Alexander said and put his hand on my shoulder.

'Go away, you monster,' I sobbed and shook his hand off.

'I'm sorry,' he said timidly, 'I didn't mean . . .'

'I said go away, you dirty animal.'

I burst into floods of tears again. A minute or two later he tried to touch my shoulder again.

'I asked you three times,' he said.

'Are you trying to be funny?'

'What do you mean? I told you. About the bestial body, about physical intimacy. Didn't I?'

'How was I supposed to guess?'

'Well, for instance, from the smell.'

'Foxes don't have any sense of smell.'

'I understood all about you straight away,' he said, stroking my arm awkwardly. 'In the first place, people don't smell like that. And in the second place, Mikhalich has been dinning it into my ears. "Comrade lieutenant general, I've looked at the recording – you've got to sort this dame out properly. She stands on all fours, with her eyes blazing, I've never seen eyes so terrible, and on her back she has this huge red lens. And she uses that lens to burn right through our consultant's brain! She turned the beam on him, and he was totally zonked . . ." At first I thought the ketamine had sent him totally insane. But then I watched the recording, and there it was . . . He took your tail for a lens.'

'What recording's that?'

'Your client, the one you lashed until he bled, was shooting amateur porn. With a concealed camera.'

'What? When I was working on credit?'

'Well, I wouldn't know about that, that's your business. As soon as he came round he brought the tape to us.'

'The fucking intelligentsia,' I said, unable to restrain myself.

'Yes,' he agreed, 'not very nice. But that's what people are like. You mean Mikhalich didn't show you the photos? He had a whole file of them, specially printed for your conversation.'

'He didn't have time . . . You mean Mikhalich is going to watch all the vile things you just did with me?'

'I don't have a single camera here, relax, my darling.'

'Don't call me darling, you beast,' I sobbed. 'You filthy

depraved male. Nobody's done that to me in the last . . .' – for some reason I suddenly decided not to mention any dates – 'ever done that to me in my life. How vile!'

He pulled his head down into his shoulders, as if he'd been lashed with a wet rag. That was curious – although my tail apparently had no effect on him, it seemed that my words affected him quite powerfully. I decided to test this observation.

'I'm so tender and delicate down there,' I said in a pitiful voice. 'And you've torn everything with your huge prick. I'll probably die now . . .'

He turned pale, unbuttoned his tunic and took a huge nickel-plated pistol out of its holster. I was afraid he was going to shoot me, the way Robert De Niro shot that tedious woman he was talking to in Tarantino's film, but fortunately I was wrong.

'If anything happens to you,' he said in a serious voice, 'I'll blow my brains out.'

'Put it away,' I said, 'put it away . . . So what if you do blow your stupid brains out? What good will that do me? I told you, don't!'

'I thought,' he said quietly, 'that you were just being coy.'

'Coy? Your dick is three times the size of that pistol, you wolf! I wasn't being coy, I just wanted to stay alive! Nowadays they even teach children in school that if a girl says "No", it means precisely "No", and not "Yes" or "Oh, I don't know". All the rape cases in the West are centred round that. Didn't they explain that in the FSB Academy?'

He shook his head dejectedly from side to side. It was a pitiful sight. I felt the time had come to stop, or I might overdo it. That recollection of Tarantino had been no accident.

'Do you have some bandages and iodine?' I asked in a weak voice.

'I'll send Mikhalich,' he said, jumping to his feet.

'I don't want Mikhalich here! The last thing I need is

Mikhalich giggling over me . . . Can't you go to the chemist's yourself?'

'Yes, I can.'

'And don't let that Mikhalich of yours come in here while you're gone. I don't want anyone to see me in this state.'

He was already at the lift.

'I'll be quick. Hold on.'

The door closed behind him and I breathed a sigh of relief.

As I've already said, foxes don't have any sexual organs in the human sense. But we do have a rudimentary cavity under our tails, an elastic bag of skin that's not connected with any other organs. It's usually squeezed into a narrow slit, like the bladder of a deflated football, but when we experience fear it expands and becomes slightly moist. It plays the same role in our anatomy as a special hollow plastic cylinder does in the equipment of employees in a great ape reserve.

The great apes employ the same technologies of social control as are found in criminal and political circles: the males who are in charge ritually humiliate other apes who they think are aspiring to an unjustifiably high status. Sometimes outsiders like electricians and laboratory workers find themselves in this role (I mean in special reserves). In readiness for such a turn of events, they carry an empty plastic cylinder suspended on straps between their legs, and this cylinder is known by the glorious name of a 'prick-catcher'. It is their guarantee of safety: if a large male obsessed by a sense of social justice jumps them, all they have to do is bend over and wait a few minutes – while the ape's indignation is expended on the cylinder. Then they can continue on their way.

And now I could do the same – continue on my way.

It led me into the bathroom, where the first thing I did was to examine my body. Apart from the fact that the rudimentary cavity under my tail was chafed and reddened, there was no problem. True, my posterior section ached as if I'd been riding a crazed horse for at least an hour (which was a fairly accurate description of what had happened), but that couldn't really be called an injury. Nature had definitely prepared foxes for encounters with werewolves.

I'd sensed earlier that I would have to wash myself in his mother-of-pearl bath – and my premonition had not deceived me. My entire tail, back, stomach and legs were covered in that wolf's filthy muck, which I carefully washed off with shampoo. Then I quickly dried my tail with a hairdryer and got dressed. It suddenly occurred to me that it would be a good idea to search the premises.

There was practically nothing to search in that luxurious, empty barn of a place – no cupboards, no sideboards, no drawers that opened. The doors leading into the other rooms were locked. But even so, the results of the search were interesting.

Standing on the desk beside the elegant all-in-one computer was a massive silver object that I had taken at first glance for a figurine. On closer inspection the object turned out to be a cigar clipper. It was a figure of Monica Lewinsky lying on her side with one leg raised towards the ceiling to act as a lever, and when it was pressed (I couldn't resist it) not only did the guillotine in the ring between her thighs snap into action, but a tongue of blue flame appeared out of her open mouth. It was a great little gadget, to my mind the only superfluous touch was the American flag that Monica was holding in her hand: sometimes just a tiny weight is enough to shift the balance and transform a piece of erotica into kitsch agitprop.

The silver Monica was holding down a big loose-leaf binder on the desk. Inside it there was a pile of very different-looking papers.

To judge from its high gloss, the paper lying on the very top was a page from some illustrated art book. Staring out at me from it was a huge, yellow-eyed wolf with a rune that looked like the letter 'F' on his chest – it was a photograph of a sculpture made of wood and amber (the eyes were the amber part). The caption said:

FENRIR: Son of Loki, an immense wolf who pursues the sun across the sky. When Fenrir catches the sun and devours it, Ragnarek will begin. Fenrir is bound until Ragnarek. At Ragnarek he will kill Odin and be killed by Widar.

It wasn't clear from the caption just how Fenrir was going to catch the sun and devour it, if he was bound until Ragnarek, and Ragnarek would start when he caught the sun and devoured it. But then, it could well be that our world had only continued to exist so far thanks to inconsistencies of that kind: it was frightening to think just how many dying gods had cursed it.

I remembered who Fenrir was. He was the most fearsome brute in the Nordic bestiary, the central character of Icelandic eschatology: the wolf who would eat the gods when the northern project was shut down. I wanted to believe that Alexander didn't identify too closely with this creature, that the yellow-eyed monster was simply an unattainable aesthetic ideal, something like a photo of Schwarzenegger hanging on the wall in a novice bodybuilder's room.

Further down the pile there was a page from a book with Borges's miniature piece 'Ragnarek'. I knew the story, which had astounded me with its somnambulistically precise depiction of something important and terrible. The hero and his friend witness a strange procession of gods returning from centuries of exile. A wave of human adoration carries them out on to a stage in a hall. They look strange:

One was holding a branch, something out of the uncomplicated flora of dreams; another flung a clawed hand forward in a sweeping gesture: Janus's face glanced repeatedly at Tot's crooked beak with a certain apprehension.

A dream echo of fascism. But then something very interesting happens:

> Probably roused by the applause, one of them – I don't remember now exactly who – suddenly broke into a triumphant screeching, unbearably harsh, as if he were either whistling or clearing his throat. From that moment everything changed.

From then on the text was covered with marks and notes. Words were underlined, framed with exclamation marks and even ringed – evidently to convey the relative intensity of emotion:

> It began with the suspicion (evidently exaggerated), that the Gods could not talk. Centuries of wild and nomadic life had <u>destroyed in them all that was human: the Islamic crescent moon and the Roman cross</u> had shown no condescension to the exiled. The low sloping foreheads, yellow teeth and thin moustaches of mulattoes or Chinese and the out-turned lips of animals spoke of the <u>decline of the Olympic breed</u>. Their clothing was out of keeping with their modest and honest poverty and put me in mind of the dismal chic of the gambling houses and bordellos of Bakho. A carnation bled out of a buttonhole. The outline of a knife-handle was discernible beneath a close-fitting jacket. And then we realized that !<u>they were playing their last card!</u>, that they were !<u>cunning, blind and as cruel as mature, powerful beasts when they are flushed out of the bushes!</u>, and – !<u>IF WE GAVE WAY TO FEAR OR COMPASSION – THEY WOULD ANNIHILATE US!</u>
>
> And then each of us <u>took out a heavy revolver</u> (the revolvers appeared from somewhere in the dream) <u>AND WE SHOT THE GODS WITH DELIGHT.</u>

After that there were two pages from the Elder Edda – apparently from a prophecy by Velva. They had been torn out of some gift edition: the text was printed in large red script on glazed paper in a very wasteful manner:

> The wind raises
> Waves to the sky,
> Casts them on to the land,
> The sky grows dark;
> The blizzard hurtles along,
> Swirling furiously:
> These are the portents
> Of *the death of the gods*.

'The death of the gods' in the last line had been underscored with a fingernail. The message of the text on the second page was equally morose:

> But there is yet to come
> The most powerful of all,
> I dare not speak
> His name;
> Few are those who know
> What will come to pass
> Following the battle
> Between Odin and the Wolf.

All the rest was in the same vein. In one way or another most of the papers in the file related to northern myth. The one I found most depressing was a photograph of the German submarine *Nagelfahr* – in Scandinavian mythology that was the name of the god Loki's ship, which was made out of the nails of the dead. A highly appropriate name for a Second World War submarine. The unshaven crew members smiling from the bridge looked perfectly likeable – they reminded me of a detachment of modern 'greens'.

As I got closer to the end of the file, there were fewer marks on the sheets of paper: as if the person who had been leafing through them and thinking about the collection of material had rapidly lost interest or, as Borges put it in a different story 'a certain noble impatience' had prevented him from leafing through all the way to the end. But the guy's pretensions had been serious, especially by the standards of our mercenary times ('the age of swords and pole axes' as it was described in one of the extracts in the file, 'the time of cursed wealth and great lechery').

The last item in the file was a lined page torn out of a school exercise book. It had been inserted into a transparent plastic envelope to protect it. The handwritten text on the page was something like a gift dedication:

> *To Sashka, a memento.*
> *Transform!*
>
> *WOLF-FLOW!*
>
> Colonel Lebedenko

I closed the file and put it back under Monica, then continued with my search. I wasn't surprised when I found several CDs beside the music centre, all with various performances of the same opera:

RICHARD WAGNER
DER RING DES NIBELUNGEN
Götterdämmerung.

The next curious item that caught my eye was a thick, grey notebook. It was lying on the floor between the wall and the divan – as if someone had been looking through it before going to bed, fallen asleep and dropped it. On its cover was written:

'Shitman' Project
Top secret.

Copy No. 9
not to be removed from the building

At that moment I didn't make any connection between this strange title and the story about the Shakespeare specialist that Pavel Ivanovich had told me. My thoughts followed a different route – I decided it was yet another proof of the power of American cultural influence. Superman, Batman, another couple of similar films, and the mind begins to stereotype reality in their image and likeness. But then, I thought, what could Russia put up against this? The Shitov Project? Who would be willing to spend nights sweating over that for low pay? That Shitov in a poor suit had been responsible for the collapse of the Soviet empire. The substance of life doesn't change much from one culture to another, but the human soul requires a beautiful wrapper. Russian culture, though, fails to provide one, and it calls this state of affairs *spirituality*. That's the reason for all the disasters . . .

I didn't even bother to open the notebook. I'd had a horror of secret documents ever since Soviet times: they did you no good and they could snow you under with problems, even if you had FSB protection.

My eye was caught by several graphic works on paper that were hanging on the walls – runes that had been roughly drawn with either a broad brush or a paw. They reminded me a bit of Chinese calligraphy – the crudest and most expressive examples. Hanging between two of these runes there was a branch of mistletoe – I learned that from the caption on the wall: to look at, it was simply a dry, pointed stick.

The design on the carpet was curious, it showed a battle

between lions and wolves – it looked like a copy of a Roman mosaic. The books on the only bookshelf were mostly massive illustrated editions (*The Splendour of Rome*, *The New Revised History of the Russian Soul*, *The Origin of Species and Homosexuality* and other, simpler titles about cars and guns). But then, I knew that the books on shelves like that had nothing to do with the taste of their owners, because they were chosen by the interior designers.

Having concluded my inspection, I went across to the glass door on to the roof. The view from there was beautiful. Down below were the dark pits of pre-Revolutionary courtyards improved by restoration work. Towering up above them were a few new buildings of the phallic architecture – an attempt had been made to insert them smoothly and gently into the historical landscape, and the result was that they looked as if they were smeared with some kind of personal lubricant. After them came the Kremlin, proudly thrusting up to the clouds its ancient dicks with the gold balls sewn into their tops.

This damned job, I thought, it's terrible how badly it's perverted my perception of the world. But then, has it really perverted it all that much? It's all the same to us foxes – we pass through life and barely touch it, like a light shower of rain in Asia. But to be a human being here is hard. Take one step away from the secret national gestalt, and this country will screw you over. A theorem that has been proved by every life followed through to the end, no matter how many glamorous coverlets you spread over the daily festival of life. I should know, I've seen plenty of it. Why? I have my own suspicions, but I won't go into the subject. People probably aren't simply born here by chance, it's no accident . . . And no one is able to help anyone else. Could that be the reason why Moscow sunsets always make me feel so sad?

'A great view from up here, isn't it?'

I swung round. He was standing by the door of the lift with a tightly packed plastic bag in his hand. The design on the bag was a green snake wound around a medical chalice.

'There wasn't any iodine,' he said anxiously, 'they gave me fuxidine. Said it was the same, only orange. I think that's even better for us – it won't stand out so much beside the tail . . .'

I felt like laughing and turned away towards the window. He walked across and stood beside me. We looked at the city for a while without speaking.

'It's beautiful here in summer,' he said. 'Put Zemfira on the player, watch and listen: 'Goodbye, beloved city . . . I almost found a place among your annals . . . What do you think she meant – something like she's been in deep shit for far too long?'

'Don't try to soft-soap me.'

'You seem to be feeling better.'

'I want to go home,' I said.

'But . . .'

He nodded towards the plastic bag.

'No need, thanks. When they bring you in a wounded comrade, you'll be able to treat him. I'm off.'

'Mikhalich will drive you.'

'I don't want your Mikhalich, I'll manage.'

I was already at the lift.

'When can I see you?' he asked.

'I don't know,' I said. 'If I don't die, call in three days.'

* * *

After copulation, all animals are sad – so the ancient Romans used to say. Apart from foxes, I would have added. And apart from women. I knew that for certain now.

I don't mean to say that women are animals. Quite the contrary – men are much closer to the animals in every respect: the smells they give off and the sounds they make, their type of phys-icality and the methods they use to fight for personal happiness (not to mention what they actually think of as happiness). But the ancient Roman who described his own mood after the act of love in metaphorical terms was evidently such an entirely organic sex-chauvinist that he simply failed to take woman into account, and that means I have to restore justice.

Generally speaking, there could be at least four explanations for this saying:

1) the Romans didn't think woman was *even* an animal.

2) the Romans thought woman was an animal, but they copu-lated with her in a way that really did make her sad (for instance, Suetonius tells us that the law forbade the killing of virgins by strangulation, and the executioner used to ravish them before the execution – how could you help feeling sad?).

3) the Romans didn't think woman was an animal, they assumed that only man was. For this noble view of things, the Romans could be forgiven a great deal – apart, of course, from those foul-ups of theirs with virgins and strangulation.

4) the Romans had no penchant for either woman or metaphor, but they did for livestock cattle and poultry, who did not recip-rocate and were unable to conceal their feelings.

There could be an element of truth in each of these explana-tions – no doubt all sorts of things happened in the course of several centuries of empire. But I was a happy animal.

For the last fifteen hundred years I'd had an old maid complex – not, of course, in relation to human beings, to whose opinion I was profoundly indifferent, but within our small community of foxes. It had sometimes seemed to me that I was the butt of secret mockery. And there were good grounds for these thoughts of mine – all my sisters had lost their virginity in ancient times, in the most varied of circumstances. The most interesting story was what had happened to sister E – she had been set on a stake by a nomad leader, and she had honestly acted out her agony for three days. She had to wait until the nomads drank themselves into a stupor before making good her escape into the steppe. I suspected that this was the origin of the insatiable hatred for the aristocracy she had manifested for so many centuries in her most whimsical escapades . . .

But even so I was just a little bit sad. As the grammar-school girl Masha from Nikolaev, one of my colleagues on the game in the year 1919, said, there's a good angel who abandons us when we lose our virginity. But the sadness I felt was radiant, and on the whole I was in an excellent mood.

There was one suspicion clouding it, though. I had the feeling that I'd been treated the same way I had been treating others all my life. Perhaps the whole thing was a suggestion that had been planted in my mind? It was pure paranoia – we foxes can't be hypnotized. But there was a certain vague unease gnawing at my heart.

I couldn't understand the transformation that Alexander had gone through. Foxes also undergo a supraphysical transformation, which I will tell you about later. But it never goes so far – what Alexander had done was mind-blowing. There was an ancient mystery still alive in him, something that foxes had already forgotten, and I knew that I would keep coming back to it in my thoughts for a long time.

And I was also afraid that the loss of virginity might affect my ability to implant suggestions. I had no grounds for any such concerns, but irrational fear is always the hardest to shake off. I knew I wouldn't calm down until I'd tested my powers. And so when the phone rang with an offer, I decided right away to go.

From his manner of speaking the client sounded to me like a bashful student from the provinces who had saved up enough money for a ritual of farewell with his childhood. But something in his voice made me check the number that lit up against the database I keep in my computer. It turned out to be the nearest militia station. Obviously the fuzz were calling me out for a *subbotnik* – a working Saturday in honour of the spring – the kind of event I simply couldn't stand ever since Soviet times. But today I decided to enter the beast's lair voluntarily.

There turned out to be three cops. There was no shower-room in the station, and I had to prepare myself for battle in a toilet with a cracked toilet-bowl that reminded me vividly of the Cheka's place in Odessa during the revolutionary years (they used to hold people's heads down over a toilet bowl like that when they executed them – to avoid getting blood on the floor). My fears, of course, proved entirely unfounded – all the militiamen sank into a trance just as soon as I raised my tail. I could have gone back to the equestrian complex, but an interesting idea occurred to me.

Early that morning I'd been thinking about Rome and remembering Suetonius, and clearly that was the reason for my sudden flash of ingenuity. I remembered a story about Tiberius's orgies in Capri: it mentioned the so called 'spintrii', who inflamed the ageing emperor's sensuality by conjoining themselves three at a time in front of him. This story fired my imagination – in my own mind I even translated 'Splinter Cell' (the title of an innocent computer game about Tom Clancy) as meaning 'The Sect of the Splintrii'. Now that I found myself in the company of three moral outsiders, I couldn't resist trying an experiment. And I managed it perfectly! Or rather, they did. Though I must say, I failed to understand what Tiberius found so arousing in this crude spectacle – to my mind it looked more like an illustration of the first noble truth of Buddhism: life is *dukha* – suffering and pain. But I already knew that, without a triad of copulating militiamen.

In the station I discovered four thousand dollars, which couldn't have come at a better time. And as well as that, I came across a scholarly large-format volume on criminal tattoos, with photographs, which I enjoyed leafing through. The tendency that this genre had followed in its evolution matched the development of world culture perfectly: religious consciousness was reclaiming the positions it had lost in the twentieth century. Naturally, the manifestations of this consciousness were not always recognizable at first sight. For instance, I didn't immediately realize that the words 'SWAT SWAT SWAT' tattooed under a blue cross that looked more like a German military award than a crucifixion were not meant to be the name of the Los Angeles Police Department's special assault force, but the Russian phrase 'Svyat, Svyat, Svyat' (meaning 'Holy, Holy, Holy') written in Latin letters.

The photograph that made the biggest impression on me was a man's back with a diptych depicting heaven and earth. Heaven was located between his shoulder-blades – the sun was shining and there were angels who looked like postal pigeons flying about. The earth level looked like the official crest of Moscow, with the dragon-killer mounted on his steed, except that instead of a lance, there was a bundle of different-coloured rays emerging from the horseman's hand, and there were lots of little dragons – spiteful little ones, crooked squashed ones and some who looked quite nice, all crawling along an alleyway planted with trees. The whole scene was entitled 'Saint George driving the lesbians off Tverskoi Boulevard'.

Flicking through several pages with the traditional Stalins, Hitlers, snakes, spiders and sharks (under one of them it said 'deep is my motherland', instead of 'broad is my motherland' as in the old patriotic song), I came across the religious theme again: someone's back decorated with a panoramic view of hell with sinners in torment. I was especially impressed by Bill Gates being devoured by worms and Bin Laden blazing on a bonfire in a frivolous white T-shirt with the emblem:

I ✈ NY

The final page showed a pale, dystrophic shoulder with the mushroom cloud of a nuclear explosion, in which the cap of the mushroom had been replaced by the NIKE streak with the word *NUKE* in it – evidently a memory of the future.

With the groaning and panting of the *spintrii* in the background, all this seemed particularly dismal. Where was humanity going? Who was leading it? What was going to happen on earth in fifty years? A hundred years? My springtime mood was spoiled, despite the good haul I'd made. But at least my conscience was clear. I didn't consider that I was stealing anything – I'd just taken payment for my services. The fuzz had got their sex, I'd got my money – and I'd never concealed the fact that my prices were high.

* * *

On the way home I thought about tattoos. I like them, but I almost never have any done. On foxes they don't last more than twenty years. And apart from that, they often blur in the weirdest way. It's something to do with the rather different nature of our physical being. In the whole of the last century, I only had one tattoo – two lines that the poet W. H. Auden burned into my heart for ever, and the one-eyed tattooist Slava Kosoi inscribed temporarily on my shoulder:

I am a sex machine.
And I'm super bad.

Below the words there was a large blue tear, which for some reason my clients used to take for either an onion or an enema syringe – as if the inhabitants of the shabby Soviet paradise really didn't know what it was to be sad.

That tattoo caused me a whole heap of problems – during the struggle against the Soviet Teddy boys – the '*stilyagi*' – I used to get stopped all the time by the fuzz and the public order squads, who wanted to know what that inscription was in the language of the supposed enemy. I had to work a few Saturday freebees a lot tougher than this one. In short, they put me right off the idea of wearing sleeveless dresses. I still avoid them, even today, although the tattoo faded away ages ago, and the supposed enemy crept up unnoticed and became a supposed ally just as soon as the dust had settled a bit.

When I got home I switched on the TV and tuned in to the BBC World Service. First I watched their review of the Internet, presented by a guy who looked like an immoral version of Bill Clinton, and then the news began. I could tell from the presenter's dynamic expression that they had a good catch.

'Today in London an attempt was made on the life of the Chechen essayist in exile, Aslan Udoev. A terrorist suicide bomber from a militant Shiite organization tried to blow him up. Aslan Udoev himself escaped with a minor concussion, but two of his bodyguards were killed at the scene.'

The camera showed the cramped office of a police official who carefully measured out his words into the black gun-barrel of a microphone:

'We know that the assailant attempted to get close to Aslan Udoev when he was feeding the squirrels in St James's Park. When Udoev's guards spotted the terrorist, he detonated his bomb . . .'

A correspondent appeared on the screen – he was standing on a lawn, with the wind ruffling his yellow hair.

'According to other sources, the device went off prematurely, before the suicide bomber had reached his target. The explosion took place at precisely twelve noon GMT. However, the police have so far declined to make any comment. Witnesses to the event said that before the explosion, instead of the usual "Allah u Akbar", the suicide bomber shouted "Same Shiite, Different Fight!" But on this point the testimony of witnesses varies slightly, possibly because of the terrorist's strong Arab accent. It was reported earlier that "Same Shiite, Different Fight" was the name of a Shiite terrorist organization which has stated that its goal is to open a second front of the jihad in Europe. In its ideology this group is close to the Mahdi Army of the radical cleric Mokhtad Al-Sadr.'

The camera showed the police official squeezed into his narrow little space once again. The correspondent's voice asked:

'We know that the Chechens belong to the Sunni branch of Islam. And the attacker was a Shiite. In this connection, can we say, as many analysts are already doing in their commentaries, that clashes between Shiites and Sunnis are now taking place in London?'

'We are avoiding any hasty conclusions concerning the motives for the crime and whoever is behind it,' the police official replied. 'The investigation has only just begun. And in addition, I should like to emphasize that at the present time we have no concrete information on the programme and goals of any terrorist group called "Same Shiite, Different Fight", or about any militant Shiite groups in England.'

'Is it true that the terrorist had wires embedded in his head?'

'No comment.'

Aslan Udoev appeared on the screen. He was walking along a hospital corridor, squinting hostilely at the camera and holding his bandaged forehead in his hand.

After that they started talking about some footballer's marriage.

I turned the television off and sat there in a state of prostration for a few minutes, trying to think. It was hard to think – I was in shock. I imagined the possible future: a special clinic, a zombifi-cation operation, a command cable installed in your head (I recalled the flesh-coloured wire in the ear of the security guard in the National hotel). And then – your mission. For instance, throw yourself under a tank with a mine on your back – like some heroic German shepherd during the Second World War . . . No, tanks were irrelevant now. Let's say, under a yellow 'Hummer' on Fifth Avenue. That was a more picturesque option, but I didn't like it much better. As they say, same shite, different Shakespeare specialist . . .

Go away? I could do that – I had a false passport for foreign travel. But where to? Thailand? London? Most likely London . . . I'd been meaning to write a letter to E Hu-Li for a long time, but never got round to it. Now I had a good reason. I sat down at the computer and focused my mind, recalling all the things I'd wanted to tell her just recently. Then I started typing:

Hello, Red,

How are you? Still the same old mischievous smile and those heaps of corpses behind your back? :))) Be careful. But then, you're the most careful of all of us, so I have nothing to teach you there.

I recently got a letter from our sister U, whom you visited. How I envy her modest, but pure and happy life! She com-plains that the work makes her tired. It is probably a blissful kind of tiredness – like a peasant's tiredness after a day's work in the field. Tiredness like that heals spiritual wounds and helps you to forget your sorrows – it was what Leo Tolstoy was pur-suing across the fields with his plough. In the city you get tired in a different way. You know, there are some horses who walk round and round a well, pumping water. If you think about it, you and I are the same kind of beast. The difference is that a well horse drives away the horseflies that feed on it with its tail, but you and I use our tails to lure the horseflies who feed us. And apart from that, the horse contributes to people's well-being. As for us . . . Well, let's say people contribute to ours. But I know you can't stand moralizing.

U Hu-Li wrote that you have a new husband, a lord. Do you at least keep count of them? I'd love to get just a brief glimpse of him while there's still something to see :)))) From what she said, just recently you've been taking a serious interest in the subject of the super-werewolf. And you obviously didn't ask me about that demolished church out of idle curiosity.

It is true that the prophecy of the super-werewolf says he will appear in a city where a church or shrine will be restored after not a single stone of it was left standing. But the prophecy is about two thousand years old, and at that time similes and metaphors were the common manner, and everything that was important was always expressed allegorically. Prophecy was written in the language of ancient alchemy – 'city' means a soul and 'a shrine that is destroyed and restored' means a heart that has fallen under the power of evil and then returned to good. Please do not seek for any other meaning in these words.

I will risk making one suggestion – only, please, do not be offended. You have lived in the West for a long time, and the Christian mythologeme has imperceptibly taken root in your mind. Think about it: you are waiting for some super-were-wolf to appear, atone for the sins of the foxes and make our souls pure, as they were at the very beginning of time. Listen. No messiah will ever come to us were-creatures. But each of us can change ourselves by exceeding our own limits. That is the meaning of the expression 'super-werewolf' – one who has passed beyond his own boundaries, exceeded himself. The super-werewolf does not come from the East or from the West, he appears from within. And that is the atonement.

There is only one path that leads to him. Yes, those same old prescriptions that make you sick:

1) compassion;
2) causing no harm to the weak of this world, animals or people – at least not when it can be avoided;
3) most important of all – the striving to understand one's own nature.

To put it very briefly, in the words of Nietzsche (adapted slightly to suit our case), the secret is simple – transcend the bestial! I have no doubt that you have already transcended the human :)))

Remember the lessons in meditation that we took with the teacher from the Yellow Mountain. Believe me, in the thousand years and more that have passed since then, they still haven't invented anything better. The atom bomb, Gucci cologne, condoms with ribs and notches, CNN news, flights to Mars – this entire motley array of wonders has not had the slightest effect on the scales in which the essence of the world is weighed. And therefore, return to the practice, and in only a couple of hundred years you will have no need of any super-werewolf. If I have wearied you, forgive me – but I was sincerely thinking of your own good as I wrote these lines.

And now for the most important thing. In recent years things have not been going well for me. My basic earnings used to be provided by a paedophile financier who was certain he could be arrested for what he was doing. A school satchel, a report book with C grades – you understand. He was sentimental – while he was waiting for our meetings, he shuddered every time a siren sounded. Yes, he was repulsive. But I only used to go out to work once a month. And then he was paralysed and I had to look for different options. For more than a year my top spot was the hotel National. But I ran into serious problems there when a certain client slipped off the tail. And now I'm surrounded by problems on every side. I'm not sure that you can understand them. The specifically Russian flavour is too strong. But they are very, very serious.

I realize you have no time for other people's troubles. But I'd still like to ask for your advice and, perhaps, assistance. Should I move to England? I'm sure I would get on with the English – I've seen quite a few of them in the National and they seem like a quite decent people to me. I'm often paid in pounds, so I wouldn't suffer any culture shock. Write quickly and tell me if there is a quiet spot in London for A Hu-Li.

Heads and tails,

A.

As soon as I sent the letter, my mobile rang. There was no number displayed, and my heart skipped a beat, I guessed who it was before I heard the voice in the phone.

'Hello,' said Alexander, 'you said three days, but that's too long. Can I see you tomorrow? At least for five minutes?'

'Yes,' I said, before I'd even thought about it.

'Then I'll send Mikhalich. He'll call you. I kiss you.'

* * *

The door of the lift opened, and Mikhalich and I entered the penthouse. Alexander was sitting in an armchair in his general's uniform, watching television. He turned towards us, but it wasn't me he spoke to.

'Right, Mikhalich, I see your lot's fucked it up again!' he said cheerfully, with a nod at the long liquid-crystal panel that was showing two channels simultaneously – on one half of the screen there were red and white footballers running about, and on the other Aslan Udoev, who looked a bit like Bluebeard, with his dark purple beard and a sticking plaster on his forehead: he was muttering something into a microphone.

'Yes sir, comrade lieutenant general,' Mikhalich replied, embarrassed. 'The entire crew's made a real bollocks of it this time.'

'Don't swear in front of the girl.'

'Yes, sir.'

'But what the fuck went wrong?'

'We can't tell. Unforeseen interference. Apparently something distorted the precise time signal.'

'Always the same story,' said Alexander. 'As soon as there's a fuck-up, they blame it all on the technical department.'

'Yes sir, comrade lieutenant general.'

'Don't you regret the waste of an operative?'

'We've got any bloody amount of Shakespeare specialists like that, comrade lieutenant general. But somehow no Shakespeares.'

'I told you quite clearly, Mikhalich, don't swear here.'

Mikhalich squinted sideways at me.

'Yes, sir. Shall I draw up a report?'

'I don't want a report. It's none of my business, the ones who thought it up can take the consequences. I don't like bits of paper. On paper everything always comes out right, but in life' – Alexander nodded at the screen – 'you can see for yourself.'

'Yes, sir, comrade lieutenant general.'

'You can go.'

Alexander waited until Mikhalich closed the door, then got up out of his chair and came over to me. I guessed he hadn't wanted to show his feelings in front of a subordinate, but even so I pretended to be offended and when he put his hand on my shoulder I moved away.

'You could have said hello to me first. And then you go and chat with that jerk about football. And in general, turn the television off!'

Udoev was no longer on the screen – he had been replaced by a smart young man with a motor-trike, who exclaimed boisterously:

'Today we're lighting it up with the Marlboro youth team!'

And then he disappeared in a pool of darkness.

'I'm sorry,' said Alexander, tossing the remote control back on to the coffee table. 'Hello.'

I smiled. We looked at each other in silence for a few seconds.

'How are you feeling?' he asked.

'Better now, thank you.'

'And what's that basket you're holding?'

'I brought that for you,' I said shyly.

'Right, let me have it . . .'

He took the basket out of my hands and tore open the packaging.

'Pies?' he asked, looking back up at me in bewilderment. 'Why pies? What for?'

I looked away.

His face slowly lit up.

'Wait . . . I was wondering why you were wearing that red hood. Ah-ha-ha-ha!'

He burst into peals of happy laughter, put his arms round me and sat me down beside him on the divan. He made the movement very naturally, too quickly for me push him away, although I'd been intending to play hard to get for a little longer. But then, I'm not sure that I really wanted to.

'It's like the joke,' he said. 'About Little Red Riding Hood and the wolf. Little Red Riding Hood says: "What big eyes you have, wolf!" And the wolf says: "All the better to see you with." Little Red Riding Hood says: "What big ears you have, wolf!" "All the better to hear you with," the wolf replies. And then Little Red Riding Hood says: "What a big tail you have!" "That's not a tail," says the wolf, and blushes . . .'

'Phoo!'

'Isn't it funny?'

I shrugged.

'It's not realistic. For a wolf to blush. His entire face is covered with fur. Even if he does blush, how can you see it?'

Alexander thought about it.

'I suppose that's right,' he agreed, 'but it's a joke.'

'It's a good thing you know who Little Red Riding Hood is, at least from jokes,' I said. 'I thought you might not get the hint. You don't look like someone who reads too many books.'

He blushed, just like in his own joke.

'That's where you're wrong. I read every day.'

He nodded towards the coffee table, which had a paperback detective novel lying on it. The title was *Werewolves in Shoulder Straps*.

'Is it an interesting book?' I asked.

'Not really. Nothing special.'

'Then why are you reading it?'

'To understand why it's called that. We check out every hostile comment.'

'Who's "we"?'

'That's not important,' he said. 'It's got nothing to do with literature.'

'Detective novels don't have anything to do with literature either,' I said.

'You don't like them?'

I shook my head.

'Why?'

'They're boring to read. You know from the first page who killed who and why.'

'Yes? If I read you the first page of *Werewolves*, will you tell me who the killer is?'

'I can tell you now. The author did it, for money.'

'Hmmm . . . Well yes, I suppose. But then what is literature?'

'Well, for instance, Marcel Proust. Or James Joyce.'

'Joyce?' he asked, moving closer. 'The one who wrote *Ulysses*? I tried to read it. It's boring. To be honest, I don't know what books like that are any good for.'

'How do you mean?'

'Nobody reads it, that *Ulysses*. Three people have read it, and then they live off it for the rest of their lives, writing articles and going to conferences. But no one else has ever got through it.'

'Well now,' I said, throwing *Werewolves* on to the floor. 'Let me tell you that the value of a book doesn't depend on how many people read it. The brilliance of the *Mona Lisa* doesn't depend on how many people file past her every year. The greatest of books have few readers, because reading them requires an effort. But it's precisely that effort that gives rise to the aesthetic effect. Literary junk-food will never give you anything of the kind.'

He put his arm round my shoulders.

'I already asked you once, speak more simply.'

'Speaking in very simple terms, I can say this. Reading is human contact, and the range of our human contacts is what makes us what we are. Just imagine you live the life of a long-distance truck driver. The books that you read are like the travellers you take into your cab. If you give lifts to people who are cultured and profound, you'll learn a lot from them. If you pick up fools, you'll turn into a fool yourself. Wasting time on detective novels is . . . it's like giving an illiterate prostitute a ride for the sake of a blowjob.'

'And who should I give rides to?' he asked, slipping his hand under my T-shirt.

'You should read serious, profound books, without being afraid to spend time and effort on it.'

His open hand froze on my stomach.

'Aha,' he said. 'So if I'm a long-distance truck driver I should take some bald-headed winner of the Schnobel Prize for literature into my cab, so that he can shaft me up the backside for two weeks while I dodge the oncoming traffic? Did I get it right?'

'Well, you know, you can vulgarize anything like that,' I said and stopped talking.

But would you believe it, I'd used the same example of a blowjob in a long-distance truck that had made me almost kill poor Pavel Ivanovich. And I couldn't have come up with anything more stupid than my comment about prostitutes – after all, Alexander knew what I did for a living. I could only hope that it would pass for an expression of humility. Judging from his reply, it had.

We foxes have one serious shortcoming. If someone says something memorable to us, we almost always repeat it in conversation with other people, regardless of whether what was said was stupid or clever. Unfortunately, our mind is the same kind of simulator as the sack of skin under our tail that we use as a prick-catcher. It's not a genuine 'organ of thought' – we have no need for that. Let human beings 'think' in the course of their heroic slalom from the vagina to the grave. A fox's mind is simply a tennis racket you can use to keep bouncing the conversation from one subject to another for as long as you like. We give people back the ideas and opinions that we have borrowed from them – reflecting them from another angle, giving them a different spin, sending them into a vertical climb.

Let me remark modestly that my simulated thought almost always turns out better than the original. To continue the tennis analogy, my return improves on every hard shot. Of course, inside people's heads every shot is a hard one. But what I can't understand is – who serves all these shots? One of the people? Or should the server be sought in some completely different place, which isn't even a place at all?

I'll have to wait until I have a conversation on this subject with some intelligent person. Then we'll see which way I drive the ball. That's the way I've been discovering the truth for more than a thousand years now.

While I was finishing this thought, he had almost managed to remove my dress. I didn't resist, I just raised the very ends of my eyebrows with a martyred air, like a little ballerina being raped yet again by a big red-necked SS man on her way to the philharmonia. What's to be done, comrades – this is occupation . . .

Today, to be sure, the little ballerina had prepared for the encounter. I was wearing underwear – lacy white panties, in which I had cut a hole for my tail with scissors. And three identical lacy bras, size zero. The two lower ones had nothing to support, but they pressed into my body slightly and created a certain small content for themselves. Of course, I wasn't actually trying to make any special concessions to lupine demands. It was an ironic postmodern comment on what was happening, a variation on the theme of the Beast that he had talked about so much during our last meeting.

I didn't know if he would like my joke and I was a bit nervous. He liked it. In fact he liked it so much that he started to transform.

I wasn't so scared this time and I studied the transformation more closely. First of all the grey, shaggy tail sprang out. It looked rather sexy – as if a spring that he couldn't hold back inside his spine any more had suddenly straightened out. Then his body arched over and his tail and head jerked towards each other like the ends of a bow drawn together by an invisible string. And then he sprouted fur all over him.

The word 'sprouted' isn't entirely appropriate here. It was more as if his tunic and trousers crumbled into fur – as if the shoulder straps and stripes were drawn in watercolour on a solid mass of wet hair that suddenly dried out and layered off into separate hairs.

At the same time, in some very natural manner, he inflated and grew. There are no wolves that large in nature, he looked more like a bear that has managed to slim a bit. But his body was real, physical and substantial – I felt its weight when he leaned his paw on my hand: it sank a long way into the divan.

'You'll crush me, you animal,' I squealed, and he took his paw away.

He was obviously excited by the sensation of his own strength and my weakness. Leaning his huge, monstrous jaws down over me (his breath was hot, but fresh, like a baby's), he bit through all three of my bras, pulling them off with his terrible hairy fingers.

My heart stopped every time his teeth clicked together so close to me. They were razor-sharp – I couldn't think why he bothered to keep that Monica Lewinsky cigar-clipper on his desk. But then, I suppose he probably smoked cigars in his human form.

After doing the same thing with my panties, he pulled away from me and began growling, as if he was about to tear me to shreds. Then he went down on his knees in front of me and lowered his immense paws on to my fragile collarbones, like some infernal organist. This is the end, I thought.

But he avoided causing me pain. In fact, to my mind, he could have behaved a little more aggressively – I was prepared for it. But this wasn't too bad either. I mean I'd geared myself up in advance for pain and suffering and was prepared to put up with more. However, the ordeal proved not to be as painful as I'd been expecting.

But I did things right anyway and groaned from time to time:

'Oh, that hurts! Don't pound so damn hard, you ugly monster. Gently, smoothly . . . That's right.'

* * *

The letter from E Hu-Li was a long one.

Hello, Ginger,

So nice to see that you haven't changed at all and are still try-ing to guide my lost soul out on to the true path.

You write that the clouds are gathering over your head. Are you serious about that? As far as I recall, the clouds have been gathering over your head for seven hundred years already; experience shows that in most cases you simply need to start thinking about something else. Maybe everything's not so terri-ble this time either?

Do you seriously want to come to England? Do you think you'll be better off here?

Understand this – the West is just one big shopping mall. From the outside it looks magical, fantastic. But you had to live in the Eastern Bloc to take its shop windows for the real thing. Perhaps that was the only meaning of your life – do you remember that Soviet song, 'We were born to make the fairy tale reality'? That's what you always did quite well – 'in your head, in your head', as the song goes. In actual fact, there are three roles you can play here – the buyer, the seller, or the prod-uct on the shelf. To be a seller is vulgar, to be a buyer is boring (and you still have to earn your living as a seller), and to be the product is repulsive. Any attempt to be anything else actually means 'not to be', as the market forces are quick to teach any and every Hamlet. All the rest is simply show.

Do you know what the secret horror of life here is? When you buy yourself a blouse or a car, or anything else, you have in your mind an image, implanted by advertising, of some won-derful place you will go wearing that blouse or driving that car. But there is no such wonderful place anywhere, apart from in the advertising clip, and this black hole in reality is lamented by every serious philosopher in the West. The joy of shopping can-

not conceal the unbearable awareness that our entire world is one huge ski shop standing in the middle of the Sahara desert. You don't just have to buy the skis, you have to buy the imitation snow as well. Do you understand the metaphor?

Apart from that, there is a specific difficulty for us foxes. With every year that passes it becomes harder and harder to maintain your identity and feel that you are a prostitute, so fast is everything else being prostituted all around you. If you hear an old friend's voice speaking in confidential tones, you can be sure it is advising you to buy two bottles of anti-dandruff shampoo so that you can get the third one free. I remember a certain word that you always used to try to introduce into the conversation whether it was relevant or not – 'uroborus'. I think it means a snake biting its own tail. When that snake's head and tail only exist as special effects in an advertising clip, it's no great comfort to know that the body is alive and fat. That is, maybe it is a comfort, but there's no one to experience it.

Your world will soon be like ours (at least, for those who are kept on to service the extraction and export of oil), but as yet it still has twilight zones where a salutary ambivalence is the rule. And that is precisely where a soul like yours can be, if not happy, then at least in balance. If these zones of ambivalence are created for you by others, then enjoy them while they still exist. The world will not always be like that. This is me preaching to you in response to your lectures.

Now about English men. Don't judge them from your brief encounters in the National. They're quite different here. Do you remember the writer Yuan Mei, whom our sister U married in 1739? I don't expect you've forgotten him – a scholar from the Hanlin Academy who studied the Manchurian language and collected stories about evil spirits . . . By the way, he knew who our sister really was. That was precisely why he married her.

140

His book (it was called What Confucius Did Not Speak Of) is half made up of stories, but it also contains some intriguing ethnographic sketches. In those times England was known as the 'Land of the Redhairs'. This is what Yuan Mei wrote about the English – I cite the passage in full:

'407. INHABITANTS OF THE LAND OF THE REDHAIRS SPIT AT YOUNG SINGERS

The inhabitants of the Land of Redhairs often engage in dissolute behaviour with young singers. When they arrange their carousals, they invite young singers, undress them then sit round them and spit at their secret place. They do not require any greater intimacy. When they have finished spitting, they let them go, with a generous reward. This is called "money from the common pot".'

This story, which might appear to be historically inaccurate, in fact reflects very accurately how an English aristocrat deals with a woman's soul when it opens itself to him (fortunately, the system of privileged education here transforms most of them into homosexuals). Before, when I observed the English, I used to wonder what was hidden beneath that impenetrable armour-plating of hypocrisy forged over the centuries. And then I realized – it was precisely that simple act. There is nothing else there, and that minimalism is what guarantees the stability of the order of things here.

Believe me, if you come to London, you will feel like a spittoon wandering alone among snipers who hawk and spit into your very soul, men for whom equality for women means only one thing – the chance to save a bit on 'the money from the common pot'.

As for the super-werewolf . . . You know, it seems to me you have become too bogged down in introspection. Think – if everything that is most important were inside ourselves, then

why would we need the external world? Or do you believe that
it no longer holds any possible surprises for you and it is
enough simply to sit by the wall on a dusty meditation rug,
pushing away the thoughts that crowd round you, like a swim-
mer pushing away dead jellyfish? What if one of them turns out
to be a golden fish that grants wishes? I think it is still too soon
to give up on this world – by doing that you might find you
have given up on yourself. You know what my hubby said to
me yesterday? 'The super-werewolf will come, and you will see
him as clearly as you see me now.' Even if in my heart of hearts
I agreed with you, how would I dare to argue with the head of
the house of Cricket? :-=))). But let us discuss this when we
meet, my dear. In a week Brian and I shall be in Moscow –
don't turn your mobile off!
    Heads and tails,
    E

When I finished reading the letter, I shook my head. Someone
was in for it soon. The doodle :-=))), which looked like the war
criminal Hitler grinning, was an ominous sign that E Hu-Li used
– it meant that she had bleak and cruel intentions in mind. But
what else was to be expected from the most pitiless fox in our
entire family? She's the same in everything, I thought. Ask her
for help, and she advises you to think about something else. The
clouds, she says, are just an illusion . . .

    Although, perhaps she's right? After all, things aren't nearly as
bad as I thought only yesterday. I was bursting with the desire to
tell someone about the affair I had been forced to start. But
who? Of course, I could spill the whole thing out to a taxi driver,
and then make him forget what he'd heard. Only it was dangerous to play pranks like that on the road. No, I have to wait for
E Hu-Li, I thought. She'll certainly be interested in listening to
me. And apart from that, she had been making fun of my virgin-

ity for so many centuries that it would be a pleasure to throw the news in her face. For all her sophistication, she had never had any lovers like that, except perhaps for one yakshi-devil in the sixteenth century. But compared to Alexander, even he seemed pitiful . . .

At this point I came back to my senses – my sister's letter had reminded me about the most important thing of all.

I had known for a long time that the moment when you are overflowing with the joys or sorrows of life is the best time to practise meditation. I turned off the computer and laid out a foam plastic rug on the floor. It's absolutely fantastic, a real gift for a meditator, it's a shame there weren't any in ancient times. Then I put a cushion filled with buckwheat husks on it and sat on the cushion in the lotus position, with my tail lowered on to the floor.

The spiritual practice of foxes includes 'contemplation of the mind' and 'contemplation of the heart'. Today I decided to begin my session with contemplation of the heart. The heart plays no part in this practice, apart from a metaphorical one. It's an accident of translation: the Chinese hieroglyph 'xin', which stands for 'heart' here, has many different meanings and 'contemplation of the innermost essence' would probably have been a more accurate translation. And from a practical point of view, it would have been more correct to call the technique 'tugging the tail'.

Every child knows that if you tug a dog or a cat by the tail, they feel pain. But if you pull a fox by the tail, then what happens is beyond the understanding of even the most intelligent tailless monkey. At that moment the fox feels the full weight of all her bad deeds. This is because she uses her tail to commit them. And since every fox, apart from the total failures, has a whole heap of bad deeds to her name, the result is an appalling attack of conscience, accompanied by terrifying visions and insights so overwhelming that the fox loses the very desire to carry on living. The rest of the time our conscience doesn't bother us at all.

A lot here depends on the strength of the tug and how unexpected it is. For instance, when we happen to snag our tails on a bush during a chicken hunt (I'll tell you about that later), we also experience light pangs of conscience. Only while we are running, the corresponding muscles are tensed, and so the effect is not so pronounced. But the essence of the practice of 'tugging the tail' lies in giving your own tail a powerful tug at a moment when the area of the tail muscles is as relaxed as possible.

Not everything here is as simple as it seems. In actual fact 'contemplation of the heart' cannot be separated from 'contemplation of the mind', because the correct performance of the techniques requires consciousness to be layered off into three independent streams:

1) the first stream of consciousness is the mind which remembers all its dark deeds from time immemorial.
2) the second stream of consciousness is the mind which spontaneously and unexpectedly makes the fox tug her own tail.
3) the third stream of consciousness is the mind as the abstract observer of the first two streams and itself.

Speaking very approximately, this third stream of consciousness is also the very essence of the technique 'contemplating the mind'. All of these practices are preliminary – you have to perform them for a thousand years before moving on to the most important, which is called 'tail of the void' or 'artlessness'. This is a secret practice that is not entirely clear even to foxes like me, who have completed the thousand-years preliminary cycle a long time ago.

And so, I sat in the lotus position, placing my left hand on my knee and my right hand on my tail. I concentrated and began remembering my past – the layers of it that are usually concealed from me by the stream of everyday thoughts. And suddenly, entirely out of the blue, my right hand jerked and tugged. I felt a pain in the base of my spine. But that pain was nothing compared with the stream of repentance, horror and shame for what I had done that flooded over me with such great power that tears sprang to my eyes.

The faces of those who had not survived their encounter with me floated past in front of my face, like yellow leaves drifting past a window in an autumn storm. They emerged from non-existence for only a second, but that second was long enough for each pair of eyes to sear me with a glance full of bewilderment and pain. I watched them, remembering the past, with the tears pouring down my cheeks in two great streams as repentance tore my heart apart.

At the same time I was serenely aware that what was taking place was simply the insubstantial play of reflections, the rippling of thoughts that is raised by the habitual draughts of the mind, and that when these ripples settled down, it would be clear that there were no draughts and no reflections, and no mind itself – nothing but that clear, eternal, all-penetrating gaze in the face of which nothing is real.

That is the way I have been practising for about twelve centuries.

* * *

From the very beginning Alexander and I had an unspoken agreement not to pester each other with questions. I wasn't supposed to ask about things that he couldn't talk about because of the non-disclosure agreements he'd signed and all the other FSB garbage. And he didn't ask any unnecessary questions, because my answers might have placed him in an ambiguous position – for instance, what if I suddenly turned out to be a Chinese spy? Things could quite easily have been made to look that way, after all, I didn't even have an internal passport, and only a fake one for foreign travel.

I wasn't really happy with this situation: there were lots of things I wanted to find out about him. And I could see he was consumed by curiosity too. But we were getting to know each other gradually, groping our way along – the information was provided in homeopathic doses.

I liked to kiss him on the cheek before he transformed into a beast (I could never bring myself to kiss him on the lips, and that was strange, considering the extent of our intimacy). But then, the caresses didn't last for long – a few touches were enough to trigger the transformation, and after that kissing became impossible.

For so many centuries a kiss had been simply one element of hypnotic suggestion to me, but now I *myself* was kissing, even if it was in a childish fashion . . . There was something dreamlike about that. His face was often hidden by a gauze mask, and I had to move it aside. One day I couldn't stand it any more, I tugged on the lace of the mask that had slipped off his face and said:

'Maybe you could not put it on when we're together? Who do you think you are, Michael Jackson?'

'It's because of the smell,' he said. 'It has a special chemical that doesn't let smells through.'

'And what can you smell up here?' I asked, surprised.

We were sitting by the door to the roof, which was open (he avoided going out of his mirror-walled birdhouse, because he was worried about snipers, or photographers, or avenging lightning from the heavens). Apart from a very faint whiff of exhaust fumes from the street, I couldn't detect any smells at all.

'I can smell everything in the world up here,' he said with a frown.

'Such as?'

He looked at my white blouse and drew in a deep breath through his nose.

'That blouse of yours,' he said. 'Before you, it was worn by a middle-aged woman who used home-made eau-de-cologne made from Egyptian lotus extract . . .'

I sniffed my blouse. It didn't smell of anything.

'Seriously?' I queried. 'I bought it in a second-hand shop, I liked the embroidered pattern.'

He drew in another breath of air.

'And what's more, she diluted the extract with fake vodka. There's a lot of fusel oil.'

'What are you saying?' I asked, nonplussed. 'I feel like taking the blouse off and throwing it away . . . So what else can you smell?'

He turned towards the open door.

'There's a terrible smell of petrol. Bad enough to give you a splitting headache. And there's a smell of asphalt, rubber, tobacco smoke . . . And of toilets, human sweat, beer, baking, coffee, popcorn, dust, paint, nail varnish, doughnuts, newsprint . . . I could go on and on with the list.'

'But don't these smells get mixed up together?'

He shook his head in reply.

'It's more as if they're layered over each other and contained in each other, like a letter in an envelope that's lying in the pocket of a coat that's hanging in a wardrobe, and so on. The worst thing by far is that very often you find out lots of things you absolutely didn't want to know. For instance, they give you a document to sign, and you can tell that yesterday there was a sandwich with stale salami lying on it. And that's not all, the smell of the sweat from the hand that gave you the document makes it clear that what it says in the document isn't true . . .

And so on.'

'And why does this happen to you?'

'It's just the usual lupine sense of smell. It often stays with me even in the human phase. It's tough. But I suppose it saves me from lots of bad habits.'

'For instance?'

'For instance, I can't smoke hash. And definitely not snort cocaine.'

'Why?'

'Because from the first line I can tell how many hours the mule was carrying it up his ass on his way from Colombo to Minsk. And that's nothing, I even know how many times that ass of his was . . .'

'Don't,' I interrupted. 'Don't go on. I'd already got the idea.'

'And the worst thing is, I never know when it's suddenly going to overwhelm me. It's as unpredictable as a migraine.'

'You poor thing,' I sighed. 'What a pain.'

'Well, it's not always a pain,' he said. 'There are some things about it I really enjoy. For instance, I like the way you smell.'

I was embarrassed. A fox's body really does have a very faint aroma, but people usually take it for perfume.

'And what do I smell of?'

'I can't really say . . . Mountains, moonlight. Spring. Flowers. Deception. But not a wily kind of deception, more as if you're having a joke. I really love the way you smell. I think I could breathe that smell in all my life and still keep finding something new in it.'

'Well that's nice,' I said. 'I felt very awkward when you said that about my blouse. I'll never buy anything in second-hand shops again.'

'Don't worry about it,' he said. 'But I would be grateful if you'd take it off.'

'Is the smell that strong?'

'No, it's very weak. It's just that I like you better without any blouse.'

I thought for a moment and then pulled the blouse off over my head.

'You're not wearing any bras today,' he laughed.

'Right,' I said. 'I read that when a girl goes to see her young man and something is supposed to happen . . . You know, if she is ready for something to happen . . . Then she doesn't put one on. It's a kind of etiquette.'

'Where did you read that?' he asked.

'In *Cosmopolitan*. Listen, I've been wanting to ask you for a long time. Do you mind that I have small breasts?'

'No, I really like that,' he said. 'I just want to go on and on kissing them for ever.'

It seemed to me that he was talking with an effort, as if his jaws were being cramped by a yawn. That was what usually happened just before the transformation. Despite his reassuring declaration about 'going on kissing them for ever', we rarely got that far. But then, his hot wolf's tongue . . . But I won't transgress the bounds of propriety, the reader understands perfectly well without that.

He barely had time to take my knickers off before it all happened: sexual arousal triggered the mysterious mechanism of his metamorphosis. Less than a minute later, standing there in front of me was a sinister, handsome beast, whose most astounding asset was his instrument of love. Every time I found it impossible to believe that my simulacrum pouch was really capable of accommodating that hammer of the witches.

When he turned into a wolf, Alexander lost the ability to speak. But he could understand everything he heard – although, of course, I had no guarantee that his wolfish understanding was the same as his human one. His remaining communicative capabilities were inadequate for conveying the complex motions of the soul, but he could reply in the affirmative or the negative. 'Yes' was signified by a short, muffled roar:

'Gr-r-r!'

And he expressed the meaning 'no' with a sound like something halfway between a howl and a yawn.

'Whoo-oo-oo!'

I found this 'whoo-oo-oo' rather funny – it was more or less the way a dog whines in the heat when its masters have locked it out on the balcony. But I didn't tell him about this observation of mine.

His hands didn't turn into wolf's paws, they were more like the fantastic extremities of some movie Martian. I found it impossible to believe those claws were capable of tender touching, even though I knew it from my own experience.

And so, when he set them on my bare stomach, as always, I felt a bit uneasy.

'What do you want, beastling?' I asked. 'Shall I lie on my side?'

'Whoo-oo-oo!'

'On my tummy?'

'Whoo-oo-oo!'

'Kneel down?'

'Gr-r-r!'

'All right, only be careful, okay?'

'Gr-r-rrrrrr-r!'

I wasn't entirely certain that last 'grrrr' meant 'yes', and not just 'grrr', but even so I did as he asked. And I was immediately sorry: he took hold of my tail with his paw.

'Hey,' I said, 'let go, you monster!'

'Whoo-oo-oo!'

'Really, let go,' I repeated plaintively.

'Whoo-oo-oo!'

And then what I was most afraid of happened – he pulled my tail. Not very hard, but still hard enough for me suddenly to remember the Sikh from the National hotel. And when he jerked my tail a little more sharply, I felt so ashamed for the role I'd played in that man's fate that I sobbed out loud.

Alexander hadn't deliberately pulled my tail. He was just holding it, quite gently in fact. But the blows of his hips pushed my body forward, and the result was as if he was trying to rip my tail out of my body. I tensed all my muscles, but I just wasn't strong enough. With every jerk my soul was inundated by waves of unbearable shame. But the most terrible thing was that the shame didn't simply sear my heart, it also mingled into a single whole with the pleasure I was getting from what was going on.

It was something quite unimaginable – truly beyond good and evil. It was then that I finally understood the fatal abysses trodden by De Sade and Sacher-Masoch, who I had always thought absurdly pompous. No, they weren't absurd at all – they simply hadn't been able to find the right words to convey the true nature of their nightmares. And I knew why – there were no such words in any human language.

'Stop,' I whispered through my tears.

'Whoo-oo-oo!'

But in heart I didn't know what I wanted – for him to stop or to carry on.

'Stop,' I repeated, gasping for breath, 'please!'

'Whoo-oo-oo!'

'Do you want to kill me?'

'Gr-r-r!'

I couldn't hold back any longer and I started crying. But they were tears of pleasure, a monstrous, shameful pleasure that was too enthralling to be abandoned voluntarily. I soon lost any idea of what was happening – perhaps I even lost consciousness too. The next ting I remember is Alexander leaning down over me, already in his human form. He looked perplexed.

'Did I hurt you?'

I nodded.

'I'm sorry . . .'

'Promise me one thing,' I whispered. 'Promise that you'll never pull my tail again. Never, do you hear?'

'My word as an officer,' he said and set his hand on his medal ribbons. 'Was it really bad?'

'I felt ashamed,' I whispered. 'You know, I've done a lot of things in my life that I don't want to remember. I've done a lot of harm to people . . .'

His face suddenly turned serious.

'Don't,' he said. 'Please don't. Not just now.'

* * *

We foxes are keen hunters of English aristocrats and chickens. We hunt English aristocrats because English aristocrats hunt us, and it's a sort of point of honour. But we hunt chickens for our own enjoyment. Both types of hunting have their passionate supporters who will shout themselves hoarse defending their choice. The way I see things, hunting chickens has several serious advantages:

1) hunting English aristocrats is a source of bad karma, which is acquired by killing even the most useless of men. The karma from chickens is not all that serious.

2) to hunt aristocrats you have to travel to Europe (although some believe that the best place is a transatlantic cruise ship). You can hunt chickens anywhere you like.

3) while hunting English aristocrats, foxes don't undergo any physical changes. But when we hunt chickens something happens that bears a distant similarity to a werewolf's transformation – we come to resemble our wild relatives for a while.

I haven't hunted English aristocrats for many decades, and I don't regret it in the least. But to this day I'm still enthusiastic about chicken-hunting.

It's hard to explain to an outsider what chicken-hunting really is. When you cast off your clothes and your shoes and pound furiously against the ground with three paws, clutching the chicken against your breast with the fourth, its little heart beats in unison with yours, and the speed-blurred course of your zigzag run flows freely through your empty mind. At that moment you see clearly that you, and the chicken, and even the pursuers clamouring behind you are really parts of a single incomprehensible whole that dons masks and plays hide-and-seek with itself . . . You want to believe that even the chicken realizes the same thing. And if it doesn't, then in some life to come it very definitely will!

These are the basic principles of chicken-hunting:

1) you should approach the chicken coop in the guise of a extravagantly clad socialite – wearing an evening dress and high stiletto heels. Your clothes should restrict your movements as much as possible and provoke associations with glamorous fashion magazines.

2) you must attract the attention of the owners of the chicken coop – they have to see their elegant visitor steal a chicken.

3) you must not run away from your furious pursuers too fast, but not too slowly either – the most important aspect of the hunt is maintaining their confidence that they can overtake the thief.

4) when the pursuers have no strength left to continue the pursuit (and also in those cases when they suffer shock from seeing the transformation take place), you should erase their memory of what has happened with a special twitch of your tail and let the chicken go free.

I introduced the last addendum myself. Only don't ask me what the chicken will do with this freedom. You can't just wring its neck, can you? Of course, it sometimes happens that the chicken passes on during the chase. But would it be any better for its evolution to end this life in suburban soup?

Some of us extend the same logic to the English aristocrats, but I don't agree with that – theoretically speaking, any English aristocrat could become a Buddha in this life, and you can't deprive him of that chance just for the sake of idle amusement.

Ninety-nine per cent of aristocrat-hunting is a tedious social exercise that differs little from a formal tea party. But sometimes the most hard-bitten of my sisters, those with whom I want absolutely nothing to do, gather together in a pack and arrange battues, in the course of which many English aristocrats depart this life at once. In these cases events become quite picturesque, and the concomitant hallucination can be experienced by many thousands of people at the same time – you can get some idea of what I mean from the story of the so-called Battle of Waterloo. But the most shocking details remain hidden from the public.

I realize how hard it must be to believe in the possibility of such appalling mass deceptions, but the important point here is that when one and the same hallucination is induced simultaneously by several foxes, its power increases proportionately to their number cubed. That is, one and the same suggestion, implanted simultaneously by three foxes, will be almost thirty times as powerful as an illusion created by one of them on her own. This is achieved with the use of secret methods and practices – first the foxes study together how to visualize an object that they have just seen, then an object that they haven't seen, and then they make others perceive objects that don't exist, and so on. A complex technique, and the training for it lasts several centuries. But if ten or twelve foxes who have mastered it get together . . . Well, you can see what they're capable of.

Some might ask why, in that case, the foxes are not yet the rulers of this world. There are two reasons:

1) foxes are not so stupid as to take on that heavy burden.
2) foxes are very egotistical and incapable of reaching long-term

agreements with each other about anything, except for the collective hunting of English aristocrats.

These days people possess many new tracking and monitoring devices, and so foxes avoid interfering in human history and solve the problem in a simpler way. In the north of England there are several privately owned castles where aristocrats are bred from the finest stock and raised specially for hunting by foxes – the output isn't all that large, but the quality is excellent. There are similar nurseries in Argentina and Paraguay, but the conditions there are appalling, and the English aristocrats, who are bred en masse using artificial insemination (so far attempts at cloning have been a failure) are only good for helicopter safaris: they talk like gauchos, drink tequila by the bucketful, require more than three attempts to draw their family tree, and as their last wish just before they die they ask to hear the song 'Un Hombre', dedicated to Che Guevara. Evidently, even in their final moments they are mimicking the portfolio investors whom they aspired to become.

There is another school of hunting, in which an English aristocrat is individually selected, and the fox herds him along his final road for several years – she becomes his mistress or wife and is there beside him right down to the moment of truth, which in this case is rather horrific. One day, during a thunderstorm or at some other dramatic moment, the fox reveals the whole truth to him and exposes her tail – not in order to implant a suggestion of one more dose of family happiness, but to strike him dead . . . This is the most complicated form of hunting, and it requires a virtuosic mastery of social manners, in which there is no one who can compare with my sister E Hu-Li, who has lived in England for many centuries and attained genuine perfection in this sport.

The greatest advantage of hunting chickens consists in the

155

supraphysical transformation that we undergo. The chicken is required as a living catalyst who helps us to achieve it – in thousands of years of civilized life foxes have almost lost this ability and, like Dante, we require a guide to lead us into the lower worlds. The transformation does not always take place, and it doesn't last long in any case, but the sensations it induces are so powerful that you are energized by the memories for many days afterwards.

Something similar happens to foxes when we are badly frightened, but that process is uncontrollable, whereas the art of chicken-hunting lies precisely in controlling our fear. You have to allow the pursuers to get close enough to trigger the mechanisms of internal alchemy which for a few seconds will turn you into a predatory beast, free from good and evil. Naturally, to avoid being freed from good and evil permanently, you have to maintain a safe distance. Basically, it's pretty much like surfing, only the price paid for losing your balance is very much more serious. But the positive emotions are far stronger too – nothing is so refreshing for the soul as risk and pursuit.

It sometimes happens that dogs trail after me, but they immediately give up once they realize who I am. Dogs are just as easily to hypnotize as people. And in addition, they have a special system for spreading information, something like the Internet, only based on smells, so that news travels fast in their circles. After one courageous Rottweiler, who tried to play with me was raped by two Caucasian brothers (I mean sheepdogs), the dogs in the Bitsevsky forest began avoiding me. They're intelligent beasts, capable of tracing the causal link between a certain Rottweiler growling as he attacks a beautiful red-haired sportswoman and all the male dogs, who are two heads taller than the said Rottweiler, suddenly taking him for a wide-eyed, lovesick bitch in full heat.

My decision to take Alexander hunting had nothing to do

with any desire to boast. A fox's transformation during a chicken hunt doesn't go as far as what happens to a wolf, so there was nothing to boast about. But I thought that if I were to undergo the supraphysical shift while Alexander was watching, it would be the best way of saying to him, 'you and I are of the same blood'. Perhaps it would extinguish the remnants of mistrust between us and bring us closer – that was what I was vaguely counting on.

I'd picked out the place for the hunt a lot earlier. One of the tracks that wound through the Bitsevsky forest emerged from the trees at a wooden house in which a forester lived (I'm not sure that's the correct term, but the man's job definitely had something to do with the park). Beside the house there was a chicken coop – a very rare thing in modern Moscow. I'd spotted it when I was riding my bike through the forest, and now I decided to make use of my discovery. But first I had to check everything one more time and determine my lines of retreat. Having devoted an entire day to reconnaissance on my bike, I established the following:

1) there were chickens in the chicken coop, and also people in the house; and so the two essential ingredients for the hunt were present.

2) I should bolt along the road that led into the forest.

3) I needed to escape from pursuit before the track emerged from the forest on the other side – there were always a lot of people strolling along the edge of the trees, mostly young mothers with prams.

In addition, I discovered how to drive a car almost right up to the chicken coop – although the forester's house looked as if it was lost in the forest, the city began only three hundred metres away: the forest was cut short by a line of six-storey concrete buildings. I noted down the address of the block closest to the chicken coop. Now everything was ready for the hunt.

My bicycle reconnaissance trip also produced another result. On my way home I rode along a track I didn't know and discovered a wonderful place where I'd never been before. It was a wide waste lot, actually more like a field, sloping down on one side to a small river and surrounded by the forest. The field was criss-crossed by narrow tracks, and on the slope leading down to the river there was a bike ramp for jumping – a steep embankment of earth worn smooth by numerous tyres. I didn't dare jump, all I did was ride up it slowly, imagining how it would feel to pick up speed and go soaring into the air. But I wasn't sure that I would be able to land.

Not far from the ramp I discovered a strange sculptural composition. A number of grey logs of various lengths had been set into the ground. Their tops had been chiselled into images of the faces of warriors. The warrior-logs stood tight against each other, and coarse, solid benches had been laid out around them. Standing at the outer perimeter, orientated towards the four points of the compass, were four simple gateways made of one log set across the tops of two others, as grey, monolithic and cracked as all the other elements. The whole thing was reminiscent of a wooden Stonehenge that had already suffered damage in its battle with eternity: the logs had been mutilated by campfires lit on them by the local kids. But despite the black scorch marks and a host of empty beer bottles, the site had beauty and even some vague kind of grandeur.

I sat down on one of the logs, fixed my gaze on the red disc of the sun (in Moscow you only get sunsets like that in May) and withdrew into thoughts of the past. I remembered a man I had met more than a thousand years earlier – he was called the Yellow Master, after the name of the Yellow Mountain on which his monastery stood. I only spent one night in conversation with him, but it was a conversation that I shall never forget – I only had to close my eyes and I could see the Yellow Master's face as clearly as if he were there beside me. And yet I had encountered so many people from day to day over so many years – and they hadn't left the slightest trace in my memory . . . My sister E knew the Yellow Master too, I thought. I wonder if she remembers him? I'll have to ask her.

Just at that moment my mobile phone rang.

'Hello,' I said.

'Hello, Red.'

I couldn't believe my ears.

'Sister E? How wonderful! I was just thinking about you . . .'

'So that's why my tail's itching,' she laughed. 'I'm already in Moscow.'

'Where are you staying?'

'In the National hotel. What are you doing tomorrow at one?'

* * *

I was afraid I'd have problems getting into the National, but none of the security men took any notice of me. Maybe that was because I was met by a young female administrator who looked like a Scharführer holding a board with the words 'Valued guest of Lady Cricket-Taylor'. She showed me to one of the de luxe suites. All that was missing was a guard of honour with an orchestra.

E Hu-Li received me sitting on a stripy divan in the suite's drawing room. I was bothered by the suspicion that I had once met a client in this apartment, either a businessman from South Korea or an Arab arms-dealer. But it might just have been that stripy divan, they have those in lots of the rooms there. When she saw me, my sister stood up to greet me and we embraced tenderly. A transparent plastic bag appeared in her hands.

'This is for you,' she said. 'Not expensive, but elegant.'

The bag contained a T-shirt with one word on it in Russian and English:

КОКНИ
COCKNEY

'They sell them in London,' she said. 'In all the different languages. But in Russian the effect is especially nice.'

And she laughed quietly. I couldn't help myself and I laughed too – 'cockney' in Russian spells and sounds like 'whack' in the imperative mood; I never noticed that before.

E Hu-Li looked exactly the same as she had in 1929, when she came to Russia on business for the Comintern, which was fashionable at the time. Only now her hair seemed to be cut just a little shorter. As always, she was dressed absolutely impeccably.

E Hu-Li's style hadn't changed for the last thousand years – it was a kind of extreme radicalism, disguised as utilitarian minimalism. I envied her bold taste – she was always half a step ahead of the fashion. Fashion is cyclical, and over the long centuries my sister E had developed the knack of riding the crests of these cycles with all the skill of a professional surfer – in some miraculous way she was always at the precise point that all the fashion designers were desperately trying to identify.

And right now she was wearing a mind-blowing waistcoat that looked like a huge bandolier with lots of different-coloured appliqué pockets that were embroidered with tiny green Arabic script and the big words 'Ka-Boom!' in orange. It was a variation on the theme of the Muslim radical's explosive belt – the way it would have been made for him by a libertine Japanese designer. At the same time it was a very convenient item – the owner of a waistcoat like that had absolutely no need for a handbag.

'Isn't that a little too bold for London?' I asked. 'Doesn't anyone wax indignant?'

'Of course not! The English expend all their spiritual energy on hypocrisy. There's none left over for intolerance.'

'Is everything really as dismal as that?'

She waved her hand dismissively.

'If I had my way, I'd introduce a new term to emphasize the scale of the problem: "Hippopocrisy".'

I can't stand it when someone speaks badly about entire nations. In my opinion, such a person is either a loser or has a guilty conscience. There was no way sister E was any kind of loser. But as for her conscience . . .

'But why can't you be the first to stop being hypocritical?' I asked.

'Then that would be cynicism. And who can say which is worst. All in all, the closet's dark and damp.'

'What closet?'

'I mean the English soul, it reminds me of a closet. The best of the English spend all their lives trying to get out of it, but as a rule they only manage it at the moment of death.'

'How do you know?'

'Do you have to ask? I can see from the inside, I'm English myself. Well, of course, not entirely – about as much as you're Russian. We could say that you're Russian, couldn't we?'

'I suppose so,' I agreed and sighed quietly.

'And what is the Russian soul like?'

I thought about it.

'Like the cab of a long-distance truck. The driver took you in so that you could give him a blowjob. And then he died, so you're left in the cab on your own, surrounded by nothing but the boundless steppe, the sky and the road. And you have no idea how to drive.'

'And is the driver still in the cab, or . . .?'

I shrugged.

'That depends.'

'Yes,' said E Hu-Li. 'So it's the same thing, then.'

'What's the same thing?' I asked.

'We have a saying: "Everybody has his skeleton in the closet." It was Lord Byron who said that. When he realized he had strangled the homosexual in himself.'

'Poor fellow.'

'Poor fellow?' E Hu-Li echoed, raising her eyebrows. 'You don't understand anything. All his life he tormented and tortured that homosexual in himself, but he only finished him off just before he died, when he realized he was going to kick the bucket soon. But as it happens, all his verses and poems were really written by that homosexual. Two American scholars have proved that, I read it myself. That's the kind of people there are in England! Better your dismal nightmare in the cab of a truck.'

'Why call it a dismal nightmare? I think there's a lot of beauty in it.'

'In what? In the skeleton riding beside you?'

'No,' I replied. 'In the Russian soul. Just imagine, you have absolutely no idea how to drive, and you're surrounded by the open steppe and the sky. I love Russia.'

'And what exactly is it about her that you love?'

I pondered that question for a while. Then I replied rather uncertainly:

'The Russian language.'

'You do right to induce that feeling in yourself,' said E Hu-Li. 'Otherwise you would find it unbearable to live here. As I do in England.'

She stretched like a cat and looked into the distance, and for a brief moment there was a lazy, dreamy look in her eyes. I had a sudden vision of a predatory, sharp-toothed gaping maw superimposed on her face, the way it happens in the twenty-fifth shot on a film. I wanted to say something mildly sarcastic to her.

'I think you induce in yourself the idea that you live among hypocrites and fiends.'

'Me? Why would I do that?' she asked.

'They say no one can commit murder unless they ascribe some bad quality to their victim. Otherwise their conscience will torment them. But when there's a whole series of murders, one after another, it's convenient to extend those qualities to the entire target group. It makes the idea of retribution less frightening.'

A shadow ran across E Hu-Li's face.

'Is this a lecture on morality?' she asked. 'Even some human beings understand that in reality there is no good or evil. But you and I are foxes. After death there is no retribution for evil, and no reward for virtue, only the universal return to the Ultimate Supreme Limit. All the rest was invented to keep the people in submission and fear. What are you talking about?'

I realized how stupid I was being – angering a sister from whom I wanted to ask advice. Who was I to reproach her with anything? Was I even a single iota better? If I really did consider myself better, then I was even worse. I had to reduce the whole thing to a joke.

'How serious we are,' I said playfully. 'That's what we get for cohabiting with the tailless monkey for all these years. You've even started thinking like they do.'

E Hu-Li looked at me suspiciously for several seconds, knitting her downy eyebrows together. It suited her really well. Then she smiled.

'So you decided to make fun of me? Well, make sure you don't turn your backside towards me . . .'

As used by foxes, this phrase is based on different references than among humans, but the general meaning is pretty much the same. I had no intention of turning my backside towards her, especially since she was quite capable of tugging on my tail – it had happened once in the fifteenth century, and I still remembered it. But the phrase suddenly reminded me of my last meeting with Alexander, and I blushed. It didn't escape my sister E's keen eye.

'Oho,' she said, 'you still blush the same way you did a thousand years ago. How I envy you. How do you manage it? I suppose for that you have to be a virgin?'

The really interesting thing is that I only blush in the company of other were-creatures. When I'm associating with people, it never happens. It's a great pity – I could really hike up my rates.

'But I'm not a virgin any more,' I said, and blushed even more deeply.

'Really?' E Hu-Li was so astonished she slumped back against the divan. 'Come on, tell me all about it!'

I'd been longing to share my story for ages, and I spent the next half-hour pouring out everything that my heart had been full of for so long.

While I was recounting the details of my giddy affair, E Hu-Li frowned, smiled, nodded and sometimes raised one finger, as if she were saying: 'Aha! And how many times have I told you that!'

When I finished she said: 'Well then. So it's finally happened, even to you. A thousand years one way or the other – what's the difference? Congratulations.'

I picked up a paper napkin off the table, crumpled it into ball and threw it at her. She dodged it nimbly.

'Experience of life really is a great thing,' she said. 'Who could have even imagined anything of the sort in the days of our youth? You seduced him so professionally that it's not even clear who raped who.'

'What?' My jaw dropped in amazement.

She chuckled.

'At least among friends you could drop the mask of offended innocence. You provoked him.'

'What do you mean? When did I provoke him?'

'When you came leaping out of the bathroom naked and stood on all fours with your backside towards him.'

'You think that's provocation?'

'Of course. The question is, why did you turn your backside towards him?'

I shrugged.

'For greater accuracy.'

'What makes that especially accurate?'

'The tail's closer to the target,' I said, rather uncertainly.

'Oh yes. But you have to look over your shoulder. Tell me honestly, have you ever done that before, for greater accuracy?'

'No.'

'So why did you suddenly decide to start?'

'I . . . I just thought the occasion was very important. And I couldn't afford to fall flat on my back. I mean, flat on my face.'

E Hu-Li burst out laughing.

'I can't believe this,' she said, 'did you really do the whole thing on autopilot?'

I definitely did not like the way the conversation was going.

'I know you are prejudiced against it,' she went on, 'but if you have a talk with a good psychoanalyst, you'll realize your true motives straight away. And by the way, you can talk to an analyst about anything you like without feeling embarrassed – that's what he's paid for. Of course, you don't have to tell him about your tail. Although you could mention it, as if it were a fantasy. But then ignore everything he tells you about penis envy . . .'

To bare my soul to my friend and hear that. I was furious.

'Listen,' I said, 'doesn't it seem to you that it's high time to take an aspen stake and stuff all this psychoanalytical discourse up the cocaine-and-amphetamine sprinkled backside that produced it?'

She gaped at me in amazement.

'Okay, I understand about the amphetamines. After all, I was friends with Jean-Paul Sartre for two years, in case you didn't know. And I understand about the backside, for the same reason. But what has cocaine got to do with it?'

'I can explain,' I said, delighted that the conversation was moving away from a slippery subject.

'So explain.'

'Dr Freud was not only a cocaine freak himself, he prescribed it for his patients. And then he drew his conclusions. Cocaine is a powerful sexual stimulant. And so all that stuff Freud invented – all those oedipuses, sphinxes and sphincters – they all exist exclusively in the mental space of a patient whose brains have been scrambled by cocaine. In that state a man really does have only one problem – what to do first, screw his mummy or waste his daddy. Naturally, that's only until the cocaine wears off. But in those days there was no supply problem.'

'I'm not talking about . . .'

'But as long as your daily dose is less than three grams,' I continued, 'you don't have to worry about all that stuff he discovered. Basing the analysis of your own behaviour on Freud is about as helpful as relying on Carlos Castaneda's peyote trips. As least Castaneda has heart, poetry. But all this Freud has is his pince-nez, two lines of coke on the sideboard and a quiver in his sphincter. The bourgeoisie love him *because* he is so loathsome. For his ability to reduce everything in the world to the asshole.'

'But why should the bourgeoisie love him for that?'

'Because portfolio investors need prophets who will explain the world in terms they can understand. And who will prove yet again that nothing threatens the objective reality in which they have invested so much money.'

E Hu-Li gave me a rather mocking look.

'But what do you think?' she asked. 'Is the tendency to deny objective reality really based on sexual deprivation?'

'Eh?' I was flummoxed.

'To put it more simply, do you agree that the world is regarded as an illusion by those who have problems with sex?' she said, in the tone of a genial TV presenter.

This was a view of the world that I'd often come across in the National. Supposedly only sexually hung-up losers took refuge from the invigorating clamour of the market in mysticism and obscurantism. It was especially amusing to hear this from a client squirming all over the bed in splendid isolation: if you thought about it, it was the same thing that happened to the poor guy all the rest of the time, only instead of a fox's tail it was the *Financial Times* that was bamboozling him, and his loneliness was not relative, as it was in my company, but absolute. But to hear such things from my own sister . . . That's what the consumer society does to us.

'It's all the other way round,' I said. 'In actual fact the tendency to associate the spiritual search with sexual problems is based on the frustration of the anal vector of the libido.'

'How do you mean?' asked sister E, raising her eyebrows.

'It's obvious . . . Those who say that should do what they've always secretly wanted to do – screw themselves.'

'What for?'

'When they start doing something they understand, they'll stop discussing things that they don't understand. The way a pig's neck is made means it can't look at the sky. But it certainly doesn't follow that the sky is a sexual neurosis.'

'I get it . . . Did you pick all this stuff up from the wolf?'

I didn't answer.

'Well, well, well,' said my sister E. 'And can I get a look at him?'

'Why the sudden interest?' I asked suspiciously.

'No need to be jealous,' she laughed. 'I'd just like to see who it is your heart took such a shine to. And apart from that, I've never seen any werewolves, I've only heard that they can be found somewhere in the north. By the way, the super-werewolf that you're always lecturing me about is actually more likely to be a wolf than a fox. At least, that's what my husband thinks. And so does his occult lodge the Pink Sunset.'

I sighed. It was simply incomprehensible to me how E Hu-Li, so astute in some matters, could be so absolutely ignorant in others. How many times did I have to explain the same thing to her? I decided not to get involved in an argument. Instead I asked:

'Do you think the super-werewolf could turn out to be my Alexander?'

'As far as I understand it, the super-werewolf is not simply a wolf. He's something as far removed from a wolf as a wolf is from a fox. But a super-werewolf is not an intermediate stage between a fox and a wolf. He is far *beyond* a wolf.'

'I don't understand a thing,' I said. 'Where beyond a wolf?'

'You know, I can't really explain that coherently. Poor Brian has collected all the available material on the subject. Would you like him to give a brief lecture while he's still alive to do it? We just happen to have some free time tomorrow afternoon. And you bring Alexander along – I think he'll find it interesting too. And you can show him to me at the same time.'

'That would be great,' I said. 'Only Alexander's English isn't so good.'

'Never mind. Brian's a polyglot and he speaks five languages fluently. Including Russian.'

'All right,' I said, 'let's give it a try.'

E Hu-Li raised her finger.

'And your lieutenant general will do us one favour in return.'

'What's that?'

'Brian and I have to get into the Cathedral of Christ the Saviour at night. And it has to be the night from Friday to Saturday, around the time of the full moon. Will he be able to arrange that?'

'I think he will,' I said. 'He's certain to have contacts in the Orthodox Patriarchate. I'll try having a word with him.'

'Then I'll remind you,' said E Hu-Li.

That's always the way with her. She solves her problems at your expense and at the same time makes you feel that she's done you a favour. Although on the other hand, I was terribly curious to get a look at Lord Cricket – the occultist, patron of the fine arts and lover of fox-hunting.

'Tell me,' I said, 'does your husband have any idea? You know, about you?'

'No. Are you crazy, or what? This is a hunt. The rules say he must only learn the whole truth at the very last moment.'

'How do you manage to keep it all secret for so long?'

'The formalities of English life are helpful. Separate bedrooms, the Victorian horror of nakedness, the demure ritual of preparing for bed. In aristocratic circles it's easy – all you have to do is establish a definite routine, and then stick to it. The really difficult thing isn't that, it's constantly postponing the finale. That really does strain all your emotional faculties.'

'Yes,' I agreed, 'your stamina is really amazing.'

'Brian is my Moby Dick,' E Hu-Li said and laughed. 'Although the poor soul's dick really isn't all that moby . . .'

'How long have you been herding him now? Five years? Or six?'

'Six.'

'And when are you planning?'

'Some day soon,' said E Hu-Li.

I shuddered in surprise. She put her arm round my shoulders and whispered.

'That's the reason we're here.'

'Why did you decide to do it all here?'

'It's less dangerous here. And then, it's such an incredibly convenient situation. Brian doesn't merely know the prophecy –

according to which the super-werewolf is supposed to appear in this very city – he intends to become the super-werewolf himself. For some reason he's certain that in order to do that, you have to hold something like a black mass in the church that was destroyed and restored, following the methodology of his idiotic sect. It all has to happen without any witnesses. I'll be his only helper, since I've been initiated into the mystery.'

'How?'

'He initiated me.'

I was struck by a sudden conjecture.

'Hang on now . . . Do *you* believe in the super-werewolf?'

'In what sense?'

'That he will come, and we shall see him clearly, and all the rest of it – you know, what you said in your e-mail?'

'I didn't say I believed it. I said that was what Brian said. I'm not interested in all that mysticism. The super-werewolf can come or not come, I couldn't care less about him. But I could never find a better opportunity for . . .' – she snapped her fingers to make sure I understood what she meant.

'Why, you cunning beast!'

E Hu-Li smiled enchantingly.

It was only now that I understood her plan. A novice chess-player probably feels something of the kind when a brilliant strategy unfolds before his eyes. The denouement promised to be dazzlingly dramatic, just as the rules of the hunt required: it was hard to imagine a better setting for the final blow than a church at night. And apart from that, from the very beginning there had been a ready-made, bizarre but plausible cover-story to explain the event. In fact, it wasn't really a cover-story, it was the absolute truth, which the star of the festivities himself believed – and so had I, only a minute ago. How could the investigating authorities suspect anything?

Elegant and natural, without even a hint of falsehood. A masterly plan. Of course, I didn't approve of this sport, but I had to give my sister her due. E Hu-Li was undoubtedly the finest hunter in the world, the only sportsfox at such a high level. I cleared my throat respectfully.

'And who's your next in line? Or haven't you decided yet?'

'Oh, I'm really spoilt for choice. There are some extraordinary possibilities, quite unexpected.'

'Such as?'

E Hu-Li half-closed her eyes and sang in a high, crystal-clear voice:

'Don't question why she needs to be so free . . .'

'Mick Jagger?' I gasped. 'How dare you even think of it?'

'Why not?' E Hu-Li asked impassively. 'He's "Sir Mick" now, after all. A legitimate target. And then, surely you don't still find those words touching? I think they started sounding like an advert for an aircraft-carrier ages ago.'

* * *

Lord Cricket was a man of indeterminate age. And sex, I feel like adding to make the description more precise. My sister E said that he came from a family with a military tradition, but his appearance gave no indication at all of that. My first look at him even put me in mind of that politically correct expression 'war hero or shero' – despite his shaved head and goatee beard. His facial expression was interesting – as if in his youth his soul had aspired towards freedom and light, but failed to break through his armour of self-control and duty and ended up frozen in an interrogatory bubble, puffing out his face into a grimace of dis-affected surprise.

He was dressed in a dark suit and white shirt with a wide tie in an extremely delicate shade of green. There was a small enamel badge glinting on the lapel of his jacket. It looked like the enamel images of Mao Tse-tung that people used to wear in China, only it wasn't Mao's face smiling out of it, but Aleister Crowley's (I wouldn't really have recognized the British Satanist myself – E Hu-Li told me).

Alexander and Lord Cricket reacted to each other cautiously. When he saw the military uniform, Lord Cricket smiled. It was an amazing smile, with just the faintest hint of irony that, nevertheless, you couldn't possibly fail to notice, no matter how hard you tried. How many centuries of effort must have gone into trimming that lawn! At the sight of Lord Cricket, Alexander nervously drew in the air through his nose and closed his eyes; his face darkened, as if he'd just remembered something upsetting.

I was frightened that they would argue. But they quickly got into small talk about the Middle East, Shiite terrorism and the oil business. I must have been looking dour, because Lord Cricket asked me the classic question:

'Why do you Russians smile so little?'

'We don't need to be so competitive,' I said morosely. 'We're a nation of losers in any case.'

Lord Cricket raised one eyebrow.

'Come now, you exaggerate,' he said.

But he seemed to be satisfied by my answer and he went back to his conversation with Alexander.

Having made sure they were talking about subjects that were safe, I started getting to grips with the video projector hired from a local business centre. Of course, there was something absurd about an occult Power Point presentation. But then, the whole field of human occultism was such a profanation that not even Microsoft could do anything to debase it.

While we were fiddling with the equipment, I succumbed yet again to the temptation to inoculate my sister E with the germs of moral principle.

'You can't possibly imagine,' I said quickly in a low voice, trying to squeeze as much useful information as possible into the seconds allotted to me, 'how liberating Kant's categorical imperative is for the soul. I felt as if I'd grown wings when I realized – yes, yes, don't laugh now – that for us foxes man can be not just a means to achieve the aim, but the aim itself!'

E Hu-Li frowned. And then she said:

'You're right. As soon as I'm done with Brian, I'll fly to Argentina for a safari. I've wanted to go shooting from a helicopter for a long time.'

What on earth could I do with her?

We just couldn't get the projector hooked up to the laptop. The Bluetooth refused to work, and I'd never had anything to do with it before. For a while I became completely absorbed in technical matters and stopped paying attention to what was happening in the room. And when I finally managed to solve the problem, Lord Cricket and Alexander were already going at it hammer and tongs – about values.

'Do you seriously believe,' Lord Cricket was asking, 'that there is any better way of organizing society than liberal democracy?'

'We don't want any of those liberals here, thank you very much! We've suffered enough in ten years. We've only just started to draw breath again.'

I realized it was time to interfere.

'Excuse me,' I said, showing my fist to Alexander where Lord Cricket couldn't see it, 'but I think you're misunderstanding each other. It's purely a matter of language.'

'How's that?' Lord Cricket asked.

'There are quite a number of sound combinations that mean completely different things in different languages. For instance, the Russian word "Bog", meaning "God", means a swamp, a "bog" in English. And the English word "God" means a calendar year in Russian. The sounds are the same, but the meaning is completely different. It happens with people's names too, it can be very funny sometimes. And it's exactly the same with the word "liberal". It's a classical inter-linguistic homonym. For instance, in America it means someone who is in favour of firearms control, single-sex marriage and abortion and feels more sympathy for the poor than the rich. But here in Russia . . .'

'Here in Russia,' Alexander interrupted, 'it means an unscrupulous weasel who hopes someone will give him a little money if he makes big round eyes and keeps repeating that twenty greasy parasites should carry on squeezing Russia by the balls, simply because at the beginning of so-called privatization, they happened to be barbecuing grills with pissed Yeltsin's daughter!'

'Phoo, how crude,' I said.

'But it's the truth. And the tragedy of Russian liberalism is that nobody's ever going to give the weasel any money anyway.'

'Why not?' I asked.

'Because ten years ago those greasy parasites were choked with greed, now they are shitting their pants in fear, and in ten years they won't have any money at all.'

It's a rare thing, I thought, for all three tenses in Russian to be combined in a single sentiment as hopelessly gloomy as that.

'Do you favour a review of the results of privatization?' asked Lord Cricket, who was listening carefully.

'And why not?' put in E Hu-Li. 'If you analyse it properly, the whole of human history for the last ten thousand years is nothing but a constant revision of the results of privatization. History is hardly likely to come to an end because a small number of people have stolen a large amount of money. Not even if the small number of people hire themselves three fukuyamas apiece!'

My sister E occasionally liked to express some radical, even seditious views – it suited her predatory beauty and instantly enchanted her future victim. And now I noticed how admiringly Alexander was gaping at her.

'Precisely!' he said. 'I ought to write that down. A pity, I haven't got a pen. But what's a fukuyama? Some sort of geisha?'

'Pretty much,' said E Hu-Li and turned so that Alexander could see her profile. In profile she is absolutely irresistible.

Why you toad, I thought. After you promised . . . But even so I couldn't help admiring her: my sister E understood nothing about Russian affairs, but she sensed instinctively what to say in order to slip the noose over a man's head at the first attempt. Alexander was gazing at her with his mouth wide open and I realized I had to rescue him in a hurry. I had to say something even more radical.

'And so all these arguments about liberalism,' I said, as if I were closing the subject, 'are simply a case of linguistic confusion. And although we greatly respect liberal democracy as a principle, in Russian the words will give off a bad stink for another hundred years or so!'

Alexander switched his adoring gaze from E Hu-Li to me. Then back to E Hu-Li. Then back to me again. The boy's having a real feast today, I thought.

'Yes, yes,' he said. 'You're right about the words. It's so easy to hide behind them. One of those offshore fat cats arrives in America, says he's a liberal, and the oppressed blacks think he's in favour of legalizing cannabis . . .'

'Tell me, is your professional activity not hindered by such an emotional attitude to the subject?' Lord Cricket asked.

Alexander didn't appreciate the irony.

'Don't misunderstand me. I don't mean to say that democracy is bad. It's good. What's bad is when villains and swindlers try to exploit it. So democracy has to be helped to move in the right direction. That's what we think.'

'That's no longer democracy,' said Lord Cricket. 'It's in the essence of democracy that no one helps it, it helps itself.'

'No one helps it? In translation that means we sit on our back-sides and watch while we're shafted in every orifice by various beneficiary owners with double chins and triple citizenships. We watched for twenty years. They'd already drawn up the plans to divide Russia into three parts and started to train the Russian-speaking staff, we know, we know . . . We've read the instructions. Do you think we started tightening the screws just for the love of it? If so, you're mistaken. It's just that if we had-n't, we'd have been gobbled in three years.'

'Who would have gobbled you up?' Lord Cricket asked in sur-prise. 'Democracy? Liberalism?'

'Democracy, liberalism – those are just words on a signpost, she was right about that. But the reality is more like the micro-flora in your guts. In the West, all your microbes balance each other out, it's taken centuries for you to reach that stage. They all quietly get on with generating hydrogen sulphide and keep their mouths shut. Everything's fine-tuned, like a watch, the total balance and self-regulation of the digestive system, and above it – the corporate media, moistening it all with fresh saliva every day. That kind of organism is called the open society – why the hell should it close down, it can close down anyone else it wants with a couple of air strikes. The question is, how do you arrive at this condition? What they taught us to do was to swallow sal-monella with no antibodies to fight it, or other microbes to keep it in check at all. Not surprisingly we developed such a bad case of diarrhoea that three hundred billion bucks had drained out before we even began to understand what was going on. And we were only given two choices – either to run out completely once and for all through some unidentified asshole, or take antibiotics for ages and ages, then slowly and carefully start all over again. But differently.'

'Well, you've never had any shortage of antibiotics in your

country,' said Lord Cricket. 'The question is – who's going to prescribe them?'

'People will be found,' said Alexander. 'And none of your World Bank or IMF, who first prescribe salmonella and then set the basin under your backside – we don't need any consultants. We've been through that already. Soar boldly over the edge of the cliff, they say, come down smack on to the ground as hard as you can, and then you'll hear the polite applause of the international community. Maybe we'd be better off without the applause or the cliff? After all, for a thousand years Russia decided for itself how to live, and it worked quite well, you only have to look at the map to see that. And now they say it's time for us to go into the melting pot. We'll see whose turn it is for the melting-pot. If someone wants to melt us down that badly, maybe we'll be the ones to send him up in black smoke. We still have the means, and we will for a long time yet!'

Alexander smashed his fist down deafeningly on the desk, making the projector and the laptop bounce into the air. And then silence fell and I could hear a fly that had lost its way fluttering between the windowpane and the blind.

There were times when I myself couldn't understand what roused the greatest turmoil in my heart – the monstrously huge instrument of love that I had to deal with when he changed into a wolf, or these wild, genuinely wolf-like views on life that he expressed when he was a man. Perhaps I found the latter just as fascinating as, as . . . I didn't pursue my thought to the end – it was too frightening.

Especially since there was nothing to be fascinated by. For all his apparent radicalism, he only ever talked about the consequences and didn't even mention the cause – the 'upper rat', engaged in slobbering self-satisfaction (that's why I hate the word 'blowjob', I thought, there you have it – the psychopathology of everyday life). In fact, Alexander probably understood everything, but he was just being cunning, the way a werewolf is supposed to be: you can only live in Saudi Arabia and not notice the sand for big money, and he certainly had that. Or perhaps he wasn't being cunning . . . After all, I'd only really understood everything about the 'upper rat' and the 'oligarchy' when I tried to explain it all in a letter to my sister U. And I still didn't know how a wolf's mind worked.

The first to recover his composure was Lord Cricket. His face assumed an expression of sincere sadness (of course, I didn't actually think that it was sincere – it was simply that the British aristocrat's mimetic skill required that precise word). He looked at his watch and said:

'I can understand your feelings to some extent. But, to be honest, I find it boring to pursue the path along which your mind is moving. It's such a barren desert! People spend their entire lives engaged in arguments like that. And then they simply die.'

'So,' said Alexander, 'do you have other options to suggest?'

'Yes I do,' said Lord Cricket. 'Take my word for it, I do. There are creatures living among us who are of a different nature. I understand that you take a keen interest in them.'

'That's right,' said Alexander. 'What do you know about them?'

'First of all,' said Lord Cricket, 'I know that they are not occupied with the petty matters of which you speak with such fervour. They simply do not notice the mirages that make us turn crimson and hammer our fists on the table . . .'

Alexander lowered his head.

'It is unlikely that you could even explain to them,' Lord Cricket continued, 'exactly what it is that makes you feel so bitter. As Thoreau put it, they march to the sound of a different drummer . . . Or perhaps it is better to say that they don't march at all. They have no ideology, but that does not mean their lives are diminished. On the contrary. Their lives are far more real than those of human beings. For, after all, what you were just talking about is no more than a bad dream. Take a fifty-year-old newspaper and read it. The truncated, silly-looking letters, the paltry ambitions of dead men who don't yet know that they are dead men . . . Everything that you are so concerned about now is in no way different from what set minds seething then – except, perhaps, that the order of the words in the headlines has changed. Wake up!'

Alexander's head had sunk right down into his shoulders now – he was totally embarrassed. Lord Cricket apparently knew how to go for the jugular.

'Surely you would like to find out who these beings of a different nature are? And understand how they differ from human beings?'

'Yes, I would,' Alexander muttered.

'Then forget all this nonsense, and let's get down to business. Today I'm going to tell you about what lies concealed behind the ability of certain people to transform themselves into animals – an ability that is real, not metaphorical. Anthy, is everything working? Then turn off the light, please . . .'

* * *

'What you are about to hear,' said Lord Cricket, 'is normally regarded as esoteric knowledge. Therefore I ask you to keep what you hear secret. The information I intend to share with you originates from the Pink Sunset Lodge, or, more precisely, from Aleister Crowley, Aldous Huxley and their line of secret transmission. The condition of secrecy that I have mentioned is essential, not so much for the sake of the lodge, as for your own personal safety. Do you accept this condition?'

Alexander and I exchanged glances.

'Yes,' I said.

'Yes,' Alexander repeated, after a brief pause.

Lord Cricket touched one of the keys on his laptop. A diagram appeared on the wall – a man sitting in the lotus position, with a vertical line drawn along his spine. Set along this line were symbols marked with Sanskrit characters, looking like different-coloured cogwheels with various numbers of teeth.

'No doubt you are aware that a human being is not merely a physical body with a nervous system, restricted to the perception of the physical world. On the subtle plane a human being is a psycho-energetic structure consisting of three channels of energy and seven psychic centres called chakras.'

Lord Cricket ran his finger down something rather like a bicycle chain connecting the cogwheels on the spine.

'This subtle structure not only regulates a human being's spiritual life. It is also responsible for the way in which he or she perceives the surrounding world. Each chakra is related to a specific set of psychic manifestations, which I won't go into just now. What is important for us is that, according to the traditional occult view, spiritual progress consists in the ascent along the central energy channel of a force known as "kundalini", or "snake energy".'

A part of the previous diagram appeared on the screen, showing an inverted triangle at the very base of the spine.

'In its coiled state, Kundalini slumbers in this triangular bone called the "sacrum". The sacrum is located at the base of the spine – in fact, it is its first bone. Or its last, depending on your point of view. In traditional occultism it is believed that the gradual charging of the chakras with the kundalini force is the essential aspect of the journey from a philistine who is indifferent to spiritual matters, to a saint who has achieved unity with the godhead . . .'

Lord Cricket paused for effect.

'In most occult schools it was usually assumed that kundalini can only rise upwards through the central channel. Nowhere in any openly available sources do we find any mention of the snake energy being able to move downwards. Nonetheless, it is possible for the energy to move in this manner.'

The following diagram was like the first, except that the vertical line continued below the seated man's crossed legs and three new cogwheels, all black, had appeared on it. There were no Sanskrit characters beside them – only numerals. The one closest to the man's body was marked '1', the next was marked '2', and the one furthest away was marked '3'.

'I'm not going to talk about how the kundalini can be made to move downwards. That requires a degree of initiation that no one present here today possesses . . .'

'Oh, Brian,' E Hu-Li interrupted, 'really, what are you saying. Tell them.'

'Anthy,' said Lord Cricket, 'everything that can be said, will be said. And so, as a result of a certain procedure, the kundalini surges down along the shadow projection of the central channel. When this occurs, it can halt at three points, which are mirror reflections of the three lower chakras – *muladhara, swadhishtana* and *manipura*.'

He drew his finger down through the three black cogwheels. I noticed number one had four petals, which made it look like the blades in a kitchen mincer. Number two had six petals, and it looked like a martial arts weapon for throwing. And number three consisted of two stars, one superimposed on the other, each with five projections, folded over slightly – ten petals in all.

'As I have already said, the movement of kundalini upwards along the central channel leads to unity with the godhead and likeness to god. It is logical to assume that the result of the snake force moving downwards must be the direct opposite. And at this point, I would like to draw your attention to a certain extremely interesting circumstance, of which I was reminded by our enchanting guest, when she spoke about the meaning of words in different languages . . .'

Lord Cricket bowed briefly in my direction and smiled. I smiled in reply and whispered to Alexander:

'Learn some manners, you oaf.'

'We heard about the Russian word "Bog" and its English equivalent "God". If you read "God" backwards, you get "Dog". You must understand that this coincidence is not simply an accident. It is possible to argue which came first – the language or the reality that it reflects. But that is merely the old chestnut about the chicken and the egg.'

The silhouettes of three animals appeared on the screen – a wolf, a dog and a fox.

'The word "werewolf" means a human being who can assume the form of a wolf, or perhaps some other animal. In Chinese, however, the corresponding term is associated more closely with foxes. But there is no fundamental contradiction in this – the fox, like the wolf, is a member of the class of canines. They are still "God" spelt backwards, still the same highly charged black mass, the same downwards shift of kundalini.'

'A highly charged black mass,' E Hu-Li repeated in a low voice, giving her husband a respectful look.

'The question that arises is how the kundalini travels once it leaves the body. After all, it can't actually move through empty space. And here we reach the most interesting part. Again, it is possible to argue at length about what is the cause and what is the effect, but the emergence of kundalini from the body is accompanied by a physical mutation. Something quite incredible takes place. Do you remember those films about volcanic eruptions? Sometimes there are scenes in them where you can see lava flowing down a slope and burning out a channel that wasn't there a moment earlier. The kundalini creates a physical channel for itself in exactly the same way. As soon as it moves below the *muladhara* – the lowest human chakra, located at the base of the spine – the were-creature starts to grow a tail!'

Two tails – a wolf's and a fox's – appeared on the screen. The fox's tail was drawn with absurd mistakes. The next slide showed the man in the lotus position again, but now he had a shaggy tail, with three black cogwheels on it.

'It is through the tail that the kundalini energy descends into the three lower infra-chakras. These centres do not have any Sanskrit names. They are conventionally referred to as "the position of the fox", "the position of the wolf" and "the abyss". The infra-chakra closest to the body is the position of the fox.'

He pointed to the black blades from the kitchen mincer, with the number '1' beside them.

'This is considered to be a point of stable equilibrium, where the energy can be located permanently, and so the were-creature can remain in the form of a fox for an unlimited period of time. However, you should not think that at this point transformation occurs into a fox that is the animal we know. The snake energy emerges only a short distance from the body, and therefore in physical terms the were-creature differs only in insignificant ways from a human being. It is simply a rather plain creature with a tail and a few changes in the shape of the ears . . .'

I almost snorted.

'In addition to that, the shape of the pupils is transformed and the superciliary arches become slightly more pronounced, but you would probably not be surprised to meet one of these creatures on the street . . .'

'Absolutely fantastic,' said E Hu-Li.

Lord Cricket pointed to the cogwheel located in the centre of the tail.

'The displacement of the kundalini to the second infra-chakra produces a far more spectacular effect. Here we are dealing with the absolutely classic case of a "werewolf". The were-creature is not simply transformed into a wolf. He is, so to speak, a wolf writ large. He is taller than a man and incredibly strong, with huge jaws full of teeth, but he walks on his hind legs like a man – although if he wants, he can run on all four legs. The descriptions in folklore are fairly accurate, since this has always been the most widespread form of were-creature in Europe. I shall only remark upon one curious detail. It is widely believed that transformation into a werewolf is associated with a specific phase of the moon or the onset of twilight. And in the folk imagination, it comes to an end with the dawn, since evil spirits cannot bear the sunlight. In actual fact, darkness and light have nothing to do with the matter. But another, correct, observation has been made: the transformation into a werewolf is short-lived, since the infra-chakra number two is a point of unstable equilibrium, where the kundalini cannot be located for a long period of time . . .'

'But what does that mean,' asked E Hu-Li, 'stable equilibrium, unstable equilibrium?'

Lord Cricket leaned down over his laptop.

'Just a moment,' he said, 'I have a slide on that subject here somewhere . . .'

An image of Stonehenge appeared on the screen, followed by an advertisement in various shades of green for a trailer home with a vase of narcissi pasted lovingly, but not very professionally in its window, and finally a black sine curve.

'There,' said Lord Cricket, 'please pardon the confusion.'

There was a blue ball lying in the hollow of the curve, and a red ball poised on its crest. The balls had little arrows of the same colours pointing away from them to indicate their direction of movement.

'It's very simple,' said Lord Cricket. 'Both balls are in a state of equilibrium, but if you move the blue ball, it will return to the point from which it started. That is stable equilibrium. However, if you move the red ball, it will not return to that point and will roll downwards. That is unstable equilibrium . . .'

'I have a question,' said Alexander. 'May I?'

'By all means.'

'Why is the first ball blue, and the second one red?'

'I beg your pardon?'

'And the arrows are the same colours. Why those two colours in particular?'

'But what difference does it make?'

'No difference at all,' said Alexander. 'I'm just curious. Perhaps you haven't heard, but in Russian the word for blue – "goluboi" – means "homosexual". I've been wondering for a long time about why the arrows on all the campaign maps are always blue and red. As if history consisted primarily of a struggle between the queers and the communists. I thought perhaps you might know?'

'No,' Lord Cricket replied politely, 'I don't know why precisely those two colours are used. May I continue?'

Alexander nodded. The tail with the black infra-chakras appeared on the screen again.

'As I have already said, the second position, at which the transformation into a wolf takes place, is unstable. If we superimpose the curve on the drawing, you can see that the neighbouring positions – numbers one and three – must be stable. Number one is the position of the fox, which we have already discussed. You probably have a question about position number three?'

'Yes,' said E Hu-Li. 'What is it, Brian?'

'I have already mentioned that the three infra-chakras of a were-creature are located symmetrically to the lower three chakras of a human being. The final infra-chakra, located at the very tip of the tail, is a mirror reflection of the Manipura, located between the navel and the heart. At this point the central channel is interrupted. The kundalini cannot move on to the upper chakras unless the region around the Manipura, known as the "ocean of illusions" is charged with the energy of a genuine spiritual mentor. According to the principle of Hermes Trismegistus, the same applies to the were-creature's infra-chakras. In order to move the kundalini to its lowest possible point, an involtation of darkness is required, the spiritual influence of a superior demonic entity that fills the so-called "desert of truth" – the rupture in the shadow central channel – with its vibrations . . .'

'And what exactly is a superior demonic entity?' I couldn't help asking.

Lord Cricket smiled.

'That depends on your personal contacts,' he said. 'The possibilities here are different for everyone . . . And so, we have come to the end of what I am permitted to tell you. I can only add one thing: position number three, the so-called abyss, is the point at which the transformation to the super-werewolf takes place.'

'And has anyone ever succeeded in completing that manoeuvre?' I asked.

'According to certain sources, in 1925 one of your compatriots, the anthroposophist Sharikov, succeeded. He was a disciple of Dr Steiner, and a friend of Maximilian Voloshin and Andrei Bely. As far as we know, Sharikov was taken into the Cheka, and the whole business was kept top secret. And the secrecy was taken very seriously: suffice it to say that the manuscript of *A Dog's Heart* – a story by the well-known writer Bulgakov that was based on rumours about the event – was confiscated. After that no one ever saw Sharikov again.'

'But what exactly is a super-werewolf?' Alexander asked.

'I don't know,' said Lord Cricket. 'At least, I don't know yet. But you have no idea how impatient I am to find out . . .'

* * *

'What are you doing wearing an evening dress first thing in the morning?' Alexander asked. 'And high heels?'

'Why, don't they suit me?'

'Black suits you very well,' he said, and cautiously rubbed his cheek against mine. 'But then, so does white.'

Instead of kissing we sometimes used to rub our cheeks together. I found this manner of his funny at first – there was something childish, puppyish about it. Then he confessed that he was sniffing my skin, which had an especially tender smell just behind my ear. After that, I used to experience a vague displeasure during this procedure – I had the feeling that I was being used.

'Are we going to the theatre?' he asked.

'Something a bit more interesting than that. We're going hunting.'

'Hunting. But who are we going to hunt?'

'Chickens,' I declared proudly.

'Are you feeling hungry?'

'That's not funny.'

'Then why do you want to go hunting chickens?'

'It's just that I want you to get to know me a little bit better. Get ready, we're going out of town.'

'Right now?'

'Yes,' I said, 'only first read this. Someone has a commercial proposition for you.'

I handed him a print-out of an e-mail letter I'd received from E Hu-Li that morning.

Hi there, Red,

I tried to reach you on the mobile, but the voice said that the 'number is temporarily blocked'. Looks like your sponsor in uniform isn't very generous . . .

Pursuant to our meeting (so charming!) of yesterday's date, it appears that when we left our boys alone after Brian's lecture and started reminiscing about old times, they had a quarrel about art. Let me tell you what happened. Brian showed Alexander photographs of some works that he is planning to exhibit jointly with the Saatchi gallery. First and foremost among them is the installation 'The Liberation of Babylon', which uses a model of the Gates of Ishtar as the background for Scottish bagpipers parachuting in with their kilts hiked up. These plaster figures convey their own state of sexual excitation to the viewer, attacking his perception and transforming him into another object put on display. In this way, the observer is made aware of his own physical and emotional presence in the space distorted by the gravity of that artistic object . . . Alexander liked 'The Liberation of Babylon', which cannot be said for all the other pieces.

Have you seen the hit of the last Venice Biennale – the haystack in which the first Belarussian postmodernist, Mikolai Klimaksovich, hid from his local police inspector for four years? Alexander called this work plagiaristic and told Brian about the similar haystack famously used before the revolution by Vladimir Lenin. Brian observed that repetition is not necessarily plagiarism, it is the very essence of the postmodern, or – to put it in broader terms – the foundation of the modern cultural gestalt, which is manifested in everything, from the cloning of sheep to remakes of old movies, for what else can you do after the end of history? Brian said it was precisely Klimaksovich's use of quotation that made him a postmodernist, not a plagiarizer. But Alexander objected that no quotations would ever have saved this Klimaksovich from the Russian police, and history might have come to an end in Belarus, but there was no sign of it breaking down yet in Russia.

Then Brian showed Alexander a work by Asuro Keshami,

one which he regards with especial affection, not least owing to the serious investment required for its production and installation. Keshami's work, inspired by the oeuvre of Camille Paglia, of whom you must have heard, consists of an immense tube of red plastic with projections on the inside in the form of white fangs. It is proposed to install it in the open air in one of London's sports stadiums.

And now I'm getting to the point. One of the most serious problems in the world of modern art is the invention of original and fresh verbal interpretations of a work. Literally just a few phrases are required, which can then be reprinted in the catalogues and reviews. This apparently trivial detail can often decide the fate of a piece of art. It is very important here to be able to perceive things from an unexpected, shocking angle, and your friend, with his barbarically fresh view of the world, does this quite remarkably well. Therefore, Brian would like permission to use the ideas expressed by Alexander yesterday for the conceptual support of the installation. The accompanying text which I include below is by way of being a fusion of Brian's and Alexander's ideas:

Asuro Keshami's work 'VD-42CC' combines the languages of different areas – engineering, technology and science. At the base level the subject-matter is the overcoming of space: physical space, the space of taboo and the space of our subconscious fears. The languages of engineering and technology deal with the material from which the object is constructed, but the artist addresses the viewer in the language of emotions. When the viewer learns that certain people have given this little queer fifteen million pounds to stretch out a huge imitation-leather cunt above an abandoned soccer pitch, he remembers what he does in his own life and how much he is paid for it, then he looks at the photo of this little queer in his horn-rimmed spectacles and

funny jacket, and experiences confusion and bewilderment bor-
dering on the feeling that the German philosopher Martin
Heidegger called 'abandonment' (Geworfenheit). The viewer is
invited to concentrate on these feelings, which constitute the
precise aesthetic effect that the installation attempts to achieve.

Brian would like to offer Alexander a fee of one thousand
pounds. Of course, this is not a large sum, but this version of
the accompanying text is not final, and it is not absolutely cer-
tain that it will be used. Have a word with Alexander, okay?
You can reply directly to Brian at this address. I am a little
miffed with him just at the moment. He is in a bad mood – last
night he was refused entrance to the establishment known as
'Night Flight'. First he was stopped by the face control (they
didn't like his sports shoes), and then some Dutch pimp
emerged from the depths of this den of iniquity and told Brian
to dress 'more stylish'. Brian has been repeating the same thing
all day long today: 'Stylish? Like the one who went in just
ahead of me? In a green jacket and blue shirt?' And he is taking
out his bad mood on me. Ah well, never mind :-=)))
    The most important thing is, don't forget about the pass for
the Cathedral of Christ the Saviour!
    Heads and tails,
    Your E

Alexander read the print-out carefully. After that he folded the
sheet of paper in two, then folded it in two again, and then tore
it in half.

'A thousand pounds,' he said. 'Ha! He obviously doesn't
understand who he's dealing with here. You know what, you
write to him. Your English is better, anyway.'

'Thanks,' I said modestly. 'What shall I say? He didn't offer
enough?'

He looked me up and down.

'Fuck him out of it from every possible angle. Only make it sound aristocratic and elegant.'

'That's not possible,' I said. 'No matter how much I'd like to.'

'Why?'

'In aristocratic circles they don't fuck each other out of it. It's just not done.'

'Then fuck him whatever way it is done,' he said. 'But hard enough to crack his arse open. Go on, put in that sarcasm of yours that has corroded my soul so thoroughly. Let it do some good for once.'

Something in his tone of voice prevented me from asking exactly what good he had in mind. He was touching in his childish resentment, and part of it was transmitted to me. And if we're being entirely honest – does a fox really need to be asked twice to fuck an English aristocrat out of it?

I sat down at the computer and started thinking. My internationalist feminist component required my reply to be structured round the phrase 'suck my dick', in the style of the most advanced US feminists. But the rational part of my ego told me that would not be enough in a letter signed by Alexander. I wrote the following:

Dear Lord Cricket,

Being extremely busy, I'm not sure that you can currently suck my dick. However, please feel encouraged to fantasize about such a development while sucking on a cucumber, a carrot, an eggplant or any other elongated roundish object you might find appropriate for that matter.

With kind regards,
Alexandre Fenrir-Gray

I deliberately put 'Alexandre', in the French manner, instead of

'Alexander'. I came up with the surname 'Fenrir-Gray' at the last moment, in a fit of inspiration. It definitely had an aristocratic ring to it. Of course, it immediately brought to mind 'Earl Grey' tea, and that gave the signature a faint aroma of bergamot oil, but the name was only a one-off anyway.

'Well?' he asked.

I read the text in Russian.

'Can we do without the "kind regards"?'

'Then it won't be aristocratic.'

'Oh, all right,' he sighed. 'Send it off . . . and then come over here, the Grey Wolf has a proposal for Little Red Riding Hood.'

'What would that be?'

'We're going to have, you know . . . A colloquium on the psychoanalysis of Russian folktales. We're going to throw pies into Little Red Riding Hood's basket. Unfortunately, we only have one pie today. So we'll have to throw it into the basket over and over again.'

'Phoo, how vulgar . . .'

'Are you going to come here or do I have to come and get you?'

'I'll come. Only let's do it real fast. It's already time we were going. And don't you bite through any of my clothes today, I went to a lot of trouble to buy new knickers, all right? Not all of them suit me.'

'Uhu.'

'And one more thing, while you can still talk . . .'

'What?'

'Tell me why every time you have to introduce that apologia for fatuous militant ignorance into the conversation?'

'How do you mean?'

'Like all that about Little Red Riding Hood and psychoanalysis. It sometimes seems to me that you're trying to shaft the whole of history and culture in my person.'

'As far as culture goes, there's something to that,' he said. 'But what's history got to do with it? What are you, a Sphinx? Just how old are you, anyway? I'd give you sixteen years. But what's your real age?'

I felt my cheeks getting hot, very hot.

'Mine?'

'Yes.'

I had to come up with something to say.

'You know,' I said, 'I once read some poems by a public prosecutor in an obscure journal published by the ministry of justice. There was one about a young defender of the Motherland that began with the words "I would never have given him more than fifteen".'

'I get it,' he said, 'the son of the regiment. So what have these poems got to do with anything?'

'I'll tell you. When a man in your uniform says "I'd give you sixteen years", the first thing you wonder is – under what article of the criminal code.' And the second thing is – how big the pay off might be.'

'If you find this uniform irritating,' he said, 'take off your stupid dress, and soon there'll be soft fur instead of shoulder straps. Yes, that's nice. What a good girl you are today . . .'

'Listen, are you going to get them a pass for the Cathedral of Christ the Saviour?'

'Woo-oo-oo!'

'No? You're right, too. We've just written a reply to that Brian. Although . . . Do you want to stick it to him in really aristocratic fashion?'

'Gr-r-r!'

'If after this letter, where you explained everything to him, you still got him a pass anyway, that would be really high class.'

'Gr-r-r!'

'So we'll do it, then?'

'Gr-r-r!'

'Good. I'll remind you later . . . What a fool you are, eh? I told you not to bite through anything! Buy yourself a plastic bone in the dog shop and chew it as much as you like, when I'm not here. Cutting your teeth, are you. You big bad wolf . . . And get a move on, we have to be in the forest in an hour.'

* * *

The car stopped at the edge of the forest, not far from the section-built six-storey house I had noted as my initial reference-point.

'Where to now?' asked Alexander.

He was acting in the condescendingly buddy-buddy manner of an adult being drawn into a meaningless game by children. That irritated me. Never mind, I thought, we'll see what you say in an hour's time . . .

I picked up the plastic bag with the champagne and glasses and got out of the car. Alexander said something to the driver in a low voice and got out after me. I set off towards the forest at a stroll.

In the forest it was already summer. It was that astonishing period in May when the greenery and the flowers seem immortal, as if now they are victorious for ever. But I knew that in just another two or three weeks there would be a presentiment of autumn in the air.

Instead of admiring the natural surroundings, I watched my feet – my stiletto heels were sinking into the ground, and I had to be careful where I stepped. We reached a bench standing between two birch trees. That was the next reference point. From there it was only a few short steps to the forester's house.

'Let's sit down,' I said.

We sat down on the bench. I handed him the bottle and he opened it deftly.

'It's nice here,' he said, pouring the champagne. 'Quiet. It's still spring, but everything's in full bloom already. Flowers . . . But up north there's snow everywhere. And ice.'

'Why did you suddenly remember the north?'

'Don't know, really. What are we drinking to?'

'To good hunting.'

We clinked glasses. When I finished my champagne, I smashed my glass against the edge of the bench and used the sharp edge to cut through the strap of my dress above my right shoulder. He followed my movements with dour disapproval.

'Are you going to pretend to be an Amazon?'

I didn't answer that.

'And listen, why are you all in black? And dark glasses? Is it a spoof on *The Matrix*?'

I didn't answer that either.

'Don't get me wrong. Black really does suit you, only . . .'

'I'll go on from here on my own,' I interrupted.

'And what do I do?'

'When I start to run, you can run after me. But somewhere off to one side. And I beg you, please don't interfere. Not even if you see something you don't like. Just keep out of it and watch.'

'Okay.'

'And keep your distance. Or you'll frighten the people.'

'What people?'

'You'll see.'

'I don't like any of this,' he said. 'I'm worried about you. Maybe you shouldn't do it?'

I stood up with a determined air.

'No more. We're starting.'

As I have already said, the goal of chicken hunting is supraphysical transformation, and the correct preparatory procedure is very important. In order to trigger the transformation, we put ourselves in an extremely embarrassing situation, the kind in which your own idiocy is so breathtaking and you feel so ashamed you wish the earth would open and swallow you up. That is precisely what the evening dress and the high-heeled shoes are for. We take the situation to such absurd lengths that we are left with no other option but to transform into an animal. And the chicken is required as a biological catalyst for the reaction – without it the transformation is impossible. It is extremely important for the chicken to remain alive until the very end – if it dies, we rapidly resume our human shape. And so it's best to select the bird that is healthiest and strongest.

When I reached the chicken coop, I looked at the forester's house. The sun was reflected in the window, and I couldn't see if there was anyone there behind the glass. But there were definitely people in the house. I could hear music coming from the open door, with stern male voices (I think it was a monks' choir) singing: 'The good night . . . the peace of God . . . the mantle of God above the sleeping earth . . .'

I needed to hurry.

The chicken coop was a planking hut with an inclined roof made of plywood covered with polythene. I drew back the bolt, flung open the door, which scraped across the ground, and immediately spotted my prey in the foul-smelling semi-darkness. She was a brown chicken with a white side – when all the other chickens made a dash for the corners, she was the only one who stayed put. As if she was waiting for me, I thought.

'Co-co-co,' I said in a hoarse, insincere voice, then quickly bent down and grabbed her.

The chicken turned out to be very meek – she twitched once to adjust a wing that was caught awkwardly, then froze. It seemed to me, as it always does at such moments, that she understood the nature of what was happening perfectly well, and her own role in it. Pressing her against my chest, I backed out of the chicken coop. One shoe got stuck in the ground, twisted over and slipped off my foot. I kicked the other one off as well.

'Hey, daughter,' a voice called to me.

I looked up. There was a man of about fifty, wearing a tattered, old padded work-jacket, standing on the porch. He had a thick, drooping moustache.

'What do you think you're up to?' he asked. 'Are you off your head?'

A younger man, about thirty years old, appeared behind the first. He had a moustache too – he was obviously the first man's son. He was wearing a blue tracksuit with the large letters 'CASC', for 'Central Army Sporting Club'. I noted that they were both too thickset to be fast runners.

The moment of truth was nigh. Looking at them with a mysterious smile, I opened the zip on the right side of my dress. Now it was only held on by the left shoulder-strap, and I easily slipped out of it, letting it fall to the ground. I was left in nothing but a short orange nightdress which didn't hinder my movements at all. A light breeze caressed my semi-naked body.

A third spectator came out on to the porch – a boy of about eight, carrying a plastic sword. He stared at me without the slightest surprise – to him I probably looked like a picture from the television, come to life, and he'd seen more amazing things on TV.

'Aren't you ashamed of yourself?' asked the head of the household with the droopy moustache.

He'd hit the bull's eye there. At that moment my soul was overflowing with shame. It was no longer shame – it was disgust with myself. I felt as if I were standing at the very epicentre of global infamy and it was not only the offended chicken-owners who were looking at me – all the hierarchies of the heavens and myriads of spiritual beings were gazing at me from their fathomless worlds with furious contempt in their eyes. I began slowly backing away from the chicken coop.

The father and son exchanged glances.

'You let go of that chicken,' the son said and stepped down off the porch.

The boy with the sword in his hand opened his mouth in anticipation of a bit of amusement. And now I realized, not with my mind, but with every last cell in my body, that there was only one way out of this cocoon of intolerable indignity – the track leading away into the forest. And I turned and ran.

After that developments followed the classical sequence. The first steps were painful because the branches and stones stuck into my bare feet. But after a few seconds the transformation began. First I felt my fingers fusing together. It became harder to keep hold of the chicken – now I had to press it against my chest as hard as I could, and I had to avoid smothering it accidentally at the same time. Then I stopped feeling any pain in my feet. And another few seconds after that I was already rushing along on three paws without any feeling of discomfort at all.

By that stage it was impossible not to notice the changes that had taken place in me – and they had been noticed. I heard voices hallooing behind me. I glanced round and bared my teeth. Both chicken-owners, father and son, were chasing me. But they were falling a long way behind. I slowed down a bit to disentangle myself from the night-dress (it wasn't difficult – my body had become lean and flexible), allowed them to get a bit closer and then ran on.

What makes a man run after a fox in a situation like this? Of course, it's not a matter of trying to recover the stolen property. When the fox undergoes the supraphysical transformation, her pursuers see something that demolishes all their ideas about the world. And then what they run after is no longer the stolen chicken, but that miracle. They are pursuing the glimmer of the impossible that has illuminated their dull lives for the first time. And that is exactly what makes it so difficult to get away from them.

Fortunately, the track into the forest was empty (throughout the entire chase I didn't meet anyone coming the opposite way). I knew Alexander was somewhere nearby – I could hear branches cracking and leaves rustling as they were parted off to one side of the path. But I couldn't see anyone – just once or twice I thought I glimpsed a shadow through a gap between the bushes.

The older chicken-owner began falling behind. When it became clear that he would never manage to close the gap, he gave up and dropped out of the race. His son kept up a good pace for about another kilometre, and then slowed down a lot. I shifted into an easy trot, and we ran about another five hundred metres. Then my pursuer started panting for breath, and soon he had no strength to run any further – I suspect he was a smoker. He stopped, with his hands propped on his knees and his dark eyes goggling at me, and I was immediately reminded of the deceased Sikh from the National hotel. But I suppressed my personal feelings – they were inappropriate here.

If my goal had been to escape, the chase would have ended there (thus does the miraculous disappear from human life). But I had another goal – the hunt. I stopped. There was no more than twenty metres left between us.

As I have already said, if the fox releases the chicken, then a minute later, at most, all the supraphysical changes disappear. Naturally, the fox can no longer run faster than a man. And so the manoeuvre I had decided to perform was risky – but I was spurred on by the awareness that Alexander was watching what I was doing. I let go of the chicken. She took a few faltering steps across the asphalt and stopped (during the hunt they go into a special kind of trance and their reactions are inhibited). I counted to ten, grabbed her again and hugged her against my chest.

My pursuer couldn't bear to be mocked like that – gathering all his strength, he came dashing after me again, and we ran another three hundred metres at a very good pace. I was happy – the hunt had definitely been a success.

And then something unexpected happened. As we ran past a fork in the track, where the trees were marked with blue and red arrows (probably for skiers – although I don't know what Alexander would have thought), I heard my pursuer shout out:

'This way! Help!'

Glancing round, I saw him waving to someone. And then two mounted militiamen rode out of the sidetrack that we had just passed.

I don't know how to express the terror and the majesty of that moment. There's something similar in Pushkin's 'Bronze Horseman', but there was only one rider there, and here there were two of them. Like a slow-motion sequence from some terrible dream, they swung round, pointed their four faces – two belonging to the militiamen and two to the horses – at me, and came dashing in pursuit.

Why do we hate English aristocrats so much? If, for just a few seconds, you had been in my skin (and at this point I was already covered by it, but rather unevenly, in patches), you would never need to ask that question again. Cops are stupid and they do what they're told, what can you expect from them? But how can you excuse educated people who have turned another creature's agony into entertainment and sport? That's why I don't condemn my sister E – although, of course, I would never do the things that she does.

It was almost a hundred years since the last time I'd had to escape from mounted pursuers (that was near Melitopol during the Russian Civil War). But when I heard the heavy hoof-beats behind me, I immediately recalled that day. The memory was vivid and terrifying – I even thought for a moment that I had simply imagined the entire twentieth century owing the heat and the oxygen deficiency, and in reality I was still running with all my might from a group of drunk Red cavalrymen who were pursuing me along the dusty road, intent on killing me. An appalling feeling.

The fright lent me strength. And as well as that, fear made my supraphysical transformation go very far, much farther than during an ordinary hunt. At first I thought this was an advantage, since now I could run faster. But then I realized that it would be the death of me. The paw with which I was clutching the chicken to my breast changed into a normal fox's limb, which is useless for holding anything. And I had lost control of the process. I was slipping inexorably towards the edge of the precipice: a few more seconds of agony, and I dropped the chicken. It somersaulted through the air and landed on the side of the track, clucking in outrage. I had already become an absolutely genuine fox – but now I wasn't going to stay that way for long.

And at this point I suddenly noticed something very strange.

I suddenly realized that my tail, which wasn't supposed to be doing anything, was working.

A fox will understand immediately what I mean, but it's hard to explain to a human being. Alexander once told me a joke about a certain libertine whose penis was so long that he could scrape it along the windows of the nightclubs. 'Ooh, I think I'm in love with someone . . .' Take away the erotic connotations, and what I felt was something similar.

Apart from that, I realized that I had always done this. The clandestine stream of hypnotic energy that I was broadcasting into the world around me had not changed in such a long time that I had completely stopped being aware of it: it was like what happens to the hum of the fridge – you only notice it when it suddenly stops. I followed the direction of the beam, to see who the suggestion was aimed at – and I realized it was directed . . . at me.

BANG, as they write in the comic books.

My self-control didn't desert me at that moment. I remained as aware as ever of what was going on – both around me and inside my own mind. One of my internal voices recited in deep bass tones the words that Laertes spoke to Hamlet after the fatal hit with the rapier: 'In thee there is not half an hour of life . . .'

'Why half an hour? What kind of poison was it on the rapier?' another voice enquired.

'It would be interesting to discuss that with the Shakespeare scholar Shitman,' a third remarked, 'only the poor fellow's no longer with us . . .'

'Then you'll get a chance soon enough!' barked the fourth.

I felt afraid: there's a popular belief among foxes that before they die, they see the truth, and then all their internal voices start talking at once. Was this really it? No, I thought, any time but now . . . But I didn't have thirty minutes, like Hamlet. I had thirty seconds at most, and they were quickly running out.

The forest came to an end. The track broke off at its edge, along which, as always, there were women from the local houses strolling with their prams. They spotted me and began squealing and screaming. With a desperate final effort I tore past the strolling women, spotted another track leading back into the forest and swerved on to it.

But my body was already betraying me. I started to feel pain in my palms, stood upright and started running on my hind legs – actually on my only pair of ordinary girl's legs. Then I trod on an especially prickly pine cone, squealed and fell to my knees.

When they reached me, the militiamen dismounted. One of them took hold of my hair and turned me to face him. His face was suddenly contorted in fury. I recognized him – he was one of the spintrii from the militia station where I had done my 'working Saturday'. He had recognized me too. We stared into each other's eyes for a minute. It's pointless even trying to tell the uninitiated what takes place between a fox and a man at a moment like that. It's something you have to experience.

'What a fool I am,' I thought despairingly, 'there's a saying, after all – don't screw where you live, don't live where you screw. It's all my own fault . . .'

'Got you now, you bitch, haven't I?' the militiaman asked.

'Do you know her?' the other one asked.

'I should say so. She worked a subbotnik at our place. I still can't rid of the herpes on my arse.'

The militiaman demonstrated an inability to understand the link between cause and effect that was exceptional even for his species, but I didn't find it funny. Everything was happening exactly the same way as that other time, near Melitopol . . . Perhaps I really was still there, and everything else was a just terminal hallucination?

Suddenly there was the deafening roar of a shot somewhere nearby. I looked up.

Alexander was standing on the track in his immaculately ironed grey uniform, with a pistol in his hand and a black bundle under his arm. I hadn't noticed him appear there or how.

'Both of you come here,' he said.

The militiamen walked meekly towards him – like rabbits towards a boa constrictor. One of the horses whinnied nervously and reared up.

'Don't be afraid, don't be afraid,' I whispered, 'he won't eat you.'

That was actually an assumption on my part: Alexander hadn't shared his plans with me. When the militiamen got close, he put his gun in its holster and said something in a quiet voice, I thought I heard '. . . report on the situation'. First he listened to them, and then he started talking himself. I couldn't make out any more words, but it was all clear from the gesticulations. First he held out his open right hand, as if he were tossing a small object up and down on his palm. Then he turned it palm-down and made a few circular movements, flattening something invisible. This had the most magical effect on the militiamen – they turned and walked away, forgetting not only about me, but about their horses too.

Alexander looked at me curiously for a few seconds, then walked up and held out the black bundle. It was my dress. There was something wrapped in it. I unfolded it and saw the chicken. It was dead. I felt so sad that tears sprang to my eyes. It wasn't a question of sentimentality. Not long ago we had been a single whole. And this little death seemed to be half mine.

'Get dressed,' said Alexander.

'Why did you . . .' I pointed at the chicken.

'What, was I supposed to let it go?'

I nodded. He spread his arms in bewilderment.

'Well, in that case I don't understand anything at all.'

Of course, it was stupid of me to reproach him.

'No, I'm sorry. Thank you,' I said. 'For the dress, and in general.'

'Listen,' he said, 'don't ever do that again. Ever.'

'Why?'

'Don't take offence, but you don't look very good. I mean, when you turn into . . . I don't know. Anyway, it's not your thing.'

'Why don't I look good?'

'You're pretty mangy. And you could be three hundred years old at least.'

I felt myself turning red.

'I see. Like a woman driver, is that it? Every second word you speak betrays the repulsive chauvinism of the male . . .'

'Let's not have any of that. I'm telling you the truth. Gender has nothing to do with it.'

I got dressed quickly and even managed to tie the cut shoulder strap in a knot above my shoulder.

'Will you take the chicken?' he asked.

I shook my head.

'Then let's go. The car will be here in a moment. And tomorrow at twelve hundred hours, be ready to leave. We're flying up north.'

'What for?'

'You showed me the way you hunt. Now you can take a look at the way I do it.'

* * *

I'd never flown in any planes like the Gulfstream Jet before. I'd never even seen any – life had never taken me to the special airports for the *upper rat*. I felt nervous because there were so few people in the cabin – as if the safety of a flight depended on the number of passengers.

Maybe that's true, by the way. After all, everyone has his own guardian angel, and when you get several hundred passengers crammed into an Airbus or a Boeing, if the hordes of invisible winged protectors don't actually increase the uplift of the plane's wings, they must at least insure it against falling. Probably that's why there are more crashes involving the small private flights used by various newsmakers heavily burdened with evil (even if some victims don't belong to this elite niche, they become newsmakers when they crash).

The passenger cabin was like a smoking room with leather armchairs. Alexander sat beside me. Apart from us, the only person in the cabin was Mikhalich – he'd made himself comfortable in the armchair furthest away and was shuffling through some papers or other. He hardly spoke to Alexander at all – just once he turned to him and asked:

'Comrade lieutenant general, it says here in a document "sheikh-ul-masheikh". Do you know what that means?'

Alexander thought about it.

'I think that's from forty kilograms of plastique and upwards.

But check it out just to be sure when we get back.'

'Yes, sir.'

Moscow floated down and away, and then it was hidden by the clouds. Alexander turned away from the window and took out a book.

'What are you reading?' I asked. 'Another detective novel?'

'No. This time I took a serious, intelligent book, on your advice. Do you want something to read too?'

'Yes,' I said.

'Then take a look at this. So you'll understand what you're about to see. It's not exactly the same case, but it's pretty similar. I brought it especially for you.'

He put a tattered volume on my knees. The title *Russian Fairy Tales* was written in red letters – it was the same book I'd seen on his desk.

'The page is marked,' he said.

The bookmark was at the story called 'Little Khavroshka'. It was a long time since I'd held any Russian children's books in my hands, and I noticed one strange thing immediately – because the print was so large, I perceived the words quite differently from in adult books. As if everything they denoted was simpler and purer.

The fairy tale turned out to be rather sad. Little Khavroshka was a northern clone of Cinderella, only instead of a fairy god-mother she was helped by a brindled cow. This cow did all the impossible jobs that Khavroshka was given to do by her step-mother. The wicked sisters spied on Khavroshka to see how she managed to keep up with all her work and they told the step-mother about it. The stepmother ordered the brindled cow to be slaughtered. Khavroshka found out and told the cow. The cow asked Khavroshka not to eat her meat and to bury her bones in the garden. Then an apple tree with jingling gold leaves grew out of the bones, and the tree made Khavroshka's fortune – she managed to pick an apple, and the reward for that was a fiancé . . . I found it interesting that the stepmother and the sisters weren't punished, they simply didn't get any apples, and then they were forgotten about.

I had absolutely no desire to analyse this fairy tale from the positions of the asshole-amphetamine discourse or rummage about in its 'morphology'. I didn't need to guess what it was really about – my heart understood. It was the eternal Russian story, the final cycle of which I had witnessed only recently, at the end of the last century. As if I personally had known the brindled cow to which children complained about their woes, who worked simple miracles for them and then quietly died under the knife, only to grow out from under the earth as a magical tree – a golden apple for every boy and girl . . .

The fairy tale contained a strange truth about the very saddest and most mysterious side of Russian life. How many times that brindled cow had been slaughtered. And how many times it had returned, either as a magic apple tree or an entire cherry orchard. Only where had all the apples gone? You couldn't find them anywhere. Except maybe by calling the office of United Fruit . . . But no, that was nonsense. 'United Fruit' was last century, but now any call you made would get lost in the wires on its way to some company in Gibraltar that belonged to a firm from the Falkland Islands that was managed by a lawyer in Amsterdam in the interests of a trust with an unnamed beneficiary owner. Who, of course, is known to every dog on the Rublyovskoe Highway where the *upper rat* lives.

I closed the book and looked at Alexander. He was asleep. I carefully took the *serious, intelligent book* from his knees and opened it:

No, the Money Tree looks different from the way certain frivolous writers of the last century thought of it. It doesn't fruit with gold ducats in the Field of Miracles, as they assumed. It sprouts through the icy crust of the permafrost in a blazing fountain of oil, a burning bush like the one that spoke with Moses. But although there are many a Moses crowding round the Money Tree today, the Lord remains significantly silent . . . The reason for his silence must be that he knows the tree will not be allowed to flutter its smoky flames in freedom for long. Calculating men will haul a slaking apparatus on to the crown of fire and force the Tree's black trunk to grow into a cold steel pipe stretching right across the Country of Fools to the port terminals, to various Chinas and Japans – so far that soon the Tree will be unable to recall its own roots . . .

After I'd read a few more paragraphs in the same fussy, obscure style, I began to feel sleepy. I closed the book and put it back on Alexander's knees. Then I slept through the rest of the flight.

I slept through the landing as well. When I opened my eyes, there was the snow-covered airport terminal building, looking more like a railway station, drifting past outside the window of the Gulfstream as it taxied along the runway. There was a long poster hanging on the building: 'Welcome to Nefteperegonievsck!' There was snow everywhere, as far as the eye could see.

At the bottom of the steps we were met by several military men in winter kit without any badges of rank. They greeted Mikhalich and Alexander like old friends, but they glanced at me, or at least I thought they did, in bewilderment. Nonetheless, when Mikhalich and Alexander each received an officer's greatcoat, I was also issued with warm clothing – a military padded jacket with a light-blue collar of synthetic fur and a cap with earflaps. The jacket was too big, and I literally drowned in it.

Three cars had come to meet us. They were black Geländewagens, just like the ones in Moscow, except that they were driven by soldiers. There was hardly any conversation at all when we were met: the men limited themselves to greetings and a brief discussion of the weather. It seemed like the local men knew all about why their visitors from Moscow were there.

The town that started immediately outside the airport had a rather phantasmagorical appearance. The buildings in it reminded me of cottages for the middle class outside Moscow. There was only one difference – these cottages were raised above the ground in an absurd fashion, on stilts that were like the hut's chicken legs in the fairy tale. That was the precise association evoked by the combination of the piles hammered into the permafrost and the red crests of the tiled roofs, and it was impossible to free myself of it: the houses became rows of chickens with their hindquarters raised high to display the black openings of the doors. Evidently I was still under the impression of the previous day's hunt and the resultant shock.

In between the 'eurohuts' I could see figures of street traders selling something from pieces of oilcloth spread out directly on the snow beside their Buran snowmobiles.

'What's that they're selling?' I asked Alexander.

'Reindeer meat. They bring it from the tundra.'

'Don't they ship supplies up here?'

'Yes, of course they do. It's just that reindeer meat's in fashion. It's stylish. And then, it's an environmentally clean product.'

I was very impressed by the Calvin Klein boutique, located in one of the cottages on piles. Its very presence in this place was impressive – it was probably the most northerly outpost of lesser Calvinism in the world. And apart from that, the sign over its door fulfilled several functions at once – shop name, geographical reference point and advertising concept:

NefteperegonievsCK

I couldn't help noticing a large children's playground crowded with structures that looked like the frameworks of tents – the children hanging on them, swaddled in warm clothing, were like fat little sloths. The playground reminded me of an ancient hunters' camping ground preserved amongst the snow. The entrance arch was painted with snowflakes, baby animals and red-nosed clowns, and above them there was a jolly inscription:

KUKIS-YUKIS-YUPSI-POOPS!

It was hard to understand what this was:

1) a nonsense rhyme intended to put the children in a good mood.
2) a list of sponsors.
3) a protest in Aesopian language (are we coming back to that so soon?) against the oppressive tyranny of the authorities.

Everything in Russian life had shifted around so much that it was hard to reach any final conclusion. And I didn't have the time: we didn't slow down anywhere and soon this tapestry of the north had dissolved in the white dust behind us. The snowy expanses of evening closed in on us from all sides.

'Put on my favourite,' Alexander said to the driver.

He looked sullen and intense, and I thought it best not to distract him by making conversation.

An old song by Shocking Blue came on:

> *I'll follow the sun*
> *That's what I'm gonna do,*
> *Trying to forget all about you . . .*

I couldn't help thinking that 'trying to forget all about you' referred to me – the female psyche does that sort of thing automatically without bothering to consult its owner. But I thought the oath to follow the sun, confirmed by the words 'that's what I'm gonna do', in the manner of the ancient Vikings, had a certain exalted beauty to it.

> I'll follow the sun
> Till the end of time
> No more pain and no more tears for me.

Naturally, when I heard the end of time mentioned, I recalled the caption under the picture of a wolf that I'd seen at Alexander's place:

FENRIR: Son of Loki, an immense wolf who pursues the sun across the sky. When Fenrir catches the sun and devours it, Ragnarek will begin.

That changed the picture somewhat . . . What a child he is after all, I thought with a tenderness that I was still not consciously aware of, what a funny little boy.

Soon it started getting dark. In the moonlight the landscape outside the car window had an unearthly look – it seemed strange that people should fly to other planets, when they had places like this right here beside them. The ground only a metre away from the invisible road might well never have been touched by the foot of man, or any foot or paw, come to that, and we would be the first . . .

When we reached our destination, it was already completely dark. Outside the car there were no buildings, no lights, no people, nothing – just the night, the snow, the moon and the stars. The only thing interrupting the monotony of the landscape was a nearby hill.

'Out we get,' said Alexander.

* * *

It was cold outside. I raised the collar of my padded jacket and tugged the fur cap further down over my ears. Nature had not designed me for life in these parts. What would I have done there, anyway? The reindeer herders don't seek amorous adventures among the snows, and even if they did, I doubt if I would be able to spread my tail in frost like that. It would probably freeze immediately and snap off, like an icicle.

The cars lined up so that their powerful headlights lit up the entire hill. Men began bustling about in the pool of light, unpacking the equipment they had brought with them – instruments of some kind that were a mystery to me. One man in the same kind of padded military jacket I was wearing, with a black bag in his hands, came up to Alexander and asked:

'Can I set it up?'

Alexander nodded.

'Let's go together,' he said, and turned towards me. 'And you come with us too. The view's beautiful from up there, you'll see.'

We set off towards the top of the hill.

'When did the pressure fall?' Alexander asked.

'Yesterday evening,' one of the officers replied.

'Have you tried pumping in water?'

The officer waved his hand dismissively, as if that wasn't even worth mentioning.

'How many times is it that the pressure's fallen in this well?'

'Five,' said the officer. 'That's it, we've squeezed it dry. The reservoir, and the whole of Russia.'

He swore quietly.

'We'll soon see about the whole of Russia,' said Alexander. 'And watch your tongue, we have a lady with us, after all.'

'Oh, a new member of the team?'

'Something of the sort.'

'That's good. We can't expect much from Mikhalich . . .'

We reached the top. I saw low buildings in the distance, pin-points of blue and yellow electric light, latticework metal structures, smoke or steam rising in some places. The moon lit up a labyrinth of pipes extending across the surface of the ground – some of them plunged into the snow, others stretched all the way to the horizon. But all this was too far away for me to make out any details. I didn't notice any people anywhere.

'Are they on the line?' Alexander asked.

'Yes,' the officer replied. 'If anything happens, they'll let us know. What are the chances?'

'We'll see,' said Alexander. 'What point is there in guessing? Let's get ready.'

The officer put his bag down on the snow and opened it. Inside there was a plastic case about the same size and shape as a large melon. Catches clicked, the melon opened and I saw a cow's skull that looked very old lying on red velvet. In some places it was cracked and held together by metal plates. The bottom of the skull was set in a metal frame.

The officer took a black cylinder out of the bag and opened it up to form something like one of those telescopic sticks for trekking. It had a round flange at one end. He took a swing and thrust the pointed end of the stick in the snow, then checked to make certain it was secure. It was, very. Then he picked up the skull, set its metal base over the flange on the end of the stick and connected them with a faint click.

'All set?' asked Alexander.

He hadn't been following the manipulations, he was watching the distant lights and the pipelines, like a general surveying the site of an imminent battle. The officer turned the empty eye sockets of the skull towards the oilfield. I couldn't understand what he was intending to film with this weird camera.

'Yes, sir.'

'Let's go,' said Alexander.

We walked down the hill towards the men waiting for us by the cars.

'Well then, Mikhalich,' said Alexander, 'why don't you go first? Give it a try. And I'll back you up if need be.'

'Straight away,' said Mikhalich. 'Just give me a couple of minutes, I'll just pop into the car to make sure I don't freeze my ass off.'

'You mean you can't manage at all without ketamine?'

'Whatever you say, comrade lieutenant general,' said Mikhalich. 'Only I'd like to do it according to my own system. And I've already switched to injecting into the muscle.'

'Well, do it your way then,' Alexander muttered in annoyance. 'Go on. We'll see. It's time you learned to walk without crutches, Mikhalich. Have faith in yourself! Let it all out! Wolf-flow! Wolf-flow! What will you do if your dealer gets banged up? Is the whole country going to pay the price?'

Mikhalich cleared his throat, but didn't say anything and walked round behind the cars. As he walked by, he winked at me. I pretended not to notice.

'One minute to go,' said a loud voice amplified by a megaphone. 'Everybody withdraw behind the perimeter.'

The cluster of men in the light of the headlights walked quickly away into the darkness behind the cars. The only one left standing with us was the officer who had helped Alexander install the skull on the hilltop. I didn't know if the command meant me as well and I looked enquiringly at Alexander.

'Have a seat,' he said, pointing to a folding chair nearby. 'Mikhalich is going to perform now. Just be sure not to laugh, he's sensitive. Especially when he's taken a shot.'

'I remember,' I said and sat down.

Alexander settled down on the chair next to mine and handed me a pair of field binoculars. The metal casing was searingly cold to the touch.

'Which way do I look?' I asked.

He nodded in the direction of the pole with the skull, which was clearly visible in the headlights.

'Fifteen . . .' said the megaphone behind the cars. 'Ten . . . Five . . . Start!'

For a few seconds nothing happened, then I heard a dull growl and a wolf appeared in the pool of light.

He was very different from the beast that Alexander changed into. So different, in fact, that he seemed to belong to a different biological species. He was smaller, with short legs, and entirely lacking in the dangerous charm of a deadly predator. The elongated barrel-shaped trunk of his body was too cumbersome for life in the natural wilderness, especially under conditions of natural selection. This corpulent body put me in mind of ancient outrages, of Christian martyrs and Roman emperors feeding their enemies to a wild beast. What he looked most like . . . Yes, most of all, he resembled a huge overfed dachshund with a wolf's skin transplanted on to it. I felt frightened I wouldn't be able to stop myself laughing. And that made everything seem even funnier. But fortunately I managed to restrain myself.

Mikhalich trudged up the hill and stopped beside the skull on the pole. He paused deliberately, then raised his face towards the moon and started howling, wagging his stiff tail like a conductor's baton.

I got the same feeling as I did when Alexander transformed: as if the wolf's body was a false appearance, or at best merely an empty resonator, like the body of a violin, and the mystery lay in the sound produced by an invisible string stretched between the tail and the face. The only real thing was this string and its appalling appassionato, everything else was an illusion . . . I felt my kinship with this creature: Mikhalich was doing something close to what foxes do, and his tail was helping him to do it in exactly the same way.

His howling roused a poignantly meaningful echo, first at the base of my own tail, and then in my conscious mind. There was meaning in the sound, and I understood it. But it was hard to express this meaning in human language – it resonated with such an immense number of words, that it wasn't clear which I should choose. Very approximately, and without any claims to accuracy, I would have expressed it as follows:

Brindled cow! Do you hear, brindled cow? It is I, the vile old wolf Mikhalich, I am whispering in your ear. Do you know why I am here, brindled cow? My life has become so dark and terrible that I have abandoned the Image of God and become a pseudo-wolf. And now I howl at the moon, the sky and the earth, at your skull and all that exists, so that the earth may take pity, open up and give me oil. You have no reason to pity me, I know. But even so, have pity on me, brindled cow. If you do not have pity on me, no one in the world will. And you, earth, look on me, shudder in horror and give me oil, for which I will receive a little money. Because to lose the Image of God, become a wolf and not have money is unbearable and unthinkable, and the Lord, whom I have denied, would not allow such a thing . . .

The call was full of a strange, enchanting power and sincerity. I felt no pity for Mikhalich, but his plaint sounded perfectly justified in terms of all the central concepts of Russian life. If I can put it that way, he was not demanding anything excessive from the world, everything was logical and well within the bounds of the modern metaphysical proprieties. But nothing happened to the skull, which I was watching through the binoculars.

Mikhalich howled for another ten minutes or so, in pretty much the same vein. Sometimes his howling was pitiful, sometimes menacing – I even felt a bit afraid. But then I didn't know what was supposed to happen, if anything – I was waiting for it, because Alexander had told me to watch the skull. But from the brief comments exchanged by Alexander and the officer, it was clear that Mikhalich had been unsuccessful.

Perhaps the reason for that was a certain unnatural, chemical tone in his howling. It wasn't noticeable at first, but the longer he howled, the more clearly I sensed it, and by the end of his performance it was so strong that I felt an unpleasant lump low down in my throat.

The howling broke off, I lowered the binoculars and saw there was no wolf on the hill any longer. Instead, there was Mikhalich, down on all fours. He was clearly visible in the headlights – right down to the last crease in his greatcoat. Despite the cold, his face was covered with large beads of sweat. He stood up and trudged down the hill.

'Well?' he asked when he reached us.

The officer held a walkie-talkie to his ear, listened for a while and lowered it again.

'No change,' he said.

'Because this is the fifth time we've worked this deposit already,' said Mikhalich. 'The second time round I always make it work. And the third time almost always. But the fifth . . . It's kind of hard to think of what to howl about.'

'Guys, we have to think of something,' the officer said, concerned. 'Almost all the wells in the sector are on their fourth cycle. If we don't get the fifth moving, then NATO will cut us in three pieces in two years, the maths are as simple as that. Any ideas, Alexander?'

Alexander got up off his chair.

'We'll soon find out,' he said. He stood there, looking at the skull through narrowed eyes and estimating the distance. Then he set off up the hill. Halfway to the skull he tossed the greatcoat off his shoulders and it fell in the snow with its arms outstretched.

'Like Pushkin walking to his last duel,' I thought, then looked at the greatcoat and thought: 'or like Dantes . . .'

The military uniform made the second seem more accurate. I suddenly understood that Pushkin was killed by a homonimic shadow of Dante – though the coincidence of names wasn't complete, it still looked eerie. As if one poet served another as a guide to the beyond again, I thought, this time with full board accommodation . . . But I had no time to reflect on this insight properly before Alexander reached the pole.

He cautiously set his hands on the skull and turned it through a hundred and eighty degrees so that it was staring directly at me – through the binoculars I could clearly see empty eye sockets and a metal cleat holding together a crack above one of them.

Alexander started down the hill. When he reached his greatcoat he stopped, raised his face to the sky and howled.

He started to howl when he was still a man, but the howling transformed him into a wolf faster than amorous arousal. He arched in a bow and tumbled over on to his back. The transformation occurred so rapidly that he was almost completely a wolf when his back touched the greatcoat. Without stopping its howling even for a second, the wolf floundered in the snow for a few moments, raising a white cloud all around itself, and then got up on to its legs.

After the barrel-shaped, flabby Mikhalich, it was particularly striking just how handsome Alexander was. He was a noble and terrible beast, one that the northern gods might really be afraid of. But his howling wasn't fearsome, like Mikhalich's. It sounded quieter and seemed sad, rather than menacing:

Brindled cow! Do you hear, brindled cow? I know I must have lost all sense of shame to ask you for oil yet again. I do not ask for it. We do not deserve it. I know what you think of us – no matter how much you give them, Little Khavroshka won't get a single drop, it will all be gobbled up by all these kukis-yukises, yupsi-poopses and the other locusts who obscure the very light of day. You are right, brindled cow, that is how it will be. Only, let me tell you something . . . I know who you are. You are everyone who lived here before us. Parents, grandparents, great-grandparents, and before that, and before that . . . You are the soul of all those who died believing in the happiness that would come in the future. And now see, it has come. The future in which people do not live for something else, but for themselves. And do you know how we feel swallowing sashimi that smell of oil and pretending not to notice the final ice-floes melting under our feet? Pretending this is the destination towards which the people have striven for a thousand years, ending with us? It turns out that in reality only you have lived, brindled cow. You had someone to live for, but we do not . . . You had us, but we have nobody apart from ourselves. But now you feel as miserable as we do, because you can no longer grow apples for your Little Khavroshka. You can only give oil to ignominious wolves, so that kukis-yukis-yupsi-poops can shell out to its lawyer and the lawyer can give the head of security a kick-back, the head of security can grease his hairdresser's palm, the hairdresser can grease the cook's, the cook can grease the driver's, and the driver can hire your Little Khavroshka for an hour for a hundred and fifty bucks . . . And when your Little Khavroshka sleeps off the anal sex and pays off all her cops and bandits, maybe she'll have enough left over for the apple that you wanted so much to become for her, brindled cow . . .

I felt as if the cow was looking at me with its empty eye sockets. And then, through the binoculars, I saw a tear well up on the edge of one of those sockets. It ran down across the skull and fell off into the snow, and then a second one appeared, and then a third . . .

Alexander carried on howling, but I couldn't make out the

meaning any more. Perhaps there no longer was any – the howling had turned into weeping. I started to weep too. We were all weeping . . . And then I realized we were howling rather than weeping – Mikhalich, the officer who had set up the pole on the hill, the men in the darkness behind the cars – we were all howling, with our faces turned to the moon, howling and weeping for ourselves and for our impossible country, for our pitiful life, stupid death and sacred hundred dollars a barrel . . .

'Hey,' I heard someone say, 'wake up!'

'Ah?'

I opened my eyes. Alexander and the officer were standing beside my chair.

'That's it,' said the officer. 'The oil's flowing.'

'How you howled!' said Alexander. 'We were simply spellbound.'

'Yes,' said Mikhalich, 'the girl came in useful all right. I didn't understand why you brought her at first, comrade lieutenant general.'

Alexander didn't answer – one of the men who had stood behind the cars during the performance had come up to him. He was dressed in a military uniform without any badges of rank – just like all the others.

'This is for you,' he said and handed Alexander a little box. 'The medal for Services to the Motherland. I know you have a lot of these things. We just want you to remember how highly the country values you.'

'Thank you,' Alexander said indifferently, putting the little box in his pocket. 'Glad to serve.'

He took me by the arm and led me towards the car. When we'd moved away from the others, I whispered:

'Tell me honestly, wolf to fox. Or if you prefer, were-creature to were-creature. Do you really think kukis-yukis is to blame for Little Khavroshka not getting an apple, and not that rotten fish-

220

head that sometimes pretends to be a bull and sometimes a bear?'

He was flabbergasted.

'What kukis? What fish-head?'

It was only then I realized just how crazy what I'd just said sounded. Yes, it was stress – I'd stopped feeling the difference between the world and what I was thinking about it. Alexander hadn't actually said anything – he had simply howled at the cow's skull, and all the rest had been my personal interpretation.

'And you threw in a bear too,' he muttered.

Yes, indeed, it was really stupid of me. I hadn't even discussed the bear and the fish-head with him.

'It's the fairy tales that did it,' I said guiltily. 'The ones I was reading in the plane.'

'Ah. That explains it.'

However, there was one question I could ask without being afraid it would sound crazy. This time I gauged the impression my words might make in advance, before I opened my mouth:

'You know, I have the feeling that you showed me to the skull as Little Khavroshka. Am I right?'

He laughed.

'And why not? You're so touching.'

'Take a good look at me,' I said. 'What sort of Little Khavroshka am I?'

'You could be Mary Magdalene,' he said. 'What difference does it make? It's my job to get the oil flowing. And for that, the skull has to cry. What's to be done if it doesn't cry for Mikhalich any longer, even when he injects five cc's of ketamine?'

'But then it . . . It was a lie,' I said, bewildered.

He chortled.

'So you think art should be the truth?'

The only answer I gave was to blink several times. The absurd thing was that I really did think that. Suddenly I could no longer tell which of us really was the cynical manipulator of other minds.

'You know what,' he said, 'you try selling that concept to the Saatchi gallery. Maybe they'll put it on show beside the pickled shark. Or maybe Brian will buy it. The guy who offered me a thousand pounds.'

* * *

Alas, Brian couldn't buy anything any longer . . . But then, that commonplace about someone who is dead is outmoded nowadays. Sometimes a client dies and his brokers carry on playing the stock market. And when the sad news finally reaches them, a computer program everyone has forgotten about carries speculating for a long time in cyberspace, buying and selling the pound and the yen when they reach the threshold levels . . . But Brian probably really couldn't buy anything from me. And certainly not the idea that art should be the truth.

Moscow greeted me with the sad news. The article on the rumours.ru site, whose address had mysteriously written itself back into my home page, had the following headline:

ENGLISH ARISTOCRAT FOUND DEAD
IN CATHEDRAL OF CHRIST THE SAVIOUR

A feeling rather like nausea prevented me from reading the entire article – I only had the strength to run my eyes over it diagonally, picking out the substance from under the journalistic clichés: 'the grimace of inexpressible terror frozen on his face', 'the tears of the inconsolable widow', 'the representatives of the embassy', 'investigation of the circumstances'. I wasn't concerned about what would happen to E Hu-Li – this was all business as usual for her. The investigators of the circumstances were the ones to be concerned about – in case that grimace of inexpressible terror froze on one of their faces too.

I should have felt sorry for Lord Cricket though. I concentrated, but for some reason instead of his face, all I could recall was documentary footage of a fox hunt – a little bundle of red-brown fur dashing across a field, totally defenceless, quaking in horror and hope, and riders in their elegant caps in pursuit . . . But I recited the requiem mantra anyway.

The next thing that caught my eye was a column heading:

SICK PREDATOR TAKES REFUGE
IN BITSEVSKY PARK

This magnum opus contained one incredibly impudent paragraph that concerned me personally:

> The fox, covered with numerous bald spots or, more precisely, still covered with fur in places, inspired in those who witnessed the incident not only an intense feeling of pity, but also the suspicion that there was a radioactive waste dump somewhere nearby. Perhaps the old, sick animal had come to people, hoping for the coup de grace that would put an end to its suffering. But one cannot expect even that kind of favour for free from the hardhearted Muscovites of today. Two mounted militiaman set off in pursuit of the sick animal, but how the chase ended remains unknown.

What a filthy liar, I thought, it's obvious that none of the witnesses said anything about a radioactive waste dump, and he made it all up himself, just to have something to fill up his column. But then the Internet columnists write about everything in the same vile way – about politics, culture, and even the conquest of Mars. And this time about foxes. This particular rumour-monger had a special trick of his own. When he wanted to cover someone in shit from head to foot, he always mentioned an intense feeling of compassion. I had always been amazed by this ability to take the most exalted of all human feelings, and turn it into a poisonous barb.

But then, if you just thought about it, there was nothing surprising about that. What was an Internet columnist, after all? A creature somewhat more advanced than a prison-camp guard dog, but very, very inferior to a were-fox.

1) the similarity between an Internet columnist and a prison-camp guard dog consists in the ability to bark into a strictly defined sector of space.
2) the difference is that a guard dog cannot guess for itself which is the correct sector to bark into, but an Internet columnist is often capable of this.
3) the similarity between an Internet columnist and a were-fox is that both try to create mirages that human beings take for reality.
4) the difference is that a fox is able to do this, but an Internet columnist isn't.

The last point is hardly surprising. Would anyone who was able to create plausible mirages work as an Internet columnist? Unlikely. An Internet columnist can't even convince himself that his inventions are real, I thought, clenching my fists, let alone other people. That's why he ought to sit quietly and only bark when . . .

Then I forgot about Internet columnists and prison-camp guard dogs, as the light of truth suddenly flashed in my head.

'Convince himself that his inventions are real,' I repeated. 'That's it. Why, of course!'

Quite unexpectedly for myself I had solved the riddle that had been tormenting me for ages. My mind had been creeping up on it for many days, first from one side, then from the other – and all in vain. But now something turned and clicked, and everything suddenly fell into place – as if I'd put a jigsaw together by chance.

I realized how we foxes differ from werewolves. As is often the case, this difference was no more than a mutated similarity. Foxes and wolves were closely related – their magic was based on the manipulation of perception. But the means of manipulation were different.

A brief theoretical digression is required here, or else I'm afraid what I say will be incomprehensible.

People often argue about whether this world really exists, or is something like *The Matrix* movie. It's a very stupid thing to argue about. All problems of this kind derive from the fact that people don't understand the words they use. Before discussing this subject, the first thing people ought to do is get to grips with the meaning of the word 'exist'. Then a lot of interesting things would become clear. But people are rarely capable of correct thinking.

Of course, I don't mean to say that all people are total idiots. There are some among them whose intellect is almost the equal of a fox's. For instance, the Irish philosopher Berkeley. He said that to exist means to be perceived and all objects exist only in perception. You only have to think calmly about the subject for three minutes to realize that any other views on the matter are like the cult of Osiris or belief in the god Mithras. In my view, this is the only true thought that has visited the Western mind in its long and funny history: all the Humes, Kants and Baudrillards are only embroidering the canvas of this great insight in a fussy satin stitch.

But where does an object exist when we turn away and stop seeing it? After all, it doesn't disappear, as children and Amazonian Indians think, does it? Berkeley says that it exists in the perception of God. But Cathars and Gnostics believe that it exists in the perception of the diabolical demiurge, and their arguments are no worse than Berkeley's. From their point of view, matter is an evil that shackles the spirit. By the way, reading Stephen Hawking's horror stories, I often used to think that if the Albigenses had had a radio telescope, they would have declared the Big Bang a cosmic photograph of Satan's rebellion . . . There is a middle way through this morass of idiocy – to believe that part of the world exists in the perception of God, and part in the perception of the Devil.

What can I say to this? From the point of view of us foxes, there never was any Big Bang, just as the Tower of Babel that Breughel painted never existed, even if there is a reproduction of the painting hanging in a room that you dream about. And God and the Devil are simply reproductions that are dreamed by some people to hang in a room of the tower on the picture hanging on the wall in a room they dream about. Berkeley assumed that perception has to have a subject, and so the coins that rolled under the cupboard and the socks that fell behind the bed were solemnly interred in the cranium of a Creator specially created for that purpose. But how do we deal with the fact that Berkeley's God, in whose perception we exist, Himself exists mostly in the abstract thinking of certain representatives of the endangered European race? And he doesn't exist at all in the consciousness of a Chinese peasant or a little bird which is unaware that it is God's? How do we deal with this if 'to exist' really does mean 'to be perceived'?

We don't, say the foxes. Foxes have a fundamental answer to the fundamental question of philosophy, which is to forget this fundamental question. There are no philosophical problems, there is only a suite of interconnected linguistic cul de sacs created by language's inability to reflect the truth.

But it is better to run into one of these cul de sacs in the first paragraph, rather than after forty years of searching and five thousand pages of writing. After Berkeley finally got the point, the only thing he wrote about was the wonder-working properties of the tincture of bitumen that he'd come across in North America. And as a result, ever since then he has been mocked by various philistines, who aren't aware that in that distant time bitumen was produced in America from a plant called Jimson Weed, or Datura.

Religious hypocrites accuse us were-creatures of addling people's brains and distorting the Image of God. The people who say this have a rather poor idea of the Image of God, since they mould it after their own sanctimonious mugs. In any case, talk of 'distortion' and 'addling' is too judgemental; language like that shifts the question on to the emotional plane and prevents any understanding of the real nature of the matter, which is as follows (please pay close attention to the following paragraph – I have finally reached the most important point).

Since the existence of things consists in their perceptibility, any transformation can occur by two routes – either through the perception of transformation or the transformation of perception.

In honour of the great Irishman, I would like to call this rule Berkeley's Law. It is absolutely essential knowledge for all seekers of truth, gangsters and extortionists, marketing specialists and paedophiles who wish to remain at liberty. And so, in their practice, foxes and wolves exploit different aspects of Berkeley's Law.

We, the foxes, use *transformation of perception*. We influence our clients' perception and make them see what we want them to see. The illusion we induce becomes absolutely real for them – the scars on the unforgettable Pavel Ivanovich's back are the best possible proof of that. But we foxes continue to see the initial reality just as, according to Berkeley, God sees it. That is why we are accused of distorting the Image of God.

This, of course, is a hypocritical accusation, based on a double standard. The transformation of perception is the basis not only of foxes' witchcraft, but also of many marketing techniques. For instance, Ford takes the cheap F-150 pick-up truck, gives it a lovely new front grille, restyles the bodywork and calls the resultant product the 'Lincoln Navigator'. And no one says that Ford is distorting the Image of God. I won't say anything about politics, everything's clear already in that area. But somehow it's only we foxes who provoke indignation.

Unlike us, werewolves use *perception of transformation*. They create an illusion, not for others, but for themselves. And they believe in it so strongly that the illusion ceases to be an illusion. There's a passage in the Bible on that subject – 'if you have faith as a mustard seed, you shall say to this mountain, "Move from here to there, and it shall move; and nothing shall be impossible to you."' The werewolves have this mustard seed. Their transformation is a kind of alchemical chain reaction.

First a werewolf makes himself believe that his tail is growing. And the emerging tail, which in wolves is the same kind of hypnotic organ as it is in foxes, exerts a hypnotic influence on the wolf's own consciousness, convincing him that he really is undergoing transformation and so on until he is completely transformed into a beast. Technologists call this positive feedback.

Alexander's transformation always began in the same way: his body curved over, as if some invisible cable joining his tail and his cranium were being drawn taut. Now I'd realized what was happening. While foxes directed energy at other people, wolves trained it on themselves, inducing a transformation, not in others' perception, but in their own, and only afterwards, as a consequence, in that of others.

Can we call such a transformation real? I have never completely understood the meaning of this epithet, especially since every historical age fills it with its own meaning. For instance, in modern Russian the word 'real' is employed in four basic ways:

1) as a battle cry uttered by bandits and FSB agents during the ritual change-over of the *roof*, or protection provider.
2) a jargon term used by the *upper rat* and *oligarchy* in conversations about their offshore accounts.
3) a technical term applied to immovable property.
4) a widely used adjective with the meaning 'having a dollar equivalent'.

The latter meaning makes the term 'real' a synonym for the word 'metaphysical', since nowadays the dollar is an occult, mystical unit based entirely on the belief that tomorrow will be like today. And mysticism is something that should be practised not by were-creatures, but by those who are professionally obliged to do it – the PR consultants, political technologists and economists. That is why I did not wish to call the werewolf's transformation 'real' – if I did, it might give the impression that it involves cheap human black magic. But two things were undoubtedly true:

1) a wolf's transformation was qualitatively different from a fox's illusion, although it was based on the same effect.
2) the lupine metamorphosis consumed an immense amount of energy – far more than we foxes expended on a client.

That was why wolves could not remain in their bestial body for long, and folklore linked their transformation with various forms of temporal limitation – the hours of darkness, the full moon or something of that kind.

I remembered the strange sensation I had experienced while hunting – when for the first time in my life I became aware of the relict radiation from my tail, directed at myself. But exactly what suggestion had I been implanting in my own mind? That I was a fox? But I knew that without any suggestion . . . What was going on? I felt as if I were standing on the threshold of something important, something that could change my entire life and lead me, at long last, out of the spiritual impasse in which I had spent the last five hundred years. But, to my disgrace, the first thing that I thought about was not spiritual practice at all.

I'm ashamed to admit it, but the first thought that came into my mind was about sex. I remembered Alexander's coarse grey tail and realized how to raise our erotic sensations to a totally new level. It was all very simple. The mechanisms for influencing consciousness employed by foxes and wolves were identical in all major respects – the only elements that differed were the intensity of suggestion and its target. I, so to speak, served my client champagne and it made him tipsy. Alexander swallowed an entire bottle of vodka all on his own, which made everyone else around horrified. But the effective substance, alcohol, was the same.

And so, by combining our resources, we could mix lots of very different cocktails out of champagne and vodka. After all, sex is more than just the simple conjunction of certain parts of the body. It is also a connection between the energies of two beings, a joint trip. If we could learn to combine our hypnotic impulses in order to immerse ourselves in an amorous illusion together, I thought, we could set ourselves up with our own *tea for two*, in which every drop would be worth its weight in polonium.

There was only one problem. First we had to agree on what we wanted to see. And not just in words – words were an unreliable prop. If we relied only on them, we could imagine the final destination of our journey very differently. Some ready-made image was required, one that would serve as the starting point for our visualization. For instance, a picture . . .

I tried to imagine an appropriate classical canvas. But unfortunately, nothing interesting came to mind – all I could recall was Picasso's early masterpiece *An Old Jew and a Boy*. Many years earlier I had used a postcard of that picture as a bookmark in Freud's *Psychopathology of Everyday Life*, which I simply couldn't get through, and ever since then I had remembered every detail of those two sad, dark figures.

No, pictures were no good. They didn't give any idea of how an object appeared in the round. Videos would be much better. And Alexander has such a big television, I thought. Surely it ought to be put to good use?

* * *

There's a kind of chewing gum that comes with cards showing pairs of loving couples in various humorous situations. These drawings are captioned 'Love is . . .' and I often used to see them stuck to the walls in lifts and cinemas. If I wanted to draw my own version of these cartoons, it would show a wolf and a fox sitting in front of a TV with their tails intertwined.

The technology of a miracle proved to be simpler than I was expecting. It was enough to bring our hypnotic organs together in any pose that allowed us to do it. Only our tails had to touch: we had to follow what was happening on the screen, and any closer proximity was a hindrance.

It developed into a ritual surprisingly quickly. Usually he would lie down on his side, with his legs hanging down on to the carpet, and I would sit down beside him. We set the film going and I caressed him until the transformation began. Then I put my legs up on his shaggy side, we joined our antennas together, and what began then was totally insane, something that no tail-less creature could ever understand. Sometimes the feelings were so intense that I had to apply a special technique to calm myself and cool off – I looked away from the screen and recited part of the 'Heart Sutra' to myself, a mantra as cool and deep as a well: I could dissolve any emotional upheaval in those Sanskrit syllables. I liked to look at the way our tails combined – the red and the grey. As if someone had set fire to a rotten billet and it had been engulfed by dancing flames and sparks . . . But I never shared this simile with Alexander.

However, while the technical aspect of the whole thing proved to be elementary, the choice of a route for our outings always involved arguments. Our tastes didn't just differ, they belonged to different universes. In his case it was hard even to speak of taste in the sense of a definite system of aesthetic guidelines. Like a schoolboy, he liked everything to be heroic and sentimental, and he made me sit for hours watching samurai dramas, westerns and something that I simply couldn't stand – Japanese cartoons about robots. And then in our dream we played out the secondary love themes that the directors had had to use to provide at least some respite between the killing and the fighting. Actually, at first it was quite interesting. But only at first.

As an experienced professional, I soon wearied of the standard quickies – I had induced more dreams on that subject than mankind had made porn films about itself. I liked to roam through the terra incognita of modern sexuality, to explore its border regions, the backyard of social morality and mores. But he wasn't ready for that, and although no one in the world could have witnessed our joint hallucinations, he was always stopped dead by his internal sentry.

He would either respond to my appeals to embark on some unusual journey with an embarrassed refusal or he would suggest something that was unthinkable for me. For instance, to turn ourselves into a pair of cartoon transformers who discover their attraction to each other on the roof of a Tokyo skyscraper . . . How dreadful! But when I wanted to become the German major in *Casablanca* and take him from behind while he was the black pianist Sam playing it again, he was as horrified as if I'd been urging him to sell out the motherland.

That would have been another interesting topic for Dr

Spengler: most Russian men are homophobic because the cancerous cells of the criminal code of honour are still deeply embedded in the Russian psyche. Any serious man, no matter what he does for a living, subconsciously measures himself against a prison bunk and tries to ensure that his service record doesn't include any conspicuous violations of prison taboos that he might have to pay for with his arse in a very direct manner. This means that a Russian macho man's life is like a permanent spiritualist seance: while the body is wallowing in luxury, the soul is doing time in the prison camps.

I happen to know why this is the way things are, and I could write a big, thick, clever book about it. Its basic idea would be as follows: Russia is a communal country, and when the Christian peasant commune was destroyed, the criminal commune became the source of the people's morality. The proprieties of the underworld occupied the place where God used to live – or, to put it more correctly, God Himself was incorporated into the notional rules as a top criminal authority. And when the final religious prosthesis, the Soviet 'internal Party committee' was dismantled, a cheap guitar tuned for prison songs set the musical range of the Russian soul.

But no matter how sickening prison morality may be, there is no other morality left at all, only the simulacra produced either by FSB prison guards or *sprintii* journalists specializing in the propaganda of liberal values . . .

Oh. I deliberately won't cross out that last sentence, let the reader admire it. There you have it, the vulpine mind. After all, we were-foxes are natural liberals, in pretty much the same way as the soul is a natural Christian. And what do I write? *What do I write?* It's terrifying. At least it's clear where it all came from – I got the stuff about the sprintii journalists from the FSB prison guards. And the stuff about the FSB prison guards from the sprintii journalists. There's nothing to be done: if a fox has heard an opinion, she is bound to express it in the first person. We can't help it. We don't have any opinions of our own on these human-related subjects (that's the last thing we need), but we have to live among people. So we just return the serves. Yes, it's a good thing I don't have to write a book about Russia after all. What sort of Solzhenitsyn would I make? But I am digressing again.

I didn't often discuss the nature of Alexander's homophobia with him (he didn't like to talk about it), but I was sure its roots had to be sought in the criminal catacombs of the Russian mind. His homophobia went so far that he rejected anything that was even remotely gay.

'Why do you dislike gays so much?' I asked him once.

'Because they go against nature.'

'But it was nature that created them. So how do they go against nature?'

'I'll tell you how,' he said. 'Children are hidden in sex, like the seeds in a watermelon. And gays are people fighting for the right to eat a watermelon without seeds.'

'Who are they fighting against?'

'The watermelon. Everybody else stopped caring a damn long since. But a watermelon can't exist without seeds. And that's why I say they go against nature. Will you say they don't?'

'A certain watermelon I used to know,' I replied, 'believed that the propagation of watermelons depends on their ability to implant in man's mind the suggestion that it's healthy to swallow the seeds. But watermelons overestimate their own hypnotic abilities. In actual fact the propagation of watermelons takes place through a process of which the watermelons are com-pletely unaware, because they are unable to observe it. Because this process only begins where the watermelon ends.'

'There you go tying those fancy knots again, Ginger, I can't follow,' he grumbled. 'Save it. Let's do without all this tricky queer stuff.'

Alexander particularly disliked Luchino Visconti. Any suggestion to put on something by this director (whom I consider one of the greatest masters of the twentieth century) was taken by him as a personal insult. I still have fragments of one of our arguments on tape. While the other dialogues in my journal are reproduced from memory, this one is absolutely accurate – the conversation was accidentally recorded on a dictaphone. I include it here because I would like to hear Alexander's voice again – I can listen to it while I type.

AS: *Death in Venice.* This is getting tiresome, Ginger. What do you think I am, some kind of queer?
AH: Then how about *Conversation Piece?*
AS: No, let's have Takeshi Kitano. Zatoichi punishes the geisha-assassin . . . And then the geisha-assassin punishes Zatoichi.
AH: I don't want that. Let's try *Gone with the Wind* again.
AS: Come off it. That staircase is too long.
AH: What staircase?
AS: The one I have to cart you up to the bedroom. And to add to the agony you make it five times longer. I was soaked in sweat last time. Seriously. Even though we never got up off the divan . . .
AH: I have to be spoiled sometimes . . . Okay, this time we'll have a short staircase. All right?
AS: No, let's . . . I fancy something with shooting.
AH: Then let's have *Mulholland Drive!* There's shooting in that. Oh, please!
AS: Back to the same old thing. I won't do it, how many times do I have to tell you? Find yourself a queer out on the avenue and watch it with him.
AH: What's that got to do with it? It's lesbians in the film.
AS: What's the difference?
(Here there is a pause in the recording, during which you can hear rustling and tapping as I rummage through the video discs scattered on the floor.)

235

AH: Listen, there's a film from one of Steven King's books. *Dreamcatcher*. Have you seen it?

AS: No.

AH: Let's try it. We won't be people, we'll be aliens.

AS: What kind of aliens are they?

AH: They have a vertical mouth full of teeth running the entire length of their bodies and eyes on their sides. Imagine how bloody a kiss could be? And cunnilingus at the same time. I think that's the way they reproduce.

AS: Darling, I get to see enough stuff like that at work. Let's have something more romantic.

AH: Romantic . . . Romantic . . . Here's *The Matrix-2*. How would you like to screw Keanu Reaves?

AS: Not a lot.

AH: Then I can screw him.

AS: Rejected. Is the third *Matrix* there?

AH: Yes.

AS: There could be an interesting possibility there with those machines.

AH: Which ones?

AS: You know, those humanoid robots with people sitting in them. They use them to fight off those black octopuses. Just imagine it, one of those robots has caught a black octopus, and . . .

AH: Listen, how old are you, twelve?

AS: Okay, let's forget *The Matrix*.

(Some kind of rustling again. I think I move on to another heap of DVDs.)

AH: How about *Lord of the Rings*?

AS: You'll only come up with something weird again.

AH: Well I'm not going to spread my legs for a hobbit, that's for sure. How come you're so afraid of everything? Do you think they'll find out at work? Your moral character?

AS: Why do think I'm afraid? I don't want to, that's all.

AH: Listen, there are some films in English here. An interesting selection.

AS: What have you got?

AH: *Midnight Dancers* . . . *Sex Life in LA* . . .

AS: No.

AH: *Versace Murder*?

AS: No.

AH: Why?

AS: Because.

AH: Do you know what the gays in Miami say instead of 'vice versa'? 'Vice Versace'. Just think of all those dark, convoluted meanings . . .

AS: First one of them shafts another up the backside, and then they swap places. That's all your convoluted meanings.

AH: I'll put it on then?

AS: I already told you. Go to the that cafe at Tverskaya, Gifts of the Sea or whatever they call it, find yourself a queer and have your fun.

AH: Listen, stop being such a reactionary. There are homosexual animals in wild nature, I've read about them. Sheep. Monkeys.

AS: As far as monkeys are concerned, I hardly think that's an argument in favour of gays.

AH: Oh you've been well trained. No reforming you. What's that disc you've got there?

AS: *Romeo and Juliet.*

(You can hear me snort contemptuously.)

AH: Bin it.

AS: Can't we watch it just once more?

AH: How many times?

AS: Just one last little time. Come on! You're a dead ringer for Juliet in that T-shirt.

AH: What can I do with you, Romeo? Go on. Only on one condition.

AS: What's that?

AH: Afterwards it's *Mulholland Drive.*

AS: Gr-r-r!

AH: Darling, really? So soon?

AS: Gr-r-r!

AH: Hang on, hang on. I'm putting it on. I'll know this off by heart soon . . . 'From ancient grudge break to new mutiny, where civil blood makes civil hands unclean . . .'

AS: Whoo-oo-oo!

AH: I'm not criticizing your organization, you beast. Relax. That's Shakespeare.

* * *

Love and tragedy go hand in hand. Homer and Euripides wrote about that, so did Stendhal and Oscar Wilde. And now it's my turn.

Until I learned from my own experience what love is, I thought of it as a specific kind of pleasure that tailless monkeys can derive from being together, in addition to sex.

I formed this impression from the numerous descriptions I had come across in poems and books. How was I to know that the writers were not describing love as it actually is at all, but constructing the verbal imitations that would look best on paper. I thought of myself as a professional of love, since I had been inducing the experience in others for so many centuries. But it's one thing to pilot the B-29 flying towards Hiroshima, and quite another to watch it from the central square of the city.

Love turned out to be nothing like what they write about it. It was ludicrous, rather than serious – but that didn't mean it could be dismissed out of hand. It was not like being drunk (the most popular comparison in literature) – but it was even less like being sober. My perception of the world didn't change: I didn't think Alexander was anything like a fairy-tale prince in his Maibach. I could see all the sinister sides of his character but, strangely enough, those things only added to his charm in my eyes. My reason even came to terms with his barbarous political views and began to discover a certain harsh northern originality in them.

Love was absolutely devoid of any meaning. But it gave meaning to everything else. It made my heart as light and empty as a balloon. I didn't understand what was happening to me. But not because I had become more stupid – there simply was nothing to understand in what was happening. They may say that love like that doesn't run deep. But I think that anything that is deep isn't love, it's deliberate calculation or schizophrenia.

I myself wouldn't even attempt to say what love is – probably both love and God can only be defined by apophasis, through those things that they are not. But apophasis would be wrong, too, because they are everything. Writers who write about love are swindlers, and the worst of them is Leo Tolstoy, clutching his programmatic bludgeon 'The Kreutzer Sonata'. Although I have a lot of respect for Tolstoy.

How could I have known that our romantic adventure would prove disastrous for Alexander? Oscar Wilde said: 'Yet each man kills the thing he loves . . .' He was a writer who lived in an era of primitive anthropocentrism, hence the word 'man' (sexism was also easy to get away with then, especially for gays). But in everything else, he was spot on. I killed the beast, the Thing. Beauty killed the beast. And the murder weapon was love.

I remember how that day began. After I woke up, I lay on my back for a long time while I surfaced from the depths of a very good dream that I couldn't remember no matter how I tried. I knew that in cases like that the thing to do was to lie without moving or opening your eyes, in the same position you woke up in, and then the dream might surface in your memory. And that was what happened – after about a minute, I remembered.

I had been dreaming of a fantastic garden, flooded with sunlight and filled with the chatter of birds. In the distance I could see a strip of white sand and the sea. Immediately in front of me there was a sheer cliff, and in the cliff there was a cave, sealed off with a slab of stone. I was supposed to move the slab, but it was too heavy, and there was no way I could possibly do it. Summoning up all my strength, I braced my feet against the ground and strained every muscle in my body as I pushed on the slab. It fell away to one side and the black hole of the entrance was revealed, belching out damp air and an old, stale stench. And then, rising up out of the darkness towards the sunny day, chickens appeared – one, two, three . . . I lost count, there were so many of them. They just kept on walking towards the light and happiness, and now nothing could stop them – they'd realized where the way out was. I saw my chicken among them – the brown one with the white patch, and I waved my paw to her (in the dream I had paws instead of hands, like during the supraphysical transformation). She didn't even look at me, just ran straight past. But I wasn't offended at all.

What an amazing dream, I thought, and opened my eyes.

There was a little patch of sunlight trembling on the wall. It was my own virtual place in the sun, acquired without any struggle at all – it was produced by a little mirror that cast the ray of light falling from above against the wall. I thought about Alexander and remembered our love. It was as certain as that yellow patch of sunlight quivering on the wall. Something incredible had to happen between us today, something truly miraculous. Without even thinking what I was going to say to him, I reached for the phone.

'Hello,' he said.

'Hello. I want to see you.'

'Come on over,' he said. 'But there's not much time. I'm flying north this evening. That only leaves us three hours.'

'That's enough for me,' I said.

The taxi drove me slowly, the traffic lights took an eternity to change, and at every crossroads I felt my heart would leap out of my chest if I had to wait just a few more seconds.

When I got out of the lift he removed the gauze mask from his face and took a deep sniff.

'I'll probably never get used to the way you smell. It seems like I remember it, and yet every time it turns out the memory in my head is nothing like it. I'll have to pull a few hairs out of your tail.'

'What for?' I asked.

'Well . . . I'll wear them in a locket on my chest,' he said. 'Take them out sometimes and smell them. Like a medieval knight.'

I smiled – his ideas about medieval knights were clearly derived from jokes. Perhaps that was the reason they were fairly close to the truth. Of course, the hairs that medieval knights carried in their medallions didn't come from tails – who would have given them those? – but by and large the picture was accurate enough.

I noticed an unfamiliar object beside the divan – a floor-lamp in the shape of an immense Martini glass. It was a cone studded with light bulbs, set on a tall, thin leg.

'That's a really lovely thing. Where did it come from?'

'It's a gift from the reindeer-herders,' he said.

'The reindeer-herders?' I said, amazed.

'Or rather, the reindeer-herders' leadership. Some funny guys from London. Good, isn't it? Like a dragonfly's eye.'

I wanted so badly to throw myself on him and hug him really tight that I could hardly keep still. I was afraid – if I took another step towards him there would be a shower of sparks between us.

He clearly felt something too.

'You're kind of strange today. Haven't been dropping anything, have you? Or sniffing anything?'

'Afraid?' I asked, glowering at him.

'Ha,' he said. 'I've seen more frightening things.'

I started walking round him slowly. He chuckled and set off in the opposite direction round the same circle, without taking his eyes off me, as if we were a pair of fencers from one of the Japanese action movies that he liked watching so much in his lupine form, clutching on to me with his shaggy grey tail hooked over. Then we both stopped at the same moment. I took a step towards him, put my hands on his shoulder straps, pulled him towards me and, for the first time in our relationship I kissed him on the lips – the way that people kiss.

I'd never kissed anyone like that before. I mean physically, using my mouth. It was a strange feeling – wet, warm, with a gentle knocking of teeth against teeth. I put all my love into my first kiss. And a second later the transformation began.

At first everything looked exactly as usual – Alexander's tail extended (or rather, tumbled) out of his spine, curled over, and an invisible thread of energy stretched between it and his head. After that he usually became a wolf in just a few moments. But this time something went wrong.

He jerked convulsively and fell on his back, as if his tail had suddenly become so heavy that it had pulled him over. Then he began rapidly jerking his arms and legs about in a horrible way (like people with craniocerebral injuries do), and in a few seconds he was transformed into a perfectly ordinary mongrel from the street or the local rubbish tip – a *dog*.

Yes, a dog. He was as big as an Alsatian, but clearly a mongrel. His plebeian proportions betrayed a mixture of numerous different breeds, and his eyes were clear and almost human in their anger, like the eyes of some wandering dogs who sleep in the entrances of the Metro with the homeless tramps. And this dog was blue-black, in fact purple-black, exactly like Aslan Udoev's beard.

Maybe it was the colour, maybe it was the pointed ears that seemed to be straining after some distant sound but I thought I sensed something diabolical about this dog: thoughts came into my head about crows and gallows, about demonic possession . . . I realize that when a creature like me says 'thoughts came to me about demonic possession' it sounds rather strange, but what can I do about it, if that's the way it was. But the most macabre thing was the groan of horror that I either imagined or really did hear from every side – as if the earth itself had groaned.

I was so frightened that I started squealing. He jumped away from me, turned towards the mirror, saw, shuddered and started whimpering. Only then did I recover my wits. At that point I'd already realized that something terrible had happened to him, some kind of catastrophe, and it was my fault. The catastrophe had been caused by my kiss, by that electrical circuit of love that I had closed when I pressed my lips against his mouth.

I squatted down beside him and put my arms round his neck. But he tore himself away, and when I tried to hold him back, he bit me on the hand. Not really hard, but it started to bleed in two places. I gasped and jerked away. He dashed to the door into the other room, slammed his paws against it and disappeared inside.

He didn't come out for an entire hour. I realized that he wanted to be left alone and I didn't intrude on his solitude. I was terrified, afraid that any moment I would hear a shot (he had once promised to shoot himself for an absolutely trivial reason). But instead of a shot I heard music. He'd put on 'I Follow the Sun'. He listened to the song once, then put it on again. His soul was clearly in need of oxygen.

I was left there, sitting on the carpet in front of the divan. As soon as I calmed down a little bit, I began getting ideas about what might have happened. The first thing I remembered was the deceased Lord Cricket and his lecture about the snake force descending through the tail. Naturally, once I heard the word 'super-werewolf', I had regarded all his theories as crazy nonsense, a garland of foul-smelling bubbles in the swamp of profane esotericism. But one aspect of what had happened lent a certain weight to what his lordship had said.

Before his transformation, Alexander had fallen on the floor, just as if someone had tugged on his tail. Or as if his tail had become incredibly heavy. In any case, something unusual had happened, something that had taken him by surprise – and it had something to do with his organ of hypnotic suggestion. And Lord Cricket had said that the transition from a wolf to what he called the 'super-werewolf' took place when the kundalini descended to the very tip of the tail. And as well as that . . .

This was the most unpleasant part. As well as that, he had mentioned an 'involtation of darkness' that was necessary for this to happen, the spiritual influence of a 'senior demonic entity . . .'

Little me?

It was hard to believe it. But on the other hand, what the deceased lord had said could well have contained a grain of truth picked up from somewhere by that Aleister Crowley of his. All sorts of secret gatherings and mystical rituals were held in the world – it couldn't all be absolute charlatanism, could it? One thing was certain – I had played a fatal part in what had happened. Apparently I had been the catalyst for some obscure alchemical reaction. As Haruki Murakami said, the force emanating from a woman is not very great, but it can certainly move a man's heart . . .

The most terrible thing was the realization that what had happened was irreversible – a were-creature never makes mistakes about things like that. I could tell that Alexander would never again be the way he used to be. And it wasn't just supposition on my part, I knew it with my tail. It was as if I'd dropped a precious vase that had shattered into a thousand fragments, and now it could never be glued back together again.

I plucked up my courage, walked over to the door through which he had disappeared and opened it.

I'd never been in there before. What I found behind the door was a small space, like a dressing room, with a table, an armchair and cupboards running right round the walls. There was a small digital recorder lying on the table. It was playing the Shocking Blue song again, promising to follow the sun until the end of time.

Alexander was unrecognizable. He had already changed his clothes – now, instead of a general's uniform, he was wearing a dark grey jacket and a black turtleneck. I'd never seen him dressed like that before. But the most important thing was the elusive change that had taken place in his face – the eyes seemed to have moved closer together and faded somehow. And their expression had altered too – a new despair, balanced by fury, had appeared in them: I don't think anyone else but me would have been able to separate out these components of his outwardly calm gaze. It was him, but not him. I felt afraid.

'Sasha,' I called softly.

He looked up at me and asked: 'Do you remember the story about the Little Scarlet Flower?'

'Yes,' I said.

'I've only just realized what it really means.'

'What?'

'Love doesn't transform. It simply tears away the masks. I thought I was a prince. But it turns out . . . This is what my soul is like.'

'Don't dare talk like that,' I whispered. 'It's not true. You didn't understand a thing. It has absolutely nothing to do with your soul. It's . . . it's like . . .'

'It's like hatching out from the egg,' he said sadly. 'You can't hatch back into it.'

He had expressed my own feeling with astonishing precision. So the change really was irreversible. I didn't know what to say. I wanted to fall through the floor, then through the ground, and keep going to infinity . . . But he didn't think it was my fault. On the contrary, he made it clear that he thought the cause of what had happened lay in him. What a noble heart he does have, really, I thought.

He stood up.

'Now I'm going to fly north,' he said, running his fingers tenderly over my cheek. 'Come what may. We'll see each other in three days.'

* * *

He appeared three days later.

I wasn't expecting him that morning, and my instinct had given me no warning. The knock at the door sounded strangely weak. If it had been the militia, the fire inspectors, the public health inspectors, the district architect or any other bearers of the national idea, it wouldn't have sounded like that – I knew how people knocked when they came for money. I thought it must be the old cleaning lady who cleaned the stand. She sometimes came to ask for hot water. I'd given her an electric kettle twice, but she still came anyway – probably out of loneliness.

Alexander was standing outside – deathly pale, with blue circles under his eyes and a long scratch on his left cheek. He was wearing a crumpled summer raincoat. I could smell alcohol on him – not old, stale fumes, but the way an open bottle of vodka smells. I'd never known him to drink before.

'How did you find me?' I asked.

It would have been hard to think of a more stupid question.

He didn't even bother to answer.

'There's no time. Can you hide me?'

'Of course,' I said. 'Come in.'

'This place is no good. Our people know about it. Have you got somewhere else?'

'Yes I have. Come in and we'll talk about it.'

He shook his head.

'Let's go right now. Another five minutes and it will be too late.'

I realized the situation was serious.

'All right,' I said. 'Will we be coming back here?'

'Probably not.'

'Then I'll take my bag. And my bike. Will you come in?'

'I'll wait here.'

A few minutes later we were already walking away from the equestrian complex along a forest path. I was pushing my bike along by the handlebars: I had an extremely heavy bag hanging over my shoulder, but Alexander didn't make the slightest attempt to help me. That wasn't really like him – but I sensed that he could hardly even walk.

'Will it take much longer?'

'About half an hour, if we don't hurry.'

'What sort of place is it?'

'You'll see.'

'Is it safe?'

'They don't come any safer.'

I was taking him to my own personal bomb shelter.

It often happens that preparations made in case of war are actually used by a later age for a different purpose. In the eighties many people had been expecting the Cold War to end in a hot one – there were at least three portents that indicated such a development was imminent:

1) bully beef from the strategic reserves of Stalin's time – which were assembled in case there was a third world war – appeared on the shelves in shops (the cans were easily identifiable by the lack of any markings, the distinctive yellowish tinge of the metal, a thick layer of Vaseline and their completely tasteless, almost colourless contents).

2) the American president was called Ronald Wilson Reagan. Each word in his name contained six letters, giving the apocalyptic number of the beast – '666' – a fact that was frequently mentioned with alarm by the journal *Communist*, where many architects of the future reform worked at the time.

3) the surname Reagan was pronounced exactly like 'ray gun' – a fact that I noticed myself.

It became clear several years later that these signs did not portend war, but the end of the USSR: the *upper rat* had chickened out, thereby fulfilling the first part of its great geopolitical mission. But at that time a war had still seemed very likely, and I was thinking about what I would do when it started.

These thoughts led me to a simple decision. I was already living close to Bitsevsky Park and in its secret depths, criss-crossed with gullies, I often came across concrete pipes, shafts and service ducts. It was clear from the different sorts of concrete that these incomplete underground structures came from various periods of Soviet power. Some were elements of a drainage system, some had something to do with underground heat pipelines and cables, and some were simply unidentifiable, but looked like something military.

Most of them were in open view. But one of these boltholes proved suitable for my purposes. It was located in impassable thickets, too remote for teenage drinkers or courting couples to use as a meeting place. There were no forest tracks leading to it, and there wasn't much chance of anyone who happened to be out walking passing that way. This is how it looked: there was a concrete pipe about a metre in diameter protruding from the earth in the side of a gully. The bottom of the opposite slope of the ravine was only a few steps away, so it was difficult to spot the pipe from above. Under the ground it branched into two small rooms. One of them had a power distribution box hanging on the wall, and even a socket for a light bulb hanging on a spike hammered into the concrete – evidently there was an underground power cable running nearby.

When I discovered this place, there were no signs of life in it, only garbage left over from the construction work and a rubber boot with a torn top. Bit by bit I brought in a lot of canned food, jars of honey, Vietnamese bamboo mats and blankets. Only instead of war, perestroika broke out, and I had no more need for a bomb shelter. But even so I still used to inspect the place from time to time, thinking of it as my 'bunker'.

Of course, all my reserves had rotted, but the spot itself had remained undiscovered: only once in the entire democratic period did a tramp attempt to move in (he obviously must have been crawling along the bottom of the gully in a delirious state and then clambered into the pipe). I had to give him a rather severe hypnotic session – I'm afraid the poor man forgot about plenty of other things as well as the gully. After that I hung a protective talisman at the entrance, something I usually avoid doing, since sooner or later you have to pay for magic that changes the natural course of things with your own death. But in this case the intervention was minimal.

When Alexander asked me to hide him, I realized immediately that I couldn't possibly think of any better place than this. But getting there turned out not to be so easy – he was walking slower and slower, with frequent stops to catch his breath.

Eventually we reached the gully, which was concealed by a proliferation of hazel bushes and some umbrella-shaped plants with a name I could never remember – they always grew to a monstrous size here, almost like trees, and I was concerned that the reason might be radiation or chemical pollution. Alexander scrabbled down into the gully, bent over and climbed into the pipe.

'Right or left?'

'Left,' I said. 'I'll just switch on the light.'

'Oho, so there's even light. Real luxury,' he muttered.

A minute later I helped him take off his raincoat and laid him out on the bamboo mats. It was only then I noticed that his grey jacket was soaked in blood.

'There are bullets,' he said. 'Two or three. Can you get them out?'

Fortunately, I'd put my Leatherman in the bag. And I had a bit of medical experience, although the last time I'd practised was a very long time ago, and it wasn't bullets I removed from a man's body, it was arrowheads. But there wasn't really much difference.

'All right,' I said. 'Only don't squeal.'

During the procedure – which proved to be rather long – he didn't make a single sound. After one particularly clumsy turn of my instrument his silence became so oppressive, I was afraid he might have died. But he reached out for his bottle of vodka and took a swallow. Finally it was all over. I'd really hacked him about, but I'd got all three lumps of silver out – there were still black hairs embedded in two of them, and I realized he had been shot when he was . . . I didn't know what to call his new form – the word 'dog' seemed insulting to me.

'That's it,' I said. 'Now we have to bandage it up with something sterile. You lie here for a while, and I'll go to the chemist's. Shall I get you anything?'

'Yes. Buy me a leash and a collar.'

'What?'

'Never mind,' he said and tried to smile. 'I'm joking. Don't worry about any medicine, dogs heal fast. Buy a few disposable razors and a can of shaving foam. And some mineral water. Do you have money?'

'Yes. Don't worry.'

'And don't go home. Not on any account. They're bound to be waiting for you.'

'You don't need to tell me that,' I said. 'Listen . . . I've just remembered. Mikhalich has this instrument that locates things. From a sensor. What if there's one of those sensors in my things?'

'Don't worry about that. He was just bragging to impress you. We don't have any instruments like that. They found you through the cleaning lady who gets hot water from you. She's been working for us since eighty-five.'

You learn something new every day.

When I came back a few hours later with two plastic bags full of shopping, he was asleep. I sat down beside him and looked into his face for a long time. He was sleeping as peacefully as a child. And standing on the floor was a glass, with three bloody silver buttons lying in it. It's hard to kill a werewolf. Take Mikhalich – the more you smash him over the head, the jollier he gets. The champagne's gone to my head, he says . . . Witty fellow. Of course this was a case of bullets, not champagne – but even so you couldn't get my Sashenka with a little thing like that.

The myth that a werewolf can only be killed with a silver bullet is very helpful to our community.

1) the wounds never fester and no disinfection is required – silver is a natural antiseptic.
2) fewer bullets are fired at us – people economise on the expensive metal and often go out hunting with only a single bullet, assuming that any kind of hit will be fatal.

But in real life the shot is far more often fatal for the hunter. If people would just use their brains for a moment, then of course they would guess who spreads these rumours about silver bullets. People might think a lot, but they think in a perverted way, and not about the right things.

The plastic bags I had brought contained food and a few small household items. As I went down into the gully and dragged them into the pipe, I suddenly thought that basically I was no different now from thousands of Russian girls who were married and whose frail shoulders had assumed the burden of running the home. It had all happened so suddenly and it was so different from the roles that I had previously played, that I wasn't sure yet if I liked it or not.

* * *

It is usually assumed that were-creatures are not concerned about spiritual problems. People think you turn into a fox or a wolf, howl at the moon, tear someone's throat out, and all the great questions of life are instantly answered, and it's clear who you are, what you're doing in this world, where you came from and where you're going . . . But that's not the way it is at all. We are far more tormented by the riddles of existence than modern humans. But the cinema continues to depict us as complacent, earth-bound gluttons, nonentities who are indistinguishable from each other, cruel and squalid consumers of the blood of others.

I don't actually think this is a conscious attempt by people to insult us. It's more likely a simple consequence of their own limitations. They model us according to their own likeness, because they have no one else to take as a prototype.

Even the little bit that people do know about us is usually distorted and vulgarized beyond all recognition. For instance, according to the rumours about were-foxes, they live in human graves. When they hear that, people imagine bones and stench, decomposing corpses. And they think – what repulsive creatures these foxes must be if they live in a place like that . . . Something like a large coffin of worms.

Of course, this is a mistake.

A good ancient grave was a complex structure consisting of several dry, spacious rooms illuminated by sunlight, which was directed into them by a series of bronze mirrors (there wasn't a lot of light, but it was enough to work by). A grave like that, situated far away from human dwellings, was ideally suited as a home for a being indifferent to the vanity of the world and inclined to solitary contemplation. There are almost no suitable graves left now: they've been ploughed up, canals and roads have been built through them. And in the modern communal apartments of the afterlife, even the dead feel cramped.

But sometimes even now nostalgia still drives me to a nearby cemetery – simply to stroll along the avenues and ponder the eternal. I look at the crosses and the stars, read the names, gaze at the faces on the faded photographs and feel so sorry for all these people I never met. Mr Keufer understood so much about life . . . And Mr Solonyan understood even more then Mr Keufer . . . And Mr and Mrs Yagupolsky understood even more then Solonyan and Keufer taken together . . . They understood everything, apart from what is most important. And the most important thing was so inexpressibly close. Sad.

Long before I came to Russia I lived for several hundred years in a Han period grave not far from the spot where the great city of Luoyang once used to stand. The grave had two spacious chambers in which various items had been preserved – beautiful gowns and shirts, a harp, a flute and lots of different kinds of dishes – basically, everything that was necessary for a home and a modest life. And people were afraid to approach the grave, since it was rumoured that a fierce and vicious demon lived there. Which, if you set aside the superfluous emotional assessment, was quite true.

In those days I practised my spiritual exercises intensively and associated on a regular basis with a number of learned men from the villages round about (Chinese students usually lived in rural areas with their families, travelling to the city to sit their exams and later, after serving their term as an official, they returned to the family home). Several of them knew who I was and they would pester me with questions about the ancient times – were there any errors in the chronology, who had organized the palace coup three hundred years earlier, and so on. I had to strain my memory and answer them, because in return the scholars would give me old texts which I sometimes needed to check my spiritual practice.

Others, bolder in spirit, used to visit me for a little wanton lechery among the ancient graves. The Chinese artists and poets valued a secluded rendezvous with a fox, especially in a state of intoxication. And in the morning they liked to wake up in the grass beside a mossy gravestone, jump to their feet and scream in horror as they ran to the nearest shrine with their hair fluttering loose in the wind. It was very beautiful – I used to watch from behind a tree and laugh into my sleeve . . . And a couple of days later they would come back again. What exalted, noble, subtle people there used to be then! Often I didn't even take money from them.

Those idyllic times flew past quickly, and they left me with the very best of memories. Wherever life cast me up after that, I always felt slightly homesick for my cosy little grave. And so for me it was a delight to move into this little nook in the forest. I thought the old days had come back. Even the floor plan of the double burrow in which we lived reminded me of my ancient refuge although, of course, the rooms were smaller and now my days were not spent in solitude, but with Alexander.

Alexander quickly grew accustomed to the new place. His wounds healed – it was enough for him simply to turn into a dog for one night. In the morning he stayed like that and went off for a walk along the gully. I was glad he wasn't ashamed of this body – he seemed to find it entertaining, like a new toy. What he liked was evidently not the form itself, but its permanent stability: he could only be a wolf for a short while, but now he could be a dog for just as long as he wanted.

Apart from that, this black dog could even speak after a fashion, although the way it pronounced the words was very funny and at first I used to laugh until I cried. But Alexander didn't take offence, and I soon got used to it. During the early days he ran around in the forest a lot, getting to know the surrounding area. I was concerned that his ambitions might lead him to mark too large a sector of the forest, but I was afraid to wound his pride by telling him so. And if anything happened, we could stand up for ourselves. 'We' . . . I simply couldn't get used to that pronoun.

It was probably because our home reminded me of the place where I had spent so many years striving for spiritual self-improvement that I felt the desire to explain to Alexander the single most important of all things that I had understood in life. I had to try at least – otherwise what was my love worth? How could I possibly abandon him alone in the glacial glamour of the progressively advancing hell that began just beyond the edge of the forest? I had to offer him my tail and my hand because, if I didn't do it, no one else would.

I decided to reveal the innermost essence of things to him. This required him to master several ideas that were new to him and then use them, like steps, to ascend to the higher truth. But even explaining these initial notions was difficult.

The problem is that everybody knows the words that express the truth – and if you don't, you can easily find them in five minutes via Google. But hardly anyone at all actually knows the truth. It's like one of those 'magic eye' pictures – a chaotic jumble of coloured lines and spots that can be transformed into a three-dimensional image by focusing your vision correctly. It all seems very simple, but you can't focus someone else's eyes for them when they look, no matter how well-disposed you are towards them. The truth is a picture just like that. It is there right in front of everybody's eyes, even the tailless monkeys'. But there are very few who actually see it. Although many think that they understand it. This, of course, is nonsense – the truth is like love, there is nothing to understand. And what is usually taken for the truth is some kind of intellectual dross.

One day I noticed a tiny grey pouch hanging round Alexander's neck on a grey string. I guessed that the colour had been chosen to match a wolf's fur – so that the pouch would not be visible when he turned into a wolf. But now it stood out against his black fur. I decided to ask him about it that evening, when he was in a benign mood.

He was in the habit of smoking a malodorous Cuban cigar before bed – a Montecristo III or Cohiba Siglo IV. I knew the names, because I had to go to get them. That was the best time to talk to him. In case you didn't know, smoking triggers a discharge of dopamine into the brain – and dopamine is the substance responsible for a feeling of well-being: a smoker borrows this well-being against his own future and transforms it into problems with his health. That evening we settled down in the doorway of our home and he lit up (I wouldn't allow him to smoke inside). I waited until his cigar was half burnt away and asked:

'Tell me, what have you got in that little pouch hanging round your neck?'

'A cross,' he said.

'A cross? You wear a cross?'

He nodded.

'But why hide it? It's okay to wear them now.'

'It may be okay,' he said. 'But it burns my chest when I transform.'

'Does it hurt?'

'It doesn't really hurt. It's just that every time there's a smell of scorched fur.'

'If you like, I can teach you a mantra,' I said, 'so that no cross will ever burn you again.'

'Oh, sure! I'm not going to recite your infernal mantra so my cross doesn't burn my chest. Don't you realize what a sin that would be?'

I looked at him incredulously.

'Hang on. So maybe you're a believer too, are you?'

'What of it,' he said. 'Of course I'm a believer.'

'In the sense of the Orthodox Christian Cultural Heritage? Or for real?'

'I don't understand the distinction. In the Holy Writ it says: "Even the demons believe and tremble!" That's about us, and that's what I do – believe and tremble.'

'But you're a werewolf, Sasha. So according to all the Orthodox precepts your road leads straight to hell. Tell me, I'd like to know, why would you choose a faith in which you have to go to hell?'

'You don't choose your faith,' he said morosely. 'Just like you don't choose your motherland.'

'But the reason religion exists is to offer hope of salvation. What are you hoping for?'

'That God will forgive my evil deeds.'

'And what evil deeds have you got?'

'That's obvious. I've lost the image of God. And then there's you . . .'

I almost choked in indignation.

'So you don't think I'm the brightest and purest thing in your entire lupine life, on the contrary, I'm an evil deed for which you'll have to atone?'

He shrugged.

'I love you, you know that. It's not a matter of you personally. It's just that the two of us live, you know . . .'

'What do I know?'

He released a cloud of smoke.

'In sin . . .'

My anger instantly evaporated. And instead I felt more like laughing than I had for a long time.

'No, come on, tell me,' I said, feeling the bubbles of laughter rising in my throat. 'So I'm your sin, am I?'

'Not you,' he said in a quiet voice, 'it's that . . .'

'What?'

'Tailechery,' he said in a very quiet voice and lowered his eyes.

I bit my lip. I knew that whatever I did, I mustn't laugh – he had shared his most intimate feelings with me. And I didn't laugh. But the effort was so great it could easily have made a new silver hair appear in my tail. So he'd even invented a term for it!

'Don't take offence,' he said. 'I'm being honest with you, saying what I feel. I can lie if you like. Only then there won't be any point in talking to each other.'

'Yes,' I said, 'you're right. It's just that this is all rather unexpected.'

We sat in silence for a few minutes, watching the tops of the prolific umbrella plants swaying in the wind.

'And have you been . . . a believer for long?' I asked.

'It's five years now.'

'To be honest, I thought you were more into the Nordic gods. You know, Fafnir, Nagelfahr, Fenrir, Loki, Baldur's dreams . . .'

'That too,' he said with a selfconscious smile. 'Only that's external, a shell. A sort of frame, aesthetic decoration. You know, like the sphinxes on the banks of the Neva in Petersburg.'

'And how did you end up in this state?'

'In my younger days I used to be keen on Castaneda. And I read in one of his books that awareness is the food of the Eagle. The way I understood it, the Eagle's some obscure thing they have instead of God. I'm no coward, far from it. But that made me feel afraid . . . Anyway, I turned to Orthodoxy. Even though the situation was rather ambivalent. I was already a wolf then, it was three years since I'd been accepted into the pack. We still had a pack in those days. Colonel Lebedenko was still alive . . .'

He gestured helplessly.

'Awareness is the food of the Eagle?' I asked.

'Yes,' said Alexander. 'That's what the magicians of ancient Yucatán believed.'

What a little boy he still is, really, I thought tenderly.

'Silly boy. It's not awareness that's the food of the Eagle. It's the Eagle that's the food of awareness.'

'Which Eagle exactly?'

'Any. And the magicians of ancient Yucatán too, with all their business seminars, workshops, videodiscs and ageing Naguals. Every last one of them is the food of awareness. Including you.'

'How's that?' he asked.

I took his cigar and blew out a cloud of smoke.

'You see that?'

He watched as it swirled and evolved.

'Yes,' he said.

'Are you aware of it?'

'Yes.'

'A werewolf is like that cloud of smoke. He lives, changes his form, his colour and volume. Then he disappears. But when the smoke dissipates, nothing happens to awareness. Something else just appears in it instead.'

'But where does awareness go after death?'

'It doesn't have to go anywhere,' I said. 'You're not going anywhere, are you? You're sitting there, you're smoking. And it's the same.'

'But what about heaven and hell?'

'They're smoke rings. Awareness doesn't go anywhere. On the contrary, anything that does go anywhere immediately becomes its food. Like that smoke there. Or like your thoughts.'

'But whose awareness is it?' he asked.

'That's the food of awareness as well.'

'No, you don't understand the question. Whose is it?'

'And that too,' I said patiently.

'But there has to be –'

'And that,' I interrupted.

'Then who . . .'

At this point he suddenly seemed to get it – he took his chin in his hand and stopped talking.

It's really difficult trying to explain these things in abstract terms. You can get tangled up in the words: 'In perception there is neither subject nor object, but only the pure experience of the transcendent nature, and this experience is everything – both physical objects and mental constructs, which include the ideas of a perceived object and a perceiving subject . . .' After the first three words you can't tell what it's all about any more. But with an example it's easy – one good puff of smoke and that's it. So now he understood. Or almost understood.

'Then what do you reckon this is, all around us?' he asked, taking back his cigar. 'Is it like *The Matrix*?'

'Almost, but not quite.'

'So what's the difference?'

'In *The Matrix* there's an objective reality – a warehouse out-side town with the bodies of the people stacked in it. Otherwise the portfolio investors wouldn't have put up the money for the film, they're very strict about that sort of thing. But in fact every-thing's like in *The Matrix*, only without that warehouse.'

'How do you mean?'

'There's a dream, but there isn't anybody dreaming it. That is, they're part of the dream too. Some say the dream dreams itself. But strictly speaking there isn't any "itself".'

'I don't understand.'

'In *The Matrix* everybody was connected by wires to something real. But in actual fact everybody's connected to the same kind of pipedream as they are themselves. And since all the dreamers see more or less the same, this pipedream is also a joint dream, and that's why people call it real. The dream only lasts for as long as the connection continues. But once it stops, there's no hardware left behind for the court bailiffs to inventorize. Or any body for them to bury.'

'Now that's where you're wrong,' he said with a grin. 'More often than not, that's exactly what does happen.'

'You know what they say – leave the virtuals to bury their virtuals. The buriers and the buried are only real in relation to each other.'

'How can that be possible?'

'Take a look around.'

He thought for a while without saying anything. Then he nodded sullenly.

'A pity you weren't around to explain that. And what good is it now . . . It's too late to change my life now.'

'Yes, you're really stuck, you poor sod,' I sighed. 'Why don't you try moving your assemblage point in the position of holy life?'

'Are you laughing at me?' he asked. 'Well laugh, Ginger, go on. It's stupid, I don't deny it. Do you believe in God yourself?'

I was really taken aback by that.

'Do you believe?' he repeated.

'Foxes respect the religion of Adonai,' I replied diplomatically.

'Respect isn't where it's at. Can you tell me if you believe or not?'

'Foxes have their own faith.'

'And what do they believe in?'

'The super-werewolf.'

'The one Lord Cricket talked about?'

'Lord Cricket was way off beam. He didn't have a clue about the super-werewolf.'

'But who is the super-werewolf?'

'There are several levels of understanding. At the most primitive one, he is the messiah who will come and tell all the were-creatures what the score is. This interpretation has been influenced by human religion, and the central profane symbol corresponding to it was also taken from people.'

'And what is this central profane symbol?'

'An inverted five-pointed star. The humans don't understand it correctly. They draw a goat's head into it with the horns at the top. They like to see the devil everywhere, except in the mirror and on TV.'

'So what does this star really mean?'

'It's the vulpine crucifix. Something like the St Andrew's Cross with a crossbar for the tail. Of course, we have no intention of crucifying anyone, we're not people. All this signifies a symbolic atonement for the sins of foxes, of which the most important is ignorance.'

'And how is the super-werewolf going to atone for the sins of foxes?'

'He will give foxes the *Sacred Book of Werewolf.*'

'What kind of book is that?'

'The general belief is that it will reveal the central mystery of all were-creatures. Every were-creature who reads it will be able to comprehend this mystery five times.'

'And what's this book going to be called?'

'I don't know. Nobody does. They say its title will be a magical pentagrammaton, a spell that annihilates all obstacles. But all this is no more than legend. The concept of the super-werewolf has a true meaning that has nothing to do with all these fairy tales.'

I was expecting him to ask about this true meaning, but instead he asked about something else.

'What does that mean – you'll "be able to comprehend this mystery five times". Once you've understood something, why do you need to understand it another four times? You're already in the know, aren't you?'

'On the contrary. In most cases, if you've already comprehended something, you'll never be able to comprehend it again, *precisely* because you think that you know everything already. But in the truth there isn't anything that can be understood once and for all. Since we don't see it with our eyes but with our minds, we say "I understand". But when we think we've understood it, we've already lost it. In order to possess the truth, you have to see it constantly – or, in other words, comprehend it over and over again, second after second, continuously. And that's a very rare ability.'

'Yes,' he said, 'I understand.'

'But that doesn't mean you'll understand it in two days' time. You'll be left with the dead husks of words, and you'll think there's still something wrapped up in them. That's what all the humans think. They seriously believe that they possess spiritual treasures and sacred texts.'

'So what you're saying is that words can't reflect the truth?'

I shook my head in confirmation.

'Two times two is four,' he said. 'That's the truth, isn't it?'

'Not necessarily.'

'Why?'

'Well, for instance, you've got two bollocks and two nostrils. Two times two. But I don't see any four in that.'

'What if we add them up?'

'How are you going to add nostrils to bollocks? Leave that sort of thing to humans.'

He thought about it. Then he asked: 'And when's the super-werewolf supposed to come?'

'The super-werewolf comes every time you see the truth.'

'And what is the truth?'

I didn't answer.

'What is it?' he repeated.

I didn't say anything.

'Eh?'

I rolled my eyes up. That's a facial gesture that really suits me.

'I asked you a question, Ginger.'

'Surely it's clear enough? My silence is the answer.'

'But can you answer in words? So that I could understand?'

'There's nothing there to understand,' I replied. 'When you're asked the question "what is truth?" there's only one way you can answer it without lying. You must see the truth within yourself, on the inside. But on the outside you must keep silent.'

'And do you see this truth within yourself?' he asked.

I said nothing.

'All right, I'll put it a different way. When you see this truth within yourself, what exactly do you see?'

'Nothing,' I said.

'Nothing? And that's the truth?'

I said nothing.

'If there's nothing there, then why do we talk about truth at all?'

'You're confusing the cause and the effect. We don't talk about truth because there's something there. On the contrary, we think there must be something there because the word "truth" exists.'

'Exactly. The word exists, doesn't it? Why?'

'Just because. Forever wouldn't be long enough to untangle all the cunning tricks words play. You can think up an infinite number of questions and answers – you can put the words together this way and that way, and every time some kind of meaning will stick to them. It's pointless. That sparrow over there doesn't have any questions for anybody. But I don't think he's any further away from the truth than Lacan or Foucault.'

I thought he might not know who Lacan and Foucault were. Although they supposedly had that counter-brainwashing course . . . But in any case I knew I ought to express myself more simply.

'In short, it's all because of words that the humans are stuck up shit creek. And the were-creatures with them. Because even though we are were-creatures, we speak their language.'

'But words exist for a reason, don't they?' he said. 'If people really are stuck up shit creek, we need to understand why, don't we?'

'When you're up shit creek, there are two things you can do. First – you can try to understand why you're up there. Or second – you can get out of there. The mistake that individuals and entire nations make is to think these two actions are somehow interconnected. But they aren't. And getting out of shit creek is a lot easier than understanding why you're stuck up it.'

'Why?'

'You only have to get out of shit creek once, and after that you can forget about it. But to understand why you're stuck up it takes a lifetime. Which you'll spend stuck up there.'

We sat in silence for a while, gazing into the darkness.

Then he asked: 'But even so. What do people have language for, if it gives them nothing but grief?'

'In the first place, so they can lie. In the second place, so they can wound each other with the barbs of venomous words. In the third place, so they can discuss what doesn't exist.'

'And what does exist as well?'

I raised one finger.

'What's this?' he asked. 'Why are you giving me the finger?'

'I'm not giving you the finger, I'm pointing. There's no need to discuss what does exist. It's right there in front of you anyway. It's enough just to point to it.'

We didn't talk any more that evening, but I knew the first seeds had fallen on fertile ground. All I could do now was wait for the next opportunity.

* * *

In case anyone thinks our way of making love is a perversion (*tailechery*, he'd called it eh? You couldn't forget that in a hurry) I advise them to take a closer look at what people do to each other. First they wash their bodies and remove the hairs from them, then they spray liquids on themselves to kill their natural smell (I remember Count Tolstoy was particularly outraged by that) – and all in order to make themselves fuckable for a short while. And after the act of love they immerse themselves once again in the humiliating details of personal hygiene.

Even worse than that, people are ashamed of their own bodies or dissatisfied with them: men pump up their biceps, women go to any lengths to lose weight and they have silicone breast implants put in. The plastic surgeons have even invented an illness, 'micromastia' – that's when the breasts are smaller than a pair of watermelons. And they've started elongating men's penises and selling special tablets so that they'll still work afterwards. If there were no market in illnesses, there wouldn't be any market in medicines – that's the Hippocratic secret that doctors swear a solemn oath never to reveal.

Human amorous is an extremely unstable feeling. It can be killed by a few stupid words, a bad smell, sloppily applied make-up, a chance intestinal spasm, or absolutely anything at all. Moreover, this can happen instantaneously, and no human being has any control over it. And this impulse typically contains – to an even greater degree than everything else that is human – a bottomless absurdity, a tragicomic abyss, which the mind only finds so easy to bridge because it doesn't even see it.

The best description I ever heard of this abyss was given by a certain red commander in autumn 1919 – after I fed him the magic mushrooms that I had collected right beside the wheels of his armoured train. He put it this way: 'Somehow I can't understand any more why it is that just because I like a girl's beautiful and soulful face I have to fuck her wet, hairy cunt!' It's put in a coarse, peasant fashion, but the essential point has been grasped precisely. And by the way, before he ran off forever into the rain-soaked expanse of autumn fields, he expressed another interesting thought: 'If you think about it, a woman's attractiveness has less to do with her hairstyle or the lighting than with my balls.'

But people still indulge in sex – although, of course, in recent years mostly through a little rubber sack, to prevent anything encroaching upon their solitude. This sport, which was dubious enough to begin with, has now become like a downhill slalom: the risk to your life is about the same, except that it's not the twists and turns in the piste that you have to watch, you have to make sure your ski-suit doesn't come off. I find anyone who indulges in this activity absurd in the role of a moralist, and it's not for him to judge what's perverted and what isn't.

Were-creatures' attraction to each other is less dependent on impermanent external allure. But of course, it does play a part. I guessed that what had happened to Alexander would affect our intimate relations. But I didn't think the trauma would go so deep. Alexander was as caring with me as ever, but only within strict limits: it was as if a barbed-wire fence had been erected at the point where formerly his affection had spilled over into intimacy. He evidently thought that in his new form I didn't find him attractive. He was partly right – I couldn't say that this black dog aroused the same feelings in me as the mighty northern wolf, one glimpse of which was enough to take my breath away. The dog was very cute, it's true. But no more than that. It could count on my affection. But not my passion.

Only that was simply not important. We had abandoned vulgar human-style sex when we realized how far we could be transported into a fairy-tale fantasy by our intertwined tails. And so his metamorphosis was no more serious an obstacle to our passion than, say, the black underwear that he started wearing instead of grey. But he didn't seem to understand this, imagining that I identified him with his physical receptacle. Or perhaps the sense of shock at what had happened and his irrational feeling of guilt were so intense that he had simply forbidden himself to think about pleasure – after all, men, with or without tails, are far more psychologically vulnerable than we are, for all their show of toughness.

I didn't take the initiative. But not because I didn't find him attractive any more. It's always nice when the man takes the first step, and I instinctively followed that rule. Perhaps, I thought, he's feeling miserable, and he needs time to come round. But one day he asked a question that allowed me to guess where his problems lay.

'You were talking about that philosopher Berkeley,' he said. 'The guy who thought that everything only exists when it's perceived.'

'Yes, I was,' I agreed.

I really had tried to explain it to him, and I thought I'd achieved a certain degree of success.

'So then sex and masturbation are the same thing?'

I was dumbfounded.

'Why?'

'If everything only exists by virtue of perception, then making love to a real girl is the same as imagining that girl.'

'Not entirely. Berkeley said that objects exist in the perception of God. The idea of a beautiful girl is simply your idea. But a beautiful girl is God's idea.'

'Both of them are ideas. Why is it good to make love to God's idea, and bad to make love to your own idea?'

'And that's Kant's categorical imperative.'

'I see you've got all the bases covered,' he muttered, disgruntled, and walked off into the forest.

After that conversation I realized he was in urgent need of my help. But I had to help him without wounding his pride.

When he came back from his walk in the forest and lay down on a bamboo mat in the corner of my room, I said:

'Listen, I was going through the DVDs we managed to bring with us. It turns out we have a film that you haven't seen.'

'And what are we going to watch it on?' he asked.

'On my notebook. It's a small screen, but the quality's good. We can sit close.'

'What's the film?'

'*In the Mood for Love*, Wong Kar Wai. A pastiche of nineteen-sixties Hong Kong.'

'And what's it about?'

'It's all about us,' I said. 'Two people living in rooms next door to each other. And gradually they start feeling fond of each other.'

'Are you kidding?'

I picked up the box of the DVD and read the brief blurb out loud:

'"Su and Chow lived in neighbouring rooms. Su's husband and Chou's wife are away all the time. Chow recognizes Su's handbag, a gift from her husband. His wife has one just like it. And Su recognizes Chow's tie, a gift from his wife. Her husband has one just like it. Though they say nothing, they realize that their marriage partners are being unfaithful with each other. What should they do? Perhaps they should simply surrender to the sweet music of the mood for love?"'

'I didn't understand a thing,' he said. 'All right then, let's surrender . . .'

I put the laptop on the floor and put the DVD in the disc drive.

For the first twenty minutes or so he watched the film without saying anything or reacting in any way. I knew the film off by heart, and so I didn't really watch it, I watched him instead – out of the corner of my eye. He looked relaxed and calm. When I got the chance, I moved closer to him, sank my hand into his fur and turned him over on to his side, so that he was lying with his tail towards me. He growled quietly, still watching the screen, but didn't say anything.

That's a fine little phrase – 'he growled quietly, but didn't say anything'. But that's the way it was. Trying not to startle him, I lowered my jeans, freed my tail and . . .

Ah, what an evening that was! Never before had we plunged so deep into the abyss. During our previous erotic hallucinations I had always remained conscious of what was happening and where. But this time the feelings were so intense that there were moments when I completely lost all idea of who I really was – a Hong Kong woman with the Russian name Su, or a Russian fox with the Chinese name A Hu-Li. There were several occasions when I felt genuinely afraid, as if I'd bought a ticket for a roller-coaster that was too fast and too steep.

The reason for this lay in Alexander – the hypnotic fluence that emanated from him now was so powerful that I was unable to resist it. If only for a short while, I myself fell victim to suggestion and became completely immersed in the illusion. Once he bit me gently on the lobe of my ear and said:

'Don't scream.'

I hadn't even realized I was screaming . . . In short, it was a total blast. I realized now what our clients went through every time we put our tails to work. People had good reason to be wary of us. On the other hand, if I'd known what far-out feelings we gave them, I would have charged at least twice as much.

When it was all over, I was left lying beside him on the bamboo mat, gradually coming round. It felt like I had pins and needles all over my body – I had to wait for the circulation to restore itself. Eventually I felt strong enough to speak. By that time he had already become human.

'Did you like it?' I asked.

'Not bad. Good surveillance work. I mean, camera work. And the director's no slouch either.'

'No, I didn't mean the film.'

'What did you mean then?' he asked, raising one eyebrow. I realized he was feeling more cheerful.

'You know what, Sasha, you know what.'

'If you mean you know what, then I liked the song a lot. Let's put it on again, shall we?'

'Which song exactly?'

'About the bandit Los Dios.'

I wrinkled up my forehead.

'What?'

'It's got this name in it,' he said in a slightly embarrassed voice. 'Maybe this Los Dios is not a bandit, I just thought so for some reason.'

'Bandit Los Dios? Where's that? Ah, I understand: "Y asi pasan los dias y yo desperando . . ." That's Spanish. "And so the days pass by, and I am in despair . . ."'

'Yes?'

'Yes. I can see now how people get prison terms in this country.'

'Just can't help teasing, can you,' he said amiably. 'So are we going to put it on? Or maybe we should watch the whole film again?'

The next day we watched the film again, then again and again. And every time that maelstrom reduced my soul to the same sweet desolation as the very first time. We lay side by side for a long time, resting. We didn't talk, there was nothing to talk about, and we had no strength left.

I liked to put my feet on him when he curled up into a big, black doughnut – sometimes he growled for effect, but I knew that he liked it just as much as I did. How fondly I recall those days now! It is wonderful when two beings find a way to bring each other happiness and joy. And what a prude you have to be to condemn them for not being like everybody else!

How many of those blissful moments were there, when we lay on the bamboo mat, relaxing, unable even to move? I think they add up to infinity. On every occasion, time simply disappeared, and we had to wait for it to work back up to its usual speed. How wisely life is arranged, I used to think in lazy contentment, as I listened to Nat King Cole singing our favourite song. He used to be so big, grey and rough. He was going to devour the sun. And he probably would have. But now there was a placid black dog lying at my feet, calm and quiet, and asking me not to tease him. Behold the ennobling influence of the female guardian of hearth and home. Such was the beginning of civilization and culture. And I had never even suspected that I could find myself playing this role.

Ah, dear Sasha, I used to think, you've never mentioned it. And I can't bring myself to ask about it . . . But you don't miss your old life as a wolf – so lonely and rootless, do you? You're happier with me than on your own – aren't you, darling?

Eh?

. . . Y *tú, tú contestando:*
Quizás, quizás, quizás . . .

* * *

I often wondered what sort of dog this was, as far removed from a wolf as a wolf from a fox. There were numerous mythological parallels, but I myself had never come across such a strange variety of were-creature. This blue-black canine seemed to be an inoffensive creature, but I had a gut feeling that there was some terrible secret concealed within him. The truth eventually emerged by accident.

The day had begun with a slight quarrel. We went out into the forest for a walk and sat down on a fallen tree, and I decided to amuse him by singing Li Bo's old Chinese song 'The Moon Above the Mountain Frontier Post'. I actually sang it quite well only, perhaps, in too high a voice – in ancient China that was prized especially highly. But my skill took a tumble at the cross-cultural barrier – when I'd finished singing, he shook his head and muttered:

'How did a Russian officer ever end up living like this?'

I was so offended I could feel myself flush.

'Don't give me that, what kind of Russian officer are you? You're the captain of the hitmen's brigade.'

'We don't kill anybody who's innocent,' he said icily.

'And who was it that sent the Shakespeare specialist Shitman to his death? Do you think no one knows?'

'What Shakespeare specialist Shitman?'

'And you don't even remember? The one who used to do blowjobs for a cigarette . . .'

'Listen, I reckon you've got psychological problems. First you have a fish head working as a bear, and then some Shitman dies, and I'm to blame for everything.'

'I just wanted to say that I know what you were doing at work. Yet I still love you.'

'That's the root of all my problems,' he said in a low voice. 'That you love me.'

I couldn't believe my ears.

'What? Just you say that again!'

'I'm joking, I'm joking,' he said hastily. 'You're always joking, so I thought I'd try it.'

The terrible thing was that what he'd said was absolutely true. And we both realized it. There was a heavy silence.

'And we didn't send Shitman to his death, we sent him to glory,' he said after a minute. 'And don't you go besmirching his memory.'

He was right, we had to change the subject.

'You mean to say he knew?' I asked.

'He must have, with some part of his mind.'

'So you have nothing to reproach yourself with?'

Alexander shrugged.

'In the first place,' he said, 'we have his application, the one he wrote in the insane asylum: "I want to see London and die", dated and signed. And in the second place, we had an expert consultation on the humanitarian aspect. The consultant said everything was okay.'

'Was that Pavel Ivanovich?' I guessed.

Alexander nodded.

'How did he ever come to work for you? Pavel Ivanovich, I mean.'

'He felt it was important for him to let us know about his repentance. A strange business, of course, but why turn a man away? Especially if his repentance is sincere. We always need information, you know – about cultural stuff, so we can tell who's with us and who isn't. And humanitarian consultations as well. So he became part of the team . . . Okay, let's drop it. Shitman's in God's hands now. That's if the Imams are telling the truth, of course.'

After that we didn't say a single word to each other all day until the evening – I was sulking with him and he was sulking with me: both of us had said enough. In the evening, when he was fed up with the silence, he started asking me the clues for a crossword.

That evening he was in his human body, and that made the room feel especially cozy. I was lying on a bamboo mat under a lamp and reading another of Stephen Hawking's books – *The Theory of Everything* (no more and no less). Alexander's questions distracted me from my reading, but I answered them patiently. I found some of them even more amusing than the book.

'What's the right spelling – hynaecological or gynaecological?'

'Gynaecological.'

'Gynaecological. Then it all fits. And I thought there was an "h" at the beginning.'

'That's because subconsciously you think of women as hyenas.'

'That's not true,' he said, and suddenly started laughing. 'Well, look at that . . .'

'Now what have you got there?'

'Gynaecological stomatology.'

'What – "gynaecological stomatology"?'

'There are two words in a line in the crossword. "Gynaecological" and "stomatology". If you read them together, it's funny.'

'You only think it's funny because you're ignorant,' I said. 'But that particular culturological concept actually exists. There's an American writer called Camille Paglia. She had this . . . No, it's not that she had one herself. Let's put it this way, she operates with the concept of the "vagina dentata". The vagina with teeth is a symbol of the formless, all-consuming chaos that opposes the Apollonian male principle, which is typified by the urge towards formal precision.'

'I know,' he said.

'Where from?'

'I've read about that. Lots of times.'

'In Camille Paglia?' I asked, incredulous.

'Nah.'

'Where then?'

'At the FSB Academy.'

'Counter-brainwashing?'

'Nope.'

'Then where exactly?' I persisted.

'In the wall newspaper,' he said reluctantly. 'It had a humour section called "smiles of all latitudes", and there was this joke in it: "What's scarier than an atom bomb? A cunt with teeth."'

I'd been expecting something of the sort.

'But why lots of times?'

'The wall newspaper was never changed in three years.'

'Okay,' I said. 'I get the picture.'

Evidently my tone of voice must have stung him.

'Why do you always have to reproach me for my ignorance,' he said irritably. 'Of course, you know more about all these "discourses" than I do. But I'm no knucklehead either, you know. It's just that my knowledge is in a different area, it's practical. Which happens to make it a lot more valuable than yours.'

'It depends how you look at it.'

'Whichever way you look at it. Supposing I learned this Camille Paglia off by heart. Then what would I do with her?'

'That depends on your inclinations, your imagination.'

'Can you give me even one example of how reading Camille Paglia has helped someone in real life?'

I thought about it.

'Yes, I can.'

'Well?'

'I had a client who was a spiritualist. He used to read Camille Paglia to the spirit of the poet Igor Severyanin during his spiritualist séances. And Igor Severyanin used to tell him, through the saucer, that he liked it very much and he'd always suspected something of the kind, only he'd never been able to formulate it. He even dictated a poem:

> *Ah, vagina dentata, this fleeting*
> *assignation is strife.*
> *Unforgettable is our meeting.*
> *Clean and chaste is my life.*

'There you see,' he said, 'I managed to lead this clean and chaste life perfectly well without any of your gynaecological stomatology, just as a soldier. And I helped my motherland.'

'And she paid you back, the way she usually does.'

'That's not something I need to be ashamed about.'

'Nobody's going to feel ashamed about it. Haven't you realized yet what kind of country you are living in?'

'No,' he said. 'And I never will. The world I live in is one I create for myself. By what I do in it.'

'Get you,' I said. 'If your FSB pals could have heard you now, they'd probably give you another medal. So you created this place for us, did you?'

'More like you did.'

I came to my senses.

'Yes, I'm sorry. You're right. Forgive me, please.'

'It's all right,' he said, and went back to his crossword.

I felt ashamed. I went over, sat down beside him and put my arms round him.

'What are we arguing about, Sasha. Let's have a howl, shall we?'

'Not right now,' he said, 'tonight, when the moon rises.'

I was left sitting there beside him, with my arm round his shoulders. He didn't say anything. After a minute or two I felt his body trembling slightly.

He was crying. I'd never seen him do that before.

'What's happened?' I asked affectionately. 'Who's upset my little boy?'

'No one,' he said. 'It's just me. Your Camille Paglia's to blame, with the teeth you know where.'

'But why should she make you cry?'

'Because,' he said, 'she's got teeth there, and now I've got claws there.'

'Where?'

'You know where,' he said. 'When I transform. Like a fifth leg. I couldn't bring myself to tell you.'

That was when everything became clear – that new secretiveness of his, and that aura of irrational dread that surrounded him when he became a dog. Yes, everything fell into place. The poor thing, how he must have suffered, I thought. Above all, I had to make him feel that he was dear to me even like that – if he couldn't see it for himself.

'You silly thing,' I said. 'So what? Grow a cactus there if you like. As long as your tail's safe and sound.'

'You really don't mind?' he asked.

'Of course not, darling.'

'And it's enough for you . . . You know, what we do?'

'More than enough.'

'Honestly?'

'Well since you've brought it up, I'd like to swap places. So that sometimes you can be Su and I can be Chow. I'm always Su.'

'No, I'm sorry, don't you go trying to turn me into a queer, on top of this business with the claws . . .'

'If you say so,' I said, 'I don't insist. You asked, and I told you.'

'Are we talking frankly now?'

I nodded.

'Then tell me, why haven't you given me a single blowjob all the times we've been in Hong Kong? Because I'm really a black dog?'

I counted up to ten to myself. After all, the fact that I couldn't stand the word 'blow-job' was my problem, not his – there was no point in taking offence.

'So you think you really are a black dog?' I asked.

'No,' he said, 'this black dog thinks that I really am him.'

'And that's why you're so rarely human nowadays?'

He nodded.

'I don't even want to be. After all, I've got nothing left here, apart from you. Everything's on that side now . . . And it's not mine, it's his. You were right when you said that words just mess with your head. So what about that blowjob?'

I counted to ten again, but I still couldn't help myself.

'Can I ask you please not to use that word in my presence?'

He shrugged and gave a crooked smile.

'Now I'm not even allowed to use words. Only you can do that, is that it? You're always putting me down, Ginger.'

I sighed. When it comes down to it, all men are the same, and they only want one thing from us. And it's a good thing if they still want that, said one of my inner voices.

'Okay, put the movie on. But not from the beginning, from track three . . .'

As always, following our insane and shameless Hong Kong rendezvous we took a long rest. I looked up at the ceiling, at the rough concrete lit by the electric bulb, resembling the surface of some ancient heavenly body. He lay beside me. What a sweetie, I thought, how touching his love is. After all, this is all so new to him. Compared to me, that is. It's a tough break for the poor boy, with those claws. But I once heard something about a dog with a fifth leg . . . Only what was it exactly? I can't remember.

'Hey!' he said to me. 'How are you doing?'

'Fine,' I replied. 'Did you enjoy that?'

He looked at me.

'Honestly?'

'Honestly.'

'It was just the complete *pizdets*.'

He uttered the Russian obscene word, which was commonly used in two senses – 'total fuck-up' and 'unsurpassable excellence, in some way related to a total fuck-up'. Yet it had one more rare meaning that I suddenly recalled. I sat upright.

'That's it, I've remembered!'

'What have you remembered?'

'I've remembered who you are.'

'And who am I?'

'I read somewhere about a dog like you with five legs. The Dog Pizdets. He sleeps up among the eternal snows, and when enemies descend on Russia in their hordes, he wakes up and . . .'

'Treads on them with his leg?' he asked.

'No. He . . . He kind of happens to them. Like shit happens, you know. That's it. And I think in the northern myths he's called "Garm". Have you come across him? The Nordic project's your area, after all.'

'No,' he said, 'I haven't. It's interesting. Tell me more.'

'He's a truly fearsome dog. The wolf Fenrir's double. He'll come into his own after Ragnarek. But in the meantime he guards the house of the dead.'

'What other information do you have?'

'Something else a bit vague . . . Like he's supposed to spy on men to see how they make fire and pass the secret on to women . . .'

'Skip this,' he growled. 'What else?'

'That's all I remember.'

'And what are the practical consequences here?'

'Concerning Garm, I don't know. You need to go to Iceland for a consultation. But concerning Pizdets . . . Try to happen to something.'

I said that to him as a joke, but he took my words absolutely seriously.

'To what?'

I was suddenly infected with his seriousness. I ran my eyes over the surrounding space. The laptop? No. The electric kettle? The light bulb?

'Try happening to the light bulb,' I said.

A second went by. Then suddenly the light bulb flared up in a bright bluish glare and went out. Everything went dark. But for a few more seconds the spiral of wire, photographed by my retina, continued to illuminate my inner world with an echo of its extinguished light. When that imprint faded, the darkness became total. I got up, fumbled on the wooden crate that served us as a table to find the torch, and turned it on.

There was no one else in the room.

* * *

He didn't come back for two days and nights. I was sick with worry and exhausted by the uncertainty. But when he came in I didn't reproach him, not a single word. Chekhov was right: a woman's soul is essentially an empty vessel that is filled by the sorrows and joys of her beloved.

'Well, how was it? Tell me!'

'What point is there in telling you?' he said. 'This I have to show you.'

'Have you learned to do it?'

He nodded.

'And what can you happen to?'

'Why, to anything,' he said.

'Anything at all?'

He nodded again.

'Even me?'

'Well, not unless you ask me to.'

'Can you happen to yourself?'

He gave strange sort of chortle.

'That's what I did first of all. Straight after the light bulb. Otherwise, what kind of Pizdets am I?'

I was intrigued and even a little frightened – after all, this was a serious metaphysical action we were talking about here.

'And what kind of Pizdets are you?' I asked in a voice hushed with respect.

'Total,' he replied. 'Absolute, final, complete and irreversible.'

At that moment he exuded such romantic power and mystery that I couldn't restrain myself and reached out to kiss him. He turned pale and stepped back, but then apparently realized that wasn't the way real machos behaved, and allowed me to finish what I'd begun. Every muscle in his body tensed up, but nothing terrible happened.

'I'm so happy for you, darling!' I said.

Not many were-creatures know what it is to feel happy for someone else. And tailless monkeys know even less about it, all they know how to do is smile broadly in order to boost their social adaptability and increase the volume of sales. While imitating the feeling of happiness for someone else, the tailless monkey actually experiences envy or, in the best case, remains indifferent. But I really did experience that feeling, as pure and transparent as the water in a mountain stream.

'You can't imagine how happy I am for you,' I repeated and kissed him again.

This time he didn't move away.

'Really?' he asked. 'But why?'

'Because after all this time you're in a good mood. You're feeling better. And I love you.'

His face darkened a little.

'I love you too. But I keep thinking that you're going to leave me. You'd probably be better off if you did. But I won't feel any happiness for you.'

'In the first place, I'm not planning on going anywhere,' I said. 'And in the second place, the feeling you speak of isn't love, it's a symptom of egoism. To the male chauvinist in you, I'm merely a toy, a piece of property and a trophy status symbol. And you're afraid of losing me in the same way a property owner is afraid of being parted from some expensive item. You can never feel happy for someone else that way.'

'So how do you feel happy for someone else?'

'For that you have to want nothing for yourself.'

'You're telling me you don't want anything for yourself?' he asked suspiciously.

I shook my head.

'But why?'

'I told you that once already. When you look inside yourself for a long time, you realize that there's nothing there. How can you want something for that nothing?'

'But if there's nothing inside you, there's nothing inside anyone else either.'

'If you think about it properly, there's nothing real anywhere,' I said. 'There's only the choice with which you fill emptiness. And when you feel happy for someone else, you fill emptiness with love.'

'Whose love? If there isn't anybody anywhere, then whose love is it?'

'That doesn't matter to emptiness. And don't you get hot and bothered about it either. But if you want a meaning for life, you'll never find a better one.'

'But love – isn't that emptiness too?'

'Sure.'

'Then what's the difference?'

'The difference is emptiness too.'

He thought for a moment.

'But can you fill the emptiness . . . with justice?'

'If you start filling the emptiness with justice, you soon end up as a war criminal.'

'You're getting something confused there, Ginger. Why a war criminal?'

'Well, who's going to decide what's just and what isn't?'

'People.'

'And who's going to decide what the people should decide?'

'We'll think of something,' he said and glanced at a fly soaring past. The bluebottle dropped to the floor.

'What are you doing, you brute? Do you want to be like them?'

I nodded in the direction of the city.

'I am like them,' he said.

'Like who?'

'The nation.'

'The nation?' I echoed incredulously.

I think even he was embarrassed by the pomposity of the phrase, and he decided to change his tone.

'I was just thinking, maybe I ought to go to work. To find out how things are going.'

I was staggered.

'Are you serious? Aren't three bullets enough for you? You want more?'

'You get these misunderstandings in our profession.'

'What misunderstandings?' I groaned. 'It's the system! You thought the system needed bright individuals, did you? It needs everyone grunting along together!'

'If necessary, I'll grunt with the rest. You just think, what are we going to do when the money runs out?'

'Oh, that's not a problem. Don't worry about that. When I go to the shop I can do some streetwalking.'

He knitted his eyebrows in a frown.

'Don't you dare talk like that!'

'And don't you dare say "don't you dare" to me, all right?'

'My girl's going to sell herself . . . I can't get my head round that.'

'"My girl, my girl . . ." Exactly when did you privatize me?'

'Are you going to earn money from prostitution? And feed us with it? Like something out of Dostoevsky.'

'Oh fuck your Dostoevsky,' I exploded. 'And I have.'

He looked at me with interest.

'Well, how was it?'

'Nothing special.'

We both laughed. I don't know what he was laughing at, but I had a good reason. I won't include it in these pages, out of respect for Russian literature, but let me just say that the red spider in *The Possessed* once crawled across the hem of my sarafan . . . Ah, all the titans of the spirit to whom I have given my amusing little gift! My only regret is that I never raised to Vladimir Vladimirovich Nabokov's lips the goblet that he described so magnificently. But in Soviet times leaving the country was a problem. Let this be yet another villainous outrage on the conscience of the baleful communist regime.

Fortunately the nascent quarrel had ended in laughter. I had almost made a mistake – you should never directly contradict a man, especially if he is tormented by doubts about his own worth. I ought to have found out what was on his mind first.

'Do you want to go back to pumping oil?' I asked.

'No, not there. Mikhalich does the howling there now.'

I guessed that during his absence he had been in contact with the outside world – he might have seen someone or spoken with them on the phone. But I didn't show the slightest curiosity about that.

'Mikhalich? But when he howled, the skull didn't cry.'

'They've come up with a new technology. Take five ccs of ketamine, add two ccs of pervitine, inject and then apply an electric current.'

'To the skull?'

'To Mikhalich.'

'The perverts.'

'Too true,' he said. 'It'll be curtains in a year like that.'

'For Mikhalich?'

'Nah, it makes no difference to Mikhalich. Curtains for the skull. It's already covered in cracks from all those tears . . . Caliphs for an hour . . . As long as the oil's flowing, the money's rolling in, they're doing fine. But nobody wants to think about what's going to happen tomorrow.'

'Listen, what kind of skull is that?' I said, finally asking a question that had been tormenting me for ages.

'That's something I can't tell you,' he said, suddenly turning sombre. 'It's a state secret. And in general, don't talk about my job.'

I wasn't surprised that he still thought of the old firm as his work. There are some jobs you can't resign from of your own free will. But I hadn't expected him to want to go back to the people who had put three silver bullets in him. Although I didn't know what had really happened then – he never shared it with me.

'Where will you go, if not to the oilfield?' I asked.

'They'll find something for a super-werewolf to do.'

'What?' I said with a frown. 'What super-werewolf?'

'Me,' he replied, surprised.

'Since when did you become a super-werewolf?'

'Since when? As if you haven't seen.'

'You think you're a super-werewolf?'

'What do you mean – think? I know.'

'From what?'

'From this,' he said. 'Watch.'

Another fly zooming along just below the ceiling dropped to the floor. It was strange to watch – the flies didn't drop vertically, they followed parabolic curve, continuing their forward motion, and they looked like microscopic kamikaze planes, nose-diving at the enemy from on high.

'Stop showing off,' I said. 'What does one thing have to do with the other?'

'Meaning?'

'Well, let's accept you can kill these flies. Let's accept that you're Pizdets and Garm. But why have you suddenly decided that on top of all that you're the super-werewolf as well?'

'Then who is the super-werewolf, if not me?'

'I told you already,' I said. 'The super-werewolf is a metaphor. To call some individual creature the super-werewolf means to descend to a very primitive level.'

'Okay, then I'll be him on that primitive level,' he said in a conciliatory tone. 'You got a problem with that, Ginger?'

'No, we can't leave things like that. Let's analyse this question properly.'

He sighed.

'Go on, then.'

'Imagine I buy myself a uniform on Arbat Street and start walking round town in it, making out that I'm a general in the FSB. You tell me I'm not a general, and I say, ah, go on, let me be a general for a bit, what's your problem?'

'That's an entirely different matter. The rank of general is awarded by a specific structure.'

'Right. That's what I'm talking about. Now think how you found out about the super-werewolf. You didn't hear it from Mikhalich, did you?'

'No.'

'Then there's probably some system of values that the word came from. Super-werewolf is the same kind of rank as general. Only it's awarded by tradition. And you have about as much to do with that tradition as I do with your firm. Do you understand that, grey one?'

'And I suppose you, Ginger, do have something to do with this tradition, right?'

'Not only do I have something to do with it,' I said. 'I'm the carrier of the tradition. The line holder, to use the correct term.'

'What line's that?'

'The line of transmission.'

'You mean you're the absolute authority here as well?' he asked. 'Straining yourself a bit, aren't you? Think you'll be able to *hold up the roof*?'

He seemed to be genuinely irritated – he even used an expression from the criminal jargon used by bandits and the FSB.

'Don't confuse a mystical tradition with the Shangri-La casino,' I said. 'The line holders are called that because they hold on to the line, not because they hold it up.'

My answer seemed to puzzle him.

'But what is that – a line of transmission?' he asked. 'What's transmitted along it?'

'Nothing.'

'What?'

'Like I said. Nothing. I've explained that to you so often, this kettle will understand it soon.'

'Then what is it they're holding on to, these line holders?'

'In the line of transmission there is nothing you can hold on to.'

'I don't understand.'

'There's nothing there to understand, either. Seeing that clearly is exactly what holding the line means.'

'All right,' he said, 'then tell me this, in words of one syllable. Does anyone in the world have the formal right to call himself the super-werewolf according to this tradition? Even at the most primitive level?'

'Yes,' I said.

'And who's that?'

I lowered my eyes modestly.

'Who?' he repeated.

'I know this will be a blow to your vanity,' I said. 'But we did agree only to tell each other the truth . . .'

'You again?'

I nodded. He swore under his breath.

'And who does this line of transmission run from?'

'I'll tell you about it sometime later.'

'No, let's have it right now. So you won't have time to invent anything.'

Well, okay, I thought, the truth cannot be concealed. He'll find out sometime anyway.

'All right. Then listen and don't interrupt. One evening, about one thousand two hundred years ago, in the country that is now called China, I was riding from one town to another in my palanquin. It is of absolutely no importance now which towns they were and why I was travelling. What is important is that on that evening we halted outside the gates of a monastery on the Yellow Mountain . . .'

* * *

Sometimes in ancient China there used to be misty evenings when the world seemed to reveal the face it wore in its infancy, at the very beginning. Everything all around – the houses, the walls, the trees, the groves of bamboo, the poles with lamps burning on them – changed in the most miraculous fashion, and it began to seem as if you yourself had cut all this out of coloured paper and carefully arranged it all around, and then started to pretend that it really was a big wide world through which you could roam . . . On just such an evening twelve centuries ago, I was sitting in my palanquin in front of the gates of a monastery on the Yellow Mountain. The world around me was beautiful, and I was gazing through the window in melancholy delight, and there were tears in my eyes.

It was music that had affected me so deeply. Somewhere close by a flute had been singing for a long time – singing of the very feelings that were in my heart. As if once in our childhood we had lived in a huge house and played magical games. And then we had become so lost in our games that we began to believe in our own inventions – we had gone out to have fun walking among the dolls and lost our way, and now there was no power that could lead us back home if we did not remember that we were simply playing games. But it was almost impossible to remember that, so spellbinding and horrifying had the game turned out to be . . .

I do not know if music can be 'about something' or not – the dispute over that is an ancient one. The first conversation on that theme that I can recall took place in the time of Qin Shi Huang. And many centuries later, when I came to Yasnaya Polyana in the guise of a nihilist girl student, Lev Nikolaevich Tolstoy mocked the idea all the way through supper, berating Beethoven with especial disdain – why, he asked, was it the *moonlight* sonata? On the whole, I would not claim that the sounds of the flute contained precisely that meaning. Or even that there was any meaning in them at all. But I realized that I had to talk to the flute-player straight away.

Of course, from the point of view of common sense, I ought not to have got out of the palanquin at all. When a flute plays beautifully somewhere nearby, it is best simply to listen to its sounds and not seek the company of the flautist. You cannot tell if he will say anything that is interesting or new to you, but you can be sure that he will stop playing. But all are wise in hindsight. Especially we foxes – by virtue of our anatomy.

There was mist all around: the people were in their houses, and I was not anticipating any particular danger to myself.

Jumping out of the palanquin, I set off towards the source of the sound, stopping occasionally and literally squeezing my tail tight against myself at the astounding, incomparable beauty of the evening. There have been no evenings like that since the eighteenth century – they say that the chemical composition of the air has changed. Or perhaps it is something more serious than that.

The monastery consisted of numerous buildings crowded together beside the main gates, which were huge, red and very costly. These gates were not set in a wall. Learned monks had explained to me that this was an allegorical expression of the sect's doctrine: the gates symbolized a journey leading back to where it starts, and starting from anywhere. The gates that weren't gates, the total openness and radiant space on all sides, I could even remember the hieroglyphs saying that. But I assumed there had simply not been enough money for walls. Just let someone donate the money for a wall, I thought, and changes would be introduced into the doctrine.

The flute was being played in the main building, which housed the Hall of the Transmission of the Teaching. It would never have entered my head to stick my face in there, despite the romantic lilac mist, but the music lent me courage.

If you fear tigers, do not go into the mountains, I thought – so come what may . . .

Raising the skirts of my gown so that my tail would be ready for any surprises, I walked on. In ancient China all garments were wide and spacious, and so I was in no danger from a chance encounter with one or two idle passers-by, especially in the mist.

As a general rule I did not induce any special illusion – I showed the same world that was all around, but without little A Hu-Li in it. Whenever someone saw me, their eyes would usually pop out of their heads at the sight of my ginger pride, but the next second they would be completely baffled at what could have set them trembling so badly – there was nothing anywhere nearby, only the bare, empty field, with the wind swirling the dry leaves in the air above it . . . This sounds simple, but in fact it is difficult, one of the most advanced of a fox's tricks, and if you encounter more than three people, there are problems. By the way, that is why, from the times of Sun Tzu, in time of war it was customary to place at least four guards at the entrance to a fortress: they feared my sisters, and with good reason.

In the main building one window was lit. That was where the flute was playing, there could be no mistake about that. It was a corner room on the first floor, and climbing into it presented no difficulty. I had to jump up on to the tiled canopy and follow it past the dark windows. This I did with no difficulty – I am light-footed. The shutters were raised at the window behind which the flute was playing. I squatted down on my haunches and cautiously glanced inside.

The flute-player was sitting on the floor with his back to me. He was wearing a robe of blue silk, and on his head he had a small conical straw hat. I could see that his head was shaved, although his style of dress was not like a monk's. He had broad shoulders and a lean body, light and strong – I sense such things immediately. On the floor in front of him I saw a teacup, a brush and a pile of paper. There were two oil lamps burning on the wall.

Evidently, I thought, he was engaged in calligraphy, and then decided to rest and took up his flute . . . I wonder what I shall say to him?

I had no plan at all – only some vague ideas swirling around in my head: first have a heart-to-heart talk, and then hypnotize him, that was the only way to deal with people. Although, if I had thought about it calmly for a moment, I should have realized that it would not work: no one would talk to me openheartedly, knowing that afterwards I would hypnotize them in any case. And if I were to hypnotize them from the very beginning, then what openheartedness could there possibly be?

But I was not allowed to think the matter through – the light of torches glimmered below me, I heard footsteps and voices. There were about ten men – I could not cast a spell on so many all at once. Pondering for no more than a second, I leapt in through the window.

I decided I would quickly bewitch the flute-player, then hide and, when the men had gone away, go back to my palanquin, since fortunately it was already almost dark outside. I landed on all fours without making a sound, raised my tail and called out quietly to the man sitting in the room.

'Most honourable sir!'

He calmly put his flute down and turned round. I immediately tensed my tail and focused all the power of my spirit at its tip – and then something quite new and unexpected happened. Instead of the pliable fizzy jelly which is how my tail perceives the human mind (it is pointless to attempt to explain this to someone who has never experienced it for themselves), I encountered absolutely nothing at all.

I had met many people who were strong or weak in spirit. Working with them was like drilling through walls made of different materials: everything can be drilled, only in different ways. But here I discovered nothing to which I could apply the willpower focused in the fine strands crackling with electricity above my head. In my astonishment I literally lost my balance and slumped to the floor like a fool, with my tail squeezed between my legs, which were exposed in front of me in an unseemly manner. At that moment I felt like a fairground juggler whose balls and ribbons have all fallen plop into the liquid mud.

'Hello, A Hu-Li,' the man said, and inclined his head in polite greeting. 'I am very glad that you have found a moment to call in and see me. You may call me the Yellow Master.'

The Yellow Master, I thought, drawing in my legs. Probably from the Yellow Mountain on which the monastery stands. Or perhaps he is aiming to be emperor.

'No,' he said with a smile, 'I do not wish to be emperor. But you are right about the Yellow Mountain.'

'What, did I say it aloud?'

'Your thoughts are reflected so clearly on your sweet little face, that it is quite easy to read them,' he said with a laugh.

Embarrassed, I covered my face with my sleeve. And then I remembered there was a tear in my sleeve, and began to feel completely ashamed – I covered one arm with the other. My robe at the time was a beautiful one, an imperial concubine's cast-off, but no longer new, and there were holes in it here and there.

But my embarrassment was, of course, a pretence. In actual fact I was feverishly searching for an exit, and I deliberately hid my face so that he would not read in it what I was thinking. It was not possible that I could be defeated by one man on his own. I could not feel his mind anywhere. But that did not mean that his mind did not exist at all. Clearly he knew some cunning magical trick . . . Perhaps he was showing himself in a place which was not where he really was? I had heard about such things. But he was not the only one who knew some tricks.

We foxes have a method that we can use to transmit an illusion in all directions at once, instantly subduing a human being's will. When we do this, we do not attune ourselves to a specific client, but become, so to speak, a large, heavy stone that falls on to the smooth mirror of the 'here and now', sending out in all directions ripples that make people's heads spin. And then the disoriented human mind grasps at the very first straw offered to it. This technique is called 'Storm above the Heavenly Palace'.

I applied it straight away – jumping up on to all fours, pulling up my robe and shaking my tail furiously above my head. It is not the tip of the tail, but its root that has to be shaken, that is, the point from which it grows, and therefore this action appears both indecorous and suggestive, especially with one's robe pulled up. However, we foxes overcome our innate modesty because the man has no time to see anything properly.

I mean a normal man. The Yellow Master not only saw, he laughed offensively as well.

'How very pretty you are,' he said. 'But do not forget that I am a monk.'

Refusing to capitulate, I strained my will to its very limit: and then, frowning as if he had a headache, he removed the hat from his head and flung it at me. The black string of the hat caught on my tail and the hat pinned it to the floor – as if it were not a simple cone of dry straw, but a massive millstone.

The Yellow Master followed that by picking up two sheets of paper covered with hieroglyphs, rolling them up and flinging them at me as well. Before I had time to think, they had pinned my wrists to the floor, like two shackles of iron. I tried to reach one of the sheets with my teeth (when we are badly frightened, the same thing happens to us as during a chicken-hunt – our human face grows longer and is transformed for a few seconds into a pretty, sharp-toothed little muzzle), but I could not. This, of course, was some sort of sorcery. I managed to read a few of the hieroglyphs written on the paper – 'there is no old age and death . . . and also no deliverance from them . . .'

My heart felt a little lighter at that – it was the Buddhist Heart Sutra, which meant this man before me was not a Taoist. Everything might yet be all right. I stopped thrashing about and calmed down.

The Yellow Master lifted his cup of tea and took a sip from it, looking me over like an artist surveying a picture that is almost finished and pondering where a final flourish of ink is required. I realized I was lying on my back and the entire lower part of my

body was indecently exposed. I even blushed at such humilia-
tion. And then I started to feel afraid. Who could tell what was
on this sorcerer's mind? Life is terrible and pitiless. Sometimes,
when people manage to catch one of my sisters, the things they
do to her are so terrible, it is better not even to recall them.

'I warn you,' I said in a faltering voice, 'that if you are intending to violate a virgin, the earth and the heavens will shudder at
such a sin! And in your old age you will know no peace.'

He laughed so heartily that the tea splashed out of his cup on
to the floor. In my unbearable shame, I turned my head away
and once again I saw the hieroglyphs on the sheet of paper
shackling one of my hands. This time it was the other sheet, and
the hieroglyphs on it were different: 'having taken as a support
. . . and there are no obstacles in the mind . . .'

'Shall we talk?' the Yellow Master asked.

'I am not a singer from the bawdy quarter, I do not converse
with my skirt hem pulled up,' I retorted.

'But you pulled it up yourself,' he said imperturbably.

'Perhaps I did,' I replied, 'but now I am unable to pull it down
again.'

'Do you promise that you will not attempt to run away?'

I mimicked an expression of agonizing internal struggle. Then
I sighed and said: 'I promise.'

The Yellow Master quietly muttered the final phrase of the
Heart Sutra in Chinese. All the men of learning that I knew
claimed that this mantra should only be recited in Sanskrit, since
that was the way the voice of the Victorious One had first pronounced it. But nonetheless, the hoops round my wrists instantly
released their grip and were transformed into two ordinary
sheets of crumpled paper.

I adjusted my hem, sat up on the floor in a dignified pose and
said:

'How instructive! The gentleman uses the same sutra as the

lock and the key. Or does the meaning here lie in the fact that this mantra truly does bring relief from all suffering, as the Buddha promised?'

'Have you read the Heart Sutra?' he asked.

'I have read a smattering,' I replied. 'Form is emptiness, and emptiness is form.'

'Perhaps you even know the meaning of these words?'

I gauged the distance to the window with a glance. It was two leaps away. Well, I thought, even if he were an imperial body-guard, he would never catch me.

'Of course I do,' I said, gathering myself into a tense spring. 'For instance, the fox A Hu-Li is sitting here before you. She appears to be quite genuine, she has form. But look closely, and there is no A Hu-Li before you, for she is an empty void.'

And with those words I made a sudden dash for the dark square of freedom already scattered with stars.

Anticipating later events, I should say that this was the expe-rience that subsequently helped me to understand Kazimir Malevich's picture *Black Square*. I would just have drawn in a few tiny bluish-white dots. However, Malevich, although he called himself a supremacist, remained faithful to the truth of life – for most of the time there is no light in the Russian sky. And there is nothing left for the soul to do but produce invisible stars from within itself – that is the meaning of his canvas. But these thoughts only came to me many centuries later. Just at that sec-ond I collapsed to the floor, overwhelmed by an absolutely unbelievable, unbearable sense of shame. It hurt so badly that I could not even cry out.

The Yellow Master had removed the shackles from my hands. The window was very close. But I had forgotten about the hat that was pinning my tail to the floor.

No physical or even moral pain can possibly compare with the suffering that I experienced. Everything that anchorites endure in years of repentance was packed into a single second of incredibly intense feeling – as if a flash of lightning had lit up the dark corners of my soul. I felt myself crumble like a handful of dust, and a stream of tears gushed from my eyes. There in front of my face was a crumpled page of the Heart Sutra with its indifferent hieroglyphs gazing out at me, telling me that I, my failed attempt to escape, and the inexpressible torment I was suffering at that moment were nothing but empty appearance.

The Yellow Master did not laugh, he even looked at me with an expression of something like compassion, but I could tell he was barely able to restrain his laughter. That made me feel even sorrier for myself, and I kept on and on crying, until the hieroglyphs that my tears were falling on blurred and dissolved into formless blots.

'Is it that painful?' the Yellow Master asked.

'No,' I replied through my tears, 'I feel . . . I feel . . .'

'What do you feel?'

'I am not accustomed to talking frankly to people.'

'In your trade that is hardly surprising,' he laughed. 'But even so, why are you crying?'

'I feel ashamed . . .' I whispered.

I felt so dreadful at that moment that I was not thinking of any cunning tricks, and the sympathy showed to me by the Yellow Master seemed undeserved – I knew very well what the due reward for my deeds was. If he had started skinning me alive, I believe I should not have objected greatly.

'What are you ashamed of?'

'Of all the things that I have done . . . I am afraid.'

'Of what?'

'I am afraid that the spirits of retribution will send me to hell,' I said in a very low voice.

It was the honest truth – one of the fleeting visions that had just flashed before my inner eye was this: a black wheel was turning inside an icy stone cell, winding my tail on to itself, tearing it out of my body, but the tail would not tear away, it kept on growing and growing, like the silk thread emerging from a spider's belly, and every second of this nightmare brought me intolerable torment. But the worst thing of all was the realization that it would go on like that for all eternity . . . No fox could imagine a more terrible hell.

'Do foxes really believe in retribution?' the Yellow Master asked.

'We do not have to believe or not believe. Retribution comes every time our tails are tugged sharply.'

'Ah, so that's it,' he said thoughtfully. 'So I should have tugged on her tail . . .'

'Whose tail?'

'A few years ago a highly cultured fox from the capital came here to pray for forgiveness of her sins. Unlike you, she had no fear of hell at all – on the contrary, she asserted that absolutely everybody would find their way there. She reasoned like this: even people are sometimes kind, and how greatly the mercy of heaven transcends earthly mercy! It is clear that the Supreme Ruler will forgive absolutely everybody and send them immediately to heaven. People themselves will turn heaven into hell – exactly as they have done to the earth . . .'

I am usually curious, but at that moment I was in such a terrible state that I did not even ask who that fox from the capital was. But her argument sounded convincing to me. Swallowing my tears, I whispered:

'Then does that mean there is no hope at all?'

The Yellow Master shrugged.

'The realization that everything is created by the mind demolishes even the most terrible hell,' he said.

'I understand this idea already,' I replied. 'I have read the sacred books and my grasp of them is really quite good. But it seems to me that I have a wicked heart. And a wicked heart, as that fox from the capital said so correctly, will always create hell around itself. No matter where it might be.'

'If you had a wicked heart, you would not have followed the sound of my flute. Your heart is not wicked. Like all foxes' hearts, it is cunning.'

'And can a cunning heart be helped?'

'It is believed that if its owner lives a righteous life, a cunning heart can be cured in three kalpas.'

'And what is a kalpa?'

'It is the period of time that passes between the appearance of the universe and its destruction.'

'But no fox will ever live for so long!' I said.

'Yes,' he agreed. 'A cunning heart is difficult to cure by forcing it to follow the rules of morality. Precisely because it is cunning, it will always seek a way to circumvent all these rules and make fools of everyone. But in three kalpas it can come to understand that it is only fooling itself.'

'But can it not be done any faster?'

'It can,' he replied. 'If the desire is strong and the will is determined.'

'How?'

'The Buddha gave many different teachings. They include teachings for people, teachings for the spirits, and even teachings for the gods who do not wish to be cast down into the lower worlds. There is also a teaching for magical foxes treading the path above the earth, but will you place any credence in it if you are told of it by a man?'

I assumed a highly respectful attitude and said: 'Believe me, I hold human beings in great esteem! If it sometimes happens that I sap their life-force, it is only because that is the way nature has made me. I could not have obtained sustenance for myself otherwise.'

'Very well,' said the Yellow Master. 'By a happy coincidence, I am familiar with the secret teaching for immortal foxes, and am prepared to transmit it to you. Indeed, I am obliged to do so. I shall soon leave this world, and it would be a pity if this marvellous knowledge were to disappear with me. But it is unlikely I shall meet another fox in time.'

'But what of your visitor from the capital? Why did you not transmit the teaching to her?'

'E Hu-Li is not suitable,' he said.

So that was the fox from the capital! She had come here in secret to atone for her sins in prayer. But in conversation she would not even admit that sins existed.

'Why is my sister E Hu-Li not suitable?' I asked. 'You told me yourself that she came to repent of her misdeeds.'

'She is too sly. She repents when she is plotting a dark deed that is utterly wicked. She seeks to lighten the burden of her soul, so that it may accommodate more evil.'

'I am also capable of such things,' I replied honestly.

'I know,' said the Yellow Master. 'But at the same time, you will remember that you are intending to commit a crime, and so your deception will come to nothing. But E Hu-Li, having planned her next act of villainy, can repent so sincerely of the previous one, that she will indeed lighten the burden of her soul. She is too cunning ever to enter into the *Rainbow Stream*.'

He pronounced the last two words with emphasis.

'Where?' I asked.

'The Rainbow Stream,' he repeated.

'And what is that?'

'You say that you have read the sacred books. Then you should know that life is a promenade through a garden of illusory forms that seem real to the mind which does not see their true nature. A mind that loses its way may find itself in the world of the gods, the world of the demons, the world of human beings, the worlds of animals, the world of hungry spirits or hell. Having passed through each these worlds, the Victorious Ones left their inhabitants a teaching on how finally to cure themselves of death and rebirth . . .'

'I beg your pardon,' I interrupted, wishing to demonstrate my learning – 'but it says in the sutras that a human birth is the most precious of all, since only a human being can attain liberation. Is that not so?'

The Yellow Master smiled.

'I would not reveal this secret to humans but, since you are a fox, you should know that the same assertion is made in all the worlds. In hell they say that only an inhabitant of hell can attain liberation, since in all the other places the beings spend their lives in the pursuit of pleasures, of which there are almost none in hell. In the world of the gods, on the contrary, they say that none but the gods can attain liberation, because the leap to freedom is shortest of all for them, and their fear of falling into the lower worlds is the strongest. The inhabitants of every world are told that it is the most propitious for salvation.'

'But what about animals? They are not told that, are they?'

'I am speaking of those worlds in which the inhabitants posses the concept of salvation. But where there is no such concept, it follows of itself that there is no need to save anyone.'

I see, I thought. As smart as a fox.

'And the salvation of which you speak – is it the same for all the worlds, or different in each one?'

'For human beings liberation is to enter nirvana. For those who live in hell liberation is to merge with the lilac smoke. For an asura-demon, it is to take possession of the sword of emptiness. For the gods, it is to dissolve into the diamond effulgence. When we speak of form, salvation is different in every world. But in its inner essence, it is the same everywhere, because the nature of the mind that dreams all these worlds never changes.'

'And how do matters stand with foxes?'

'Formally speaking, were-creatures do not fit into any of the six categories of which I have spoken of. You are a special case. It is believed that sometimes a mind born into the world of demons takes fright at its cruelty and goes to live on its outer perimeter, where the demonic reality borders on the world of people and animals. Such a being does not belong to any one of these worlds, since it migrates between all three – the worlds of humans, animals and demons. It is to this category that magical foxes belong.'

'Yes,' I said sadly, 'that is how it is. We fall between three stools and all because of our horror at life. Then is there a way out for us?'

'There is. The Buddha and his disciples were once fed a delicious meal by a fox, who was not, in fact, acting entirely without self-interest and had designs on the disciples. But the Buddha was very hungry, and in gratitude he left this fox a teaching for were-creatures that is capable of bringing them to liberation in a single lifetime – taking account of the fact that were-creatures live for up to forty thousand years. The Buddha was pressed for time, and therefore the teaching was brief. But since it was given by the Victorious One himself, it nonetheless possesses magical power. If you follow it, A Hu-Li, you can not only save yourself, you can also show the way to liberation for all were-creatures living on the earth.'

My head started to spin in excitement. I had dreamed of something like this all my life.

'Of what does this teaching speak?' I asked in a whisper.

'Of the Rainbow Stream,' the Yellow Master replied, also in a whisper.

I realized that he was making fun of me, but I was not offended.

'So what is this Rainbow Stream?' I asked in a normal voice.

'It is the ultimate goal of the super-werewolf.'

'And what is the super-werewolf?'

'It is a were-creature who succeeds in entering the Rainbow Stream.'

'And what else is it possible to know about the super-were-wolf?'

'Outwardly it is the same as other were-creatures, but inwardly it is different. Only there is no way the others can tell that from its external appearance.'

'And how is it possible to become one?'

'You must enter the Rainbow Stream.'

'But what is that?'

The Yellow Master raised his eyebrows in astonishment.

'I have already told you. The ultimate goal of the super-were-wolf.'

'And is it possible to describe the Rainbow Stream in some way? In order to have some idea of which way to direct one's aspiration?'

'It is not. The nature of the Rainbow Stream is such that any descriptions will only serve as a hindrance by creating a false idea of it. It is not possible to say anything certain about it, it is only possible to be there.'

'But what must a super-werewolf do, in order to enter the Rainbow Stream?'

'He must do only one thing. Enter it.'

'But how?'

'By any means that allow him to do so.'

'But surely there must be some instructions that the super-werewolf receives?'

'They consist precisely of this.'

'And that is all?'

The Yellow Master nodded.

'So it turns out that a super-werewolf is one who enters the Rainbow Stream, and the Rainbow Stream is what the super-werewolf enters?'

'Precisely.'

'But that means that the former is defined in terms of the latter, and the latter is defined in terms of the former. What meaning is there in all this?'

'A most profound one. Both the Rainbow Stream and the path of the super-werewolf lie out of this world and are beyond the reach of the everyday mind – even a fox's. But they are directly related to each other. Therefore, it is only possible to speak of the former in relation to the latter. And of the latter in relation to the former.'

'And is it possible to add anything more to this?'

'It is.'

'What?'

'That the Rainbow Stream is not a stream at all, and the super-werewolf is not a werewolf at all. One should not become attached to words. They are only required as fleeting footholds. If you attempt to carry them with you, they will drag you down into the abyss. Therefore, they should be cast off immediately.'

I took a little time to think about what I had heard.

'It is intriguing. It turns out that the supreme teaching for foxes consists of only two words that are related only to each other and are not amenable to any explanation. And in addition, even these words have to be cast off once they have been spoken . . . It would seem that the fox who fed the Buddha did not have very good karma. And did she herself succeed in entering the Rainbow Stream?'

The Yellow Master nodded.

'However, that only happened quite recently. And she did not leave behind any instructions for other were-creatures. That is why I am obliged to transmit the teaching to you.'

'It is hard to believe in the truth of such a teaching.'

'The higher teachings are called higher because they differ from those to which you are accustomed. And if something appears true to you, you may already regard it as false.'

'Why?'

'Because otherwise you would have no need of any teachings. You would already know the truth.'

That was logical. But his explanations reminded me of those philosophical syllogisms that are primarily intended to confound the mind.

'But even so,' I persisted, 'how can a teaching consist of only two words?'

'The higher the teaching, the fewer the words on which it leans for support. Words are like anchors – they appear to provide a reliable grasp on a teaching, but in reality they only hold the mind in captivity. That is why the most perfect teachings dispense words and symbols.'

'Of course, that is so,' I said. 'But even in order to explain the superiority of a wordless teaching, you have had to speak many words. How can only two words be enough for someone to guide himself through life?'

'The higher teachings are intended for beings with higher abilities. And for those who lack them, there are volumes upon volumes of nonsense, in which they can rummage for the whole of their lives.'

'And do I have higher abilities?' I asked in a quiet voice.

'You would not be sitting here otherwise.'

That altered the situation somewhat.

'And are there many super-werewolves in the world?'

'Only one. Now that is you. If you wish, you can enter the Rainbow Stream. But you will need to make an effort.'

Who would not feel flattered on hearing that she has higher abilities? And the prospect of becoming a unique being was something that completely took my breath away. I thought about it.

'And the fox who succeeded in entering the Rainbow Stream,

what is known about her?'

'Very little,' the Yellow Master said. 'Your predecessor lived in a little mountain village, practised extreme asceticism and completely forswore all contact with human beings.'

'How did she feed herself?'

'She used her tail to convince a pumpkin patch that spring had come. And then she absorbed the life-force of the pumpkins . . .'

'How terrible,' I whispered. 'And what happened to her?'

'One day she simply disappeared, and that's all.'

'And she did not leave any writings?'

'No.'

'That was rather egotistical of her.'

'Perhaps you will leave some.'

'But do I really have to switch from men to vegetables?'

'The Buddha did not leave any instructions on that score. Listen to what your heart tells you. And do not swerve from the path.'

I bowed twice.

'I promise to strive obstinately for the goal, if you will grant me the transmission of which you have spoken.'

'You have already received the transmission.'

'When?' I asked.

'Just now.'

'Is that all?'

I must have looked very perplexed.

'It is quite enough. All the rest would only introduce confusion into your ginger head.'

'Then what am I to do?'

The Yellow Master sighed.

'If you were a human being, I would simply smack you across the forehead with my stick,' he said, nodding towards his knotty staff, 'and send you to work in the garden. There is nothing higher than this teaching and some day you will understand that.

But the path of the super-werewolf is a special one. And since you are so persistent in asking me what you must do, I will tell you. You must find the key.'

'The key? To what?'

'To the Rainbow Stream.'

'And what kind of key is it?'

'I have no idea. I am not a super-werewolf. I am a simple monk. And now be on your way – your palanquin is waiting for you.'

* * *

'And ever since then I have continued on my way,' I said, and stopped speaking.

My story seemed to have made a strong impression on Alexander.

'Well?' he asked me. 'Have you found the key?'

'Of course.'

'And what is it?'

'A correct understanding of your own nature. Everything that I tried to explain to you.'

'So you've already entered the Rainbow Stream?'

'You could say that,' I replied.

'What did it look like?'

'First you have to understand what the super-werewolf is.'

'So what is it?'

'It's you.'

'That's what I keep telling you,' he said plaintively. 'But you confuse me. You say it's really you. You everywhere.'

'Again you don't understand. You think you're the super-werewolf because you can break light bulbs and knock flies down by just looking at them . . .'

'Not only flies,' he said. 'And not only by looking at them.

You can't even imagine what I can do.'

'What can you do?'

'I don't even have to look, get it? I only have to think it. For instance, yesterday evening I happened to the General Customs Inspector.'

'What, did he die?'

'What for? He just muttered in his sleep and turned over on to his other side. I wiped him clean out.'

'And what does that mean?'

He shrugged his shoulders.

'It means he'll get some obscure job in some foundation and will sit there until he fades into the wallpaper. And all his kick-backs will go to the right people now. I mean, to the honest people with clean hands.'

'What a tough guy you are,' I said. 'And how do you do it?'

He thought about it.

'It's like sex, only the other way round. It's hard to explain. You know yourself, it's all in the tail. But I haven't figured out the details yet . . . So you admit I am the super-werewolf after all?'

'You don't understand anything properly,' I said. 'Just because you can swat flies and customs officials, that doesn't make you a super-werewolf. You don't even have any right to think you're a super-werewolf yet.'

'And you do have the right to think so, do you?'

'Yes, I do,' I said modestly, but firmly.

'Seems to me you're coming on a bit too strong altogether, Ginger. There's no place left in the world for me any more.'

'This whole world is yours. Just understand who you really are.'

'I'm the super-werewolf.'

'Right. But what is a super-werewolf?'

'It's me.'

'There you go again. I thought you were a keen-eyed lion, but you're a blind dog.'

He shuddered as if he'd been lashed with a whip.

'What?'

'It's just a teaching about the gaze of the lion,' I explained hastily, sensing that I'd said too much. 'They say that if you throw a stick to a dog, it will watch the stick. But if you throw a stick to a lion, it will keep its eyes fixed on the thrower. It's a formal turn of phrase that was used in debates in ancient China when an opponent started clutching at words and stopped seeing what was really important.'

'Okay,' he said, 'let's drop it. So maybe you'll tell me what the super-werewolf is?'

'The super-werewolf is the one you see when you look deep inside yourself for a long time.'

'But you said there's nothing in there.'

'That's right. There isn't anything there. That is the super-werewolf.'

'Why?'

'Because that nothing can become anything at all.'

'How's that?'

'Look. You're a werewolf, because you can turn into, erm, a wolf. I'm a were-creature, because I'm a fox who pretends to be a human being. But the super-werewolf becomes you, me, this bag of apples, this cup, this crate – everything that you look at in turn. That's the first reason why it's called the super-werewolf. Besides, any were-creature can be caught by the tail, figuratively speaking.'

'Okay, probably,' he said.

'But the super-werewolf can't be caught by the tail. Because it doesn't have a body. And that's the second reason why it's called that. Do you understand?'

'Not entirely.'

'Remember, when we were flying back from the north, you told me that when you were a child, you used to dream about a diving suit in which you could land on the sun, dive to the bottom of the ocean, jump into a black hole and come back out?'

'I remember.'

'Well then, that's exactly the kind of diving suit the super-werewolf wears. It's simply a void that can be filled with anything. Nothing can stick to this void. Nothing can touch it or stain it, because you only have to take away what it's been filled with, and it will be the same as it was before. There's nowhere for the local cop to put a registration stamp on it, and nothing for your Mikhalich to attach his bugs to.'

'I get it. Now I get it,' he said, turning pale. 'That's really impressive. No security service could ever catch someone like that!'

'I'm glad you appreciate that.'

'And how do I become it?'

'There's no way.' I said.

'Why?'

'Think about it.'

'Because there can only be one super-werewolf, and it's already you? Do I understand things right now, Ginger?'

'No, Grey One, no. You can't become it, because you have always been it. The super-werewolf is your own mind, the same one you use from morning till night to think all sorts of nonsense.'

'So I'm the super-werewolf after all, am I?'

'No.'

'But it's my mind, isn't it? Then what's the problem?'

'The problem is that your mind isn't actually yours.'

'Then whose is it?'

'It's not possible to say that it is anybody's at all. Or what it's like and where it is. All these concepts arise within it, that is, it precedes everything else without exception. Do you understand? Whatever you imagine, consider, believe or know for sure, the mind's what will do it.'

'Are you talking about the brain?'

'No. The brain is one of the concepts that exist in the mind.'

'But the mind arises because there is a brain,' he said uncertainly.

'Those villains have really brainwashed you out of your wits,' I sighed. 'People have no idea what mind is. Instead they study the brain, or the psyche, or Freud's love letters to Einstein. And scientists seriously believe that mind is the product of certain chemical and electrical processes in the brain. That's the same as thinking that a TV set is the cause of the film showing on it. Or that a salary is the cause of human existence.'

'That's what economists do think.'

'Right. Well, let them think it. Let them generate their electrical impulses, steal tranches of credit, make official protests, measure the amplitude and the velocity, give the blowjob and take the derivative coefficient, and then determine their rating. Fortunately for this world, we foxes are here in it, as well as all those clowns. We know the secret. And now you know it too. Or you almost know it.'

'Yeah, right,' he said. 'And who else knows it, apart from foxes?'

'Only the chosen are supposed to know it.'

'And you're not afraid to reveal it to me?'

'No.'

'Why? Because I'm one of the chosen too?'

'Because only the mind can know this secret. And the mind has no one to hide it from anyway. It is one.'

'One?'

'Yes,' I said, 'one in all, and all from one.'

'Then who are these chosen ones?'

'The chosen ones are those who understand that any worm or butterfly, or even a blade of grass at the edge of the road, are chosen ones just like them, only they don't know about it for the time being, and you have to take great care in order not to offend any one of them accidentally.'

'I still don't understand what mind is,' he said.

'Nobody understands that. Although, on the other hand, everybody knows it. Because it is precisely mind that is listening to what I say right now.'

'Aha,' he said. 'I get it now . . . Maybe not everything, from beginning to end, but the way I understand it, there isn't any end to all this anyway . . .'

'That's it!' I said. If only that was always the way.

'Okay, let's say we've figured out the super-werewolf. But what's the Rainbow Stream?'

'Simply the world around us,' I said. 'You see the colours – blue, red, green? They appear and disappear in your mind. That is the Rainbow Stream. Every one of us is a super-werewolf in the Rainbow Stream.'

'You mean, we've already entered the Rainbow Stream?'

'Yes and no. On the one hand, the super-werewolf is in the Rainbow Stream from the very beginning. But on the other, it is not possible to enter it at all, because the Rainbow Stream is simply an illusion. But this is only an apparent contradiction, because you and this world are one and the same.'

'Aha,' he said. 'Interesting. Okay, carry on.'

'The real super-werewolf is a heavenly being. A heavenly being never loses her connection with the heavens.'

'What does that mean?'

'In this world there is nothing but dust. But when a heavenly being sees the dust, she remembers the light that makes the dust visible. While a tailless monkey only sees the dust on which the light falls. That's why, when a heavenly being dies,

313

she becomes light. But when a tailless monkey dies, he becomes dust.'

'Light, dust,' he said, 'so there is something there after all! There is some kind of individual personality. You've definitely got one, Ginger. I've felt that pretty strongly just recently. Or will you tell me I'm wrong?'

'This personality, with all its quirks and stupidities simply dances like a doll in the clear light of my mind. And the more stupid this doll's quirks, the clearer the light that I recognize over and over again.'

'Now you're saying "my mind". But you only just said it's not yours.'

'That's the way language works. It's the root from which infinite human stupidity grows. And we were-creatures suffer from it too, because we're always talking. It's not possible to open your mouth without being wrong. So you shouldn't haggle over words.'

'All right. But the personality that dances like a doll – that's you, isn't it?'

'No. I don't think of this personality as me, because I'm very far from being a doll. I am the light that makes it visible. But the light and the doll are only metaphors, and you shouldn't clutch at them.'

'Yes, Ginger,' he said. 'You've certainly been studying these questions for a long time . . . So tell me, how old are you really?'

'Old enough,' I said and blushed. 'And about the dog and the lion – don't be offended, please. It's a classical allegory, and a very ancient one, honestly. The dog watches the stick, but the lion watches the person who threw it. By the way, when you understand that, it makes it much easier to read our press . . .'

'I understand about the dogs and the lions, you needn't have told me again,' he replied sarcastically. 'And I know about the press without you. Better tell me which way foxes look.'

I smiled guiltily.

'We foxes keep one eye on the stick and the other on the person who throws it. Because we're not very strong creatures, and we don't just want to improve our souls, we want to live for a while too. That's the reason we're slightly cross-eyed . . .'

'I'll have to toss a couple of sticks your way and see which way you look.'

'You're in good form today, comrade lieutenant general.'

Alexander scratched his chin.

'Right, where's the main conclusion?' he asked.

'What conclusion?'

'You know, how to control all this? So that we can benefit from it.'

'It's rather hard to control,' I said.

'Why?'

'You'll run yourself ragged trying to find the controller.'

'Yes, it looks that way all right,' he said. 'I'm not sure I like it.'

'What's wrong with it?'

'The Rainbow Stream, the super-werewolf – that's all fine. Let's say we've dealt with control too. But I still don't understand the most important thing. Who creates the world? God?'

'We do,' I said. 'More than that, we create God too.'

'That's taking things a bit far, Ginger,' he chuckled. 'You'll do anything to get by without God. What do we create the world with? Our tails?'

I froze on the spot.

It's hard to describe that second. All the surmises and insights of recent months, all my chaotic thoughts, all my presentiments – they all suddenly came together into a blindingly clear picture of the truth. I still didn't understand all the consequences of this epiphany, but I already knew that now the mystery was mine. I was so excited, my head started spinning. I must have turned pale.

'What's wrong with you?' he asked. 'Are you feeling unwell?'

'No,' I said, and forced myself to smile. 'I just need to be alone for a while. Right now. Please don't distract me. It's very, very important.'

* * *

The world works in a mysterious and incomprehensible fashion. Wishing to protect frogs from children's cruelty, adults tell children not to crush them because that will make it rain – and the result is that it rains all summer because the children crush frogs one after another. And sometimes it happens that you try with all your might to explain the truth to someone else, and suddenly you understand it yourself.

But then, for foxes the latter case is probably the rule rather than the exception. As I've already said, in order to understand something we foxes have to explain it to someone. This results from the specific qualities of our intellect, which is specifically designed to imitate human personalities, and is capable of mimicking the features of any culture. To put it more simply, it is our essential nature to constantly pretend. When we explain something to others, we are pretending that we have already understood it all. And since we are very clever creatures, we usually really do have to understand it, whether we wish to or not. They say that's what makes the silver hairs appear in our tails.

When I pretend, I am always acting in a perfectly natural manner. And so I always pretend – that way everything turns out far more plausibly than if I suddenly start behaving sincerely. After all, what does behaving sincerely mean? It means expressing your essential nature directly in your behaviour. And if it is my essential nature to simulate, then for me the only path to genuine sincerity lies through simulation. I don't mean to say by this that I never behave spontaneously. On the contrary, I simulate spontaneity with all the sincerity that I have in my heart. But words are proving tricky again – I am talking about something very simple, but it makes me seem like a dishonest creature with a double bottom. But it's not like that. I actually don't have any bottom at all.

Since a fox can pretend to be anything at all, she attains to the highest truth at the very moment when she pretends she has attained to it. And the best way to do this is in discussion with a less-developed being. But when I was talking to Alexander, I was not thinking about myself at all. I really was trying as hard as I could to help him. But as it turned out, he helped me. What an astonishing, incomprehensible paradox . . . But this paradox is the principal law of life.

I had approached the truth gradually:

1) as I observed Alexander, I realized that a werewolf directs his hypnotic impulse at his own mind. The werewolf suggests to himself that he is turning into a wolf, and after that he really does turn into one.

2) during the chicken hunt I noticed that my tail was directing its fluence at me. But I did not understand exactly what I was suggesting to myself: I thought it might be some kind of feedback loop that made me into a fox. I was already only two steps away from the truth, but I still couldn't see it.

3) in the course of my explanations, I told Alexander that he and this world were one and the same thing. I had everything I needed for final enlightenment. But I still needed Alexander to speak out and call things by their real names. It was only then that I attained to the truth.

I and the world are one and the same thing . . . What was it that I was suggesting to myself with my tail? That I was a fox? No, I realized in one blinding second, I was suggesting this entire world!

When I was left alone, I sat in the lotus position and withdrew into a state of profound concentration. I don't know how much time passed – perhaps several days. In a state like that there is no particular difference between a day and an hour. Now that I had seen the way things were, I understood why I had failed to spot this uroborus before (how apt that I had repeated that word all the time). I had not seen the truth because I was not seeing anything but the truth. The hypnotic impulse that my tail was directing at my mind was the entire world. Or rather, I had taken this impulse for the world.

I had always suspected that Stephen Hawking did not understand the words 'relict radiation' that occur on every second page of his books. Relict radiation is not a radio signal that can be captured using complex and expensive equipment. Relict radiation is the whole world that we see around us, no matter who we are, were-creatures or human beings.

Now that I had understood exactly how I was creating the world, I had to learn to control this effect somehow. But no matter how hard I focused my spiritual energy, I got nowhere. I ran through all the techniques that I knew – from the shamanic visualizations that are current among the mountain barbarians of Tibet to the sacred fire of the microcosmic orbit practised by the followers of the Tao. Nothing worked – it was like trying to move a mountain by pushing against it with my shoulder.

And then I remembered about the key. Yes indeed, the Yellow Master had mentioned a key . . . I had always thought that it was simply a metaphor for the correct understanding of the hidden nature of things. But if I'd blundered so terribly concerning the most essential point, I could have been mistaken here as well, couldn't I? What could it be, this key? I didn't know. So I still didn't understand anything, then?

My concentration was disrupted and my thoughts started to wander. I remembered about Alexander, who was waiting patiently in the next room – during my meditation he hadn't made a single sound, apprehensive of disturbing me. As always, the thought of him provoked a warm wave of love.

And then at last I understood what was absolutely the most vital point:

1) there was nothing in me that was stronger than this love – and since I was creating the world with my tail, there was nothing stronger in the entire world.
2) in the stream of energy that radiated from my tail, and which my mind took for the world, love was totally absent – and that was why the world appeared to me in the way that it was.
3) love was the key that I had been unable to find.

How had I failed to understand that immediately? Love was the only force capable of displacing my tail's relict radiation from my mind. I concentrated once again, visualized my love in the form of a little red, blazing heart and began slowly lowering it towards my tail. When I had lowered the heart of fire almost as far as its base, suddenly . . .

Suddenly something incredible happened. Inside my head, somewhere between the eyes, a shimmering rainbow of colour appeared. I did not perceive it with my physical vision – it was more like a dream that I had managed to smuggle in to the waking state. The shimmering was like a stream in the sunshine of spring. It sparkled with every possible shade of colour, and I could step into the caress of that kindly light. In order for the shimmering rainbow to engulf everything around me, I had to lower the flaming heart of love further, taking it beyond the point of the Great Limit that is located just three inches from the base of a fox's tail. I could have done it. But I sensed that afterwards, among those streaming torrents of rainbow light, I would never again be able to find this tiny city and Alexander who had been left behind in it. We had to leave this place together – otherwise what was our love worth? After all, he was the one who had given me the key to a new universe – without even knowing it . . .

I decided to tell him everything immediately. But it wasn't easy to get up – while I was sitting in the lotus position, my legs had become numb. I waited until the circulation was restored, struggled to my feet and walked towards the other room. It was dark in there.

'Sashenka,' I called. 'Hey! Sasha! Where are you?'

Nobody answered. I walked in and turned on the light. The room was empty. There was a sheet of paper lying on the wooden crate that served us as a table. I picked it up and, screwing up my eyes against the harsh electric light, I read this:

Adele!

I took no notice of the fact that you were concealing your age, although recently I'd begun to suspect you were more than seventeen – you're far too smart. So what, I thought, maybe you were just well preserved and really you were already twenty-five or even almost thirty, and you had a complex about it, like most girls. I was prepared for you to be a little more than thirty. I could probably even have come to terms with forty. But one thousand two hundred years! It's best if I just tell you straight out – I can never have sex with you again. Forgive me. And I'll forgive you for that blind dog thing. Maybe I am blind compared to you. But we can't help the way we are.

I'm going back to work tomorrow morning. Maybe I'll regret this decision. Or not even have time to regret it. But if everything goes the way I intend, the first thing I'll do is clarify a few issues that have come up in our department. And then I'll start clarifying the issues that have come up in all the other places. I shall devote the glorious power you have inadvertently helped me to obtain to the service of my country. Thank you for that – from me and our entire organization, against which you are so unjustly prejudiced. And thank you for all the amazing things that you have helped me to understand – although probably not completely and not for long. Time will show who the real superwerewolf is. Goodbye for ever. And thank you for calling me Grey One to the very end.

Sasha the Black

I remember that second. There was no confusion. I had always understood I couldn't keep him near me for ever, that this moment would come. But I hadn't thought it would be so painful.

My little moonchild . . . Play then, play your games, I thought in tender resignation. Some day you'll come to your senses all the same. But what a shame you will never learn the most important mystery from me. Although . . . Perhaps I should leave you a note? It will be longer than yours, and when you read it to the end you'll understand exactly what it was I didn't get a chance to tell you before you left. How else can I possibly repay you for the freedom that you have unwittingly given me.

Right then, I thought. I'll write a book, and sooner or later it's bound to reach you. You'll learn from it how to liberate yourself from icy gloom in which the oligarchs and the public prosecutors, the liberals and conservatives, the queers and straights, the Internet communists, werewolves in shoulder-straps and portfolio investors wail and gnash their teeth. And perhaps not just you, but other noble beings who have a heart and a tail will be able to learn something useful from this book . . . But in the meantime, thank you for revealing to me what the real score is. Thank you for love . . .

I couldn't hold back any longer – the tears gushed in a torrent down my cheeks and I cried for a long, long time, sitting on the wooden crate and looking at the white square of paper with the neat lines of his words on it. Until the very last day I had called him the grey one, afraid of hurting him. But he was strong. He didn't need any pity.

That was it. Two lonely hearts met among the pale blossoms of the Moscow spring. One told the other she was older than the city around, the other confessed that he had claws on his dick. For a short while they twined their tails together, spoke of the highest truth and howled at the moon, then went on their way, like two ships passing at sea . . .

Je ne regrette rien. But I know that I shall never again be as happy as I was in nineteen-sixties Hong Kong on the edge of the Bitsevsky forest, with a carefree bliss in my heart and his black tail in my hand.

* * *

When this book was almost finished, I met Mikhalich while I was out riding my bike. I was tired of turning the pedals, and I'd sat down for a rest on one of the massive log benches standing in the empty lot beside the Bitsevsky forest. My eye was caught by the kids jumping off the ramp on their bikes, and I spent a long time watching them. For some reason the saddles on all their bikes were set very low. Probably special bikes for jumping, I thought. But in every other way they were ordinary mountain bikes. When I turned away from the jumpers, Mikhalich was standing beside me.

He had changed a lot since the last time we'd seen each other. Now he had a fashionable haircut, and he was no longer dressed in retro-gangster gear, but wearing a stylish black suit from Diesel's 'rebel shareholder' collection. Under the jacket he had a black T-shirt with the words 'I Fucked Andy Warhol'. A gold chain peeped out from under the T-shirt – not really thick, and not really thin, just exactly right. A simple round, steel watch, black Nike Air trainers like Mick Jagger's on his feet. What a very long way the security services had come since those times when I used to travel to Yezhov's dacha for the latest Nabokov . . .

'Hi there, Mikhalich,' I said.

'Hello, Adele.'

'How did you find me?'

'With the instrument.'

'You haven't got any such instrument. Don't give me that. Sasha told me.'

He sat down beside me on the bench.

'I do have an instrument, Adele, I do, my girl. It's just that it's secret. And the comrade colonel general was following instructions when he spoke to you. I disobeyed those instructions when I showed it to you. And the comrade colonel general put me right afterwards, is that clear? As it happens, I'm disobeying instructions again now when I say that I do have an instrument. But the comrade colonel general always follows them very strictly.'

I couldn't tell any longer which of them was lying.

'And does the cleaning lady from the equestrian complex really work for you?'

'We have many different methods,' he said evasively. 'We couldn't manage otherwise. It's a very big country.'

'That's true.'

We sat there in silence for a minute or two. Mikhalich observed the kids jumping off the ramp with interest.

'And how's Pavel Ivanovich?' I asked, to my own surprise. 'Still consulting?'

Mikhalich nodded.

'He came to see us just the other day. He recommended a book, now what was it . . .'

He took a piece of paper out of his jacket pocket and showed it to me. I saw the words: *Martin Wolf: Why Globalisation Works* written on it in ballpoint pen.

'He said things weren't really all that bad after all.'

'Really?' I said. 'Well, that's really great. I was starting to

323

worry. Listen, I've been wanting to ask this for a long time. All those well-known figures, Wolfenson from the World Bank, Wolfovitz from the Defence Department – or maybe it was the other way around – were they all, you know, as well?'

'There are all sorts of wolves, just like people,' Mikhalich said. 'Only now they can't even come close to us. Our department's stepped up to a completely new level. There's only one Nagual Rinpoche in the world.'

'Who?'

'That's what we call the comrade colonel general.'

'How is he, by the way?' I couldn't help asking.

'Well.'

'What's he doing?'

'He's snowed under with work. And after work he sits in the archive. Analysing past experience.'

'Whose experience?'

'Comrade Sharikov's.'

'Ah, him. The one Bulgakov wrote about in *A Dog's Heart*?'

'Don't talk about things if you don't know anything,' Mikhalich said sternly. 'There are all sorts of lies going round about him, slanderous rumours. But no one knows the truth. When the comrade colonel general first turned up for work in his new uniform, the oldest members of staff even shed a few tears. They hadn't seen anything like it since nineteen fifty-nine. Not since comrade Sharikov was killed. It was after that everything fell to pieces. He was the one holding it all together.'

'And how was he killed?'

'He wanted to be the first to fly into space. And he went, just as soon as they made a cockpit big enough for a dog to fit into. You can't hold someone like that back . . . The risk was immense – during the early launches every second flight crashed. But he made his mind up anyway. And then . . .'

'The idiot,' I said. 'The vain nonentity.'

'Vanity has absolutely nothing to do with it. Why did comrade Sharikov fly into space? He wanted to happen to the void before the void happened to him. But he didn't get the chance. He was just three seconds of arc short . . .'

'And Alexander knows about Sharikov?' I asked.

'He does now. I told you, he spends days at a time in the archives.'

'And what has he said about it?'

'The comrade colonel general has said this: even titans have their limitations.'

'I see. And what questions do the titans have for me?'

'None, really. I was ordered to convey a verbal communication to you.'

'Well, convey it, then.'

'Seems you're putting it about that you're the super-werewolf.'

'Well, and what of it?'

'I'll tell you what. This is a unique country we live in, not like the rest of the world. Here everybody has to know who they answer to. People and werewolves.'

'And how am I interfering with that?'

'You're not. But there can only be one super-werewolf. Otherwise, what kind of super-werewolf is he?'

'That trivial kind of understanding of the word "super-werewolf",' I said, 'smacks of prison-camp Nietzcheanism. I –'

'Listen,' said Mikhalich, raising his open hand, 'I wasn't sent here to jaw. I'm here to tell you.'

'I understand,' I sighed. 'And what am I supposed to do now? Hit the road?'

'No, why? Just leave it out. Remember who's the super-werewolf around here. And never put your foot in it again. So there's no confusion in anybody's mind . . . Get it?'

'I could take issue with you,' I said, 'over whose minds are filled with confusion. First of all –'

'We're not going to argue about it,' Mikhalich interrupted again. 'As Nagual Rinpoche says, if you meet the Buddha, don't kill him, but don't let him take you for a ride.'

'Okay then, if we're not going to argue, we're not. Is that all?'

'No, there's one more question. A personal one.'

'What is it?'

'Marry me.'

That was unexpected. I realized he wasn't joking and looked him over carefully.

The man sitting in front of me was in his fifties, still in robust health, braced for his final headlong rush at life, but he still hadn't understood (fortunately for him) just how that rush ended. I'd seen off plenty like him. They always see me as their last chance. Grown men, and they don't understand that they themselves are their last chance. But then, they aren't even aware what kind of chance it is. Sasha had understood something at least. But this one . . . Hardly.

Mikhalich was looking at me with insane hope in his eyes. I knew that look too. What a long time I have spent in this world, I thought sadly.

'It would be like living on your own island,' Mikhalich said in a husky voice. 'Or you could really live on your own island if you like. Your very own coconut Bounty bar. I'll do everything for you.'

'And what's this island called?' I asked.

'How do you mean?'

'An island has to have a name. Ultima Thule, for instance. Or Atlantis.'

'We can call it whatever you like,' he said with a grin. 'Is that really a problem?'

It was time to wind up the conversation.

'Okay, Mikhalich,' I said. 'This is a serious decision. I'll think about it, okay? For a week or so.'

'Do that,' he said. 'Only bear this in mind. In the first place, now I'm the big shot in the apparat when it comes to oil. That's a fact. It's my stopcock all those oligarchs suck their oil out of. And they'd suck the other thing too, if I so much as frowned. And in the second place, just remember this. You like wolves, don't you? I know about that. I'm a wolf, a real wolf. But the comrade colonel general . . . Of course, he holds a superior post, with immense responsibility. The whole department idolizes him. But just between you and me, my thing is twice as big.'

'Please don't go into detail.'

'Okay then, no detail. But you think about it anyway – maybe it's better with a decent detail after all? You know all about the comrade colonel general anyway . . .'

'I do,' I said.

'And bear in mind that he's vowed never to turn back into a man as long as the country has any external or internal enemies. Like comrade Sharikov did before . . . The whole department was in tears. But to be honest, I don't think the enemies have anything to do with it. He just gets bored now being a man.'

'I understand, Mikhalich. I understand everything.'

'I know.' He said. 'You're a clever one.'

'All right. You go now. I want to be alone for a while.'

'Why don't you teach me that thing,' he said wistfully, 'you know, the *tailechery* . . .'

'He told you about that as well?'

'Nah, he didn't tell me anything. We've got no time to waste on you now. We're up to our eyes in work, you ought to understand that.'

'And what sort of work is it?'

'The country needs purging. Until we catch all the offshore fat cats, there's no time for yapping.'

'How are you going to catch them, if they're offshore?'

'Nagual Rinpoche has a nose for them. He can smell them through the wall. And he really didn't tell me anything about the tails. I heard it on the instrument. You were arguing about them, about . . . e-egh . . . the best way to twist them together.'

'You heard it on the instrument, I see. Okay, go now, you shameless wolf.'

'I'll be waiting for your call. You be sure to keep in touch with us. Don't forget what country you live in.'

'As if I could.'

'All right then. Call me.'

He got up and walked towards the forest.

'Listen, Mikhalich,' I called to him when he was already a few metres away.

'Eh?' he asked, looking back.

'Don't wear that T-shirt. Andy Warhol died in nineteen eighty-seven. It makes it too obvious that you're getting on a bit.'

'I heard you have a few problems in that area yourself,' he said imperturbably. 'Only I still like you anyway. What difference does it make to me how old you are? Not going to shag your passport, am I? Especially since it's a fake.'

I smiled. I had to admit that he did have charm – a werewolf is a werewolf.

'Right Mikhalich, not the passport. You'll be shagging dead Andy Warhol.'

He laughed.

'Personally speaking, I've got nothing against it,' I went on. 'But it dismays me to think that you're looking for him in me. Even though I like you so much as a *human being*.'

I had hit him with the most terrible insult possible in our circles, but he simply roared with laughter. The dumb stud was probably totally impervious.

'So don't wear that T-shirt, Mikhalich, really. It positions you as a gay necrophile.'

'Can you say that in Russian?'

'Sure. A stiff-shagging faggot.'

He chuckled, stuck his tongue out, waved the end about sug-gestively in the air and repeated:

'Call, I'll be waiting. Maybe we'll get the entire department to think up an answer for you.'

Then he swung round and set off towards the forest. I watched the black square of his back until it dissolved into the greenery. Malevich sold here . . . But then, who needed these allusions any more.

* * *

I only have a very little left to say. I have lived in this country for a long time and I understand the significance of accidental meet-ings like this, of conversations ending with advice to keep in touch with the security services. I spent a few days sorting out my old manuscripts and burning them. In fact, the only sorting I did was to run my eye diagonally over the pages covered with writing before I threw them into the flames. I had accumulated an especially large number of poems:

> *She's not a wingless fly on someone's Thule,*
> *He's not a one who fears the night around.*
> *The two night prowlers are the fox A Hu-Li*
> *And her dark friend, the sudden Pizdets hound.*

It saddened me most of all to burn the poems: I never had a chance to read them to anyone. But what can I do – my dark friend is too busy. I have only one task left to carry out now, and that is already close to completion (which is why my narrative is shifting from the past tense into the present). It is the task of which the Yellow Master spoke to me twelve centuries ago. I must reveal to all foxes how they can attain freedom. In effect, I have almost done this already – it only remains to draw together everything that has been said into clear, precise instructions.

I have already said that foxes use their tails to implant the illusion of this world in their own minds. This is expressed symbolically by the sign of the *uroborus*, round which my mind has been circling for so many centuries, sensing the great mystery that is concealed within it. A snake biting its own tail . . .

The inviolable link between the tail and the mind – that is the foundation on which the world as we know it stands. There is nothing that can intervene in this circle of cause and effect and disrupt it. Except for one thing. Love.

We werefoxes are significantly superior to people in all respects. But like them, we almost never know true love. And therefore the secret path leading out of this world is hidden from us. But it is so simple that it is hard to believe: the circuit of self-hypnosis can be broken by a single movement of the mind.

I shall now transmit this unsurpassed teaching in the hope that it may serve as the cause of the liberation of all those who possess a heart and a tail. This technique, lost since time immemorial, has been discovered anew by me, the fox A Hu-Li, for the good of all beings, under the circumstances described in this book. Here is a full and complete exposition of the secret method of ancient foxes known as 'tail of the void'.

1) First the werefox must comprehend what love is. The world that we create by inertia day after day is full of evil. But we cannot break out of the vicious circle because we do not know how to create anything else. The nature of love is entirely different, and that is precisely why there is so little of it in our lives. Or rather, our lives are like that because there is so little love in them. And in most cases what people take for love is physical attraction and parental instinct, multiplied by social conceit. Werefox, do not become like a tailless monkey. Remember who you are!

2) When a werefox comprehends what love is, she can leave this

dimension behind. But first she must settle all remaining accounts: thank those who have helped her on the way and help those who need help. Then the werefox must fast for ten days, pondering on the inscrutable mystery of the world and its infinite beauty. In addition, the werefox must recall her evil deeds and repent of them. She must remember at least the ten darkest deeds she has committed and repent of each of them. While the werefox does this, genuine tears must well up in her eyes at least three times. This is not a matter of banal sentimentality – crying purges the psychic channels that will be brought into play at the third stage. 3) When the preliminary practice has been completed, the werefox must wait for the day after the full moon. On that day she must rise early in the morning, perform ablutions and withdraw to a remote spot out of sight of all people. There, having freed her tail, the werefox must sit in the lotus position. If the werefox cannot sit in the lotus position, it does not matter – she can sit on a chair or a tree stump. The important thing is that the back must be straight and erect and the tail must be relaxed and free of restraint. Then the werefox must breathe in and out several times, engender in her heart love of the greatest possible power and, shouting out her own name in a loud voice, direct the love as deeply as possible into her own tail.

Any werefox will immediately understand what is meant by the words 'direct the love into her own tail'. But this is such a bizarre and inconceivable thing to do, such a gross violation of all the conventions, that I might be regarded as insane. Nonetheless, this is exactly the way things are – this way lies the secret road to freedom. The result will be similar to what happens when an air bubble gets into a blood vessel leading to the heart. It will be enough to stall the engine of the self-reproducing nightmare in which we have been wandering since the beginning of time.

If the love engendered was genuine, then following the shout, the tail will cease creating this world for a second. This second is the moment of freedom, which is more than enough to leave this realm of suffering behind for ever. When this second arrives, the werefox will know quite certainly what she should do next.

The same technique can be used by werewolves and pizdets hounds while in their lupine form.

I have also attained to comprehension of how tailless monkeys can escape from this world. At first I intended to leave detailed instructions for them too, but I do not have enough time. I will therefore briefly mention the most important elements. The key points of this teaching are the same as in the above. First the tailless monkey must engender love in his soul, beginning with its most simple forms and gradually ascending to the genuine love that knows no subject and no object. Then he must review his entire life and grasp the futility of his goals and the villainy of his ways. And since his repentance is usually false and short-lived, he must shed tears for his own dark deeds at least thirty times. And finally, the monkey must perform a magical action similar to the one described in point three, but amended to take account of the fact that he has no tail. The tailless monkey must therefore first grasp how he creates the world and in what way he imposes the illusion on himself. This is all rather simple, but I have absolutely no time left to dwell on it.

Let me say something more important. If any werefox, walking the Way, should discover a new road to the truth, she should not disguise it in all sorts of confusing symbols and tangled rituals, as the tailless monkeys do, but must immediately share this discovery with other were-creatures in the simplest and clearest form possible. But she should remember that the only true answer to the question 'what is truth' is silence, and anyone who opens his mouth simply doesn't know the score.

Well then, I think that is all. Now Nat King Cole will sing and I shall go. It will happen like this: I shall finish typing this page, save it, throw my laptop into my rucksack and get on my bike. Early in the morning there is never anybody at the ramp on the edge of the Bitsevsky forest. I've been wanting to jump from it for a long time, only I didn't think I'd be able to land. But now I've realized how to do it.

I shall ride out into the very centre of the empty field, gather all my love into my heart, pick up speed and go flying up the slope. And as soon as the wheels of my bicycle leave the ground, I shall call out my own name in a loud voice and cease to create this world. There will be an astonishing second, unlike any other. Then this world will disappear. And then, at last, I shall discover who I really am.

Born in 1962 in Moscow, Victor Pelevin has become recognized as the leading Russian novelist of his generation. His comic inventiveness and talent as a fabulist have won him comparisons to Kafka, Calvino, and Gogol, and *Time* magazine has described him as a "psychedelic Nabokov for the cyberage." Pelevin is the author of four novels (*Omon Ra, The Life of Insects, Buddha's Little Finger,* and *Homo Zapiens*), three collections of stories (*The Blue Lantern, A Werewolf Problem in Central London,* and *4 by Pelevin*), a novella (*The Yellow Arrow*), and *The Helmet of Horror: The Myth of Theseus and the Minotaur.* In 1998, he was selected by *The New Yorker* as one of the best European writers under thirty-five, and in January of 2000 he was the subject of a *New York Times Magazine* profile entitled "Gogol a Go-Go." His 2000 novel, *Buddha's Little Finger,* was a finalist for the International IMPAC Dublin Literary Award. He is the winner of the Nonino Prize and the Richard-Schonfeld Prize for literary satire, and his novels have been published in thirty-three countries.